# PAVLOVA RISING

## MEGAN HILLS

*This book is dedicated to all those First Nations
knowledge holders who keep patiently explaining the
basics to the rest of us doofus heads in the hope that
one day we will get it.
And to Jeff, my sweetie.*

# CONTENTS

**Part 4 - Tasting**

# PART 1
# LARD & FLOUR

# CHAPTER 1

I raised my partially frozen fist to the door, ready to knock. Then I heard, 'Fuck.' The expletive from the other side could have only come from the very depths of despair. I pressed my ear to the timber, but no other sounds followed. After knocking firmly, I waited. Nothing. Taking a deep breath, I grabbed hold of the icy brass doorknob, tightened my grip on my messenger bag and headed in. The first thing that hit me was the heat. Perry was English, I reminded myself. The man understands interior temperature control. Australians are useless at this.

At this point, Perry should be doing one of three things: sitting behind the desk, standing at one of the bookshelves that lined three of the walls, or gazing out the single window, which revealed an embarrassing mishmash of architecture inflicted on the university campus over the last hundred years, and the city of Sydney beyond. But I couldn't see him. Anywhere.

'Dr Perry?'

Like most, I'd first heard about Perry from his book *Hot Culture – Art Theft in the Twentieth Century*. With large glossy colour images on even larger amounts of white space, the book had made criminal activity look like a new interior design approach. Sales had rocketed internationally. Perry was launched out of academia and onto people's coffee tables. The fine art expert had become an unlikely celebrity. His photo was everywhere, depicting a dashing dark-haired intellectual wearing a black t-shirt under a black leather jacket. Perry's blue eyes were far from angelic. His mouth had the grin of someone who had nabbed the last biscuit from the tin. Perry was forty-four years old. A tidy number, much like my own twenty-two years. Strong and perfectly balanced, I thought. Seeing the man now, other words came to me. A large, pink, sweaty face had risen from behind the desk. His crop of greying brown hair looked like a playful parent had just ruffled it. Weight gain had occurred somewhere between jobs. A lot of weight.

'Anna Lissam?'

'Er, yes,' I nodded.

'My computer has gone completely blank,' Perry said, pushing his dark-rimmed spectacles up the bridge of his bulbous nose. Can a nose put on weight? 'Blank for no reason at all,' he added.

It appeared the new faculty head had been investigating a computer cable, following its lead in the hope of a rainbow. I worked my way carefully around the desk to take a closer look. The screen was indeed at its blackest. Pressing control+alt+delete achieved nothing.

'You need to restart,' I said.

'Bugger,' Perry groaned, working his way back onto his feet.

That was when I first noticed the stain on his light blue shirt, an unfortunate brown smudge in the shape of Africa. Somalia and Mauritania peered out from either side of his red tie. The tie wasn't wide enough to hide Tasmania, let alone Africa. His corduroy jacket was too tight to be buttoned.

The computer took forever to crank back up. Being on the precipice of technological disaster, it was clear Perry was not in the mood for chitchat. Digging his fingertips deep into his cheeks, his red-tinged eyes watched the computer, waiting for it to return to consciousness. I stole another glance at his shirt. The stain looked more like shoe polish than coffee. Looking down, his brown leather shoes confirmed it, mid-tan. Had he cleaned them with his shirt and then decided to wear it?

The computer beamed back to life. A document titled 'Aboriginal Art Intro (Recovered)' automatically appeared. Nausea stirred in my stomach.

'Thank god,' Perry said. 'Actually, I should thank you. Well done.'

'Excuse me, Dr Perry,' I started, 'is this document yours?'

'Yes, indeedy,' he replied, relaxing back into the leather office chair.

I walked carefully to the other side of the desk, weighing up my next move. 'You were writing about Australian Aboriginal art?' I asked.

'Yes, for the undergrads,' Perry replied. 'Might seem a little ballsy, being a Pom fresh on Australian shores. But believe me, Lissam, I know a thing or two about Aboriginal daubs.'

That had always been the problem. A thing or two is no way near enough. The man had not yet acclimatised.

'It's getting rather warm in here, isn't it?' Perry said, wiping his brow with a handkerchief. 'Mind letting some breeze in?' His head nodded towards the window while the rest of him bent down to turn off the heater. It took some effort on his part. I walked across the room and tugged at the double hung. It was stuck. This was a building from 1848, after all. The only decent architecture in the place, despite its expanded wood-framed windows and lack of central heating. I yanked again. The frame slid upwards. An icy gust of wind promptly blew into the office, lifting a generous stack of papers off the desk and tumbling them face-first onto the floor.

'Close it!' Perry yelled as he frantically gathered his pages. I followed orders with an unintentional slam. After a moment of haphazard organisation, he leaned on his desk and said, 'Perhaps we should open the door.' Despite Perry's fall from photoshopped grace, our forthcoming conversation still warranted privacy. Duty-bound, I opened the door and then sat down, my back exposed to the hallway.

'Okay, let's get started.' Straightening himself back behind the desk, Perry began thumbing through the contents of what looked to be my file. In this screen-focused institution, it was odd to see pages still printed and housed in a manila envelope. I settled into the chair opposite and waited. 'This is a thesis meeting, me being your new supervisor...' he said, 'but I see that you are also an employee here in the faculty.'

Trying to ignore the open door behind me, I focused on matters at hand. 'Yes, I work in the digital image library, cataloguing art images and managing copyright paperwork.'

'How's it going?'

'Great, I love it.' That wasn't strictly true. I didn't really love it, but it suited me for now.

'As far as I can see from these reports, the image library's very organised. You run it well.'

'I do my best.'

'Your best is excellent, Lissam, if both this employee assessment and...' Perry opened another file, '...your academic transcripts are anything to go by. You're a high distinction student...undergrad on a scholarship…second scholarship for your masters,' he looked up. 'Impressive.'

'Thanks,' I replied. His eyebrows reminded me of beach bracken.

'From what I gather,' he continued, 'all fine art and theory masters' students are one semester into thesis writing.'

'Yes, that's right. Here is my synopsis,' I said, pulling my paper from my bag and handing it over. Perry laid the pages on the desk and folded his hands on top.

'Tell me about it,' he said.

'I am dedicating my focus to the artist Vernon Jones.'

'Never heard of him.'

'He was Australia's most prolific nineteenth-century portrait painter. Came from England in 1832.'

'A convict?' Perry asked, eyes gleaming. 'What did he do to be sent to the end of the world?'

Australians are used to their country being referred to as the end of the world, or something like it, by northern hemispherians. We take it on the chin, even revel in it. I smiled as I shook my head, 'No, Vernon was a low-level officer.' Perry visibly deflated. 'Vernon Jones didn't get paid much, so he earned money on the side painting portraits.' And then I played my trump card. 'Vernon's artistic career in London hasn't yet been properly researched, however. I've sourced some excellent contacts.' Bump up this baby to a PhD and hello, travelling scholarship. I was about to unveil my excellent London contacts, but Perry interrupted. 'Why do you want to study him?' he asked.

'Why?' I faltered for a moment. 'Well…after all this time, Vernon Jones is still waiting for the recognition his extraordinary works deserve.'

'Why do you think that he's still waiting…from his coffin?'

'He was obviously before his time. Many of the portraits are quite unflattering.'

'Got a shocker of a review by the Sydney Morning Herald in 1846.' Perry's bracken raised as he scanned the photocopy.

I sucked air through my teeth. 'As I said, he was before his time. Vernon Jones was a new kind of portrait painter. There are some examples printed on the last page of the synopsis.'

Perry flipped the pages to the back and laughed. 'Jesus.' His nostrils flared while attempting to suppress laughter. It didn't last. One snort and laughter exploded. He continued to laugh until his eyes filled with tears.

'Okay,' I said. 'At first glance, they may appear poor in technical ability.'

'Okay, I'm looking again, Lissam,' his watery eyes then met mine before dropping to the page for another dip. 'And again. That's three glances now. Still looks like doggie doo. "Poor in technical ability" is a rather generous compliment.'

Shit. The London National Portrait Gallery, my ticket out of Sydney, were interested in Vernon Jones. A new version of 'warts and all', they said. Even my previous supervisor, Hatchet, loved Jones' crap portraits. Which was something, as the man didn't love easily. Uncontrollable bursts of aggression sporadically interrupted Hatchet's cool demeanour. Hence, the students coining him 'Hatchet Herman'. But the laughter stopped in a recent class when Hatchet had two important announcements to make.

'It turns out you can't eat art,' he said. 'Well, you can if it's by Dieter Roth, but we all know how that turned out.' The class didn't. They had never heard of Dieter Roth. The urge to Google it was almost unbearable. But Googling anything in front of Hatchet never ended well. 'The Data Analytics Department delivered this to my desk this morning.' He picked up an inch-thick spiral-bound report, looked at it for an unnervingly long time, then put it down again. No one made a sound. 'After assessing employment trends worldwide, their findings summarise that only 5% of you are likely to find employment in Visual Arts History. Assuming you all successfully graduate with a master's degree. This means only two of you have a real shot at the real world.' In fact, it was only 1.5, but I wasn't going to correct him. The news was depressing enough. A lead weight fell upon the class. We were never a cocky bunch about our employment future, but this was worse than expected.

'The Data Analytics Department analysed…us?' someone from the class asked.

'It was more of a fun lunchtime exercise for them,' he said, peering across the room, he added, 'I suspect their own career prospects are a little more secure,' he said. 'Speaking of limited careers, my second announcement is that I'm retiring. Leaving at the end of the week.' Had the Data Analytics Department pushed him over the edge? Was he a rat leaving the sinking ship? But Hatchet said nothing further on the topic. Instead, he shifted focus to the 1980s and the heyday of corporate art collections, which was a kindness. Nostalgic fairy floss for art historians.

Then, a week later, Thomas Perry arrived. Nothing online had explained why Perry had abandoned his prestigious lecturing position at London's Whitlock University. Or why he had flown across the world to head the credible but modest Fine Art History & Theory department at Prescott in Sydney. Whitlock University's quarterly newsletter had divulged the most: *Professor Perry's resignation is due to an unexpected change in personal circumstances. We wish him all the best for the future.* Google had no more answers to give, nor did anyone else at Prescott.

'Maybe I should be kinder,' Perry continued. 'Did Vernon have a mental disability?'

'No,' I replied, looking at the stain on his shirt again.

A sigh escaped as Perry pushed his glasses upward. 'Why do you want to study this person, Lissam?'

'Well, no one really knows about this early Australian artist -'

'And there's an excellent reason for that. This man's paintings should be shot, burned and buried. You know that, even if Herman didn't.' We both raised our eyebrows at that last point before Perry continued. 'So why do you *really* want to study this codswallop?'

I couldn't very well say 'London research junket', so I started deliberating over a credible response. Fortunately, Perry was a man of impatience.

'A thesis must start with a question,' he said.

'A question?' I asked. 'I thought it had to be an argument.'

'No, arguments come later.' He pushed his spectacles up the bridge of his nose again. 'First, one must start with a question. What does a question require?'

'A question requires...'

Perry thumped his desk, 'Curiosity, Lissam, a lot of curiosity. And what does a lot of curiosity require?'

'Curiosity requires...'

'Passion, Lissam,' Perry thumped the desk a second time. 'You need passion.' At that, he rose from his chair and walked to the window, gesturing me to follow. 'What's that building over there, the new concrete effort with the red fins at the top?'

'G Block,' I replied, staring at the overgrown Lego set from the late 1990s.

'And what do they teach there?'

'Economics, business and marketing.'

'Lissam, if you want to fill a gap in the market, go to G Block. That's where you belong. If you want to be passionate about art and its path, stay here. Are you feeling passionate, Lissam? Are you passionate about Vernon?'

'I'm very interested to discover -'

Perry settled back behind his desk. 'But are you passionate?'

I returned to my chair and felt my lips roll inwards. All I needed was to say 'yes', but the word just wouldn't come. I had to admit it. Even if Vernon was in the vicinity of talented, I knew he would still leave me a little cold. In fact, there was something about early Australian history in general that had me doodling en masse. In the office on that clear winter morning, Perry forced me to see the disappointment I had in my own country. Australia had no Norman Conquest, no Wars of the Roses, Renaissance or monarchical dramas to call its own. Instead, Australia had bread thieves, clueless pastoralists and clunky Ned Kelly.

'No passion?' Perry eventually replied. 'Well, if you want to carry on this way, you don't belong here, no matter how good the marks are. So, one more time, are you passionate about Vernon?'

'London's National Portrait Gallery is expecting me-' It sounded good, London's National Portrait Gallery. Hatchet liked it as well. But Dr Perry didn't have the same expression. His was more Viking-with-constipation. Perhaps he didn't believe me. Remarkably, the NPG were actually expecting me. Administration had told me to get back in contact once I teed up the travelling scholarship. This was the way I saw it: Vernon was my first foothold, the National Portrait Gallery my second. Basically, I just wanted to climb out of Australia to somewhere else. Leave this godforsaken suburbanised island and start exploring. Exploring for what, I wasn't sure yet. I guess something that might actually interest me.

'*Passionate*,' Perry's fingers curled into a fist. 'That's what I'm asking.'

My head turned slowly from one side to the other, a slow denial that manifested beyond my control. Perry promptly ripped up the synopsis, London torn apart in seconds. I mustered one question that came out more like a last gasp for air. 'Are you sending me to G Block?'

'Not yet,' he replied gently. 'Find out what you are passionate about. Find out what makes you laugh hard, weak with anger, weep and ache with joy.'

'But Vernon Jones is a perfect thesis topic -'

'For someone else perhaps.' Perry's smile looked genuinely sympathetic. 'But not for you.' He then patted my file, gesturing I was destined for greater things, or that I'm a cocker spaniel.

'I don't know how exactly...'

'Do whatever it takes, my dear. Find out what really floats your boat.'

'My boat?' Sitting in the chair, I felt myself sinking.

'A master's thesis takes a lot of self-motivation. Passion will carry you through it. A doctorate takes even more, which is what I gather you wish to expand your thesis into so you can nail that international research scholarship you're chomping at the bit for.' I sat stunned. 'Am I right?' he pressed.

'...yes,' I squeaked.

'Then go forth,' he said, flinging his arms out, 'and write a thesis proposal that bursts out from the pages.' Perry then rested back in his chair. 'I think we should meet the same time next week.'

I nodded, uncertain as to whether next week was the deadline for discovering passion. Perry placed his bulky hands flat on the desktop and heaved himself from his chair. Shaken, I stood up and shook his large, fleshy hand. With a cracked voice, I found myself thanking the bastard. Lifting my messenger bag, now lead-heavy, I staggered out.

'Hello, Anna.'

I almost jumped out of my skin. I knew the voice before I saw the face. It was Marvin Brodie. He had been right outside the door, no doubt listening to the whole disaster. Now he was smirking at me. Marvin, together with his regularly self-tested IQ, trotted around campus with a permanent smirk. The smirk had become even more putrid lately. Probably because he now saw himself as the 1.5% career survivor. This was partly to do with becoming wealthy by representing various 'hot' digital media artists from across the globe. Marvin figured he could surpass his arch-rival, DAAOn (Digital Art Animation Online), by winning academic kudos. Hence, the master's degree. Like me, he was looking to bump up to a PhD. Unlike me, Marvin's thesis was probably secure. The guy was a knob, but the knob had a genuine passion for art animation.

'Brodie!' Perry yelled from his desk. Marvin promptly entered. Closing the door behind him, I noticed he had replaced the smirk with a light but confident smile.

'Welcome to Australia, Dr Perry,' I heard him say.

Goosebumps sprang up on my arms as I walked down the Siberian corridor. My throat constricted. A cold was coming, I was sure of it. Bloody Doctor Perry, I thought as my Docs squeaked on the grey linoleum. With a single week to create a Perry-proof plan, one thing was certain. Finding passion in this place was out of the question.

# CHAPTER 2

'Paaaasssshhhion.' On the evening of 'Thesis Destruction I' (I was already predicting a sequel), Maggie was on the other end of the phone nursing a jasmine tea while imitating Lawrence Olivier underwater.

'Paaaasssshhhion,' she repeated. 'The word sounds like what it is.'

'Yeah, I guess so,' I replied, clutching onto my hot water bottle while doodling Dr Perry with a chainsaw appearing at his head. The apartment was, as usual, taking an eternity to heat up. Doodling usually had a therapeutic effect, but my irritation with Thomas Perry was rising.

'Anna,' Maggie said, snapping my attention back. 'What do you think of when you hear the word "passion"?'

'Passion? The same as everyone, I guess. Nookie.'

'So perhaps your thesis could be about…nookie…in art?'

'But I don't feel excited by it,' I frowned. 'Why is that?'

Maggie could have made the comment, 'Because you haven't had any in so long, you've forgotten how to spell it.' Instead, she said, 'Maybe because sex is something that we are expected to say. That's why we immediately associate it with passion. Ironically, the predictability of this takes the passion out of it.' There was a pause on the phone before she groaned, 'You're going to hate me for what I'm about to say.'

I picked up my pencil again and gnawed at it like a beaver with damming issues. There was a possibility she might bring the subject of my unintentional celibacy into the open after all. It had been eleven months, if you call passion half-baked 'relations' in a Maserati after two bottles of sparkling wine and a handful of pebble-sized hors d'oeuvres. Contemporary wedding functions can be dangerous like that. Delicate and poorly distributed nibbles drenched in generous quantities of sub-standard alcohol had replaced the sit-down dinner. This led to an impromptu dalliance in the man's silver prestige vehicle (minimal leg room). I hadn't seen him before or since, but we were bound to meet again at another wedding, him and his wife. A gleeful bridesmaid revealed his relationship status during the honeymoon departure arch. Faith in my own judgment disappeared with the rattling of cans down the driveway.

'Impossible,' I said. 'You couldn't say anything I'd hate, Maggs. Besides, all my hate is currently being funnelled towards Dr Thomas Perry.' My doodle was evidence of this.

'Remember Dorothy Brown?' Maggie said. It wasn't really a question. She knew I would never forget Dorothy Brown.

'Dorothy Brown,' I gloomed. 'Can't believe you brought her up.'

'But you were so passionate about her paintings during your undergraduate years.'

'Well, that passion has well and truly bailed. It's possibly gone to Tasmania…to die.'

'Really? Years ago, another student heckles you…'

'Marvin Brodie,' I growled. 'Smirk-master of the century.'

'So Marvin Brodie heckles you,' Maggie persisted, 'during your talk on Dorothy Brown, and that's it? You banish her art, and all the inspiration they bring from your life?'

'His heckling was a horrific experience, granted. But I thank him for it.'

'How so?'

'He woke me up to the obvious. Never study Aboriginal art, including Dorothy Brown's paintings, unless you are Aboriginal. We have interrogated them enough. And worse,' I added. 'Speaking of which, you wouldn't believe who's giving a lecture on Aboriginal art to the undergrads.'

'Who?'

'Thomas Perry.'

'Fresh off the plane and already teaching Aboriginal art to Australians?'

'Exactly,' I said, drawing a circle that was going to be…what? The lead broke from too much pressure. 'I should have deleted his lecture notes permanently when I had the chance, for his sake.' I started stubbing out the pencil head like a cigarette. 'Maybe I'm just not a passionate person. Should calm, composed, unruffled people be barred from research?' I asked, gnawing again on the pencil.

'I think you can be passionate, Anna. And it will find you, I guarantee it.'

'But will it find me in time for the next Perry meeting?' Maggie had no answer for that. 'Thanks for listening to my whinging, Maggs.'

'You can listen to mine next time. I've got to go-'

'Hold your horses, what's wrong? I've been waiting two years for you to whinge about something.'

'Nothing really, it can wait,' she said. 'Ruben's just walked in. Time to get dinner happening.'

*Dinner.* Maggie was the kind of person who could whip up a goat's cheese soufflé in under five minutes, followed by Jaffa crème brûllé. I began to salivate.

'Come around for a feed tomorrow, after uni. I promise to complain then.'

'I'll be there, I said. 'Looking forward to that historic event.'

Just as I hung up, the front door swung open. 'I had a shocker of a day at work,' Liz announced, slamming it shut. 'The car broke down. I couldn't get an Uber, so I had to take the train and got chatted up by a bloody solicitor.' For all my time on public transport, I had never once been approached socially by anyone with an income. The report of the day continued, as my flatmate took off her clothes like a distracted stripper. Purple leather jacket, '...he said he wanted to search my trademarks...', green ankle boots '...had unique protection strategies...', red mohair skirt '... intellectual property, my arse...' A cigarette conducted her words throughout the performance. In leopard print bra and g-string, she wound up her story. 'I gave him the lowdown on infringements, let me tell you,' and made her way to the bathroom, leaving a trail of designer wear behind her.

After four years of sharing the Surry Hills apartment, I couldn't recall one evening when Liz decided to just hang out at home. She spent her time elsewhere, talking, drinking, smoking, swallowing colourful pills and snorting colourless powder. Not all at once, but she gave it her best college try. Living mostly alone didn't bother me, though it wasn't what I expected when moving to the city from my small town of Nagurra. In the country, it was also common for people living together to not like or know each other well. The difference was that they had loved each other once.

'How do I look?' Moving my eyes over Liz's Givenchy red lapel jacket, green mushroom-shaped skirt, the clang of silver banana-shaped bracelets, the ensemble reminded how much I hated that question. It looked so awkward, it must have been the height of fashion.

'Gauguin once said -'

'Who?' Liz interrupted.

'Paul Gauguin, the French Post-Impressionist artist. Painted Tahitian women in bright colours.' Liz frowned and shook her head.

'He had multiple lovers and died of syphilis.'

'Oh, *him*.' Liz smiled warmly and nodded.

'Gauguin said that beauty could come from something ugly, but never from something pretty.'

Liz was in advertising. She looked at me the way she did when her clients suggested using their children in the commercial. The expression was not pretty. 'I'm going out,' she announced unnecessarily. 'Fuck, where are my keys?'

'On the floor,' I said. 'Near the kitchen door.'

She dived on them, then was out and into the night. Two minutes later, I kicked myself. The rent was overdue. I shared an apartment with a woman who earned double of anyone I knew and yet never paid the rent on time. Scholarship stipends and digital image library wages only stretched so far. I contemplated how far Liz could've gotten in her gold platforms, but decided not to chase her. Instead, I walked into the lounge room, picked up articles of clothing and tossed them through Liz's bedroom doorway, landing them square on the bed. I had practice.

Then an urge took me. I grabbed my bag and keys, pulled my black beanie over my hair and headed for the stairs. The urge was not rent money, but art. And the possibility of a free glass of something mid-priced from the Coonawarra region. Hurrying out into the street, Liz was nowhere to be seen.

I could walk to where I was going. Puffing my warm breath into the cool air, I headed up the road towards Oxford Street. Within fifteen minutes, the run-down cottages and refurbed deco apartments had given way to establishments offering Bombay Sapphire gin, gluten-free friands, eco-furniture and tea cosy handbags. By the time I was weaving through the hords of cool hunters, my body had warmed up and was feeling a little buoyed by the bustle. Two blocks up, I ducked down a side street towards the quieter, leafier and more stately precinct of Paddington. Converted factories and warehouses freckled the streets of nineteenth century terraces. Any of them could be a private gallery and probably was.

By day, competition festered fiercely amongst the art dealers like a large dysfunctional family at a tasteful Christmas Day lunch. They would peer into each other's white spaces, wondering what artists they were missing out on, what clients to lure away. But it was also a brotherhood of sorts, formed through the struggle of selling original fine art to a nation distracted by sport.

I headed for Noah Webster Gallery. Its namesake belonged to a man who took incredible commercial risks over the five years his gallery had been in operation, and mostly won. Webster's success got up the nose of many of his Paddington 'relatives'. The gallery (post-tobacco warehouse) had an exclusive exhibition opening that night. I was, as usual, there to crash it. Walking towards the end of the street, I could make out the glowing hubbub. Some guests were milling around the industrial entrance, sipping wine from hired glasses.

You would think the laughter and chatter indicated a successful exhibition inside. Not necessarily. Alcohol is a great mis-representer of many things, including any level of genuine cultural patronage.

Edging along the cluster of soft foreign fabrics and loudly branded handbags, I made my way inside. If there was any souvenir aroma from the building's tobacco days, it was suffocating under a chemical interpretation of apple blossom, entitled *Achieve* parfum. I did my best to breathe while wedging and sliding my way between guests, finding a position close but not too close to the nearest exhibition wall. Philippa Cusack's field paintings were the excuse for tonight's celebration. I had never heard of Philippa Cusack. Chances were, many here hadn't either. Noah Webster had a reputation for pulling up-and-coming talent out of the garrets (or someone's spare room) and into The Art World. Tonight, it was Philippa's turn to be discovered. To be honest, I wasn't that interested in this new artist. Tonight was about getting a glimpse of the star-maker, Noah Webster.

I had no invitation, but private gallery openings rarely required them. The bigger the crowd, the more festive the feel, the more likely someone will buy on a whim. Paintings of fields doesn't sound all that exciting except, at first glance, you would assume Philippa Cusack's were slightly blurred photographs. They reminded me of snaps from my childhood. My father embraced the candid approach, his lens catching us with the kind of distorted expressions that would leave Picasso to shame. He is also clumsy and often trips while moving about his subjects, thereby missing us completely. The result was a collection of photos of our situ, slightly skewed and fuzzy. Sometimes he herded me and Mum into fields outside of Nagurra. If Dad tripped out there, the result looked something like a Cusack painting.

I could feel the roughness of the tall, drying grass around my ankles. Again, Webster had trumped it. This artist was going places, well beyond this regional property where she had obviously spent a good whack of time. Looking around the freeloaders hovering their hands over the circulating antipasto platters, I wondered if Cusack was here. Shimmying through the hoi polloi, I found myself in front of an autumn field with a wall of concrete looming from the right. Cusack had titled this 'Shopping Centre Entry'. The message was clear: this season was doomed to retail window posters and catalogue branding. Most of the paintings were just fields, but some played with concrete additions. Buildings, benches, runways. By the look of the red stickers, indicating sales, the exhibition had garnered some serious financial enthusiasm. I glanced at the laminated list fixed to a wall nearby. Owning a Cusack meant parting with anything from two thousand dollars to fifteen. After gallery commission, tax, material expenses such as paint and canvas, freight and travel costs, the artist wouldn't be left with much, considering the time it must have taken to paint each work. But good sales here meant an impressive start to a new artist's career.

Unless some stickers were fake. Some galleries activated the fake sticker tactic to boost buying confidence. But you could tell this practice was being carried out when all the least sale-worthy works had stickers. Anyway, sticker faking was rarely done on opening night unless the situation was desperate. And it would be surprising if Noah Webster Gallery ever had to stoop to it. From what I could see in between heads, no Cusacks were duds. Each had their own natural texture and a slightly uncomfortable atmosphere caused by its skewed shift in undramatic light.

Of course, Jan Hildebrandt was there. With ruddy cheeks, discount spectacles and ill-fitted brown suit, she stood behind the white reception desk while chatting to an older woman in a red dress scoffing a fold of prosciutto and goat's cheese. Jan was Webster's right-hand gal. As appearances go, the woman looked like she would be more comfortable behind the counter at a local bakery. But, if the art sector rumour mill was anything to go by, her knowledge of art was exceptional. I had quizzed Jan during some of my past visits to the gallery. Even though I was obviously a student, not a buyer, she always answered my questions with care, often pulling out some unusual references to explain whatever work we were looking at. *'When frustrated, she paints with marshmallows... the pinks ones...'* During my last visit, about three months ago, I laughed when Jan said, *'This artist has recently been captivated by Venus Fly Traps...'* She gave me her classic Cornish pastie smile then, as she did at Cusack's opening before continuing her conversation with red dress. 'Really?' said red dress. 'How lovely.'

*Lovely,* I thought. As descriptions go, 'lovely' was about as exciting as custard. I surmised that anyone who used the word 'lovely' had a mind resembling custard. Then I saw a waiter with a tray laden with alcohol. Scooping up a glass of Shiraz, I noticed the small video cameras installed in the ceiling corners. Were they new?

'You lucky thing.' That was Jan, now talking to a group of finely presented women all around the age of sixty. 'Travelling around Australia. Eight months, really? Merv and I were going to, but then the poor sausage passed on. Very sudden...'

'Why don't you come with us, Jan?' one of the women asked. The others nodded, their large gold earrings shining and bobbing like festive baubles.

'A generous offer but, no, I couldn't. Noah couldn't cope without me. Could you, Noah?'

And there he was. Noah Webster. Tall, possibly in his late forties, slight in build with trimmed grey hair. He had a tanned complexion that, given it was late winter, was probably assisted. Wearing a well-cut charcoal suit and a thin red tie, he smiled gently at the women and touched Jan's arm affectionately. Behind him was a tubby woman in a crushed olive-coloured linen dress, staring out wide-eyed. Philippa Cusack. It had to be her. She looked more like a wombat caught on a freeway than a sales tool. Nonetheless, Noah was steering her towards a well-dressed couple glancing at the price list. His movements were calm and considerate, but I sensed he, too, had an internal churning going on. The sort of tension that professionals 'manage'.

'Camp as a row of humpies,' a shaggy-looking guy whispered in my ear. His shagginess had been carefully designed, faux casual. Probably cost a fortune. 'Noah Webster,' he added. As if it needed clarification.

'And your point is?' I asked.

'You just looked like you were eyeing him. Thought I'd save you the trouble.'

'You're a true friend,' I said, hoping he'd get the platonic picture and if not, then the Wiltshire-sharp sarcasm. Disappointment-lite floated across his fringe-flopped face before he shrugged and moved on. Shifting my attention back, Noah was still working the couple. He was almost looking smug while doing it. Cusack had disappeared, possibly hiding in the toilet.

Thanking the gods I didn't work in sales, I discarded my empty glass and worked my way back through the hubbub to step out into the brisk night air. If smugness was something earned, then Noah Webster had earned it. Before running his own show, he had been working for Harrington's Auction House. Some fake Aboriginal paintings had slipped through his net, which created a lot of noise in the media. Disgraced, he left to never return. Learning of Noah's history brought about a kindred spirit feeling, but I kept this to myself. Of course, my heckling experience by Marvin was micro to Webster's macro. And this, I suspected, was where the comparisons with Webster and I end.

It would have been understandable if Noah had focused on tried-and-true artists, stuck in some kind of safety zone after Harrington's. But he chose to challenge himself, and collectors, by supporting relatively unknown talent. Everyone in the Australian art sector knew about the Harrington's debacle, along with some key players overseas. But then there was this unprecedented rising from the ashes: the dignified success of Noah Webster Gallery.

Meanwhile, my next project was lying in tatters in Dr Perry's wastepaper bin. Vernon Jones wasn't the equivalent of Noah Webster Gallery. My strategy was not dignified. I had nothing to feel smug about. Pulling my beanie over my ears, I walked outside, hunched against the cold, and headed home.

# CHAPTER 3

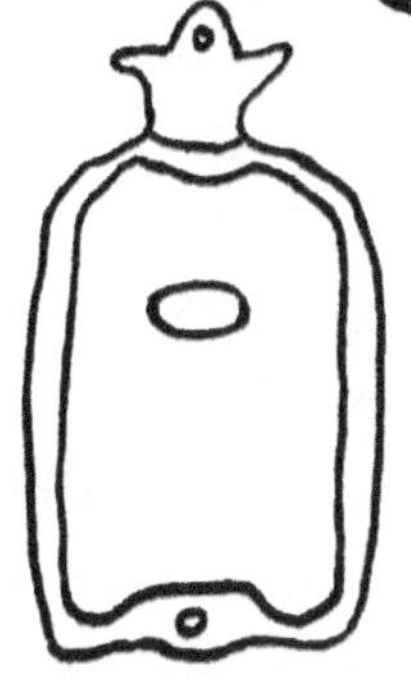

My office was once a cleaning closet. It would explain why there were no windows and why I literally had to climb into it over the armrests of my chair to sit at the desk. The chair was designed to swivel, but it was permanently jammed by exterior constraints – such as the walls, a filing cabinet and the desk. On the upside, I was warm. I had brought in a hot water bottle. Operations & Maintenance rejected my multiple requests for a heater. 'Fire risk,' they had said. Whereas Perry had permission to torch the department at will.

It was Thursday. The day I usually consider a nice mix of image library work and lectures. I looked at the two emails. Both from Sharon, the faculty administrator. Or rather, the first was from Rupert, her four-year-old son. It was a celebration of punctuation, commas, full stops and dashes. The other email was from Sharon proper, apologising for the previous email. Then something caught the corner of my eye.

'Hello Rupert,' I said. The small boy's face was covered in chocolate while his hand clutched an empty crinkled wrapper. I hoped he didn't come any closer with those sticky fingers. I tried to remain calm while clearly cornered. 'A little early to be hitting the confectionery, isn't it?'

"

Rupert paused before replying, 'Mummy sent you an email.'

'Thanks, I just saw that,' I said. 'You sent me one too, didn't you? Excellent message.' The boy nodded solemnly, then looked around my office, possibly considering his smearing options. 'You're not at childcare today?'

'No,' he replied. 'Mummy has a-a-bishon soon.'

'An exhibition?' I replied. Of course, I already knew that. Whenever Sharon's children were at work, it was always because of an upcoming exhibition. Art supplies came before childcare fees at times like these. 'Time to go back to Mummy now?' I suggested. 'I think she needs your help, doesn't she?'

'Yes…no…don't know,' his little face creased, looking more like the chocolate wrapper by the second. It was possible he might cry. Panicked, I knocked hard and fast on the wall.

'Rupert, come here,' Sharon called from the other side. Then I heard the squeak of her chair (she could swivel), as she got up and appeared at the doorway. Her legs appeared first. Sharon's legs were so long it that must have been a challenge to find an easel to fit her requirements. 'Sorry, Anna,' she said, bending her tallness down to the height of her offspring.

'No problem, he just seemed a little distressed.' Let's face it, we both were. Of course, as soon as his mother appeared, Rupert transformed. He now looked quite relaxed and satisfied with life, complete with full beard. 'I hear you have an exhibition. How is it coming together?'

'Pretty well, thanks,' Sharon nodded. 'I have to have something beyond this job.'

'Work for the soul,' I confirmed.

'Yes,' she said. 'Also trying to develop another source of income. You don't know when your number's up here.'

'I can't imagine they would ever want to retrench you, Sharon.'

Sharon looked me straight in the eye. 'Nothing is a sure thing, Anna. Believe me.'

'Even still…' I mused, watching Sharon flip to full size and leading her son away. Turning back to the computer, I deleted her messages and considered my next task. Which, as it turned out, had to do with religion.

'Jesus fucking Christ, I don't believe it!' That was Perry from two doors down. It was the brand of traumatic cry many men assume would get a woman running in support. The tactic failed. Eventually, a sterner voice called, 'Sharon, could you come in here, please?'

'On the phone,' she called back.

'What?'

'I'm on the phone.'

'It's an emergency,' he persisted. 'Technical fucking meltdown.'

I hauled myself up and over my armrest-come-pummel horse and walked down the corridor to enter the den of despair.

'May I help, Dr Perry?' I asked, jealously eyeing the bar heater currently on double beam.

'My computer screen has completely frozen,' he said. This morning, he wore a clean, albeit wrinkled, Africa-free shirt.

'How frustrating,' I said. 'Have you tried control, alt, delete?' Perry promptly took instruction and, like before, we both waited for the results. This time, I settled into the chair opposite and stared at the heater as if it were a campfire. It took an eternity for something good to happen, but it did. 'What would I do without you?' Perry said, beaming at me. I rose from my chair, thinking of all the things I could do without him. A thesis underway, a doctorate scholarship, a flight to London.

'Lissam, if you could possibly help me with something further? I need some images for this lecture. Aboriginal dot painting from the Western Desert.'

*Here we go.* 'Pardon me for saying, Dr Perry,' I said, 'but Hatch…Professor Herman usually organised a visiting expert for those lectures.' Prescott University's Indigenous Culture specialist existed only in the five-year strategic plan. It was unlikely to see the light of day.

'Expert?' Perry retorted. 'Sorry, Lissam. I can't pass up this magnificent challenge.' I stared at him, wondering why the Englishman before me hadn't had his spirit broken from the coalmines, Margaret Thatcher and Brexit. 'Besides,' he continued, 'I'm not completely uneducated about Australian Indigenous culture. You know we have some Aboriginal paintings at Whitlock University, back home. Dorothy Browns.'

I drew a breath. 'Really?'

'Good stuff, Dorothy Brown'

These were the pearls of fine art interpretation by one of the most internationally acclaimed art historians of my time: *Good stuff.*

Dorothy's diminutive dots were in neutral colours reminiscent of her ochre tradition but combined with a contemporary minimalist style. The effect was shimmering and hypnotic, like a mirage. I was not her only fan. For years, the world had been clamouring for Dorothy's sense of space like it was waterfront real estate. I shouldn't have been surprised Whitlock had some Dorothy Browns, being such a prestigious institution. Prescott University was not so lucky. No one had been so kind as to gift one to our collection, and we weren't holding our breath.

'Yes, we were rather pleased to nab some Browns,' Perry said.

'You have more than one?' *The injustice continues.*

'Yes, Whitlock has four canvases, in fact. A quadriptych series, so they must stay together,' Perry explained, 'as a tribe,' he ended with a chuckle.

'Whitlock is fortunate to have them,' I said. Dorothy had done a few different 'sets' of paintings during her career: pairs, triptychs and quadriptychs. But she was mostly known for large singular canvases. A quad was quite a coup. 'Shame she's not painting anymore,' I added.

'Yes, I remember hearing something about her pulling out of the game. When was it, do you recall?'

'2015,' I replied, as if it were my birthday, though it felt more like a death. 'The pressure to produce was too much, at least that was what the papers said.'

'Created quite a stir, didn't it? Quite odd, considering how hard it was to talk to her in the first place. She wasn't called "The Greta Garbo of the Desert" for nothing.' I looked at Perry, debating whether to bother explaining how the constant haranguing from the art paparazzi and hungry dealers drove Dorothy into hiding. But Perry ploughed on with his own contemplations. 'Wanting to be left alone was one thing,' he said. 'Removing herself completely was quite another. Put many noses out. White noses, I imagine,' Perry chuckled to himself again. 'Wasn't there talk that her own people were upset by it too?'

'I don't know for sure. That's the thing with Aboriginal culture, it's hard to know anything for sure,' I said, hoping the statement might make him think twice about the lecture. 'There is a lot in their culture that is secret. *Sacred* secrets.'

'*Terra australis incognita*,' Perry mused. 'Unknown southern land.' His mind was drifting elsewhere, possibly in a pith helmet. Wandering back to the present, he asked, 'She still alive and kicking, you think?'

'Dorothy Brown? I have no idea.' The thought of it. Dorothy dead? She didn't look like a spring chicken when she began exhibiting. But no one knows how old she is. Not even Dorothy.

'Either way, prices for her work would have skyrocketed.' Perry's chest puffed up. 'We should have them valued. Whitlock, I mean. It might be a good idea to have images of them for my lecture.'

With an overwhelming urge to find a fly for his ointment, I said, 'As long as she hasn't passed away in the last twelve months.'

Perry raised his eyebrows. 'Why is that?'

'You can't show images of the deceased or their art within a year of their passing, or use their name,' I explained. 'It's a tradition of respect.'

'You can't use their name?'

'It's called Sorry Business. Sometimes you can use their last name. It depends on the community, I think. I've also heard that you can never use their names. But then I've heard examples where the community can't say the name for five or six years. It's not a one-size-fits-all rule. Culture is complex, you see.'

'Can't use the names of the dead,' Perry mused. 'Quite the opposite to us. Still, might be a good idea to find out for certain if Dorothy is still with us. And for any Aboriginal artist that we have in the image library,' Perry shifted in his chair. 'We best be legitimate.'

'Does that include artists from the Torres Strait Islands?' That was my fly number two, hoping for stickage.

'Torres Strait Islands?'

'When we refer to Aboriginal artists, we probably should also be saying Torres Strait Islander as well. They don't identify as Australian Aboriginal.'

'Let's call them Indigenous. It covers all bases,' Perry winked. 'Anyway, I've actually already earmarked the images I wish to use on the library's database,' he said, settling back in his chair. 'There are about twenty images, I think.'

'You altered my database?' I asked. It was like saying he had rummaged through my handbag in search of Minties.

'Yes, I did it last night,' he said, pushing his glasses up the bridge of his nose.

'May I ask -,' I spluttered, 'what exactly you did, Dr Perry?'

'Added a field and put the letters "Abo" in it.'

'Abo?'

'Yes, short for "Aboriginal",' he said, as if I hadn't worked it out. 'Before I knew about this Torres Strait Islander thing. Can't say I'm all that familiar with the program, but I think it's okay.'

My stomach churned. 'I'd better go and check.'

'Don't you have a lecture to go to?'

'Lecture?' I said, looking at my watch. He was right. I had ten minutes.

'Not one of mine,' he replied. 'Still, it's important.' Perry grinned from his chair. 'Thanks for the IT support. Losing that file would have been disastrous.'

I ran down the corridor into my office, leapt over the armrest and dived onto the keyboard. Clicking madly on the icon, the database would not appear. Instead, I saw a large red cross, an error message and an undecipherable code. In a manic frenzy, I dialled the university's IT support department. As it rang, I realised my bottom was hot. Really hot. The hot water bottle was under me. I pulled it out and threw the rubber against the wall.

'Gordon will be at the crash site in fifteen minutes.' The tech coordinator giggled as he added 'Flash Gordon.'

My body began to relax despite the news that I was going to miss the lecture, whatever it was on. Besides, fifteen minutes for technical response was unheard of. An event to be witnessed. While waiting for Flash, I opened the filing cabinet (involving the yoga pose sideways dog), took out Prescott's art collection printed catalogue and typed up the names of all Aboriginal and Torres Strait Islander artists. The Gallery of New South Wales was likely to be my best source of information on artist deaths. I rang the gallery number and asked for the Curator of Aboriginal and Torres Strait Islander Art.

'She's not answering her phone,' the receptionist said. 'Would you like to leave a message? I can put you through to her voicemail.'

There were quite a few names to list, most of whom I had trouble pronouncing. I felt a twinge of embarrassment about this. For all the facts I'd learned and skills I'd developed in my life, I was completely at sea when it came to correctly pronouncing Aboriginal words. Nonetheless, I angled for the curator's coveted email address so I could just send the names through.

At that moment, a bony young man with a baby face appeared, sporting a smirk not dissimilar to Marvin Brodie's. This was Flash, and he was right on time. I climbed out of my chair and watched Flash contort his thin frame into it. 'You need a bigger office,' the genius observed. To his credit, Flash was in the database within seconds. Unfortunately, Perry's inserted field had thrown all the information askew. Gordon's smirk disappeared. He couldn't explain what Perry had done, but he was fascinated by it. I sent him down the corridor to Perry to find out. Meanwhile, I sent a grovelling email to the state gallery's curator, along with the list of First Nations' artists in the Prescott collection, adding Dorothy Brown's name at the end. The tech returned, still puzzled, but he removed the offending field without creating further chaos.

'My sincerest apologies,' Perry said over my shoulder, startling me. The bulky man moved like a spider monkey in slippers.

'You weren't to know, Dr Perry,' I replied with enforced goodwill. 'Perhaps the best thing to do is for me to email you some basic guidelines about using the database?'

'That would be lovely.'

'Lovely,' I murmured after the two men departed.

Looking at my watch, the lecture was half over, but I sprinted out the building and across the quadrangle to listen at the door.

Prescott University was one of the big eight. Meaning it was one of the country's eight prestigious sandstone universities. That said, all universities had additional contemporary architecture reeking of planned obsolescence. Art History and Theory was housed in the original sandstone section, which explained why the classrooms looked so shabby. The rickety lecture room was one of the smaller ones reserved for intimately-sized post-graduate classes. There was Professor Palmer, bunkered behind a wooden rostrum from the 1960s, anchored on the small stage in front of a whiteboard. Unfortunately, Marvin was sitting in his usual spot right at the front and spotted me. His oversized, well-groomed head kept oscillating from the lecturer to me. Palmer, distracted by Marvin's swivel-action, hauled me in front of the class like a naughty schoolchild. I dropped my hot water bottle (didn't mean to bring it with me) and mumbled, 'Had to help Doctor Perry...'. Palmer released me immediately, almost falling to the floor in apology. I straightened my coat and made my way to the back, sending a wink to Marvin on the way.

Perry followed Palmer's lecture. The break between lectures was quiet. Ninety-nine percent of the students were on their phones. Snapchat or Instagram, probably. I don't have a profile on either, can't see the point. Our new Head of Faculty arrived carrying a large case. He set it down on a nearby table and theatrically opened it to reveal a slide projector. The room was old school, but it seemed Perry was even older school. The class tittered at the ancient equipment, but he shot us a look so cold everyone clammed it. Perry instructed Marvin to dim the lights. It thrilled Marvin to oblige. The first slide projected a drawing by Matt Blackmore, a nude woman I had seen before. One line, very simple. It was a slide from my image library archive. By this time, my hot water bottle was cool, but I could feel natural heat rising in my body. Perry had raided my files again, this time from the archive cabinet.

'The line in this drawing?' Eva asked after being zoned in on by Perry.

Eva Ng was her full name. Half German, half Vietnamese. Most would mistake the name for a twilight greeting and would say 'evening' in polite return. However, when it came to meeting Eva Ng herself, most were unsure what to say. Perpetually dressed in black, Eva was five feet nine inches in height and was, as they say, built. Her face had Vietnamese features except for a nose that sported a significant bump in its centre. It was a nose that leaned forward, as if on the verge of saying something but muzzled by its owner.

'Yes, how would you describe it?' At that moment, Perry slapped his stomach, then thrust his index finger at her.

'Epicurean,' Eva replied in monotone. Like the rest of the class, I stared back at Perry. He dropped his hand from his stomach and looked back in the opposite direction towards his desk. 'Is that what you feel about it when you see this line? Try again.' Perry turned back and thrust his finger at her again.

'Sybaritic,' she said. Perry's eyes turned to meet hers. "You have an excellent thesaurus in that head. But is "sybaritic" really the

word you want to use? Come on…what do you *feel* about the line?'
Perry's eyebrows bounced suggestively. The class stayed as quiet as
collective church mice waiting for the cat to be fed by something
tinned. Meanwhile, I doodled Perry as the minimalist nude, dressed
only in glasses and forming beard. He looked suitably ridiculous.

'Very good,' Simon whispered. That morning, Simon had been
in someone else's art project. It had involved a drone shot of one hot
pink haired head amongst one hundred blonde heads. Naturally,
Simon was the pink one.

'Sensual,' Eva spat out eventually, colour rising up her throat.

'Getting warmer,' Perry said, unmoved.

'Carnal,' Simon mumbled, working his ESP skills across the
room. 'It's carnal, Eva.' He was right, as far as picking the word
Perry wanted.

Eva gritted her teeth. 'Voluptuous.'

'Noooo,' Simon tsked quietly.

Perry kept both eyebrows raised and nodded only slightly,
encouraging her to continue. She took a deep breath before playing
her final card. 'Carnal'.

Perry waved his hands above his head like a Baptist preacher,
'Ohhhhh, yeeeeeesssss,' he yelled to the heavens while the class
cheered, including Simon. Perry's eyes shifted to the back row.

'How would you describe it, Lissam?'

'Synthetic,' I replied.

'Really?' Perry asked, taking a step back. The rest of the class
turned their heads to the back. 'Why synthetic?' he asked.

'It used to be a passionate line', I explained, 'in the beginning.
But eventually it became more automatic. Something so well
practised that he could draw it with heroin in his system. That's
what we see here.'

Someone called out, 'I prefer his line of cocaine,' and the class whooped. Simon turned to me and offered a fist punch as a respectful acknowledgment of my revolutionary act. I met the punch, but it was undeserved. I'd just made my relationship with Perry even worse. But Perry's attention towards class discipline had shifted to the broader chaos. 'So is that what can happen to passion, to art?' he asked, placating the rowdy atmosphere. 'It can get drug-fucked?' The class audibly delighted in a lecturer swearing. 'I wouldn't laugh if I were you.' Shame silenced the room. 'Heroin killed Matt Blackmore. We can't paint or sculpt from the grave now, can we? Okay,' he clapped as he turned towards the slide projector. 'On to other contours…'

Perry had taken my contrary view on the chin. But it wasn't very politic of me, not if I wanted him to endorse my travel plans. In hindsight, I should've said something boring like 'erotic'.

Returning to the office late that afternoon, I checked my inbox for a reply email from the curator. There was nothing. I tapped lightly on the desk while staring at my screensaver. After Hatchet's resignation, I'd drawn a doodle of my ex-supervisor in celebration. Simon had taken the liberty of scanning the doodle and making it my screensaver. There was Professor Herman hanging from a parachute, smiling with hatchet in hand, drifting across the screen. But I wasn't really seeing it. Instead, I was imagining Perry trying to track down Dorothy Brown on Twitter. Worse, asking me to do it.

As I got out from under the desk and turned off the light, I shook my head and mumbled to myself, 'He wouldn't do anything like that.' Then looked down the dark, quiet hallway towards his office. Perry's office light was still on. 'Of course, you can,' I heard him say. Then a pause for whoever was on the phone with him. 'I won't let you off that easily,' he replied, his laugh booming like Santa Claus.

45

# CHAPTER 4

According to the label, the berry and oak got along very well. Thirteen minutes into the twenty-minute train ride, I was hanging onto the carriage's vertical bar like a burnt-out pole dancer. Reading the wine bottle in my hand was easier than attempting to find my phone in my bag while the train twisted and turned through the suburbs. Post-station, I trudged the footpath's steep inclines to get to Maggie's. Once at Maggie's heavily aged hardwood front door, thunderous sounds of Mahler were reverberating inside off the hardwood floors and high ceilings. I knocked hard, then pressed my nose against the stained glass that flanked the entrance to see if anyone had heard. No shadowy movement so far. The place was a cathedral compared to my apartment. But to most, perhaps it was simply a five-bedroom bluestone in a nice North Shore suburb. A solid house in a family neighbourhood. After pounding until my rhythms overcame Symphony Number Nine, I heard Ponty running up the hallway, yelping with idiotic excitement. The Newfoundland was only two years old but large enough to be forty and was unbearably welcoming. 'Down Ponty!' Maggie drew me in. She was wearing the frumpy moss green cardigan that always had me imagining her on 'the moors'. Once safely inside, I promptly handed over the bottle.

'Cab Sav, yum,' she said. 'Come through. Ruben's at the keyboard with Mahler.'

I hung my coat, plonked my bag amongst a collection of muddy boots and umbrellas, and followed Maggie up the hallway. Every room had ornate cornices, framed drawings, and ragged-edged Persian carpets on the hardwood floors. The house was like a well-travelled old man with an interesting perspective on society. You could smell it, feel it and hear it. Well, you could hear it when Ruben wasn't distorting the speakers with Austrian composers from the nineteenth century. Walking into the study, the amps at full tilt, we found Ruben at his keyboard playing a computer game.

'Solitaire, Ruben?' I yelled, wondering what would drive an educated person to pursue a game that was as productive as untangling spaghetti.

Maggie turned down the music.

'I was listening to that,' he said, then jutted out his chin and blew upwards, lifting his fringe. Ruben's brown hair was permanently falling over his eyes. How he could see anything was beyond me.

'Remember when solitaire was called patience?' Maggie asked me.

'No,' I frowned. I was ten years younger than Maggie and Ruben. A lot can change in a decade. 'I'm sure Liz would say 'patience' doesn't make for a good marketing buzz word.'

'Zucchini!' Maggie screamed, leaping over Ponty and running towards the kitchen, her elbow accidentally knocking the wine bottle off the desk. Ruben deftly caught and steadied it. He then asked the inevitable question. 'Tour?'

'Perhaps I should help with the zucchini?' I asked.

'Nah, she's fine.' Ruben led me out to the old glasshouse out the back. This pre-dinner tradition of being guided around Ruben's orchid collection had never been my favourite part of the evening. This evening, it also hindered finding out what Maggie had to grumble about. But here we were, breathing in fertiliser. While technology was busy outdoing itself, an orchid, given the right conditions, could live forever. This was how Ruben had first introduced his glasshouse to me when we met five years ago. The statement had some personal gravity, as Ruben lived in perpetual fear of being retrenched. He was a manager at the state library, so the fear had some weight behind it. But Ruben's fear had been around for so long, with no hint from human resources promising to validate it. Still, words like Google and Amazon weren't welcome in his presence.

'As some parts discreetly die at the back of the orchid,' Ruben had explained, 'other parts grow from the front.' Both Charles Darwin and Ruben harboured a respect for this plant above all others. The difficulty for me was a matter of aesthetics. The flowers appeared as if they were expressing every emotion at once. Looking around, I imagined Ruben's hothouse as a psych ward for foliage. We continued our walk. Then Ruben whispered, 'Do not ask how to grow an orchid. Ask "How does this orchid grow?"' It was almost like he was talking to himself, his expression one of gentle reverence.

'Dinner's ready,' Maggie yelled through the kitchen window, but Ruben didn't seem to hear it.

'We'd better go,' I said, touching his elbow.

'What?' he replied, almost shocked.

'It's time for dinner.'

'Right.' He dragged his fingers through his fringe and began walking towards the house.

At dinner, I watched Maggie pushing a portion of her spectacular roast lamb around her white plate like a hockey puck in slow motion. Ruben, equally quiet, was shovelling a forkful of perfectly stuffed zucchini into his mouth before he had finished the last mouthful. Considering instant noodles were my default meal at home (breakfast, lunch and dinner), the contents of my plate at Maggie's were, as usual, beyond my wild imaginings. But tonight, the usual chatter was absent. My Cabernet Sauvignon sat in their glasses like two mosquito-infested ponds. Even Ponty had given up begging. Instead, he posed as a deflated sphinx in the corner. There was a serious spanner in things.

'Okay, who died?' I asked. Not one of my finest moments, as it turned out.

They stared at each other before Ruben managed to swallow, then began speaking. Which was odd in itself. Usually, Maggie was the icebreaker of the house.

'Anna, you are our closest friend,' he began and then faltered before continuing. Fortunately, he was looking straight at me, and the fringe was behaving. 'We've been wanting to start a family, which has led to trying IVF for…well, for quite some time.'

'Really?' I asked, feeling numb. I always thought I was their child.

'Three specialists later,' Maggie said, then shrugged.

'It's no dice,' Ruben ended. 'We got the news a couple of days ago.'

It was assumed by everyone – including myself, especially myself – that Maggie and Ruben would have children sometime. Now the two were going to be knocking about alone in this enormous house.

'Adoption?' I asked, attempting a softening agent.

'We've talked about it,' Maggie replied. 'But it means overseas trips these days. Pulling some poor child out of their culture.'

'Sure,' I agreed, 'but what if their culture sucks? Who wouldn't want your culture, Maggie? Your culture is the best. Look how brilliant you both are. Loving, funny…well, sometimes funny. And this amazing food, this incredible house. Oh, this house. It would offer cognac and backgammon if it could.'

'And Cuban cigars,' Ruben nodded, looking around the room.

'It's too soon to discuss this,' Maggie replied, her eyes hanging down at the sides with exhausted grief. Ruben reached over to squeeze her left hand just as she reached over to gently pat mine with her right.

Maggie and I had met at a boutique bar in the city. The sort of bar with a wine list an inch thick, presented in a leather cover still smelling of leather. With our mutual friends long gone, we were researching the difference between malted and non-malted whiskey. After testing a healthy sample, I turned to the space where the bartender had been standing five minutes before and gave my conclusion.

'Scoshhh shhhonal shhhing.' Which meant 'Scottish seasonal shedding'. My words were akin to a washing machine.

'Going to the loo,' Maggie yelled over the noise of the bartender vacuuming around us. It was the first time I noticed the bar was empty. I also noticed how Maggie's thick woolly jumper was advantageous when she walked smack straight into a heavy antique cabinet, rolled off and disappeared into the ladies. The next weekend, Maggie was wearing the same jumper when she walked into Ruben. More sober, less physically damaging. Love.

Maggie began clearing the plates. I followed her into the kitchen with the silver gravy boat and plastic margarine container. I couldn't help but look at the latest of the paintings on the walls. They were from the childcare centre where Maggie worked, gifts from the kids. Butcher's paper, acrylic and crayon (in the very brightest of colours) had turned the kitchen into a psychedelic fire hazard. Still, there was something to the works that always impressed me. I figured it was hard to be creatively pretentious when you wear Thomas the Tank Engine pyjamas.

As soon as her hands were free, I gave her a hug. 'Maggs,' I said. She pecked me on the forehead before turning to fossick in the refrigerator. I put on the kettle and began supervising the boil.

'Feel like something sweet?' Maggie asked while pulling out a meringue dessert topped with cream and strawberries from the refrigerator.

'My god, pavlova,' I said. 'Haven't had one of those in years. Can I flame it with the brûlée torch?'

'No, Anna.'

'Why not?'

'Because it's not crème brûlée. It's a pav. It's perfect just as it is. A nice, light pav. Well, it's nice and light,' she carried the dish out, 'except for all the cream.' I followed with dessert plates.

'Ah, the pavlova,' said Ruben, while arming himself with a small fork and spoon. 'Australia's national dessert.'

'Is it?' I asked, distributing the plates.

'Yesterday, out of the blue, I had a yearning for it,' Maggie said, cutting slices. 'Comfort food, I suppose. I found my mum's old recipe. Pavlova was originally from New Zealand, you know.'

'Typical Australians, stealing from the poor New Zealanders,' I said. 'Why do we always do that?'

'Australia chose the name pavlova,' Maggie added as she cut the cake into slices. 'Disguising stolen goods, I suspect.'

'After the Russian ballet dancer, wasn't it? Anna Pavlova?' Ruben asked, staring at the dessert.

Maggie nodded, passing the slices around, 'Naming a dessert after her beauty while raising the kilos of anyone who looked at it.'

'Ruben, please don't give it to Ponty,' Maggie said. The dog had risen from his retreat and already began to eat from Ruben's fork.

'It's just a treat, for god's sake,' he implored.

'Alright, alright,' she said, hands in the air. Ruben stopped. He picked up a spoon and ate quietly. Maggie did the same. After a few seconds, they both laughed. Just a little.

I nursed my stomach as I rocked back and forth on the train ride home. The damage had been done over that bottle of dessert wine Ruben pulled out after the pav. A syrupy drop with a great apricot thing going. Still, dessert wine after dessert. They really do need children in order to discipline themselves better. Then I realised I'd missed Central Station. That would teach me to drink and take public transport. The next stop was Redfern, and I felt a slight panic.

I was aware, however, that it was eleven at night, I was travelling alone and just about to get off at a station right next to Eveleigh Street. My mission was to walk out on the other side of the tracks, avoiding Eveleigh Street at all costs. All I knew was that one side had Eveleigh Street, which meant The Block. And this meant Aboriginal and Torres Strait housing district with a well-publicised history of violence and crime. I'd heard they had been working to clean it up though. I didn't know who 'they' were, or what was meant by 'cleaning it up'. Usually, it involved moving people already on the back foot to somewhere worse. The details were vague, and since moving to Sydney, I had been given the distinct impression that you don't get off at Redfern station on your own late at night.

The train pulled up, and I stumbled out onto the platform. Damned if I was getting out at Macdonaldtown to wait around for another train to take me back to Central. Besides, Redfern station had enough lighting for an Olympic opening ceremony. If you had a shadow, it was somewhere else. Train stations in Sydney are much of a muchness. Asphalt platforms, mini-billboards, and yellow lines to prevent the accident prone from becoming rail kill. I followed the one person who got off with me, a middle-aged man in an ordinary brown sports coat and jeans who, by his posture, looked like he'd done six shifts back to back. Once we got to the top of the stairs, my chaperone stopped to check his phone. I wondered if I should do the same. But fatigue descended. All I wanted to do was go to bed. The cold air tightened my skin as I made my way out of the old brick station alone and onto a narrow street. I could see clearly across the road where a low concrete wall was adorned with a mural – less Banksy, more community centre.

My inner art critic barely took in the myriad of bright colours, dotted circles and wavy lines. Following the mural around a corner, a painted head of an old man with obligatory grey beard greeted me. Nodding as I passed, I continued down the one-lane road, the wall's illustrations of emus and kangaroos keeping me company. Street lighting lacked the enthusiasm of the station's illumination, but my mind was on kangaroos and emus. Those sure-footed mascots that balanced on leafy branches on our national coat of arms. Which was bizarre, as kangaroos and emus are never found on branches. 'Complete misrepresentation,' I muttered to myself before realising I had come out the wrong entrance. I was on Eveleigh Street. This must be The Block. Admittedly, spotting the six-by-ten metre Aboriginal flag painted on the side of a building was a bit of a giveaway. But by then, I was already halfway down the road, heading towards what was surely Cleveland Street. I could see the streetlights and traffic in the distance. Between me and Cleveland was a narrow, silent, empty street. Silent, except the distant electronic sounds wafting down from the station and as I walked further down, the old Tears for Fears song '*Shout, shout, let it all out.*' An oddly sweet song for a place that had been silenced.

Being under the influence didn't blunt my innate sense of direction completely. Once on Cleveland, all I had to do was turn right, which would take me straight to Surry Hills. Home free. I amped up my walking pace while passing the sort of playground that belonged in a prison for five-year-olds. I was a good runner, I reminded myself. A crap swimmer, but an excellent runner. I then passed a disused building which crouched behind weeds and chain wire fencing. The run of terraces should have made me feel at home, but the two men sitting on the front porch had me catching my breath. From the corner of my eye, I spotted a red bandana on the head of one of them, a cigarette in the mouth of the other. The next terrace had a bearded man who looked more Spanish, staring down at me over the rusted ironwork of his first-floor balcony. The scene was like something out of a play. Everyone costumed with props and in their places, me included. Still going. Doors were closed, keeping the warmth in. Someone had covered a window with a pink sheet. The three men outside said nothing. I focused straight ahead, trotting past with a smile that would suit a knife-thrower's assistant, almost tripping over a tabby cat on the way. I squinted and refocused while practically running past the darkened warehouses that edged the residential precinct.

My ears were alert for sounds, but there were no footsteps coming up behind. 'Almost home,' I coaxed myself as I broke into the light of Cleveland Street. While catching my breath, cars, trucks and buses hurtled past, almost obscuring the Dulux paint shop across the road. No one was going to hurt me. I knew that now, except perhaps my double dessert. Apricot and strawberries. I bent over and breathed in the traffic fumes before straightening up and moving on.

# CHAPTER 5

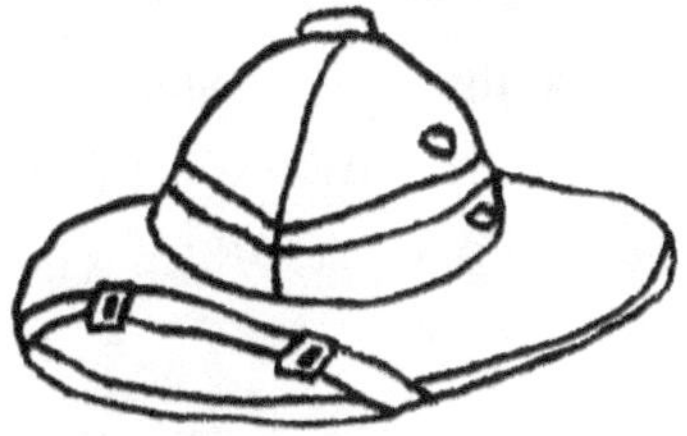

'Surely it's just a virus?' Perry scoffed.

'Unfortunately, no,' Flash Gordon replied. 'As I mentioned before, we do hold training sessions for staff.'

When Perry summoned me by phone to his office, Gordon was already at the computer, frowning. Perry had moved to the floor, working up a sweat while unfolding a printed map of Australia. The warmth of the room made this office significantly more comfortable than my ice box down the hallway. But I didn't feel more comfortable. Not at all.

'Lissam.'

'Doctor Perry.'

'Damn computer's playing up again.' Perry said before pointing his bulky index finger in the very middle of the country. 'Alice Springs,' he explained, 'the belly button of Australia.' I looked down. 'Dot paintings from the desert,' he added.

'Yes', I replied, wondering if he was going to explain it to me or whether I was to explain it to him. Gordon continued to tap on Perry's keyboard, then stopped and leaned back, folding his hands behind his head as he waited for something to finish downloading. He winked at me over the monitor. Confusing need with desire was likely to be a lifelong challenge for Gordon. I shifted my gaze back down to Perry.

'Aboriginal art in the desert region largely focuses on dot painting as a style,' he said. 'Why do you think that is?'

I reluctantly crouched down. 'There are different theories. The most obvious is because they were originally diagrams, maps and patterns drawn in the dirt. A bird's-eye view. They tell the Dreaming stories of their ancestry in this way. Which is also a kind of survival guide, I believe.'

'You learnt this at school, then?' Perry asked. Gordon returned to typing codes.

'Yep,' I replied, which was a lie. What I knew of dot painting was learnt during my undergraduate obsession with Dorothy Brown. One would think, living in a country town, I would not only learn about Aboriginal people but also hang out with one or two. I don't even remember seeing anyone Aboriginal in Nagurra. And we didn't find out much in Mrs Roberts' classes. I remember some textbook images of men with spears on a beach, but that was about it. Ned Kelly, on the other hand…

Perry pushed up his spectacles. 'Anything else?'

He wasn't letting me off the hook just yet. 'From the air,' I said, glancing up at the ceiling, wondering if it could open up and suck me into another world, 'from the air the landscape looks sort of dotted.'

'You've seen it?'

'No, just pictures.'

'You've never been to the Northern Territory?'

'No, not yet.'

'Travelled much at all?'

'Not really…my studies have been demanding,' I replied, glancing at the wastepaper bin.

'Right,' Perry said as his eyes dropped back down to the map. 'Paintings with aerial views. I imagine the desert tribes would have had trouble seeing the landscape from the air, too. You know, before they had access to aeroplanes and such.'

I drew a deep breath before answering. 'Hard to explain that one.' But there was one point I had some information on from some research during my undergrad. 'Apparently, some Aboriginal people don't like the word "tribe". They prefer clan or community.'

'Really?' he asked. 'Why?'

'"Tribe" suggests a hierarchical system which they didn't have. Don't have," I said, reminding myself that Aboriginal culture is still alive.

'I suppose they could look from mountain tops, ridges,' Perry said, gazing over the map.

'Not every area has that kind of elevation. A lot of the desert is pretty flat. The paintings – or the maps, if you want to call them that – can cover an enormous area. More than what you might see from the top of a cliff.'

'What are you saying, Lissam? That Aboriginal people levitate?' Even Gordon looked up for an answer.

'I'm not saying anything.' My glare misdirected at Gordon had him blushing before he returned to what he was doing. 'I don't know. This isn't my area.'

'Not your area?' Then Perry smarted. His hand reached up to his chest.

'Are you alright?' I asked.

'What?' Perry grimaced. 'Ah, yes. I'm fine.' Lowering his arm, he tried crossing his legs and gave up. 'Gordon, turn off that heater, will you?' Gordon complied.

Perry shifted his ankles to one side, with his body resting its weight on the trunk of his arm. 'Not your area? Then we will both be learning quickly, my dear,' Perry continued. 'Swift adaptation is the plan.'

'Adaptation?' I asked, though I also wanted to clarify the 'we'.

'Yes, adaptation,' he replied, 'to this strange place you call home.'

Gordon swore into the light of the monitor. 'Lissam,' Perry turned briskly, 'I think it's time we move to a computer that functions.'

Perry walked over the map of Australia and marched down the corridor towards my office. I raced to overtake him, ensuring my position at the keyboard. Perry dodged into Sharon's office, taking a spare chair. When we had both squeezed into my cleaning cupboard, I was instructed to check incoming emails for a response from the Art Gallery of NSW. The bulky dishevelment next to me made the room almost suffocating.

Still no reply from the art gallery curator. But there was an email from Perry himself. He had forwarded the Dorothy Brown quadriptych images from Whitlock University the night before.

'A.W. took these photos with his new digital camera and emailed them across.' Perry's chest puffed at the international network he still commanded. A.W., I soon learned, was Alistair Wilcox, a fine art lecturer at the London University. The collection's curator had been retrenched the year before, Perry explained, though distracted by the re-opening of each image.

Three of the paintings had variations of red-brown patches of semi-darkness, like the shadows of clouds. The fourth was more brown-grey and darker again, a night painting perhaps. I hadn't seen anything like it. The fine dot techniques were all archetypal Dorothy. They just didn't feel like archetypal Dorothy. Her 'signature' calm feeling was absent.

'When were these done?' I asked.

'Not sure, they can't find the info that came with them.'

'The certificates of authenticity?'

'Yes, I've ordered staff to find them or there will be trouble,' he said, breathing heavily. 'I remember when the paintings arrived in 2013,' Perry smiled, shifting into honeyed nostalgia. 'At that point I realised that thirteen was a very fortunate number indeed,' he released a light chuckle. 'The works were presented to the vice-chancellor as a gift to acknowledge some successful collaborative research project. The Arts Faculty were more excited than anyone, even though they weren't given to us officially.' He then frowned a little before saying, 'They were originally supposed to go to the vice-chancellor's boardroom, but they ended up in Engineering. The idiots accepted the canvases as if they were paper serviettes. Plebeians,' he spat. Perry then became distracted by something on the screen.

'There's no artist signature,' he said.

I shook my head, almost in pain from the naivety, which then only reminded me of my own. I might know more than Perry, but it was a measurement used to compare amoebae. 'They don't sign on the front like we do. Sometimes they write their name on the backs of the canvases. The painting itself is really the signature.' Perry shifted in his seat. 'The dots are meticulous,' he said. 'They sent out a search party to look for the paintings when I requested the photos. Found behind some filing cabinets, the four of them. Well, that's engineers for you. They can build eight-lane bridges and towering skyscrapers, but ask them to hang four paintings...'

I stared at the images, back and forth, one to the next.

'Well?' he asked with a nod and a smile. 'What do you think?'

'They are...different...good...but different.'

'What do you mean, different?' The smile dropped.

'Maybe these were done at the end, just before she left.'

'Why?'

'Ah, well...it's because...look, what do I know?'

'Spit it out, Lissam,' Perry boomed, startling me.

'They don't have the same feeling.'

'As what?'

'As Dorothy's other paintings.'

'What?' The word was almost a whisper. He pressed on. 'They look okay to me. What are you getting at?'

'Perhaps it's the reproduction. Digital cameras can alter quality.' But I knew that wasn't it. Photographic quality never affected the resonance, the feeling of the work. Not for me. Not for Dorothy's paintings.

'Don't make excuses to flatter me, woman,' he barked. 'Tell me.'

'I'm no specialist,' I started. Noah Webster was a specialist and look what happened to him. Fried by all and sundry for letting fakes through onto the auction lot. But Perry continued to look at me expectantly. I enlarged the image and looked more closely for something I already knew wasn't there. 'These paintings are technically well done, considering.'

'Considering what?'

'Considering they don't feel like the hand of Dorothy Brown.' I looked him in the eye and gave the only answer I knew. 'I'm not sure.'

Perry nodded for a moment while staring at the screen, then shrugged. 'Okay, we don't know if she's still alive, right?'

'No, the curator hasn't replied to my email.'

'Then we must take matters into our own hands,' he declared. Which meant I was to Google it. After trawling through several websites relating to Dorothy Brown, the artist had not yet been reported as deceased.

'Her ex-dealer would know for sure,' Perry said. 'Who was that?'

'I think she had a few,' I answered. Typing further, I sourced an article that appeared in the *Sydney Morning Herald*, 10 September 2005.

Dorothy Brown, a Stumpy Downs artist, had exhibited her work at Galerie Exotique in Sydney. The piece had not appeared in the arts pages, but in general news. This was not surprising. Serious art reviewers, wary of commercial kitsch, wouldn't touch a space called Galerie Exotique with a barge pole.

*New 'dot paintings' by Western Desert artist, Dorothy Brown, are being exhibited at Sydney's Galerie Exotique. Dorothy has travelled from the little-known Aboriginal community of Stumpy Downs, a three-hour drive west from Alice Springs.*

*'We don't normally hold one-man exhibitions,' said Galerie Exotique owner, Miles Porter, 'but we've made an exception for Dorothy. We are very excited to have her here in Sydney. And even though she's very shy, we are hoping Dorothy will demonstrate her painting skills for us during her stay.' The Galerie Exotique exhibition* Dot Paintings by Dorothy Brown *will close at the end of the month."*

A large photograph of a fine-boned Dorothy Brown dominated the brief article. Sitting on the gallery floor, the slight woman wore a t-shirt with the Road Runner on it. A curly mop of black hair covered her face. Squatting and standing onlookers surrounded her, hoping for the t-shirt's antithesis. Something seriously authentic and authentically Australian. Her brush hovered over abstracted ochre-coloured dots crawling across the surface. Miles Porter's wish had come true. Dorothy painted her Dreaming in Sydney. It was the second miracle at Galerie Exotique, after achieving a one-man show by a woman.

I hadn't even heard of Galerie Exotique, so I searched for it. No listing anywhere. I tried a search on Miles Porter who, according to the *Sydney Morning Herald* in 2006, had been pronounced dead.

'Leukaemia,' I read aloud.

'HIV,' Perry shrugged.

'Not these days, surely'

'It's getting rarer, granted,' Perry replied. 'But some poor sods are still falling foul of it.' Then Perry pushed to resume the research. We discovered that until Dorothy stopped painting in 2015, she moved from gallery to gallery, a nomadic trail to more reputable spaces run by more reputable dealers. No one gallery was honoured with the term 'home'. Which left Perry nowhere. Until the certificates of authenticity were found at Whitlock, it would be hard to know who to ask. So he kept asking me.

Throughout the afternoon, Perry shot questions as if hosting an Aboriginal game show. The theme on circles had been going for a good half hour: Aboriginal concepts of circular time, circular meeting places symbolised in paintings, circular body paint designs.

My ability to answer had been pitifully limited. I was fast losing points, and my PhD prize was nowhere to be seen. Sometimes I had answers but soon realised my sources may have been less than reliable. We all read things, are told things, but what do I really know? Awkwardness ate away at me every time I was forced to reply, 'I'm not exactly sure.' Doing my best to find out, I tapped at the keys for anything that might satisfy him. Perry, on the other hand, was buzzing.

After a harsh interrogation on ochre preparation, Perry was interrupted by a little girl with blonde hair, looking much like Sharon.

'Hey there, Miss Grace,' I said, but the child had already fixed her gaze on Perry. She had a small bottle in one hand and a tiny white brush in the other.

'Sharon,' Perry yelled, but Sharon didn't reply. Grace walked up and began to paint the toes of Perry's brown leather shoes with correction fluid. I sat back and watched while Perry picked up the phone and dialled the extension.

'Sharon, I really think it's time you find a solution...' he started down the receiver. There was a pause, then Perry put down the phone. Sharon soon appeared at the doorway.

'Bring back the free university crèche,' she said, ignoring her daughter, who had tossed the bottle and brush on the floor, making way for the next activity: hanging off Perry's belt.

'The crèche has nothing to do with me,' he whined while struggling to hold up his pants. Sharon picked up the bottle and brush, then held out her hand to Grace. Walking out, Sharon replied, 'Everything is connected with everything else.'

'Quoting Lenin, are we?' Perry asked. But Sharon had already left the room, trailed by Grace glaring over her shoulder. Gordon looked in to announce that the computer was back in action. Perry thanked him while pushing up his spectacles. I assumed this was Perry's cue to leave, but he remained seated and continued the roll of requests for information.

The focus became even sharper when he learned that Dorothy Brown appeared on a cover of the *Weekend Australian* magazine. In 2010, Dorothy, a tobacco-chewing grandmother from the desert, had become the darling of the New York art scene without even going there. According to the article, she was one of the highest-paid artists in Australia. Two auction houses and a dealer from Frankfurt were all given a substantial amount of column space for their critically reserved comments. However, an interview with Brenda Wood pulled the article together. Wood was a white art coordinator from Stumpy Downs. Intelligent and compassionate, the interview gave the most powerful journalistic hook of them all, the human touch.

'Many people have a romantic idea of Dorothy painting in the quiet of the desert landscape,' Ms Wood said. 'In reality, she does her best among yapping dogs, blaring music, children crying, and flies. Both the dealers and her family pressure Dorothy to produce. Dealers want more paintings and the relatives want more cars. She buys them a car a week.'

'Do they need a car a week?' the interviewer asked.

'Need?' Ms Wood asked in return. 'That's a hard question to answer. But I can tell you that there's no public transport out here.'

'What does Dorothy want?'

'I can't say for sure, she doesn't say much,' Ms Wood replied. 'If she asks for anything, it's usually more Coke Zero.'

Photographs accompanied the article, but took some time to download. The images began to appear, one by one. Rusted corrugated sheds, the flat red earth and worn-out trees under the weight of a deep blue sky. This was Stumpy Downs, the closest thing to Dorothy's studio. The artist herself appeared in bare feet, a dusty floral dress and a woollen beanie. Her small, thin frame was depicted painting outside on the ground in the red earth with seemingly happy children running around nearby. Dorothy had declined to speak.

'Look at that burnt orange dirt Dorothy's sitting on,' Perry exclaimed with delight. 'Your country's so old it is rusting, Lissam.'

A myriad of bold headlines declared Dorothy's withdrawal from the market. It was 2015. She hadn't died, but the approach was similar. They used her images everywhere.

'How strange, this disappearance,' Perry said. 'You would have thought with the recognition, the respect, the money for her family and community, that all her Christmases had come at once.'

'Maybe Dorothy doesn't celebrate Christmas,' I replied, weary from the research.

Perry glanced towards me, slightly irritated. Then he got an idea. Thumping his fist on the desk, he demanded, 'Call Swampy Downs.'

'Stumpy Downs,' I corrected, and then hesitated. Calling would be invasive, surely. Perry intercepted the handset and wiggled his finger at the screen for me to find the number. The Stumpy Downs Art Centre number came up on the screen, and Perry dialled like it was a race. And waited. And waited. And waited. Just before the call rang out, someone picked up the phone.

'Yes, is Dorothy Brown there?' he asked. I sank into the corner. 'Can you repeat that? Sorry, I'm having trouble understanding you. Look, is the art coordinator there?' Perry raised his voice, either in exasperation or for clarity. 'Brenda Wood? Is she still the art coordinator?' By this time, he was practically yelling. 'According to the *Australian* newspaper in 2010,' he said, 'Brenda Wood was…Hello?' Perry turned to me. 'They haven't hung up, just put the phone down. Probably looking for the art coordinator.' After thirteen minutes of ear-straining patience, he gave up, placing the receiver back in its cradle. 'Damn. Well, we can try later.' Perry unleashed a big stretch, cramping the space in the office further, before rising. The toes of his shoes glowed with white dabs of correction fluid. He paused at the doorway to say, 'Thank you for your assistance today. It's been most helpful.'

I nodded, wondering what I had done.

Perry reappeared at my door later that afternoon. His face had the expression of a blank Scrabble tile.

'Just had a meeting. A rather depressing one, I'm afraid. It is probably best if we both sit down.' I was already seated, clutching my hot water bottle. Perry settled back in his borrowed seat and looked at me for a moment. It was a moment with elastic. It stretched and stretched. In the end, I had to break it.

'What was the meeting about?'

'Many things.' One of those things may have been linoleum flooring, as he had shifted his gaze downward and was staring hard at it. 'Well, it was essentially about funding.' He raised his eyes back to me.

'Funding?'

'We can't financially sustain your position at the image library.' He paused for a moment, then continued. 'Professor Herman had made an effort to juggle things before his departure, trying to find another way to keep you here. He wasn't successful. Your efforts have been greatly appreciated. Be sure of that. It's down to pounds. Dollars, rather.'

I looked hard at him. The sympathy appeared genuine. He pressed on. 'Your final day is next Friday.'

'Next Friday?' I spluttered. 'I have a week?'

'You were contracted, paid weekly, as you know. There were hopes to put you on the payroll next year. Fine print bastards. I did what I could, really. I can't express how...' Perry drifted off and then came back in again. 'I do feel sincerely sorry.' He then stood and moved towards the door. 'See you next week.'

'Next week?' I asked back in a daze. I almost said *I'm not sure, but I'll try to find out* as Perry's back disappeared from view.

No, I wasn't totally rapt with the job. But the convenience and routine worked for me. It was shocking how shocked I felt. Perhaps I liked the job more than I thought.

Sitting in total silence, while Hatchet Herman drifted in his parachute across my screen, I was aware of everything. And yet had no thoughts skittling about my head. Not one. I moved my mouse not to the image database, but to the games menu. Solitaire. The game was unsuccessfully short. The cards weren't useful. There was nothing I could have done.

At the end of the day, still in a half-daze, I checked my emails. There was a message from the curator at the Art Gallery of New South Wales. According to her records, five of the artists on our list had died, but not in the last twelve months. Dorothy Brown, it seemed, was still alive. If it wasn't for my emotional anesthetization, I would have been delighted at the news that Dorothy was still out there. But no feeling came. For further confirmation on Western Desert artists, the curator offered the phone number and email address of an arts organisation in Alice Springs. *The arts centre of Australia's centre,* I thought.

I forwarded the information to Perry, shut down the computer and climbed out of the chair. Somehow, my foot caught on the armrest and my body fell, smacking my head on the hard floor. I hauled my wretched body up. No serious damage done. Perhaps I was too numb to feel it. Slipping on my suede coat and grabbing my messenger bag, I walked out with as much purpose as I could muster. It was quite a performance in confidence, but no one was watching. The corridor was empty.

Once outside, I looked back at the sandstone buildings. Perhaps it was fitting that they had always reminded me of the past. The light was dimming as I made my way across campus. Before I'd even known it, I'd made a detour along the windows where students created bizarre objects that said something about our strange lives. One student, with brown hair pulled back in a knot, was letting fly on canvas with some dark orange paint. She staggered back and then saw me looking at her and laughed. Feeling caught out, I continued to walk. And walk. Past the train station where I should have gone in. Walking further and further towards home. I arrived at my flat an hour and a half later, still numb but with the urge to eat. After consuming the remainder of the vanilla ice cream that had been sitting in the freezer for a couple of months, I wandered around the apartment feeling sick, then slumped on the couch and picked up the phone. I was going to message Maggie, but she had problems of her own. Instead, I called the only number I knew off by heart, besides my own.

The intention was to talk about them rather than me, but my mother wouldn't have it. My news always came first. While I explained the retrenchment, my father yelled questions from the background.

'What they have done doesn't seem fair,' Mum said. 'They should have given you more warning. Still, this could be leading you to something better. So darling, try not to lose faith. You have more strength than what you give yourself credit for.' It was good feedback. I just wished I could embrace it, touch it even. But the faith thing was tricky. Both my parents were churchgoers. Dad may as well have been at the TAB. He liked to cover his bets. Mum was quite different. She had leapt to the faith in her youth and had been instantly buoyed by the holy water. Eyes closed at prayer and breathing deeply, some extra oxygen was possibly being supplied on the side. Outside of church, the woman had a to-do list that rivalled the length of the Dead Sea Scrolls.

I heard gentle muffles and fumbles, and then my father.

'Hello, poppet.'

'Hello, Dad.'

'You'll find your feet again. Know why?'

'Why?'

'Because you have to.'

'Cheers, Dad.'

'Bye, poppet.'

Mum came on again. 'You know we love you. If there's anything we can do, then you must let us know. Do you need some money?'

I winced at the offer. They weren't exactly rolling it in themselves. 'No, please don't worry about that, but thanks for the thought. You're right. I'll be fine. Dad's okay, isn't he? How's the hip?'

'Getting better, despite his insistence to defy the doctor's orders at every turn.' I remembered my father's defiance after the surgery. I took the train back and forth over a couple of months to help get him moving at the hospital, then to settle him back home. It was like teaching a rabid pit bull the two-step. 'I'm getting better because I defy them. Bloody quacks!' he yelled from the faux leather recliner, no doubt. It was his favourite place, right in front of the television. I wasn't sure, but at that point I could've sworn Mum whispered 'Jesus'.

Returning to the kitchen cupboards, I bypassed the instant noodles for a packet of salt and vinegar chips. It was past the due-by date, but I figured the salt and vinegar would preserve the goodness into the next century. It had only just occurred to me I was cold. But

I couldn't be bothered doing anything about it. With gritted teeth, I turned on my laptop to face my future in advertised employment listings. It was taking longer and longer for my computer to start up. *Two years old, aged. Need a new one. But need a new job first.*

It made sense to start on ArtsHub, the online hotspot for arts opportunities. Good thing I'd kept up my student membership. But scrolling down the page had my heart bouncing out of my ribcage, before sliding through my stomach, rattling around my right knee and landing into my sock. I didn't have the experience required to fill out any of the applications. Moving onto the university's online job search section, nothing remotely in my skillset was listed. After trawling the administration, then hospitality lists of general job sites, I realised I was no longer part of the human race.

Charging into the apartment, Liz caught me swallowing the remainder of a family block of chocolate. She balanced her cigarette out of the side of her mouth while shedding her Darlita white trench coat and kicking off her citrus green boots. The cigarette moved up and down like an oar as she waded through her account of the day spent on a commercial shoot.

'And then he refused to get back into the swimming pool of mustard,' she said, wandering into her bedroom. '"It's only mustard", I said. And you can guess how much it costs to fill a swimming pool with mustard. But he kept saying the rash was getting worse. Something about an allergy. Well, I told it to him straight -' Re-emerging in a lemon-yellow tube dress and rubber boots, Liz detected that something was amiss. 'Are you okay?' she asked.

'According to my boss, there's no funding for my job. I'm out.'

'Shit, Anna. This happened today?' I nodded while balling up the chocolate wrapper and chucking it towards the kitchen. Liz didn't reply at first. She was applying lipstick. Red Inferno. 'Funding cuts, you say?'

'Yes,' I replied. 'The department's been looking for ways to extend the job…blah, blah, blah…' I plunged my head back and forth into the couch cushions, Mum's sensible words fading with every nose-dive.

'You'll be okay.' Liz patted my head awkwardly before making her way to the front door.

'The rent is due.'

'Sure, I've got this thing I have to go to right now. Shit, where are my keys?'

'On the floor, near your left foot,' Liz looked wildly. 'Next to your orange pashmina.'

'Gotcha,' she said, as if cornering a blowfly. 'Okay, I'm off. You'll be okay, sunshine.'

The front door opened again. 'Liz?' I whimpered, hoping that a wad of rent money would be thrown in my direction. But my fantasy was in vain. Instead, a nose came through the door, followed by Eva's face, followed by Simon. His pink hair had faded to fairy floss.

'Eva wanted to come out with us,' he explained.

'Come out where?' I asked.

'Out to a very nice bar I've discovered recently, to cheer you up,' he said, joining me on the couch.

'We heard,' Eva said while she remained standing.

'About what?' I asked, wondering whether it was the thesis or the retrenchment that had caught the rumour wind. Or perhaps it was that I'm still in the shackles of celibacy.

'The retrenchment, Sharon told me,' he said. 'Everyone's pissed off on your behalf, Anna. It's so unfair.' No doubt Simon was, as usual, exaggerating things a little for the sake of making me feel better. How everyone could be pissed off when hardly anyone knew me was the flaw in his fairy tale. It was then I noticed a red mark across his forehead. 'Souvenir from being masking-taped to the side of a petrol tanker. Anton's performance piece last night.' 'Sounds like a gas,' I replied. A feint attempt at levity. 'It was incredible…' he smiled, about to expand. He then remembered why he was here. 'But back to your job situation.'

'Maybe it's for the best,' I said, putting the thought out there in the hope Simon could explain why that might be.

But he simply nodded and asked, 'So what sort of work would you like to do now?'

'Preferably something not in the fast food industry.'

'Admittedly, jobs have been pretty thin on the ground lately.'

'It's apocalyptic,' Eva added.

Simon continued. 'But I've already made some calls on your behalf, as has Eva.'

'Really?' My heart levered up an inch. I appreciated Simon's generosity and his extensive network. But Eva making calls on anyone's behalf was unheard of. 'Thanks, guys. You're the best.'

A year ago, Eva had landed a job at the prestigious Tyrone Gilbert Gallery, where she sat donned in her usual black attire on a black office chair behind a large white desk in a large white space. If surrounded by monochromatic sculpture, Eva could have been confused for a display. The gallery job was not just a useful position. Eva had found her home. Like an experimental life form finding its way back to a test tube.

'Nothing specific has come up yet,' Simon continued. 'We need to be patient. In the meantime,' he got up off the couch and offered a hand, 'let's go find us some bubbles.'

Eva followed us to the door, kicking a pile of Liz's clothes out of her way.

It was eight o'clock. The bar was jammed, mostly with suits from finance management or lawyers. The volume of babble increased with every minute. Eva pointed towards people leaving a booth, and we shimmied through to it. Simon high-fived at least eight people on the way, the glaring red mark across his forehead not affecting his confidence one iota. Harrington's, the fine art auction house that almost ended Noah Webster's career, had been the making of Simon's. He had nabbed a job there by the end of his undergraduate studies. Since then, his charming, discreet, and methodical manner fast built his reputation. Yes, he carried out the expected tasks of coordinating packing and transport, writing conservation reports and assisting in research. But Simon's true talent came to the fore on auction nights. His exceptional recollection of faces and names was backed up with at least one personal reference per person. The jewel to his crown was appearing open and transparent while in custody of secrets that could cause the collapse of many a multinational, and even more marriages.

While Simon poured sparkling wine into three flutes, I haggled to pay my share. 'When you've got the new job, you'll be buying us Taittinger, darling,' he declared.

'I'll be buying Taittinger when I find a thesis topic that Perry decides to accept.'

Simon almost dropped the bottle. 'Don't tell me he didn't go for Vernon?'

'He didn't go for Vernon. My thesis is currently at campus recycling.'

'Bloody hell,' he said. Even Eva's eyes had widened. 'Well, there's another good reason for alcohol,' Simon added, filling up the glasses.

On an anti-Perry roll, I moved onto the Dorothy Brown saga. 'When I looked at the quadriptych, I felt alarm bells. Still, I'm no Aboriginal art expert.'

'Don't underestimate gut feeling, particularly yours, Anna,' Simon assured. 'You have a brilliant eye -'

Eva swallowed her entire glass in one swoop. 'Never heard of fake Dorothy Browns.'

'That's why I was so surprised,' I said.

'Well, it would be a big deal if you are right. Fake Browns,' Simon enthused, his mind ticking away at my possible fame and fortune. 'This could be it.'

'Could be what?'

'Your newfound passion. Aboriginal art, Dorothy Brown.'

'Actually, it's an old-found fear.'

'Ah, yes,' he recalled. 'The Marvin Brodie tutorial.'

'It was my tutorial.'

'It was *supposed* to be your tutorial,' Simon pointed out. 'That moron made heckling an Olympic event. But these Dorothys... faked Aboriginal paintings do circulate the market quite a bit...'

'Did Noah Webster tell you to say that?' Eva asked.

'I've never even spoken to Noah Webster,' Simon replied. 'He doesn't exactly hang around Harrington's. Wish he did, though. He's delicious,' Simon grinned before taking a sip of his sparkling. 'His fakes were more bad luck than anything. No evidence showing foul play on Noah Webster's part. Besides, he's made good with his own gallery.'

'You won't get anything out of Webster, Anna,' Eva said. 'He won't discuss anything Aboriginal.'

'I'm not touching it either,' I said, holding my hands up in defence. 'That's Perry's baby.'

'Maybe we could help Anna get a job at Noah Webster?' Simon suggested to Eva.

'Forget it,' Eva replied. 'Jan Hildebrandt is very protective of Noah. Major door Rottweiler.'

'I always thought Jan was a rather wholesome woman,' I said, 'like she should be selling pasties.' Simon and Eva looked at me as if I had just farted. 'Anyway, I overheard a conversation she was having with some older women. They were organising a trip around Australia and had offered to include her.'

'Ah, the grey nomads,' Simon said, as if he yearned to be one of them.

'Jan's becoming a grey nomad?' Eva interrupted.

'No, she declined immediately, said that Noah needed her.'

'Simulated mother-child co-dependency,' Eva said. 'Tragic.'

'So how are your topics going with Perry?' I asked, before draining my glass.

'Fine,' Simon and Eva said in unison. And why shouldn't they? Simon's topic was on AIDS art from the twentieth century: *Art Quality versus Social Cause*. Only a gay student could get away with that. Eva was surveying night paintings: *Black Isn't Black*. Dark and immediately argumentative, very Eva.

While I gazed upon my company in jealous admiration, Eva began glaring at a bowl of wedges and sour cream at the next table. Meanwhile, a man in a pinstriped suit was catching Simon's eye from the bar. 'I'll just go and get us some nibbles,' he volunteered.

'Brilliant idea,' Eva said, while moving on to her third glass. 'I could eat a horse.' I looked at her, fully believing it.

Later that evening, I stumbled up the terrazzo stairs of my apartment building, unlocked the front door (after four attempts) and fell inside directly onto the pile of Liz's clothes. The woman herself was, as usual, nowhere to be seen. While somewhat under the influence, I recalled my conversation with Eva earlier that evening.

'Working in a gallery must be *hard*,' I said with undue emphasis, focusing on her nose to keep steady. 'I mean it is ess…ess…. essentially a sales job. Trying to sell something that very, very… very few people buy.'

'Sales?' Eva retorted with a slur. 'A gallery assistant in any top gallery is lucky to sell one piece a week. Just as well they're so fucking expensive.'

I looked around for Simon, but he vanished an hour ago. 'Hey!' Eva said, drawing my attention back.

'Yes, Eva?'

'You've got to not let the big spaces get to you.'

'The big spaces?'

'The big spaces of time between all those busy little points.' Eva rubbed the tips of her fingers together frenetically in front of the bump of her nose.

'The busy little points, Eva?'

'Yes, you know, the sales, silly. The busy little points.' Eva slapped my hand, then turned sombre. 'It's all about being able to handle the big spaces, Anna. That's the secret they never tell you.'

# CHAPTER 6

The next day, something akin to a miracle occurred.

'You've got a job interview,' said the disembodied voice.

'Really?' I croaked. *Was I dreaming?* Crusty-eyed, I had accidentally rolled out of bed and onto the floor. At least my phone, still buried in my bag, was now within reach.

'Yes,' the voice said. 'Just tell them you can work full-time and can analyse data like my mother.'

'Who is this?' I replied, rubbing my eyes. My head was aching.

'Just do it, slugger,' the voice said. Eva, even more monotone than usual.

'Analyse data like your mother?' I said. 'She's the German one, isn't she?'

'Ja,' Eva replied.

'But I'm not a data analyst,' I said.

'It's at Fürst Gallery, two o'clock.'

'Fürst Gallery?' *Very prestigious.* 'This afternoon?' *Too soon.*

'Why does a private art gallery need a data analyst?'

'Market trends, external drivers. Stuff like that.'

'Wha-?'

'Just Google the basics for the interview,' Eva replied. 'Fake it 'til you make it.'

'Fake it 'til you make it…while selling authentic original art,' I murmured. During the conversation, my hangover had merged into a generalised dread of waking life. Then I remembered something. 'I can't work full-time. I have lectures,'

'You can negotiate something with them,' Eva said, 'this afternoon.'

'But they haven't even seen my résumé.'

'Tyrone pumped you up over the phone.'

'He did?' I asked, now fully awake but still very confused. 'But we haven't even met.'

'Let's just say, because you're a friend of mine, it serves him well if you're working in his main competitor's gallery.' It turned out there was such a thing as a free lunch. It just meant buying dinner. 'Anna, update your résumé and make sure you're at the gallery by two.'

After the call, I settled at my desk, googled 'data analysis private art gallery' and did my best to focus on phrases such as: *market share, product segments, revenue forecast, operating conditions and current performance.* I then created a résumé to suit. It was a glow on paper, a pathologically fake it 'til you make it glow. The last time I had worked on my résumé was for the postgraduate scholarship. 'Worked' was an overstatement. The scholarship was in the bag, purely down to my marks. But the résumé looked different now. My impressive list of scholarships had doubtful legs outside academia. Typing in the digital image library details, I embellished my skills wherever possible. As the printer rolled out the pages, my hand moved around my neck, absently feeling for a price tag.

That afternoon, I changed into the navy suit bought for the image library interview. But the interview was a mere formality.

Again, my marks and also the scholarship had oiled the way. After a deep breath, two aspirin and a dab of organic vanilla perfume, I made my way to the gallery circuit. The air outside was still chilly, but it didn't stop my hands from sweating.

Fürst Gallery was essentially a large room with white plasterboard walls and polished concrete floor and, at that moment, empty of life. A smashed-up Holden, two-thirds the actual size, was in the middle of the space. As I walked around the wreckage, I came across a man in jeans and flannelette shirt, sprawled facedown across the floor. Like the car, the human was slightly smaller than expected. The man and the car looked real, but obviously weren't. Being a car crash made looking away difficult. A ghoulish trait of the living. The reduced scale lured you to peer even harder. The man had some tattoos depicted on one arm. A configuration of a dragon, a skull and a rose. Unoriginal. *Did the flannelette shirt and boring tattoos reduce our compassion? Was he somehow the cause of the accident, not just the victim?*

I sighed, more concerned about the actual, full-scale disaster that was my life. Rubbing the perspiration off my hands and onto my jacket, I looked around for a human, a door, a bell. Anything to let the gallery staff know of my arrival. I waved at a camera fixed high in one corner. Five minutes passed before a young, frail woman with thick-framed spectacles appeared from a hidden side door. Outsmarting customers in search of assistance was definitely an architectural feature. I wondered if they were considering a moat with sharks.

The woman held out a bony hand. It was all she had to offer. I gave it a shake, which felt more like playing with a twig. 'Anna Lissam,' I said, 'for the job interview.' She nodded before leading me through the magical door. Comparing my suit to hers, I was obviously five steps behind fashion. Normal fashion, not Liz's version. These were highly visual people. I was doomed. Panic rose from my knees.

We entered a windowless room where four unintroduced staff in minimalist black dress tapped on computer keyboards and murmured into headsets. The walls were bare. However, through the doorway ahead, I glimpsed a large painting of a burning rope in a dark desert landscape. I followed the frail, bespectacled woman towards the fire, which hung behind a woman who sat behind a giant glossy black table. While in menopausal age range, the woman appeared upbeat in her green shirt and purple floral tie. A hefty gloop of product spiked her short brown crowning glory. That hair wasn't going anywhere.

'I'm Lois.' She delivered her introduction with such force I felt lassoed. I offered my hand, but Lois ignored it, making a gesture towards the chair at her left instead. I handed over the résumé and sat feeling like I'd been dropped behind enemy lines. Art museum people don't belong in the private sector, and certainly not ones pretending to be data analysts. I needed to get out. But then Lois launched. 'I need a full-time employee with the data analysis skills of Eva's mother.'

'You actually know Eva's mother?' I asked, taken aback. I'd assumed Eva had been speaking figuratively.

'Yes, but she left,' she shrugged. 'She was excellent, except for her English.'

'My English is—' Lois cut my attempt at whimsical humour short. 'The job isn't all data analysis, of course.'

'Of course.' I nodded, understanding nothing.

'There are general administration tasks, but the data analysis is important.' Lois looked at me, urging me to chime in.

'Yes, researching sharing product…product share…is a passion of mine,' I said with as much gusto as a two-day-old party balloon. 'The forecast segments, operating revenue…in the market… considering current conditions…' Lois began looking at me sideways. 'I create exceptional pie diagrams,' I lied. I hadn't even created a pie, let alone a pie diagram. Lois looked like she had just eaten a pie diagram. I needed some solid ground. 'You will see on my résumé that I have strong digital image library management experience.' I pointed to my pages in her hands. 'I can resize and file images in my sleep. And manage copyright paperwork fully awake.' Lois, indifferent to my true qualities, moved swiftly onto sales.

'Sales?' I asked. 'Is the gallery changing?' The question had slipped out from my thoughts.

'Changing?'

'About having someone in the gallery greeting visitors…buyers,' I clarified.

'People who come off the street?' Lois raised her mug to her smiling lips. As no beverage had been offered, my hands remained capped on my crossed knees. 'They're not buyers, dear.' There was a slight rolling of eyes before speaking with a deliberate emphasis on every word. 'Buyers are people who we build relationships with. They call, we call, have meetings and such. We often host art showings off premises.' The woman put her coffee mug on top of my pristine résumé. It had become a coaster.

'So why have a gallery?' I asked.

'It's a showcase to titillate, get them wanting more, wanting a relationship with us,' Lois said. 'They call when they're serious.' In other words, it was about playing hard to get. Fürst Gallery had turned playing hard to get into an art form. Pressing a hand against the belly of her tie, Lois rose from her chair. 'We will contact you in due course,' she said. But when she lifted her mug and handed back my résumé, I realised Lois would do what came naturally: creating a sense of rejection by doing nothing.

Private galleries are businesses, I reminded myself while shouldering my handbag and heading for the door. Someone once said that the trick to business was to be the centre of what's going on behind. The theory seemed logical, but it never sat comfortably with me. Now that I had experienced behind the scenes of Fürst Gallery, I had to admit, when visiting again the place would look different. Even less human than before.

It started raining as soon as I walked out. *How miserably poetic,* I thought. Picturing my compact umbrella sitting snugly in my messenger bag at home, I pulled my head down and walked fast towards the bus stop. As the rain soon became a downpour, I dived into the nearest doorway and pondered my options. I could visit Eva at Tyrone Gilbert Gallery, not far away. Thank her boss for the effort and apologise for letting the side down. But then a voice said, 'Wet out there, is it?' I looked around. Jan was beaming her Cornish pasty grin from the desk. So dazed from the interview, I hadn't even noticed I was standing in Noah Webster Gallery's doorway.

'Yes,' I replied. 'The rain has just started.' I walked inside just as Noah came out of a back office, looking just as dapper as at the opening. I felt the dampness of my suit, the black plastic résumé folder in my hand, and a strange surge of ambition.

'Noah Webster?' I asked. He turned to find my outstretched hand. 'I'm Anna Lissam, pleased to meet you.' Noah raised a smile as Jan's dropped. 'I just wanted to pass on my résumé.' I had become possessed. Conveniently leaving my soggy, badly dressed body, I observed myself continuing the impromptu pitch. 'As you will see, I'm studying for my Master's Degree in Fine Art. I've also been responsible for creating and managing the digital image library for the faculty. Now that's been successfully implemented, I'm looking for a part-time position in the commercial realm. I learn quickly.'

It was an inspired, completely spontaneous move.

'Thank you, Anna,' he said, 'but I already have an assistant. Have you met Jan Hildebrandt?' Jan had remained seated behind the desk. Her pasty presence had been replaced by something ready to be let loose off a chain.

It was a stupid, completely insane move.

'I could never expect to replace Jan, of course,' I stammered.

'We're not in need of more staff at this time,' Noah replied. 'But good luck with the search.'

Jan took the résumé from Noah and gave it the administrator's curse, 'I'll keep it on file.' Noah gestured to Jan that he would talk to her later about 'that catering invoice.' Returning to the back office, he closed the door behind him.

What I had done descended on me. Taking a breath, I turned to Jan and apologised. 'That must have looked a little…'

'Yes,' Jan replied, staring back at me. Her puce brown suit was even worse than my navy one, but this detail was not a comfort.

Steeling myself, I moved towards the desk and lowered my voice with, 'You need a holiday.'

'I beg your pardon?'

'You know, travel around Australia with your friends,' I whispered. 'Partake in the caravan convoy. I overheard you talking about it at the opening.'

'Who are you?' Jan asked with repugnance.

I pointed at the résumé by way of explanation. 'Don't you see? I can keep your seat warm.' The gallery's temperature was exceptionally comfortable. Pulling a chair up, I pushed on, unsure of where I was heading. 'Noah can set up a contract to ensure that your job will still be yours when you return. I only need something temporary.'

'Temporary?' Jan looked dubious. 'Why?'

'I'm due another scholarship in a few months.' What had come over me? It was like being channelled by a spirit with a sick sense of entrepreneurial verve. 'My focus is on a more academic path. I have no interest in working in a gallery any longer than necessary.' I finished up, almost panting. 'No offence.'

'Well, I am offended,' Jan said while smoothing out her jacket lapels. 'You think I was born yesterday? I know what's going on. You young people think you can just -'

'You have the experience, Jan. I've never worked in an art gallery before, or retail of any kind,' I replied.

'So why would Mr Webster give you the job then?'

'Because…' I faltered. 'Because he'll listen to you.'

Jan had no words for it, but the sheer disgust was hard to miss. I pressed on, a kamikaze for my own cause. 'Imagine a contract with all our signatures on it, ensuring you can have your pasty and eat it.'

'My what?'

'You get what you want, Jan. Eight months of travel and a job to come back to.'

Then the telephone rang. 'I'm going to have to ask you to leave.'

I stood up as Jan answered the phone, bumping into a large man in overalls carrying a bubble-wrapped painting. 'Watch out,' he said, saving the painting from knocking a sculpture by the door.

'Sorry,' I said, rubbing my forehead, as if I had knocked that too. Surely I had. I felt sick.

Jan glared from behind the desk while saying into the phone, 'Keeping dry, and you?'

I made it out the door, coaching myself that it had been worth a shot, then walked directly into a deep puddle. If necessity was the mother of invention, it seemed desperation was an embarrassing relative that no one wanted to know. I had offended the only person I warmed to in the private gallery industry. And now my shoes were soaked.

Dollops of rain fell from the leaves above as I walked along the street. The gods weren't angry. They were just deeply disappointed. My heavy clothes stuck to me. Exhaustion pulled at my face, hands and ankles. It had been hard work fighting for something that I didn't really want in the first place. Harder to become someone I never wanted to be.

'Soft-centred or nuts?' Maggie asked over the phone.

'I'm both,' I replied, back on the hot water bottle and feeling guilty for calling.

'Come on, Anna. Which chocolate do you prefer?'

'Haven't a clue.'

'I'll bring both.'

'Thanks, Maggs. But I just feel like being by myself for a bit.' It was a lie, but it felt virtuous saying it.

'You sure?'

'Yep.' *Bring the Green & Black's, please.* An appropriate choice. I was feeling very green in my lack of experience and deeply depressed by my shameless behaviour at Noah Webster.

'Okay, call me if you change your mind,' was the gentle reply. The retrenchment news had rocked Ruben the most. His gasp in the background had been highly audible over the phone during my conversation with Maggie. At one point, I could hear him say, 'This is just the beginning!' before a door slammed. As retrenchment loomed above Ruben at all times, he was probably the most emphatic person in my life at that moment. It just didn't feel like it.

'This is just the beginning?' I asked.

'Well, he's right. This is just the beginning of a whole new chapter in your life.'

'I don't think that's what he meant.'

'Well, he's more accurate than he knows. Beginnings are good things,' she said.

'What are you going to do now?' Maggie was sticking to her purpose like toffee.

'Now?'

'When you get off the phone.'

'I'm not ready to get off the phone,' I said, clutching the handset. 'Are you winding up my whining?'

'Not at all, but when we hang up,' Maggie said. I released a whine. 'When we hang up,' she repeated, 'watch a nice movie, get your mind off things. Start fresh on Monday.'

As it turned out, Monday had its own plans.

'Everyone lies.'

The Monday morning lecture was due to start soon, but Perry hadn't made his entrance yet. As usual, I picked up on the musty smell when I first walked into the ageing room. But forgot it just as fast. Maybe you become part of the mustiness in a place like this. I spotted Eva across the room and wandered over to thank her for the interview line-up, explaining that my promises of pie graphs didn't win me the job.

'But I fell off the career ladder completely afterwards at Noah Webster Gallery. I was there just to get out of the rain, but spontaneously pitched myself to him.'

'Wicked,' Eva replied. She was smiling, but for all the wrong reasons.

'Yes, it was wicked, Eva, in the traditional sense,' I said. 'I did it in front of Jan. It was shameless, awful behaviour.'

'You pitched in front of the Door Rotty?' Her smile morphed into shock. I'd never seen Eva so expressive. This was bad.

'I'm so embarrassed,' I said, pulling at my cheeks. But I continued the story, punishing myself with a full confession. 'Then, after Noah left, which he did very quickly, I tried to talk Jan into going on a holiday. You should have seen her face. I'll never be able to visit Noah Webster Gallery ever again.'

'Stroke of brilliance.'

'Brilliance?' I asked. 'I've been feeling sick about it all weekend.'

'You didn't do it behind her back. You were up front, and then you included her, made her a player. I would never have thought of it.'

'Well, she wasn't playing, Eva. She was highly offended.'

'She'll get over it.' Eva shrugged. 'In fact, I bet you got her thinking.'

Perry walked into the room. 'Time to go,' I said, making tracks to my spot up the back.

'Later, slugger,' Eva replied.

As I passed the front row, I could feel a hand cling to my arm. 'Marvin?'

'Heard you lost your job, Anna,' he said, smirk in place. 'Shame.'

'What is a shame, Marvin, is me knowing a brilliant underground animation artist and introducing him to DAAOn, not you.' I'd always wanted to say it, just to see the reaction.

'What?' Marvin's jaw locked in defence. 'You're bullshitting. I know everyone here who's underground.'

'He's not from here,' I said, keeping the sick fantasy alive. Marvin deserved it, but this wasn't me. I didn't recognise myself. I made my way to my usual seat at the back of the room. Simon was sitting on the far side of the classroom that day. I wasn't being ignored. He just liked to circulate. Settling into my seat, I pulled out my pad. Perry entered the room, throwing his satchel on the desk and letting it slide to the edge. He wandered around, twirling his spectacles in a propeller motion while looking over the class. I suspected that this was a kinetic prop to crank up the atmosphere. It seemed to be working. The entire class was becoming mesmerised even though nothing had actually been said. Doodles had taken up most of my page by the time Perry finally launched into concepts of perspective.

'Who's that?'

'*Christ.*' I almost leapt out of my skin. Perry was sitting next to me. It was a mystery how someone so hefty could be so nimble.

'You know, I wouldn't have picked it as Christ. Short hair, glasses, no beard, vomiting Picasso's *Guernica*. But that's no criticism, mind you,' Perry prattled. It's always challenging to have a new perspective of an old icon.' The class was in an extended state of amusement while I was in a contracted state of irritation.

'You look uncomfortable,' Perry said, but he wasn't speaking to me. He was addressing the rest of the class. 'You've twisted your bodies to look at us up the back here. Why don't you turn your chairs around? Make yourselves comfy, that's it.' The class clattered their chairs and collapsed again. 'Talking of new perspectives, let's look at this room another way.'

I was well prepared to turn my chair around, too. Looking at the wall would have suited me just fine. Instead, I sat in a quiet state of agony, hoping that Perry would leap up and move to the left or the right side of the room to keep the student perspective on a 45-degree swivel.

'Now that you are all re-seated,' Perry continued, 'what do you see that you don't normally see?'

'Anna,' Marvin spouted.

'You see Anna,' Perry repeated. 'Don't you normally see Anna, Marvin?'

'At times, yes. Just not when she's sitting there. But she always sits at the back, hidden from our view.' I rolled my eyes at the last comment, laden with tedious Marvin-drama.

'When you see Anna now, what's different?'

'She looks quite far away.' I was pleased that I was far away from Marvin. It was a good place to be.

'Anything else?'

'There's not as much light back there, so she's…she's…got a chiaroscuro appearance about her.' It was an obvious levering for extra credit by using multi-syllabic art term points.

'Chiaroscuro, emerging from the darkness, good Marvin,' Perry said. 'Anyone else?'

'Perhaps, it's the shadow…I don't know,' Marvin again, not letting anyone else speak, 'but she appears a little melancholy.' It was as if he were describing a painting, rather than a human with fully operational hearing devices. 'One could only assume something's *happened* to her.'

I could barely contain myself, but within seconds Perry had stood up and was walking down the aisle towards the rostrum. The class turned around their seats, keeping their gaze on Perry while he made his way to the front of the room. Clearly, he was used to having students on strings. I resumed doodling. Marvin is such a fool. Nothing has happened to me, nothing at all.

Leaving the lecture room after Perry had wrapped up, I looked at my phone and noticed a message. I didn't recognise the number. But listening to the message had me almost dropping the phone. It was Jan Hildebrandt asking me to call back. She sounded quite calm and not at all abusive. It was Monday. Private galleries were closed on Mondays, so the number might be her private mobile number. When I hit reply, Jan answered, pivoting on one question.

'What happens if you don't get the scholarship?'.

'It always happens,' I replied. Historically, the statement was accurate. Still, what happens next was another ballgame.

Maybe Jan sensed this because her next question was, 'But what if you don't?'

'You'll have the position secured by the agreed contract, and I'll find another job.'

'How interested in gallery work are you?'

'Not at all, as I said before. I just need a job for now.'

'This isn't your passion?'

'Passion?' I asked. 'Ah, no.'

'What do you want to do?'

Relieved Jan didn't ask what my passion was, I replied, 'Complete my Masters', then move up to a Doctorate and miraculously end up in London.'

'What's your topic?'

'My topic?' I asked, knowing exactly what she meant.

'Yes, for your thesis.'

'Well, it was going to be on Vernon Jones.'

'Who?'

'Australia's most prolific portrait artist of the nineteenth century.' I felt fatigued. 'Look, the last thing I want is for you to feel uncomfortable. I mean it, Jan. If it doesn't feel right, let's not do this.'

There was a pause. 'Leave it with me, I'll see what I can do. 'Australia's most prolific portrait artist of the nineteenth century.' I felt fatigued. 'Look, the last thing I want is for you to feel uncomfortable. I mean it, Jan. If it doesn't feel right, let's not do this.'

There was a pause. 'Leave it with me, I'll see what I can do.'


Within half an hour, Jan called back with an interview time,

'Two-thirty today at the gallery.'

'I'll be there.'

'It's my day off. The gallery's closed, so I won't be,' she explained.

'Okay.'

'Noah will make the final decision.'

'Of course,' I replied. 'Oh, Jan?'

'Yes?'

'I can only work part-time and I'm not a data analyst.'

'That's okay,' Jan replied. 'I'm only part-time and…data analyst? You don't have to worry about that. The gallery's success rests on Noah's eye.'

I lowered myself down on the couch armrest. 'Great.'

'If this is going to work, I'm going to have to leave soon.'

'I need work soon, very soon,' I replied. 'Thanks, Jan. I really appreciate it.'

'Who knows? I might be thanking you soon enough.'

I put down the phone in disbelief. The obnoxious hustle had paid off, which was both wonderful and depressing at the same time. An awkward grin appeared on my face, like something released from storage.

Donned in my navy suit once more, it was two-thirty sharp when I approached the gallery. The door was closed but unlocked. I passed the unattended front desk and wandered around the gallery, absorbing Philippa Cusack's pastoral paintings without the crush of people from opening night. There was a large painting of a windswept field – sans concrete – that hadn't yet sold. Would I be expected to find a home for it? The idea filled me with dread. Sweat sprang from my palms like a timed sprinkler system.

Noah Webster emerged from a back room. As expected, he was looking dapper in a suit tailored from a different planet than mine. 'My apologies! I didn't hear you come in. Oh, you're Anna, aren't you? Here for the interview. Goodness, is it two-thirty already?' Noah shook my hand. His shake was firm and dry, mine impersonating a pound of wet Play-Doh. Somehow, he resisted the urge to wipe his hand on his suit, or on mine. 'Come and sit down, let's chat.'

'You have a beautiful gallery. Cusack's paintings are mesmerising.'

'Philippa has sold well for only her second solo show. The work she's doing now is even more exciting. Of course, we want to sell these first.'

'Of course.' I wanted to maintain some objective distance, but instantly felt myself being drawn to his verve.

'Let me get us coffees,' he said, rubbing his hands together. 'How do you have it?'

'Just with milk, thanks,' I said.

After a few minutes, Noah re-emerged from the back room, juggling two cups and a pad and pen. 'Well, this is an unexpected turn from our last meeting, isn't it?'

'Indeed.'

'Jan – I call her my surrogate mum – has been tremendous in helping me out.' Noah handed me a cup. 'The gallery's been open for just over five years, and she's been here from the start. A holiday is well overdue.' Noah's voice hushed a little. 'She may choose to retire afterwards, I'm not sure.'

'I am applying only on the basis that Jan's position is secure for her when she returns.'

'Yes, yes of course.' Noah sipped at his cup. 'I appreciate your integrity. An excellent quality.' His relaxed features displayed no hidden or forced agenda, but he was looking across at the pages in my hands with interest.

'A more succinct, updated copy of my résumé,' I explained, handing it over. This version was honest, stripped of data analysis fabrications. 'I have references if you need them. Thomas Perry's contact details are at the back.'

'*The* Thomas Perry?'

'Yes, he's now at Prescott.'

'Really? Why on earth is he here?'

'Not sure, to be honest. He seems interested in Aboriginal art.' It was too late to take it back.

'Really?' Noah's eyes deadened before shifting focus back to the résumé. As he scanned the words, his face brightened again. 'Excellent,' he announced, before wedging the résumé between his pad and his knees. 'I'll cut straight to the chase, Anna. I could hire more staff, but I like to have just one other. Having a lean operation seems to work best for my needs. Extra staff have been hired on a casual basis to help Jan, but it never seems to work out.

'This gallery is fairly secure financially. I'm fortunate enough to have a few key clients overseas and some corporates here. I'm often in the city in meetings.'

'So why have a gallery?' I asked. 'Why not just be a dealer?'

'Cred and bread, Anna. In this virtual world, your basic shop front still counts.' Noah smiled.

'It's quite the shop front,' I said, smiling back.

'I tell my clients that art has only three basic needs: recognition of talent, appreciation of talent, and usually ten thousand dollars or more.' Noah chuckled at himself, then spoke intently to the corner of the coffee table. 'Working in contemporary art galleries may sound either glamorous or boring. But actually, it's both, plus whatever you make it.' After listing some administrative duties, he looked up and across to me in a budgie-like manner.

'There will be times when you will have to be accommodating to a client's decor, regardless of how tasteless it is. Everyone thinks they have good taste, don't they?' I nodded, straightening my navy jacket.

Noah's illustration of gallery operations could have become a mini-motivational selling seminar. Instead, he talked about the one-to-one conversations with gallery visitors, the intellectual intimacy of the experience. A light bulb went on in my brain when he said he preferred the term 'education' to 'sales'.

'I need someone who can also help with catalogue essays and media releases,' he said. 'Your academic training could be particularly useful for these tasks.' Throughout the conversation, I volunteered succinct facts about myself to which Noah would always smile and say 'Marvellous'. At least until he asked what my thesis topic was.

Replying with 'Australian art' didn't satisfy him.

'That's a broad subject, Anna,' he smiled. 'What specifically about Australian art are you interested in?'

I thought of Dorothy Brown and said, 'Australian minimalism early this century.' But really, who knew?

'Marvellous,' he grinned. Noah then switched tack, warning me he would be out much of the time. 'But I'll have my mobile if you need anything.'

'Marvellous,' I said with a smile, enjoying the idea of being left alone to work. It could be similar to the solitude of the image library, I reasoned with myself. Except for the public interrupting.

We negotiated working hours so I could attend all my lectures. Unfortunately, my thesis meetings with Perry also remained intact. 'In terms of wages,' Noah said, 'as I mentioned, this is a lean operation.' Every safety net has its holes, I thought, sinking back into my chair. 'At this stage, I can offer forty thousand pro rata. With a commission bonus of five percent of anything you sell in the gallery. That's five percent off the sale price. For instance, if you sold a three-thousand-dollar painting, you would receive one hundred and fifty dollars on top of your pay. We call it sweets.'

'Sweets?'

'Like dessert.' Seasoned on the gruel of university fare, Noah's commission-sprinkled wage package was more than I would have ever hoped for. My taste buds salivated. 'Would this arrangement be satisfactory?' he asked.

Thrusting out my hand to shake on it, Noah gave me forms to sign. The first was a confidentiality agreement. Noah hesitated before continuing. 'I believe in a team approach. I value Jan's loyalty, her discretion. Standard business practice, commercial-in-confidence stuff. I would appreciate the same approach from you.'

'Of course,' I nodded, distracted by the solicitor's letterhead resembling the US Supreme Court. There were other standard employment tax forms and an employment contract on Noah Webster Gallery letterhead, ensuring that Jan could resume the position upon her return. Taking the pen, my eyes fixed on Noah's suit. It was cut from extremely high-grade wool. Italian. I probably could have negotiated for more.

'Read these over in your own time. You can bring them back when you start.'

'Which would be…?' I was hoping for 'How about right now?'

But he replied, 'Wednesday next week. Jan's almost sorted here. Some overlap time with the two of you would have been good, but I'm sure it'll be fine. Welcome aboard, Anna.'

'I look forward to starting, Mr Webster.'

'Please call me Noah.'

'Thank you, Noah.' I rose from my chair, sending a silent thank you to Jan, wherever she was. And wondered, just for a moment, what secrets of Noah's she might be travelling with.

# CHAPTER 7

The child lounged on the large purple cushion like a sultan. An inordinate number of coloured bits of paper were scattered across the floor around him like jewels. The four-year-old stared at me, unimpressed.

'Anna, this is Flynn,' Maggie said as she tidied up the childcare centre like a cyclone in reverse. 'Flynn's mother is running a little late.'

'Hi, Flynn.'

'Hi,' the child replied without enthusiasm.

Maggie looked behind her distractedly. 'Anna, would you mind keeping an eye on this little rascal while I do a quick clean up the back?'

'No problem,' I said, turning to assess the child as he assessed me. Flynn wore a striped red and blue t-shirt, seen only through generous amounts of splattered paint that also covered his elbows and down his left leg. Green paint was smeared across his left cheek. 'You've been painting then?' I asked.

'Yes', he answered. I hoped for his embellishment, but there was none. In the far corner of the room were various coloured papers stuck onto a large sheet of butcher's paper. I walked closer to it. The colours, the placement, the feeling, it was all as I expected. Brilliant.

'That's mine,' he said.

'Nice work, Flynn.'

I was going to tell him he had a future, but the child was not interested in motivational feedback or visionary ambition. Instead, he asked, 'Why does the sky look like that?' pointing his tiny finger out the window to the increasing darkness.

I heard mopping sounds from the back room. Maggie was still busy. Flynn lowered his finger and waited for an answer.

'The sky? Well, it's a long story.'

Flynn's face brightened to the point of cracking the paint on it. 'I like stories,' he said.

I sat down next to him on a green cushion, took a deep breath, and reached past the cobwebs into my imagination. This was the story I told:


### WHY THE SKY LOOKS LIKE IT DOES

*A long, long time ago, when the earth was in the process of setting up shop, there was an artist called Tom. Although Tom was young, he was also extremely talented and many of his older colleagues had to admit that 'The kid's got what it takes.' As a result, Tom was contracted to many interesting and varied projects, such as creating lakes, rivers, and hills.*

*Tom worked hard and soon made his way up to mountains. One day on site, Tom noticed a young woman in the distance. She was wandering about without a hard hat on. So he walked up to her to warn her about the problems associated with public liability claims. Tom didn't realise that the young woman was Princess Madeleine, as few had ever seen the*

*Princess. Her father, disillusioned with the trappings of wealth and power, was an unhappy totalitarian who lived in denial and had become a dysfunctional, overprotective parent.*

*Princess Madeleine turned around, stopping Tom in his tracks. She had the clearest, brightest, bluest eyes he had ever seen. Meanwhile, the young woman measured Tom's dimensions and decided that he was definitely a stud muffin. For both, it was love at first sight. Unfortunately, Maddy's daddy had already super-glued his daughter's fate to another, more aristocratic suitor in an adjoining constituency with mountains already finished.*

*Princess Madeleine, not one to mince words, explained the dud deal to Tom. At this news, he got the blues. Madeleine was also unhappy and cried with frustration. Her tears fell on the new landscape and began to mix up some of Tom's exquisite tonal qualities. But he didn't care. He declared his love to her and then watched helplessly as she walked away.*

*The Princess meandered miserably amongst the construction. Growth surrounded her while her hopes for happiness deteriorated. She sat down and sulked. After a while, she was approached by a big, beautiful African American woman, who said to her, 'If you can't be with the one you love, honey, then love the one you're with.'*

*But Madeleine could not hang with this spiel. 'Sounds good in theory,' she replied, 'but I've just given my heart to this other guy, and it's a rent-to-buy situation.'*

*The woman waved her finger and said, 'You're in breach of contract, girl.'*

*'Don't I know it,' the Princess sighed unhappily.*

*Feminism was, at this stage, a doodle on culture's drawing board. So Princess Madeleine hummed along to the tune of parental authority as best she could. However, Tom, still young and restless, tracked down his enthroned sweetie and, after a couple of close calls with security, their secret meetings began. It wasn't exactly domestic bliss, but it was better than nothing.*

*Tom's career, at least, was moving ahead nicely as he had pitched for and landed the plum job of painting the sky. Rather than presenting proposals, models and working drawings, he decided on spontaneous instinctual expression. The source of his inspiration could be nothing but the blue eyes of Princess Madeleine.*

*When he thought the work was resolved, Tom invited his peers to view it. Looking at Tom's totally blue surface, the harsher critics called it self-indulgent. The softer critics said that, on a good day, it looked minimalist. But what they hadn't noticed was the subtle varnish Tom had applied, making the surface look cloudy when the light hit it in a certain way. This effect reflected the moment when Tom's loved one had wept. He was particularly happy with this aspect as it worked well with the irrigation requirements in the brief.*

*Still, Tom had to agree that perhaps it needed more depth through juxtaposition with its antithesis. Suddenly, he turned the painting around and vigorously slapped huge quantities of thick, black paint all over the back surface. He stopped and looked at it for a moment. He then remembered that artist Frank Stella was supposed to do this in the sixties. So, rather than spoil the fun, Tom contemplated his inspiration further. Considering the dark periods between Tom's royal rendezvous, black seemed an appropriate colour symbol. However, his love*

Maggie and another woman were standing at the doorway. Meanwhile, Flynn was flaked-out on the cushion fast asleep.

'He was riveted,' I said. 'At the start.'

'Well, if you had explained the black and blue bits in terms of football injuries, you might have had a chance,' the woman said. 'Thanks for taking care of my boy.'

'Flynn is quite the artist,' I said, pointing across the room to the masterpiece.

The mother smiled. 'I guess all kids are. Then something happens, doesn't it? We grow up.'

'Fortunately, not all of us,' Maggie laughed as I sat thinking, *Maybe we don't grow up, we just move away.*

After the wunderkind and his mum left, Maggie said 'Thank God,' and disappeared into the kitchen, soon emerging with two glasses of gin and tonic and a paté-biscuit platter. Celebratory fodder from the staff meeting the previous Friday.

'G&T in these mammoth tumblers?' I asked. 'How do you guys make any constructive decisions?'

'The meetings are more therapy. Believe me, it's required. On the minutes we call it "team-building".'

'Tumbler,' I said, sitting down on a chair large enough to support one fully grown buttock. 'What an appropriate name for a glass designed for high alcohol content.'

Looking at Maggie, I was weighing up whether I should ask about her infertility struggle. Something in me said 'no'. She appeared rather perky, balancing on her chaise petite, spreading paté onto a biscuit and handing it over. I shifted my focus to the brown dollop before me. Like sausages, it was best not to ask what it was made of. The other query was whether it should actually be eaten, after sitting in the fridge unsealed for at least three days. But I trusted Maggie. She knew her food. Closing my eyes, I took a bite. If it were goat genitals, it was still moreish. Maggie picked up the small, rounded knife and prepared a second round. Given that it was no longer suitable to probe another friend's fur for dead skin, burrs or dead leaves, as my ancestors may have done, food and disorienting substances were all we had to feel close. And the sharing of secrets.

'What's the problem?' Maggie asked. 'You've just got this great job, but you don't look like you have.'

'It is great. I am grateful. But a significant part of the position *is* sales, which is not really my area.' The career equivalent of buyer's remorse had started creeping in.

'You've never done sales.'

'I've managed to avoid it until now. Still, Noah says it's more "education" than "sales". He calls sales commission "sweets".'

'Like dessert?'

'Yes.' I nodded at my glass, then looked up at Maggie. 'Did I just get sold?'

'It's your favourite art gallery and the job's only temporary.'

'True,' I said, tilting my glass towards her in acknowledgement.

'Don't you have that meeting with that Perry fellow tomorrow... about passion?'

'Blimey, you're all over it, Maggs. Most people have trouble enough remembering their own meetings, let alone someone else's.'

'I just know this one's been playing on your mind.' I tilted my glass towards her in acknowledgement again. 'The man has just retrenched you. If he expects you to find a new thesis topic that you feel passionate about in a week, he has rocks in his head.' Maggie was right. I looked across at her, feeling the warm glow of G&T and gratitude. What a shame she wasn't going to be a mother.

The next day, I settled into the chair across from Perry, imagining I was surrounded by a protective aura of universal love. And wearing boxing gloves.

'The scans of the certificates were emailed last night, as attachments,' Perry started.

'The certificates?' I asked.

'Yes, the certificates of authenticity of the Dorothy Browns at Whitlock. A.W. found them. I haven't had a chance to look yet, shall we?' Not waiting for a reply, Perry swivelled his monitor around so I could see the screen from my side of the desk. He was trying a new method of opening attachments. One I had never seen before. Every time he pushed a button, the computer beeped like it was in pain.

'I think it's easiest if you just double click on the attachment icon,' I recommended. Perry nodded and followed through. He smiled when four typed certificates of authenticity appeared, one certificate per painting. Each page had the title 'Country', artist 'Dorothy Brown', date of the work '2005', and a short bio on Dorothy.

The only difference between each certificate was a registered number: 'DB674', 'DB675', 'DB676' or 'DB677' an allocated code per painting. The rest of the information remained the same, even for the night painting. And all were on Galerie Exotique letterhead, signed by Miles Porter.

I was more distracted by the date. 'It's surprising to see that the paintings were done in 2005.'

'Why?' he asked.

'I had assumed that, if they were hers, they would have been painted later, at the end of her career.'

'You really don't like these paintings, do you?' Perry asked with a chuckle, seemingly less defensive than before.

'It's not that I don't like them.'

'But you don't think they are Dorothy Browns?'

Shrugging, I said, 'I could be wrong.'

'But here we have certificates of authenticity. Do they not satisfy you?'

'Well, certificates have been faked too.'

'But you are a twenty…' Perry looked at a manila folder marked 'Lissam, A.' on his desk, '..a twenty-two-year-old studying fine art. How do you know? You haven't even seen the paintings in the flesh, so to speak.'

'It's hard to explain,' I mumbled.

'You are also a postgraduate specialising in art history and criticism,' Perry added with an impatient sigh. 'Try it.'

'I have a gut feeling about Dorothy's work.'

'Not good enough.'

'You're right. It's not,' I complied, hoping it would be the end of it.

'Not good enough.'

'Yes, I know. And I agree with you.'

Perry leaned back in his chair. 'I want you to prove it.'

'Why?'

'Are you going to spend the rest of your life saying I know because I know?'

'No.'

'No, of course not,' Perry replied. 'Instead, you intended to spend the rest of your life playing with this gift, your gut vision, as a secret hobby and working with conventional means of research because that's what the world expects. Secrets are heavy things to carry, Lissam, believe me.'

I stared blankly at him. 'You think I have a gift?'

'Maybe. But how would I know? You haven't proven it,' Perry said. 'What good is it if you are the only one who knows that these Dorothy Browns are fakes?'

'I've had trouble proving things before.'

'You were an undergrad before. We're now in more major league territory, Lissam. Primary research. You are now allowed to go to the source.'

'You can research it if you want to, Dr Perry,' I said. 'I don't mind.'

'No, Lissam,' Perry slammed his hands on his desk. 'For god's sake, girl, have some conviction about what you are saying. Follow through, *do* something about it.'

Perry scribbled on a blank sheet of paper and handed it over the desk.

'"Anna Lissam Proves Her Eye is Right",' it read, '"Example:
Faked Dorothy Brown Paintings at Whitlock University, London."'

'Working title,' he added, taking off his glasses and tossing them
onto the desk. 'Prove to me that your gift is real. Prove to me that
these aren't Dorothy Browns. Start with your hypothesis and follow
through with unearthing the evidence.'

'How?'

'That's up to you,' he said, looking increasingly smug. 'It's your
little project.'

'Why can't I apply the same principle to Vernon Jones?'

'Vernon Jones, the honest rather than horrendously awful
portrait painter?' Perry said incredulously. 'You'd pick him over
one of the greatest artists of our time – still living, we believe –
who is having a terrible injustice done to her and her Dreaming?'
Perry leaned forward and whispered, 'I'll tell you a secret, Lissam.' I
begrudgingly leant forward. 'If you really want to make a difference
in history, you're better off participating in the present.'

I sat, absorbed with my options. Perry waited, pressing his
fingertips together as he leaned back and gazed out the window.

'Dr Perry, I don't think I should interfere with this.'

He turned towards me, resting his hands on the arms of his
chair. I continued, 'Dorothy Brown deliberately withdrew from the
commercial world –'

'Why do you think she did that?'

'I imagine the pressure to produce was too great, that it was
not the life she wanted. The integrity of her work was obviously
diminishing as a result.'

'The integrity of her work,' Perry repeated.

'I'm *guessing* that might be part of it,' I answered. 'But I don't
know.'

'The integrity of her work,' he repeated again, this time moving his gaze back to the window, looking out at G Block. His opposing fingertips found each other again. After an inordinate slab of silence, he said, 'What if you made it your thesis topic?' My heart hit the linoleum. 'Formalise the title,' he continued, hands open and thrust wide. 'It could expand to a Phd, but you'd need to go to London to see the paintings properly, of course.'

London. I could feel a tingling sensation on my face. That was until another thought came to mind. 'What if I'm wrong?' I asked.

'You learn something,' he replied with a smile.

'What if I'm right?'

'You learn something.' Perry stopped smiling and clutched at his chest. Seconds passed before releasing a sigh. 'Just a little indigestion,' he explained, hitting a fist to his breast, much like movie ER staff do before the shock paddles arrive. I watched his reddening face and began to move towards his phone. But his free hand stretched out towards me, a gesture to stay right where I was. When Perry had resumed to near-normality, I asked, 'Shall I call someone?'

'What?' His eyes still looked a little dazed. 'God, no. Tip-top now. Okay, back to your thesis.'

'What about passion?' I asked.

Perry pulled out a handkerchief and daubed his forehead with it. 'Passion?'

'You said I had to be passionate about my topic.'

Leaning to the side momentarily, he put his handkerchief back in his trouser pocket. When straightened, he said, 'There is such a thing as quiet passion.' I stared back, trying to imagine Perry being quiet about anything.

'To be completely honest, Dr Perry,' I replied tentatively, 'I don't feel passionate about this topic, not even quietly.'

'You are,' he nodded, 'you just don't know it.' My eyebrows rose with indignation. In turn, Perry raised his hand, permitting himself to continue. 'Passion is very much linked to fear. The two are opposites that, with extremity, become very close, like the ends of a horseshoe. The more extreme they become, the closer they become,' he replied. 'You fear your lack of understanding of Aboriginal culture.'

'But -' I interrupted.

Raising his hand again, he added, 'You also fear what might happen in learning more. When all else fails, you find your passion through what you fear. This process is a very quiet one for you, Lissam. Very difficult to admit to consciously.'

I wallowed deeply in scepticism while Perry rested back in his chair. Looking up and across the desk, I sensed I was on a path, regardless of whether Perry's theory was right or wrong. And then there was London. A PhD from Whitlock? It could be a possibility if I got to know the staff there, staff like A.W. Anything was possible.

'Can you please forward to me A.W.'s email with the images and certificates? I'll have to contact A.W. about who gifted the paintings,' I said. 'Unless you recall?'

'Some pharmaceutical company...can't recall the name.'

'In 2013, you said?'

'Yes, our lucky number.' Perry smiled, turning to his screen. 'What's your email address?'

'Can I do it?' I intercepted before he could lay one finger on a key. 'It'll be ...ah...faster.'

'Be my guest,' Perry said, shifting his chair away from the computer. 'I'll let him know to expect one from you. Otherwise, the system might detect you as spam.'

'Thanks, please cc me into that message so the system will know it's me,' I said, forwarding the email to mine.

Returning to my seat, I asked, 'Do you know whether the pharmaceutical company originally purchased the paintings from Galerie Exotique?'

'Possibly,' Perry shrugged. 'The certificates have the Galerie Exotique letterhead on them.'

'The certificates travel with the paintings. They could have gone through several hands before the company purchased them.'

'Well,' Perry pondered, 'the paintings were given as a generous declaration of friendship. Whitlock wouldn't have received the receipt.'

'And I'm supposed to burrow into this gift horse's mouth?'

Perry nodded. 'Down its throat if necessary.'

I grabbed my bag and headed for the door, then stopped and turned around. 'Just to let you know, from next week I'll be working at Noah Webster Gallery part-time. But it won't interfere with lectures or our meetings.'

'Noah Webster,' Perry mused. 'Paddington gallery?'

'Yes.'

'Didn't he have some history in the auction houses, letting through dodgy Aboriginal artworks?'

'Yes,' I said, taken aback by the distance this art industry gossip managed to travel. He smiled at me, an overweight, partially bearded Cheshire cat. 'You won't find any Aboriginal art at his gallery. I guess he learned to leave it -'

'What days will you be there?' Perry interrupted.

'Wednesdays, Fridays and Saturdays.' I said, making my way out.

'Might visit you there sometime, Lissam.' Perry said good-naturedly. I felt nauseous at the thought. He was bound to mention

Dorothy Brown to Noah, and the fake paintings. 'Congratulations,' he added.

At least Marvin Brodie wasn't on the other side of the door listening in. But I no longer needed him to feel menaced. I now had Thomas Perry and his moxie for all things Aboriginal. As I walked down the stairs, my dreams of a Whitlock PhD faltered. Intuition had no place in high-profile universities. Intuition was the opposite of academic. I might as well dig a career hole and jump right in. By the time I was walking outside, I saw the words 'Anna's Lissam's future academic career' with a red rubber stamp over the top: *Terra Nullius.*

# CHAPTER 8

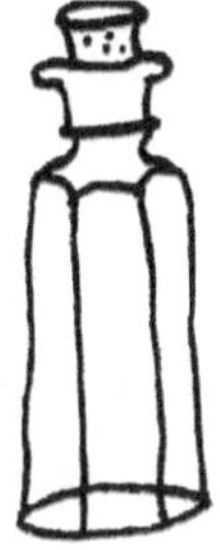

*Lovely to meet you, Anne (by email). The pharmaceutical company that gifted the Dorothy Brown quadriptych to Whitlock in 2013 was Nordon Pty Ltd. However, the company was absorbed by Dowlings Pty Ltd in 2014. The contact Whitlock University had at the time of the donation was a Mr Frederick Paymer. Frederick Paymer is no longer employed with the company and has no forwarding address. Paymer's replacement, Mr Lorenzo Farina, has no record of the Nordon's gift to Whitlock University and knows no other staff member who was involved in the purchase or presentation of the gift.*

*I'm sorry I can't offer more than this. I do wish you all the best with your research.*

*Warm regards,*

*Alistair Wilcox*

It was a nicely hedge-trimmed dead end, cc'd to Perry. Appropriate for the end of the week and the last day of my job. Perhaps it could be the end of this line of the Dorothy Brown enquiry. Knowing Perry, I doubted it. I climbed out of my chair and walked down to Perry's office. The door was open. Perry looked up from behind his desk.

'You saw the reply from A.W.?' he asked.

'Yes,' I said. 'The friendship generously declared by Nordon sounded somewhat short-lived.'

'I imagine it's challenging to sustain friendships when you're being eaten by a bigger fish, particularly the shark variety,' he replied. 'Come, sit down.'

'And yet they could afford several Dorothy Brown paintings to give away not that long before the absorption. It's strange, surely?'

'It's called being a pharmaceutical company. Not short of a buck, even the smaller fish.'

'Wouldn't some research equipment donated to the University, something to do with health, have been more appropriate? They are in the health industry after all. Why give art, and Australian art at that?'

'You're right, they usually give equipment and such,' Perry replied with a frown. Then a thought came to him. 'Dowlings might have already been breathing down their necks, had their sticky fingers on company accounts. Large gifts are usually planned, part of an exchange. Something from Nordon was possibly already expected. That's right,' Perry's posture straightened, 'I heard the company had the paintings but nowhere to put them. Couldn't believe it. You make space – build walls if you have to – for paintings like these.' Perry's expression turned to delight. 'Emu oil!'

'Emu oil?' I asked.

'Yes, the company was trying the alternative medicine market and did this huge promotion about emu oil. That's why they had the Dorothy Browns. To hang up behind the CEO for PR photography. Ah, the ol' emu oil. Good for arthritis, apparently?' He looked to me for confirmation.

'I have no idea,' I replied.

'Well, investing in novelty medicines like that might leave your company up for grabs.'

'They should have tried shark cartilage.'

'Good, is it?'

'No – well, it might be – but I mean to ward off the corporate sharks, Dowlings.'

Perry grinned. 'It's prudent PR to give a painting or sculpture on the odd occasion. The local paper can take a photo of it, keeps appearances up. Better than equipment. Makes the sharks look almost human.'

'Well, I'm not sure what I'm supposed to do now.' I shrugged, doing my best to look helpless. 'Miles Porter from Galerie Exotique is dead, Whitlock can't help…'

'Make trouble, Lissam,' he replied. 'Time to stir the water. See what comes to the surface.'

'Trouble?' I asked.

'Like your life depends on it.' Perry relaxed back in his chair and smiled, flashing his imperfect teeth.

'Surprise!'

A surprise retrenchment party. How appropriate. At twelve-thirty, Sharon asked me to come to her office. I walked in to find a good two-thirds of the faculty standing awkwardly with a sandwich in one hand and a paper cup of wine in the other. I looked back at Sharon, who had probably been lumbered with the job of organising this. She probably knew I was going before I did. Why hadn't she warned me? But then I realised she had on that morning with Rupert. *Nothing is a sure thing, Anna, believe me.* And there I was thinking she was worried about her own security. Hindsight is not a wonderful thing. It's humiliating.

Perry was there, grinning across the room before turning to reply to a lecturer who was discussing a faculty matter. Sharon thrust a plate of ham and cheese sandwiches in front of me.

The tutors standing nearest asked me about my plans for the future.

'Still studying for my Master's, of course,' I answered. I was about to mention my new job, but one lecturer cut in to ask about a photograph he had trouble sourcing from the internet.

Perry tapped at his plastic cup with a plastic fork. His cheeks and nose were flushed. 'Stop the bleeding prattle for just one second.' The room went silent. 'I haven't known Anna Lissam for long. But in the brief spell that we have shared together, I have learned many things about this remarkable staff member.' I gulped at my wine while wondering how many Perry had consumed before my arrival. 'Thanks to Anna, we now have the most remarkably efficient image library system imaginable – so accessible that we can now use it ourselves.'

'Unfortunately for Anna,' came a sarcastic comment from the back.

'Yes, perhaps,' Perry replied, eyebrows aloft. 'However, Anna has already found herself a very nice position at the esteemed Noah Webster Gallery in Paddington. A position that will present new and exciting challenges and opportunities. Why? Because true talent never sits still. It is, in a way, nomadic. True talent constantly moves onto greater things by the forces of nature -'

'And funding cuts,' came the voice again. It was a new tutor, quite young and not yet strapped in the straitjacket of university diplomacy.

'Funding is, of course, god to us at the university,' chuckled Perry, hand to chest. Half the room chuckled in return. 'The forces of nature…or god,' Perry continued, 'know when we are destined for these greater things. I don't know how many of you are aware that Anna is one of this department's highest-grading students. We are proud to have her, but soon enough she will graduate, take flight

-' *to London,* I thought, 'and spread her wings completely. Thank you, Anna, for everything that you have achieved here and good luck for what will no doubt be a very interesting journey.' At that, Perry tipped his plastic cup in my direction and gave me a wink.

'Thank you, Professor Perry,' I replied. A room of plastic cups tipped in turn and murmured, 'To Anna.' Their eyes continued to rest on me, expecting more.

I placed my cup and plate on Sharon's desk. 'And thank you,' I launched, 'to everyone here for making my time as a staff member of Prescott so wonderful…really. I will miss working at the image library.' I paused as my eyes became moist, unprepared for my own reaction. 'I-I can't tell you how much it has given me. Thank you.'

'Better take those Dorothy Brown images from Whitlock back off the database before you go,' Perry piped up. 'Don't want suspected fakes on our system, do we?'

A murmur of 'fakes?' ran around the room. I peered at Perry, who was busy squeezing another Semillon out from a cask. What was he up to? The Dorothy Browns weren't even in the system, so why say it? Was he demonstrating "trouble"? While he chortled with the young tutor, the answer came to me. Perry was close to hammered.

'Another wine?' one tutor asked at my elbow.

'I would…' I said, looking around, 'but it looks like someone's already cleared away my cup.' Letting out a nervous laugh, I added, 'I've probably had enough anyway.'

Pink-cheeked from Chateau de Cardboard, Perry announced to all and sundry that I was to be given the afternoon off. It was the least he could do, he added. I agreed. Being a fine day, I made my way to the city, enjoyed the sunlight on my face as I wandered through the sprawling lawns of The Domain. The Art Gallery of

New South Wales sat at the back of this enormous park and in front of Woolloomooloo's Finger Wharf. This large finger of over 400 metres was originally designed for handling wool exports, later to handle migrants. More recently, it had become a boutique hotel, restaurant and residential development. A playground for adults.

Between the thick sandy columns that lined the gallery's classical Greek-inspired façade, brightly coloured banners publicising the Toulouse-Lautrec exhibition flapped in the winter breeze. Being a weekday, Toulouse-Lautrec was attracting retirees, ladies of leisure and an inordinate number of school children. A swarm of grey blazers and worksheet clipboards disappeared downstairs in orderly fashion, eager to learn all about the prostitutes of Montmartre's cabaret nightclubs in the late nineteenth century. Brave teachers followed. As I had toured the Lautrecs when the show first opened, I moved on, bypassing wild abstracts from Russia, art videos from Vietnam and an enormous elephant made of paperclips. Nothing would distract me from my central focus, my ultimate mission. The whole purpose, in fact, of visiting this place. The gallery café.

The café had the best warmed apple and cinnamon muffins in the city. Washed down with a flat white made life complete. Once I drained my cup and dabbed at the crumbs from the muffin plate, I contemplated the staircase across the lily pond of tables. The stairs were the gateway to the Aboriginal and Torres Strait Islander collection. As sunlight is the cancer of art, exhibitions in basements might be considered a special gesture towards preservation. A compliment. But the placement of the Indigenous collection could also be considered buried.

I hadn't been down there for a while, not since preparing for my ill-fated tutorial on Dorothy Brown. Sitting at the café table, I pondered the idea of a second muffin as retrenchment celebration.

But the truth was staring down both barrels. Dorothy and I needed to talk. I made my way down the stairs, across the marble floor foyer, and u-turned onto the polished concrete towards Yiribana Gallery. Yiribana means 'this way' in the language of the Eora people, the coastal Aboriginal people of Sydney. An unusual name for a collection placed so far away from the rest of the gallery. Once visitors know what Yiribana means, they could be forgiven for assuming the work is all Sydney-based. But the collection is made up of paintings, drawings, photography and sculpture from Aboriginal and Torres Strait Island communities, including Stumpy Downs. The space itself is modest, given the history and diversity among different communities. I walked through the four small sections. A brightly coloured painting with the words 'PAY THE RENT' dominating its canvas. That it was in a First Nations' collection immediately brought gravity to the message. I was already familiar with this Queensland artist's work. Richard Bell was better known for a similar painting, *Scientia E Metaphysica (Bell's Theorem)*, featuring the words '*Aboriginal Art –It's a white thing*', sending the message that Aboriginal art is a commodity in a system controlled by those who aren't First People. I suspected Bell enjoyed the irony when the painting won a high-profile national award sponsored by a large telecommunications company, bringing him international prestige.

I wandered past photographs of well-known urban Aboriginal mothers and naïve paintings on cardboard about children going missing, intricately painted traditional barks and simple abstract paintings until I came to the final room. It was also the largest room, dedicated to Northern Territory artists. The display of primarily dot paintings surrounded a forest of Yolngu burial poles standing in the centre of the room. The very back wall was dedicated to Dorothy Brown's *Meeting Place*, a five-by-two metre painting. Despite its magnificent size, it was like hooking up with an old friend at a reunion. I stood there, absorbing its surface. There were no outlines of hands, symbols of waterholes, of digging sticks or spirits. Just space made up of small and meticulous dots in shimmering bronzes and browned reds, dots so fine I could barely see them. The feeling was so simple and open, so calm. Just as I remembered her.

I settled on the wooden bench in front of it. Most would call the painting an abstracted landscape. But to me, *Meeting Place* was both person and landscape. I stared at the painting for close to an hour, enjoying the rekindling feeling it gave. Then my gut sank. I imagined the woman laughing at my take on her painting, the audacity that I might have something to say about it in a thesis. I once read somewhere that Dorothy had a good sense of humour.

The caption information said 2009, though the painting still looked wet. I got up to look closer at the surface, but a burly attendant appeared out of nowhere.

'Hey, don't get too close,' he barked.

'Sorry!' I backed away so quickly I walked straight into a burial pole, which knocked over three others on its way down, missing Gloria Petyarre's *Mountain Devil* by millimetres.

'Oh dear,' the guard said, staring at the funereal catastrophe.

'I am so sorry,' I repeated. I could have said it ten more times, but doubted it would improve the situation.

'Thank Christ they aren't the real deal,' he said. 'But you'd better get out of here. The curator's going to have kittens.' He pointed to the exit while reaching for the walkie-talkie on his belt.

While exiting the gallery, a group of tourists caught and herded me towards the gallery store, weaving through Toulouse-Lautrec catalogues and posters. After an enforced tour through Europe, Asia and periodicals, I found myself in Australia. The sensible thing would have been to cut my way through the four teenage boys who had blocked my path. They were gathered around a Dali calendar like it was erotica. Melting clockfaces will do that to young males. But it was impossible for me to ignore the book on Dorothy. It was the size and weight of a large wooden chopping board. The publication had been released after Dorothy had announced her departure from the market and became a collector's item in itself, like funereal memorabilia, 'Dorothy Brown 1999-2015'. The display copy had been well thumbed. Three hundred and forty of her paintings had been reproduced, sourced from private as well as public collections. Prolific was just the beginning and, I supposed, also the end. Dorothy had done in fifteen years what would take most other artists a lifetime. Even Vernon Jones.

Heading the introduction was a photograph of Dorothy, angular, wrinkled and the colour of couverture chocolate. She was wearing a t-shirt with a print of large tropical flowers. No flowers like that were in the Western Desert, or in her paintings. Did she like the t-shirt? I wondered. Or was it just something handy to throw on? Dorothy looked straight at the photographer, eyelids drooping as if nothing else could surprise her. There was also a small twinkle in her eye, tongue in cheek. Her cheeks were large enough for ten of her tongues.

Flipping the pages from front to back, I didn't detect any fakes. Well, what I thought would be fakes. Not like the Whitlock quads. However, I could feel a chronological slide from liberty to vacuum. That signature calm was almost absent during the last phase of her illustrious career. Almost, but not quite. Dorothy Brown wasn't a martyr. She got out before she lost herself. That much was clear.

Then I saw three guards making their approach to the store, one murmuring something official into his walkie-talkie. As they entered the children's section (a reasonable starting point if looking for a burial pole vandal) I carefully lowered the book on the stack and slipped out the exit into the light of day.

On my first day at Noah Webster, Liz finally paid her share of the rent. But she had lost her keys again.

'Can't help, Liz. I have to get to the gallery,' I said.

'You're not going anywhere looking like that, young lady,' Liz replied, wincing at the navy suit. Meanwhile, my fashion critic was wearing a red gingham shirt, a pink leather miniskirt, and gold boots.

'I don't have anything else.' We returned to my wardrobe and dug deep.

'Narnia looks dull this season,' she replied. 'No, you're right. There's nothing wearable in here. I probably have something in my wardrobe -'

'No really, that won't be -' But it was too late. Liz was unstoppable, and before I could say 'ring-spun fabric', I was wearing a silver jacket with orange trousers and pink loafers. I said I wasn't sure about it.

Liz agreed. 'You are going to have to shop during your lunch break. Today.'

'Noah didn't mention lunch breaks in the contract.'

'Got to train your boss, Anna. *You* tell *him* when you are going to take your lunch break.' Liz paused. 'But it would be more effective if you were wearing sequins.'

'Shopping may have to wait till payday, I don't have any money yet.'

'Credit darling, live the lie!' Liz said, handing over purple earrings and a red and silver chiffon scarf. 'Tomorrow night is late trading, I'll consult.'

'No, really. You don't have to.' It was more of a plea.

But my flatmate would have none of it. 'I'm quite good in a crisis,' she answered, lighting a cigarette.

Liz had a client meeting at Bondi, past the gallery circuit, so she offered to drop me off – after I found her keys (behind the television). The fine weather warranted opening up the top of her black Mazda sports, so I used the scarf to hold my hair down. But it kept blowing back around my neck. Red and silver flapped into my face. It was like being attacked by Christmas tinsel.

'If I don't see you before, I'll meet you here tomorrow at five-thirty. Have a nice day, darling,' Liz yelled.

I said 'Great,' omitting the fact that I wasn't working the next day. Patting down my wind-blown hair, I walked my mismatched attire into the gallery. Noah was there, in the same state of budgie enthusiasm as before.

'Anna, hi, how are you?' I was waiting for a look of horror on his face at my attire, but the man didn't blink. 'Listen, I'm so glad you're here. I have a string of meetings, so I'll probably be out all day. But don't worry,' he continued, 'here are your keys. This one's for the security system, which is over there behind the thing,' Noah gestured to nowhere in particular. 'The artist, Cusack, won't hassle you. She's in Hong Kong for the month.' I looked at the fields and wondered how she was coping over there, away from her country life.

'My mobile number is here if you need to call me,' he said, pointing to a Post-It note. 'But don't give the number to anyone else. The air conditioning switch is near the security system. The credit card facilities are here. You know how these work, don't you?'

I didn't, but Noah was already out the door, fighting the windswept foliage and yelling, 'Just call me if you need me. Don't be a stranger!'

I had questions. Lots of questions. I immediately started dialling his mobile number, but then hung up and took a few deep breaths. After a few minutes, I realised the lights weren't on.

Why the spotlights were off was difficult to ascertain. Finding the switches was even harder. During my search, I set off the security system twice, then found them. Showtime. Settling behind the front reception desk, I discovered a bank of small security monitors depicting different areas of the gallery. I could see the entire space at a glance (I was alone). One of the screens was switched off. I tried turning it on. Nothing happened. As I was fiddling, a surge of unprompted cool air rushed through the air conditioning vent directly above my head. Shivering, I swivelled to the computer. The screen lit up, asking for a password. The cool air pumped through the vent while I searched the desk drawers for a hidden password. Within five minutes, my teeth began to chatter. I delicately tuned the unnumbered temperature dial like cracking a code for a safe. Before I detected any significant change, a well-groomed middle-aged couple walked in.

'Noah Webster, please,' the gentleman said, looking me up and down (unimpressed, quite rightly). Then the telephone rang.

'Noah's not, er, Mr Webster's not in at the moment -'

'Not in? But we have an appointment with him.'

I excused myself for a moment to answer the telephone.

'Yes, Noah Webster, please.' It was a male voice. Abrupt.

'Mr Webster is not in at the moment,' I replied. 'Can I take a message?'

'Yes, you can tell him that I waited two hours for him yesterday and I'm really *pissed off*!!'

'And who may I say is calling?'

'You can tell him it's the artist who has been saving his fucking bacon!' Before slamming down the receiver, the man added, 'He'll know who it is.'

I smiled up at the couple who had been glaring at me since I picked up the phone.

'Noah left not long ago,' I said. 'I'll try him on his mobile and let him know that you're here.' A call came through on the other line. I put Noah's mobile on hold and answered, 'Noah Webster Gallery, how can I help you?' But there was no answer, so I hung up. The other line was dead also. I dialled Noah's number again, and the same thing happened. Then it became clear. Noah had diverted his mobile to the gallery number earlier and had forgotten to take the diversion off. 'I'm afraid it's not answering. He said he might be out all afternoon.' I sent a text, but Noah didn't respond.

'I can't believe he has done this again,' said the woman.

'Can I help you at all?'

'I doubt it,' the man replied.

'Well, maybe she could,' the woman said, practically tugging his jacket sleeve.

'Don't be ridiculous, Peg.' Obviously, it was Peg who was ridiculous. I only looked it.

'Can I take down your details? I'll keep trying -'

'That won't be necessary. Just tell him he has lost a sale.'

The two walked out. I quickly tried the mobile number again, activating the circular diversion once more, boomerang-style. Sitting back, I wondered what I'd done by accepting the job, not knowing this Noah from the biblical one. Both Noahs seemed to bite off more than they could chew, though nautical Noah seemed better organised.

Irritated, I swivelled around on my chair, wondering about music. Most galleries these days were silent, keeping the art experience pure. Music could interfere with what the art was communicating. Nonetheless, there were speakers dotted around the gallery, no doubt controlled by the computer I couldn't access. I wheeled my chair across to the multi-function printer sitting on a low white cupboard. Running my fingers over the various buttons, familiarising myself with their functions, I then tried the cupboard and found it locked. I made a mental note to ask Noah about the key, passwords, and perhaps a staff orientation app Jan may have developed before packing. She had printed out the latest gallery e-news at least and left it on the desk. It was a digital invitation to the next opening. A single photograph depicted a minimalist metallic sculpture. It looked like a car bumper gently twisted and turned into a long, elegant 's' shape. The piece could have been horrendously amateur, but it worked. The caption read 'Kevin Bradley *Bumper Bar Intonation*'. I then looked back at the photo to see if I had been a little generous. The work was fine. It didn't excite me, but it looked professional enough to be sold at a gallery. Still, I would have expected something more from Noah Webster Gallery. Kevin Bradley was art at room temperature.

I wandered through the gallery towards the kitchen to fix myself a coffee. Passing Noah's office, I backtracked to his door. It was locked. In the modest kitchenette, I put on the kettle and, while waiting for the boil, looked around the stockroom nearby. The generously sized space was still barely enough for all the work that Noah had decided to store. Paintings were held in carpeted racks, most separated by large pieces of foam core or cardboard, some were completely covered in bubble wrap. Boxes of old catalogues were stacked on top of one another next to a small collection of abstract sculptural pieces, all by different artists.

I heard, 'Hi there,' by my shoulder, and yelped in shock. A short woman was standing next to me. 'Sorry, didn't mean to creep up on you,' she said. 'My name's Laura Watson.' Laura Watson was cheerful. This was bound to be temporary. 'I'm here to collect my etching.'

'Your etching?' I asked, still catching my breath.

'Noah's not here? I told him I'd be coming today.'

'No, and I'm afraid he didn't tell me about your etching 'I'm sorry, it's my first day.'

'It's probably here in the stockroom somewhere,' Laura suggested. 'I could come back later, but it's a bit of a bind. I really need it today for a client. Shall we both have a quick peek then?'

'Okay,' I agreed, grateful for the offer of assistance. I sent Noah a quick text to alert him. Again, no response. As we both walked into the stockroom, I asked, 'What does it look like?'

'Unframed, probably rolled up or between two pieces of cardboard. Yay big,' she held out her hands as if she were scoring an AFL goal. I began pawing through racks while Laura looked around some sculpture. Both of us came to the same conclusion. There was no order to the storage. Every few minutes I would run out and look down the gallery to see if anyone else had entered, then run back. We found the print rolled in tissue sitting on top of an enormous pile of used bubble wrap. To my relief, a sticker with the name "Watson" tagged it.

Back at the desk, Laura said, 'I'll pay by credit card.' There was no note of the price anywhere. Even without my coffee, the room temperature was definitely rising. At least I wasn't freezing anymore. I looked at the EFTPOS machine, pleading for it to talk to me. 'I'm sorry,' I said. 'I've never used one of these things from this side of the counter.'

'Ah, don't worry. Typical Noah, he's lovely really, but sometimes he tries us all.' The woman happily carried out her own transaction, explaining what she was doing at every step. 'It's a little warm in here, isn't it?' She was right. The Arctic temperature had become summertime in the Middle East. Laura successfully paid $450. She seemed honest enough. I started to sweat. She took her print and, with a sympathetic expression, whispered, 'Good luck!' before disappearing out the door. I wiped my brow, wondering if I was witnessing a theft. Realising I should have asked for a number or address, it was too late. Another customer, this time an elderly woman with shaky hand movements, walked into the gallery.

'I want to find something REAL, something down to earth, but it also has to be *tasteful*!'

'Have you seen the current exhibition?' I said, gesturing towards the walls. 'Philippa Cusack's work is exceptional -'

'No, no, no. It's not what I'm looking for *at all*,' she said, shaking her head violently. 'For goodness' sake, where's Noah?'

'I'm afraid Noah is not in at the moment.'

'Not in? When is he coming back?' She took a pressed white handkerchief from her purse and dabbed at her neck in exasperation.

'I'm not exactly sure. He may not be back today.'

'But I *need* him! Or Jan. Is Jan here?'

'Afraid not. She's on holidays.'

'It's very close in here, dear.'

'Close?'

'Warm, dear.' I twiddled at the dials until cool air rumbled through the vents once more. 'I'm looking for something *special*.' The woman looked at me as if the description would serve all purposes. It would have been much more helpful if the woman had said that she was looking for something *green* or *raunchy*. 'Tell Noah I need to speak with him *as soon as possible.*'

'Yes, I will. What is your name, please?'

'He knows who I am.' The woman flew out the door before I could explain that I didn't. The commercial art world was a little like the Wizard of Oz. Most people were easily categorised on appearance, but each was lacking something fundamental. On that day, I was missing food. In the rush, I had forgotten to pack a lunch. While searching for stray mints in the corner of my handbag, I found the three employment contracts, signed for Noah the night before. Placing them carefully in the second drawer of the desk, my body shivered from the cold. The temperature was dropping fast. I spent the next half hour twiddling with the air conditioning knobs and drinking endless quantities of liquid, alternating between steaming black coffee and refrigerated water. Cusack's boundless fields no longer brought me peace and calm. My skin became a sieve for perspiration.

At five minutes to close, the temperature was on a downhill slide. A young man with an unsteady smile and a large sports bag entered the gallery.

'How are you today?' he asked, rubbing one arm with the other to keep warm. The tone was rehearsed, but no amount of practice was going to hide its shallow sound.

'I don't know,' I replied. It was an honest answer. For a moment, he forgot his script. 'Um, right. Ties? I've got some ties, lovely ties. Going very cheap.'

'I don't wear ties anymore,' I replied, thinking of my school years. He shifted his weight and took out a handful of his most popular samples anyway.

'Um. Make nice gifts.' I glanced at what looked like elongated pizza toppings and shook my head apologetically.

'Any other staff here that would be interested?'

'I really wish there was,' I replied earnestly.

'No worries.' The young man gathered up his goods but then stopped. 'Aren't you cold in here?'

'Yes,' I said. 'Yes, I am.'

'You might want to look at the air conditioning,' he smiled. With the sports bag hoisted over his shoulder, the salesman headed out to his next destination. Sitting fixed behind my desk, my jaw was clenched against the cold. This was no place for hot water bottles.

# PART 2
# SUGAR & FRUIT

# CHAPTER 9

'We need obscene spenders. And, by god, we need to suck up to them.'

'I just think I make a better academic than a salesperson.' Liz was changing in her bedroom while I was sitting on the floor in the hallway, back to the wall. I was feeling heavy. Really heavy.

'It's your first day on the job, Anna. The boss pisses off, totally leaving you with the dirty – which is nothing new, by the way. You need to learn to chill.'

'Chill?' I asked, feeling a shiver. My throat started to feel sore.

Liz rummaged through her handbag for her keys. 'Bloody, bloody, bloody...' I crawled across the carpet and picked up the keys from under her bed.

'Thanks, I'm off. Oh, and don't forget tomorrow night – we're going to warm up your card! Actually...I've got something on tomorrow night...Saturday?'

'I work Saturdays now,' I replied, rubbing at my throat.

Liz clicked her fingers. 'Friday after work. There's a new mega-boutique in the city having a special opening, invite only. I'll track down an invite, then pick you up from the gallery.' Before I could answer, Liz and her glowing cigarette had already disappeared into the night. Hauling my body upright, I picked up some of Liz's clothes on the way. Then dropped them straight back onto the floor again. Unearned exhaustion pulled at every muscle. I staggered into the bathroom and ran a bath, throwing in some eucalyptus oil in the hope it would chase away what was fast descending upon me. Sinking in, I lay there, took a few deep breaths, then felt a lump forming in my throat. Nursed my foggy head until the temperature turned tepid. The soak didn't seem to help. Wrapped in my robe, I lay on the couch and flipped through a local free magazine. Being a non-news week, I was soon scanning the back section. Despite the plethora of internet dating sites, ♥Meeting Point♥ was still there. Ignoring the fact that I was shackled to the chains of celibacy, personal advertisements sometimes served as personal amusements, and I was in need of some perking up. I scanned down the first carefully chosen emboldened word highlighted at the start of each classified listing.

**A quiet,** shy, 32 yo.
**Affectionate,** outgoing...
**Anyone....**
**Broad...**
**Connoisseur...**
**Cuddly....**
**Elderly....**
**Emotional...**
**Extra** large heart...
**Heartbroken...**
**Home** alone...
**Jewish...**
Just arrived!...
Male...

Mature...

No...

Romantic...

Secret...

**Starting...**

**Trestle** table for sale...

**Truthful...**

**Unplugged...**

**Unscathed...**

**Vegan....**

**Volcanic...**

**Wanted...**

**Wild** one...

**56** Yrs. young. Not an oil painting.

I must have fallen asleep because the next thing I heard was laughter in the outside hallway, the clatter of keys, and the door opening. Liz charged through, piggybacked by a tall, well-built man in jeans and leather jacket.

Liz screamed, 'LONG LIVE THE HANKY PANKY!' and rode him into her private rooms. She soon appeared alone, however, to search for something in the fridge.

'Hey Annie, how goes it?' Liz reached for the bottle of Roederer polished off two weeks ago. 'I forgot, bugger.'

'He must be special, bringing him back here,' I said, nodding towards her bedroom.

Liz smiled in an alcoholic haze. 'Gotta buy you a boy on Sunday too, Anna. Some Chris Hemsworth-looking...what's your credit limit?' I blew my nose in response. 'Consider something casual...a fling!' Liz waved her hand and then leaned on the bench to steady herself. 'Best get back.' At that, she bounced off the hallway walls to the bedroom.

It's hard to say "Thank god it's Friday" when returning for a second day at a new job after a disastrous first day – and now feeling below par. I shuffled onto the bus as if wearing slippers. The day before had been a write-off. The head cold had its way with me while Simon kindly took mindful lecture notes on my behalf. Physically, I felt just well enough to work. Mentally, it was uncertain. As Liz was nowhere to be seen that morning, I had escaped the apartment wearing my blue suit. It had become a new comfort. The morning was crisp, cloudless, and promising warmth sometime soon. Being peak hour, the bus was full. I hung onto a rail, trying not to think of the day ahead. Explaining my first day to Noah would inevitably point an accusing finger at unprofessional behaviour. To whom, the odds were fifty-fifty. I had left written messages on the desk, but how he responded to those was yet to be discovered.

Upon arrival, Noah was nowhere in sight and, to my relief, there were no clients waiting. As I turned on the lights, a piercing scream vibrated through my bones. The alarm mercilessly continued until I was able to think through the noise and remember how to turn it off. When finally pacified, I sat down and gripped onto the silence. Which was momentary. Noah promptly bounded in, all smiles, with a younger man in tow.

'Anna, I see you've worked out that dreadful alarm system. Well done!' I smiled back weakly, wondering if he was serious. 'I'd like you to meet my friend, Robert. Robert, this is Anna, my new lifesaver.'

'Pleased to meet you, Anna.' Robert smiled and bowed slightly in a polite, gentlemanly manner. He had short-cropped dark brown hair, the beginnings of wrinkles around his eyes that were more like light sketch marks for amusement.

Noah showed Robert the printout for the next exhibition. The lukewarm one. 'The artist is a friend of Robert's,' Noah explained to me. I nodded, now clear on how Kevin Bradley made it onto the exhibition calendar. 'Jan's already sent out the eNews invite and the media release,' he said. 'I don't suppose you had a chance to go through the stock room yesterday?'

'Not properly,' I replied. 'Though I had to retrieve that print for Laura Watson.' I could feel my voice fading.

'You found the print, marvellous. Did she pay the four hundred?'

The weight slid partially off my shoulders. I'd overcharged. Or rather, the client had overcharged herself. 'She paid four-fifty,' I confessed.

'Four hundred and fifty?' Noah pondered, 'Maybe it was four fifty...'

'Other people wanted to speak with you, but they wouldn't leave their names. I couldn't reach you on the phone. Did you get my texts?'

Noah seemed surprised. 'That's right. I forgot I had the diversion for the first hour. Then I must have been out of range. The texts came through last night, meant to read them properly, but...'

'The city is always terrible for reception on your phone,' Robert said. 'I told you, it's time to upgrade.' Noah nodded, looking at his phone then shrugged. 'Still, it was a very productive day,' he said, turning to me. 'Well handled, Anna. Clients can be challenging sometimes.'

'The air conditioning was playing up a bit.'

'Yes, it does that sometimes. Don't know why, but it should be okay today.'

'Right,' I said, uncomprehending. 'Anyway, I need the password to the computer. And here are my signed contracts.' I retrieved them from the desk drawer and passed them over.

'Great, thanks,' Noah said, tucking the folded pages into his breast pocket. He clapped his hands together. 'We'll sort out the password later. Let's do the stock room tour.' All three of us wandered to the back of the gallery. Noah halted at the door. 'Before we go in, you must understand that there are some hideous works in there, some I would never show in the gallery. I keep them for special clients who have no taste.'

Noah was right. Some paintings appeared custom-made for intimate spaces in Vegas. The worst were carefully packed in bubble wrap. Less for protection, more for camouflage. I even spotted a painting of a smiling Negro boy in a pink rural setting holding a spray of purple flowers.

'Actually, that sort of thing is now considered so bad it's fashionable.' Robert said with a laugh.

I checked to see if it had been painted on velvet. No, it was Masonite.

'The artist is doing a series where the eyes and mouth glow in the dark,' Noah said. 'Jazz bar job.'

Another was of a ghostly woman's face surrounded by blue and green swirls of seaweed hair.

'Dreadful, isn't it?' Noah chirped.

'Appalling,' I agreed, daubing my nose with a tissue. The question of taste reminded me of my unfashionable attire, but neither of them had even glanced at my suit. Instead, Robert asked me, 'What do you think of this?' while wrestling a large frame out of the rack. I gasped, and the two men looked at me in surprise.

'Exquisite,' I said, still gazing at it.

An egg sat by itself against a large, blue-grey background. A glow came from the shell, unadorned and unattached. Pure. The title was 'Egg'.

'I was babysitting the gallery when the artist brought this in,' Robert explained.

'It's well painted,' Noah said, hands on hips.

'But don't you think the glow is beautiful?' Robert pursued.

'Perhaps.'

'You can say it, Noah. You're amongst friends.'

'It's beautiful,' Noah replied, while perusing some other paintings. Robert smiled at me in triumph. 'Well, if you think it's so wonderful, for god's sake go to the guy's studio and look at the rest of his stuff. He keeps calling me, and I just haven't had the time.'

'Let Anna go. He is gorgeous, Anna, you will love him.' Robert touched my arm as if he had known me for years. 'His name is John Roebelling.'

Noah rolled his eyes and turned to me. 'Go out there today if you want. I have to stay in the gallery anyway to meet Frank and his greenbacks.' Noah gave me John's number to coordinate a meeting and then disappeared into his office with Robert.


'Sorry, did I wake you?'

'Um, kind of.' I could hear a stretch through the phone.

'Hi John, my name is Anna. I'm calling on behalf of Noah Webster.'

'Noah Webster?'

'I know it's late notice, but I was hoping to visit your studio sometime today if it's convenient. If you have any more work you want to show us, that is,' I added cautiously. Robert peeked his head out of Noah's office, smiling and giving me an encouraging thumbs up.

'Today?'

'But if you're busy, we could make it another day.'

'No, today's fine. Noah can't come?'

'No, I'm afraid Noah's unable to find the time just at the moment.'

'But he trusts her judgment implicitly!' Robert yelled from Noah's door.

'That was Robert. I believe you met him when you came to the gallery.'

'Ah, yes, Robert. Who could forget?' John laughed. 'Well, what time were you thinking of coming over?'

'Where are you? It's not written down here.'

'Paradise.'

'Paradise?'

'Out west, it's in the sticks.'

'I don't believe I've been there. Sounds nice.'

'It's a hole.'

'That's okay,' I said. 'I'm sure your paintings make up for it.' I dabbed my dribbling nose silently with a tissue.

'As long as you think so,' he replied, now sounding quite alert. 'Do you know how to get here?'

'I'm sure I'll find it,' I said, certain that not having a car was going to make the excursion a challenge. John gave me the address details, and we arranged to meet in an hour. Noah and Robert emerged from the office as I was blowing my nose.

'Noah, the artist is in Paradise. That's beyond Locktown, isn't it?' I began searching the map on my phone. It looked quite a distance.

'Some artists find unusual locations for inspiration,' Noah said. 'It's very easy to get there, though. You've got a car, don't you?'

'No, not yet,' I replied. It hadn't occurred to me to consider planning towards it. I was a hand-to-instant-noodle-to-mouth person. But didn't want it to be a problem with Noah. Going out to artist studios sounded more fun than sitting in a gallery. Still, perhaps future "sweets" could change that. But that meant sitting in a gallery first.

'Well, just take the bus to Central,' Noah said as he began walking to his office, 'then the train to Locktown, and there will be a bus to take you straight to it.'

'And then what?' Robert asked. 'Noah?'

After a few seconds Noah reappeared with a pile of letters and packages. 'What?'

'How does Anna get from the bus stop to the studio?'

'She can get an Uber or cab. Or she could call him to pick her up.'

'That's ridiculous. Anna, would you like to borrow Noah's car?'

'The Audi?' Noah spun around to face Robert. Meanwhile, I searched my memory for the last time I drove.

'Anna will be fine on public transport. Won't you, Anna?'

Second day of the job, I would have to be.

'Oh, and could you drop these off at the post office? We have an account with them. Here's the bulk mail form.' Noah handed over a piece of paper, then piled up my open arms with mail. Robert looked at me with sympathy while Noah rustled about in the near-empty petty cash tin. 'Here's twenty dollars for the fares.' I did my best to hold the money along with the packages and my handbag.

'You're all heart, Noah.' Robert said as he took the mail off me and walked me out to the street. 'Don't worry, I'll take these to the post office.' He put the boxes down and said, 'Here's John's number, my mobile number and an extra twenty dollars, just in case. Call me anytime if you get stuck.'

'Thanks so much, Robert.'

'Noah's hopeless with this sort of thing,' he smiled. 'Besides, I feel like I should give you a compass and thermals.'

'I'm sure I'll manage,' I laughed. 'But, seriously, thanks again.'

'Tell you what, I'll call John back to let him know you may be late and that you will call him to rescue you from the Paradise Shopping Centre. And, darling, you *will* want to be rescued by John.' He winked before picking up the boxes and walking down the road towards the post office. I smiled at Robert's back, turned in the opposite direction and headed west.

# CHAPTER 10

The further I travelled, the slower time passed, the cheaper the shopping bags and the more my nose seemed to run. When the train stopped at one of its multitude of stations, I watched a couple around my age stumble on, laughing as they collapsed directly opposite me. As they sat, the guy's hands moved around the girl's knees, her hips, her bra straps, her neck. It was as if he had just glued her together and was working to keep the parts in place. The girl pushed him away, laughing, and he responded like elastic. Meanwhile, I blew my nose.

It felt like a solid half day before a sign saying 'Locktown' appeared through the window, and the train pulled to a halt. Leaving the carriage, I wandered around the adjacent car park until I found the bus stop to Paradise. I then stood in the queue for thirty-five minutes. Those around me didn't appear in a hurry to go anywhere. They sat in the sun, staring at their phones. Others chattered over groceries. I tried not to worry about punctuality and blew my nose instead. Finally, the bus appeared.

Happy to be moving again, I settled into my seat and looked out the window. *Charcoal Thai, Blaze Pine Furniture, Sleep City, Automobile Service (with tyre prices slashed!), The Icebox Clothing Store, Pre-Loved Bedding.* Regardless of what was in the minds of the people who christened their businesses, huge range shopping at discount prices kept the aluminium and glass doors open. Studying my phone's map, I carefully counted the streets as they passed. Houses were either hospital cornered or weed-riddled shambles. Road works on the wide streets had left uneven tar patches. Pedestrians were few and far between, mostly mothers pushing strollers flanked with shopping bags on each handle, some with children running in front. The Paradise Shopping Centre sign grew larger and larger, as did its premises. The place was so mammoth it deserved its own flag. I messaged John, and we planned to meet outside *Crazy Cow Burgers*. Fortunately, *Crazy Cow* was opposite the shopping centre, rather than in it. While waiting, I stood in the sun, leaned on four teats attached to an oversized udder of a cross-eyed cow standing on its haunches. And blew my nose.

It only took John five minutes to arrive. But any peace I had experienced from this artist's egg completely vanished when I saw John's mode of transport. He was spread out over a motorbike, an old silver Triumph, ready to be flipped over onto an operating table. If an emergency arose, I would be as useful as a baton twirler. But one emergency instruction absorbed during my school days was impossible to forget: 'If a motorcyclist has an accident, do not take the helmet off or the head may fall apart.'

I fixed my eyes on the helmet hooked through John's left leather-jacketed arm. It was meant for me – to prevent brain spillage. John placed the helmet in front of him and then pulled his own off. Squashed brown curls bobbed in limp greeting. His dark eyes did the smiling for him, but they sloped down at the sides as if in a permanent state of empathy. I gauged John to be in his early or mid-twenties. Underneath his unzipped black leather jacket peeped the obligatory old, paint-speckled t-shirt of The Artist.

'Anna of Noah Webster Gallery?' he asked.

'John of the egg,' I replied, offering my hand.

To my surprise, he gave it a firm shake. 'Here you go,' he said, handing over the helmet. I examined its interior before entering. 'Don't worry,' he smiled while helping with the chinstrap, 'I've got insurance.'

'That's a comfort.'

John didn't seem perturbed by my sarcasm. Before putting on his helmet, he said, 'Can't believe you took public transport all the way out here.' But then faltered. 'I'm trying to find somewhere, um, closer to the city, you know, closer to the galleries. It'll make it easier, I guess.'

This was possibly the beginning of an artist's version of a sales pitch. I caught his smile before he pulled down my visor. John's rambling was saved only by his assailable nature and the fact that he was ambiguously attractive. Robert, it seemed, had a good eye.

I hitched my skirt and straddled the seat behind him. My feet moved about, trying to find the right place. For a moment, I envisioned toes getting caught under the wheel and knees snapping. John took hold of my calf muscles and positioned them to safety. His hands on my legs caused a surge of intimacy, but I reasoned he did that for all his clueless passengers. *Safety first*, I said, grounding myself. And then we were off.

During the start of the trip, I held onto the bar at the back, then watched in horror as my skirt shimmied up towards my waist. Leaning forward, I hooked one arm around his waist while using the other for clothing adjustments. The scene looked like a mobile Lamaze class for 'How to Give Birth to a Professional Artist.' Then my nose ran again. After a mucus-challenged six minutes, the bike pulled up outside a large corrugated iron garage. The garage was prosaic, with the exception of the solar panels spread across the roof, glinting in the sun.

'What brought you out here?' I asked, quickly wiping nasal slime off the helmet with my sleeve before handing it back. 'Or have you always been here?'

'God no, my job was getting in the way of painting. I gave it up to focus better. The guy who owns the studio space owed me a favour. He's kind of an artist, too. More of a dabbler, really. He made some money on some skateboard designs way back. Anyway, I needed a place to crash and work full-time. I've had it for a few months free.'

'Great,' I replied as he led the way through an obscure side entrance, muffling a sniff with my elbow as I followed.

The warehouse exterior gave the impression it would be dark inside, but installed skylights and spotlighting had provided the perfect conditions for painting. I looked at the work as we passed. The paintings were a far departure from the example in Noah's stockroom. Most were medium-sized canvases with stick figures and irregular splotches of primary colour.

'Now that I've been working full-time for a few months, my work has really developed, you know. I feel that it's more, um, mature.' I stopped and peered hard at one of the paintings. 'This is Eden's work,' John clarified. 'The one who owns the studio. My work is through here.'

Breathing a sigh of relief, I wandered through the doorway to the even more expansive space. As far as details go, it looked like a typical painter's studio. Random panels of white gyprock served as temporary walls, short of reaching the corrugated ceiling by at least two metres. Some egg canvases hung, others leaning on walls. It was hard to ignore the double bed in the corner, but I moved my eyes across to John's makeshift kitchen (old sink, dented oven with a rusted two-plate stovetop, paint-smeared bar fridge). The 1950s style laminated table and matching chairs did its best to create an intimate setting within the enormity of the space.

I followed John across the paint-splattered concrete floor to an easel near the centre of the studio. The natural light from above worked well there. A side table was covered with pots of paint, brushes, wooden boards and ripped pieces of cardboard used for preparing colours and an ashtray sprouting a couple of joint stubs, one with a light smear of red lipstick. A digital camera sat on a tripod, serious equipment from the look of it. Nearby was an old wooden desk, on which John's laptop sat closed.

I turned to look at John, but something caught my eye. A billboard sized photographic image on paper was tacked on the wall with pins behind us. The image was of the food court in a shopping mall, possibly Paradise Shopping Centre. A middle-aged man and a young woman had empty food wrappers and cups before them. The man wore blue trousers and a white shirt, sleeves rolled, with a nametag pinned at his chest. The woman had black trousers and a purple short sleeved knitted top with a thin gold chain around her neck. A white handbag sat on her lap. The balance of the bodies indicated they were rising to leave. It could have been the most ordinary of snapshots. It could have fallen into the category of documentary or graphic design, rather than art. But the scale, the movement and the light made it more than that.

'This is the area that I'm working on at the moment,' John said. 'Still being developed, no titles for them yet.'

'Have you lost interest in eggs?'

'I needed something new.'

'What's newer than an egg?'

'Large-format digital prints,' he replied. 'Well, digital fine art isn't new, but the quality and size of what you see here is.' John walked closer and asked, 'Did Noah look at my website?'

'You've got a site?'

'I left my résumé with the painting – the explanation about this new work and website was on the résumé.'

No résumé had been mentioned to me. It would have been useful reading on the train. 'Noah's been very busy lately,' I fudged. 'Even I have trouble getting his attention.'

'I've scored some sales from the site,' John said, 'but it mostly helps people get an idea of what I'm doing. Gets the taste buds going, you know?'

This made sense. Apparently, there was less time to shop. Packaging and convenience had become everything. The internet was a global shopping trolley. But the idea of buying original art over the net, rather than seeing it for real, had never made sense to me. A seventeen-inch monitor would have difficulty depicting the power of the image before us. Gallery spaces still had their purpose.

'How did you manage a print-out of this size?'

'Near to here, there's a tech park. A mini Silicon Valley. Not just for software, but hardware and printing, too. They have some pretty incredible equipment,' he said. 'This is large format ink jet printing using high quality pigmented inks and archival paper.'

'So Paradise has its advantages.'

'You've found me out.'

'Wouldn't a print-out this large be expensive?'

'The Park's still playing around with the technology themselves, so I'm their guinea pig. I've put their logo on my site as a sponsor.'

I could sense him looking at me as I continued to run my eye over the image. He was holding his breath.

The work showed a greater maturity than his age, whatever that was. I rarely felt a great connection with art photography. But here, on this mammoth scale, were two ordinary people on the cusp of departure. Our everyday lives seen properly for the very first time. Uplift mixed with slight melancholia, followed by the whisper *'It's just life'*.

Then I remembered I was there on behalf of Noah Webster. The jump from painting eggs to photographing people required some explaining.

'Do you miss painting?' I asked as a lever.

'Not really,' he shook his head before glancing back at the eggs that now looked so small. 'My hand really started to ache from the brushwork. I think my wrist needs some serious physio,' he said, holding it while rotating his hand. 'Plus, the digital thing is exciting, and it's changing all the time.

'Take a chair – or rather a box,' he said, gesturing towards the pile of old wooden crates behind him. Scattered on the floor were A4 colour printouts of more shopping centre scenarios. I sat on a sturdy-looking crate and took a closer look. One photo had a woman and child in a supermarket aisle passing a stacker pushing a box of detergent onto the top shelf. Another was of a woman waiting for her shoe to be repaired, dangling her shoeless foot while she sat, a partial glimpse of a shoe store in the background. A mobile telephone saleswoman stood at a temporary booth, ignored by two passing men in suits.

For all the movement, there was stillness. For all the people, there was solitude. For all the sales signage, there was a sense of reverence. In amongst the archetypal shopping frenzy, John had managed to capture sacredness.

I turned back to the couple pinned to the wall 'The model,' I pointed to the young woman and then down to the A4 printouts.

'She appears in all of these.' Her wide-set grey eyes had been a giveaway, even when she was dressed as an Indian male packing goods in the supermarket aisle.

'You noticed. You're the first.' John rubbed at the side of his head. 'We've gone to great lengths to give Candy different personas. She's an actor and has a friend who's a terrific make-up artist. I can't afford to pay them, so I let them use these images for their portfolios.'

'Who are these other people in the print-outs?'

'Friends bought with beer,' he laughed.

Looking closer, the two people in the food court were made up of a mass of what appeared to be printing dots. 'It's an inkjet printer that you use?' I asked.

'That's right,' John replied. 'It's a super-wide format digital printer. You're looking at the circles?'

'Yes, I thought they must be printing dots, but don't inkjet printers spray jets of ink, merging the colours? There shouldn't be dots.'

'You're right. The friends who have seen this all immediately assume I used the old Ben Day dot printing process. For me, the dots are a sort of homage to the past, to the old process of printing,' John said.

'So why don't you just use the old printing process?'

'It wouldn't look exactly the same if I used Ben Day. The dots would be a collection of red, blue and yellow dots if that were the case. You'll notice these dots are made of many colours. It's like a re-enactment, which will never be exactly like the original.'

'Like the re-enactment of the people,' I said as I looked at the wall, then back at the original photo.

'That's it. Recently, Candy and I were just sitting here – admittedly, we had a few beers and smoked a couple of spliffs – and she saw what it was really about.'

'What was that?' I was curious, though also a little irritated someone called Candy saw something I missed.

'She said the dots were like molecules.'

'Molecules?'

'And I yelled, "Yes!" I was so excited. I hadn't seen it before. Molecules are the essence of us, the environment, everything. The dots throughout the image remind us that we are all made up of the same matter. Regardless of who we are or what we do.'

Candy's theory was a good one, I had to admit. She wasn't just a pretty Indian male face. Turning to John, I said, 'Noah's going to be grilling me for some basic info about you,' or so I assumed. 'I suspect most is on your website, but do you mind?'

'Sure,' he grinned shyly. 'But I'm not great with words. Particularly about my work.'

'I can help,' I smiled as I pulled out my pad and pen. 'Education?'

'One year of art school before dropping out.'

'Why did you drop out?'

'The lecturers were wankers.'

'Care to expand?'

'I learn more from the actors, the make-up artist, and the tech dudes. And also from the people who aren't involved in the process at all, people with fresh eyes and fresh brains.'

I gave a half-nod, unsure of what I just heard. I had always enjoyed the structure of university, until Perry arrived. 'Your exhibition experience?'

'Three years of small group shows.'

'Commissions and prizes?'

'None.' John had spent the majority of his time learning to paint and, more recently, using image software. 'Umm…So now that you see this, what I'm doing, you think I have a shot at getting a show?'

'The exhibition calendar is booked solid for the next few months,' I fabricated. 'But if you're going to be there, you've got to be there. And I mean for the long haul. We thought you were a painter, and now I see you're a photographer. You have to show commitment to your medium and slowly build up trust with Noah. This takes time.' It all sounded credible and logical. Second day on the job, not bad. John nodded, accepting but disappointed. 'It is early days, I guess,' he admitted.

'So how old are you, John?' It seemed an obvious question to ask in the professional context.

'Twenty-one.' John started looking through the photographs and then gazed towards the computer monitor.

'Well, you've got plenty of time to work up to where you want to be,' I shrugged.

'How old are you, Anna?' No longer distracted, he was staring right at me. The question was surely unprofessional. Pausing, I wondered how I was going to get back to the land of Noah. He held his eyes on me while I doggy-paddled in silence. Eventually, he spoke instead, although it was more of a loud whine. 'Christ, Anna, I'm really serious about this. I've exposed myself here. I'm all around you.' He bounced onto his feet. 'You can waltz in here and ask any question you want. You talk about trust. My dick's out to be sliced and you won't even say how old you are.'

'Twenty-two,' I said, recovering from his graphic analogy.

'I'm so sorry.' He sat back down again. 'I have no right to talk to you like that. I've just been working so hard and...I don't know what's wrong with me.'

'It's okay. You made a good point,' I nodded. John was looking at his shoes while I inspected the lighting. 'To be honest, I only started working for Noah yesterday. I've never worked for a gallery before.'

I wished the scene would cut to a commercial. It didn't, so I pressed on. 'I'm sorry Noah couldn't come today, and you got me instead. You and your work deserve better.' I stood up, giving the bottom of my jacket a tug as a futile professional gesture. Heading for the door, I realised I was going to have to walk back to the shopping centre.

At the door, I noticed my nose was clear. While large and unheated, the studio was possibly the cure for the common cold.

'I'm glad you came instead of Noah,' John said, following me out. 'You're the first gallery person I've met that's got that creative thing, too.'

I stopped walking. 'Creative thing?' I asked.

'Yeah, you know what I mean,' he said. 'Can I take you back to the gallery?'

'Ah-ha!' I laughed. 'So you do want to meet Noah today.'

'No, I'll just drop you off, promise,' he said, hand to his heart. 'Besides, I can't take my work on the bike.'

'It is a bit of a wind catcher,' I agreed. 'All the way to Paddington with you on the bike? Will I be safe?'

'I keep telling you,' he smiled. 'I've got insurance.'

# CHAPTER 11

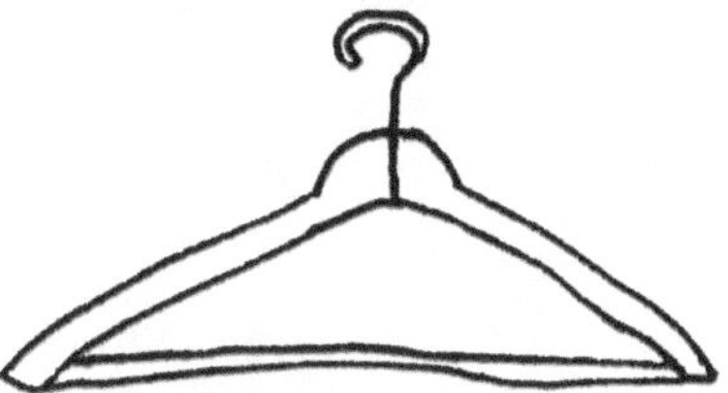

'Tonight we shop. I'll be at Nora's at five-thirty.' It hadn't taken long for Liz to find a pet name for Noah.

'Okay, but -.' Liz had already hung up.

On John's bike, I had learned how to keep my skirt down with one hand and steady myself with the other. Once at the gallery, he saluted me from the bike and blasted off into suburbia. Noah's American client had been held up in the afternoon, finally arriving just as I was hanging up the phone from Liz. He was a short, balding man, plump in a brown pinstriped suit. He nodded in my direction before spotting Noah emerging from the stockroom.

'Noah!' the man yelled while running halfway across the floor.

'Frank,' Noah called back.

Frank stopped to take a break and walked the rest of the way, gulping breaths.

'I didn't think you were going to make it,' Noah said.

'Me neither. A driver without a decent gps. What can ya do?' Noah shook his head in agreement. 'Took me the long way round. Lyin' punk. It was a freakin' nightmare, I can tell you.'

Noah steered Frank back towards the front of the gallery. 'Frank, this is Anna. Frank is from the States.'

'Welcome,' I said.

'Hey Anna, how ya doin'.' It wasn't a question.

Frank offered Noah a Cuban cigar, who refused. 'I don't know if our artist, Phillipa Cusack, would approve of cigar smoke around her paintings.'

'Tell you what, if there's any damage, I'll pay for it.'

'The cleaning or the painting itself?' Noah negotiated.

Frank chuckled. 'I'd better be careful around you.'

'Around me?' Noah asked in mock-modesty.

'Noah, I've come to Australia feeling generous.' Frank announced.

I expected them to talk in Noah's office, but the men settled into the two chairs opposite my desk. Then Frank lit up his cigar and smoked like trains used to. I drained my coffee and offered my mug as an ashtray.

'Shame you can't eat art, eh?' Frank said as he looked around the room.

'No, but it helps you to breathe,' Noah replied, trying not to cough from the cigar smoke. I left to make a pot of coffee and to inhale. When I returned, the conversation had moved on to cars. Gear shifts, carburettors, pistons and alignments. Upholstery didn't get a mention. Noah barely uttered a word.

'So Michigan's the place to be if you want to work in the car industry?' I asked after hearing it was where Frank resided.

'No, honey,' Frank said. 'Michigan's the place to be if you want to own the business. If you want to work, go to Mexico. You'll get paid in potatoes, though, or corn chips,' he chuckled. Frank noticed my frown. 'It's what they're used to,' he said, shrugging it off. I shifted in my seat while Frank took another puff and smiled a hand span. 'I bet South-East Asia loves you guys. And hates you.' When his comment failed to muster a response, Frank asked, 'So what do you drive, Anna?' It was a way of keeping the conversation on the asphalt.

'I've never owned a car.'

Frank looked at me like I had just swung down from the Starship Enterprise.

Noah asked, 'So you're in Australia for business then, Frank?'

'Not really, no. Pleasure.' Frank grinned. I assumed he had come to the other end of the world to take pleasure from others. 'Visiting a beautiful woman,' he said, moving his hands as if moulding an egg timer.

'Really? How did you meet?' Noah asked.

'On the internet,' he replied matter-of-factly. 'We met up yesterday. Turns out, she's not so beautiful after all.' By this time, Frank was speaking directly to Noah. I surveyed Frank's short legs, insulation layers of fat, the bald patch, and the unflattering brown suit. 'Penny Waters, know her?' Noah shook his head. 'Her daughter is in the art game…Ros…'

'Rosalind Waters?' Noah and I said in unison.

'Yes, that's it,' Frank nodded.

'She's one of our most influential art critics,' Noah explained. 'Quite a striking woman.'

'Well, maybe I should be dating her,' Frank smirked before moving on to the topic of mufflers. Noah pried him out of the chair and around the gallery, perhaps hoping he might damage the remaining unsold paintings.

'A bit farmyard for my taste, buddy,' Frank concluded, walking back to my desk to stub out his cigar in my coffee mug.

'This is our next show,' I said, passing over the printout for the Kevin Bradley sculpture exhibition.

'Hey, these look like car parts twisted into poetry-like,' Frank announced.

'That is exactly the impression the artist is striving to achieve,' Noah replied. 'Kevin is rather passionate about cars himself.'

'When's this?' Frank checked out the date. 'Good, I'll be back in time for the opening. I'm going to sunny Queensland tomorrow for a few days. That was where I was going to take the broad, do the exotic tour. But looks like I'm going solo,' Frank shrugged. 'Mind if I bring some business buddies along to your opening?'

'Not at all, as many as you like,' Noah said with a generous smile. I could imagine a man like Frank being unable to resist buying something big in front of colleagues. So, it seemed, could Noah. 'The more the merrier,' he added.


At ten past six, Liz sauntered into the gallery like she had just bought it for investment purposes.

'So this is it?' she asked rhetorically while looking around her, cigarette burning in hand. The cigarette matched the fox stole wrapped around her neck, but her tartan mini skirt and heeled basketball boots were on their own. Squinting her eyes while inhaling gave the appearance that she was focusing on the artworks. 'You're trying to sell these for five...some ten thousand a pop?' Liz pointed her cigarette to two abstract sculptures in the corner. 'They're lovely, Anna, but bloody hell. Well, if he can sell this crap for these prices, he can afford to give you a lunch break, can't he?'

'Ahem,' I coughed. 'Liz, this is my boss, Noah Webster.' Noah had appeared from his office. It was difficult to ascertain what he had heard. 'Noah. Ah, this is my flatmate, Liz, who was just about to put out that cigarette.' I thrust my glass of water in her direction (my mug was in the kitchen soaking in detergent, post-cigar).

But Liz just changed cigarette hands and shook Noah's with a strong pump action. 'Liz Calder, how do you do?' And resumed smoking.

'Charmed,' he replied, giving no sign that he had been.

I made departure movements. Handbag, keys, sanity. 'We're on our way now, Noah. I hope -'

'Hold it a sec,' Liz said. 'I would like Noah to explain to me the value of this work over here.' She thrust her hand over to the painting on the far wall, scattering a feathery ash trail behind.

I moved back behind the desk, wanting no part in what was about to happen.

'There certainly is value. You have an excellent eye, Ms Calder.' Noah's enthusiasm began to blot away traces of doubt. 'I'd be delighted to expand upon this particularly fascinating painting.' Noah led Liz to the painting and spoke at length about the meaning of a concrete building in a field. He outlined its dignified position in art history and delved into the sordid detail of the artist's life. Reality, as usual, was lounging somewhere in between. After five minutes of mutual nodding and pointing, Liz drew the final breath on her cigarette.

'Well, that was very interesting, Noah. I think I might buy it. How much is it?' she peered at the tag. 'Only seven thousand? I think it would go perfectly in the dining room, don't you think, Anna dear?' she said, turning towards the desk. 'Have you worked out how to use that credit card machine yet?'

I remained silent. Familiar enough with Liz Calder theatre, I knew there was no intention to buy the work. Meanwhile, Noah was rising to the occasion. 'Of course, she knows how to work the machine. She's teaching me how to use it!' Liz went so far as to shuffle through her wallet. 'Oh, dear, I didn't bring the right credit card. Anna, could I use yours? No, that won't work. You have the lowest credit limit in captivity. Never mind, I'll pop in tomorrow and we can fix it then.' She gave a large, bikini queen smile. He nodded in return. Hands clasped and knuckles white, Noah was all too aware that customers who hesitated were usually lost.

'I don't suppose you're any relation to Alexander Calder?' he asked. 'The famous American artist?'

'No, I don't believe so. What was his work like?'

'He made magnificent sculptural mobiles. Bright, colourful forms with beautiful movement.'

'Well, then,' Liz raised her eyebrows. 'Maybe I am.'

'See you tomorrow?'

'Of course.'

I stood in the middle of the street. 'I thought tonight was about *helping* me.'

'Clients let him down all the time. And Nora isn't exactly Mr Follow Through himself,' she said, lighting up another cigarette. 'Come on, Anna, it was just a bit of fun.'

Liz was right. Noah wasn't Mr Follow Through and had continued to prove it in the gallery that afternoon. I would take calls from irate unidentifiable people and Noah would wave me away, mouthing 'I'm in a meeting,' as he wandered back into his office. At one point, I had tried to discuss John Roebelling, but phone calls on his mobile intercepted my efforts.

Opening Liz's car door, I threw the rubbish from the front seat into the back (sushi container, Tiro bottle, scrunched serviette and a macramé-enhanced clog). We then made our way to the throbbing metropolis – the city of Sydney – where the cost of parking rivalled my superannuation. Liz found a free spot down a service alleyway

I'd never known existed. 'Do not, and I mean do *not*, tell anyone about this space,' she warned me before striding towards Pitt Street Mall. Liz bee-lined towards Sukka, the new mega-boutique. Much like an art exhibition opening, well-dressed people were milling around the entrance, chatting with wine glass in hand, ignoring the purpose of the place. Before following Liz inside, I noticed a handkerchief in the window masquerading on the minimalist mannequin as clothing.

'I wonder if Nora goes clubbing,' she said. 'Haven't seen him around.'

'I have no idea what he does in his spare time,' I replied. 'Or in his work time, for that matter.'

'If he died, who would take over the gallery?'

'Good god, Liz, I have no idea. Why on earth would you ask that?'

'If he goes clubbing, he could be taking Zed. And if…never mind.'

'Zed?'

'Zed. As in the letter Z. Some say Zee. That's what they call it in the States. Ends up in rap songs and before you know it, the younger ones are calling it Zee. It's totally messing with our alphabet.'

'What is it exactly?'

'It's a brand of liquid ecstasy. The gay boys love it,' Liz replied. 'There's nothing like taking Drano mixed with Mr Sheen to make a fun night out. No sugar, no calories, no hangover makes it very popular with those wanting to keep up appearances. Plus, it's only about fifteen bucks for a fish.'

'A fish?'

'You know, those soy sauce fish bottles. They often come in one of those,' she said. 'You might die, plenty do. But your innards look clean. Hey, that rhymes.

'Die?' I asked, as I followed her in, wondering if Simon took Zed. He was always so experimental.

'Sometimes you think you're getting Zed,' Liz continued, 'but it's that Bute stuff used for car repairs. Seriously lethal.'

An industrial beat pummelled my eardrums. The sales representative, sporting crop top and plaits, looked at us with a glazed expression and then returned to folding a lime green top, absorbed in the task. Meanwhile, the sounds of rusted plumbing pipes being whacked against other rusted plumbing pipes fed through speakers. I looked around, uncertain where to start. A vocalist worked her way up to screaming orgasms. The crescendos had been tampered with in the studio, cut short and repeated several times on a loop. The orgasms started to go backwards.

Liz had already grabbed a clatter of coat hangers and began moving me towards the immodest changing cubicles. I tried to pull the curtain across, but there wasn't enough material to reach. It was hard to understand how people felt too intimidated to visit private art galleries, but could shop at a place like this on a regular basis. I gulped down the last of my wine.

Finally swaddled, I looked at myself in the mirror. The pale-yellow dress had multiple straps twisting around me like Superman's path around planet Earth. The curtain flew open, and Liz moved in and shifted the straps to their proper place with one hand, wine in the other. I wondered where she got the instruction book for the dress. We both looked in the mirror.

'This colour isn't right for your skin.'

'Does it come in a different colour?'

Liz crossed her arms. 'No, you'll have to change the skin.' I laughed. 'I'm serious,' she continued. 'You should visit a tanning salon.'

'Yeah, right. And then a cancer ward,' I replied.

'It's just a spray tan, doofus,' she replied. 'Okay, try this on and this.'

'Liz, I really don't think -.' I felt cramped and wondered whether Aristotle was also in the changing room. I could hear him saying, 'Art completes what nature cannot bring to a finish.' I told him to get out.

Halfway through shimmying into tight satin black trousers, the curtain tore open and the sales representative came to life. 'Need any help?' she barked over the music. Caught topless with trousers fighting the force of my thighs, I quickly shook my head and pulled back the curtain. With some sucking and grunting, the pants moved over my hips. Hoping the teeth on the zipper would remain clenched, I tried on a white cotton t-shirt with a Bugs Bunny cartoon on the front. Looney Tunes were back in fashion, apparently. Before I could take it off, the curtain flew open again.

'Hey, that's great,' Liz exclaimed.

I nodded and yelled, 'I hate it.'

'It's a bit cas for work anyway. Try this.' Liz threw more dubious clothing onto the hook and disappeared.

I took off the t-shirt and unzipped the pants. My stomach moved forward with relief. The curtain flew back again, and I found myself in front of a stray huddle of guests. A few glanced back, including two bored-looking men. My stomach pulled in, defenceless. The sales assistant, holding the curtain out, yelled, 'UK?'

'No,' I yelled back. 'Close the curtain!'

'K,' the girl sneered and danced off, letting the curtain flap. Then Liz's head appeared around the curtain like a hand puppet.

'I'm not coping,' I said. 'Two guys out there saw more of me than my mother ever did.'

'Hey, don't fret, they're cute. And I think one of them likes you.'

'What? You're insane...and obviously the only person in this shop that hasn't seen my thighs.'

'Anna, how are men going to lust after you, if you don't lust after yourself?'

'I think it's "love", I have to love myself.'

'Yes, that, too. But at this stage I think you should just concentrate on lust.'

'Not after today...'

'Today?'

'Oh, I just met this guy, but it wasn't -'

'Wasn't what?'

'Well -'

'What?'

'He's -'

'What?'

'An artist. Does beautiful work -'

'Nice butt?'

I paused with pursed lips. 'Yes, but it gets worse.'

'He paints naked men for a living?'

'No, he's into photography and one of his models – female – is in everything. They get stoned together in the studio and talk about molecular biology.'

'Sounds riveting.'

'He's an excellent artist, very mature for his age.'

Liz held up my hair into tiny pigtails as we both looked in the mirror.

'He's younger than you? They get off on the idea of The Experienced Woman.'

'I'm only a year more experienced.'

Liz dropped the pigtails. 'This has got nothing to do with being you, or even looking like you. Opportunity needs to be created.' I must have appeared doubtful. Liz clicked her fingers and said, 'Think of it like you're applying for a government scholarship.'

In other words, look like they want you to look and then do what you wanted to do all along. With that said, taking relationship advice from a woman with the commitment level of a rabbit in the springtime was, frankly, absurd.

At the next clothes change, I bunkered in.

'Come out,' Liz said.

'No.'

'Can I come in?'

'No.'

'Anna...'

'No.'

'What's the problem?'

'You can see my bra through this thing.'

'You're supposed to. It's semitransparent,' Liz explained through the curtain. 'Have you got some nice bras?'

'It's my *underwear*.'

'It's fashionable.'

'People have recurring nightmares about wearing things like this in public.'

'Men have recurring wet dreams about women wearing things like that in public.'

Liz put the matter on simmer and started talking dresses. Both of us agreed I needed a frock for exhibition openings. Liz presented a black dress that slipped on like a glove. Somehow, every unwanted bump disappeared. A black satin ribbon tied up the halter neck at the back. Standing on my toes, pretending to have heels, I looked at myself and saw something elegant.

'It's a free cocktail dress,' Liz explained.

'The dress is free?'

'No, the dress brings you free cocktails as soon as you walk into the room.'

'Do you think this could also be a you-will-spend-up-big on art dress?'

'If you want it to be, Anna,' she replied sagely, 'then, yes, I believe it will.'

I bought the dress along with two remarkably normal-looking fitted suits. One dark olive green, the other black. Added to the ensemble were a pair of Italian leather black shoes with medium heel and a matching black leather bag. I also threw on the credit card another pair of black shoes, but with a higher heel for the opening dress. Liz enforced two of the semitransparent tops, figuring that if she was unable to remove my jacket, the young artist had a shot. After all, she said, warmer weather was just around the corner.

# CHAPTER 12

Drumroll. 'Here are the shopping centre scenes,' I explained to Noah the next day, showing him John's website. It was clean and professional in design, with a fast load time given the number of images on the site. The text was engaging, too. Usual for an artist's site, striking the balance between professionalism and warmth through John's own words.

'They look pretty good,' he said, angling his head at the photos.

'Unfortunately, you can't really feel the power of their dimension on this screen.' I had zoomed out as far as I could. Zooming in to show the contrived dots (pretend molecules), Noah nodded. But the screen constraints were failing us both.

While the site impressed Noah, it was early days for John's digital work. 'Close observation rather than a full embrace,' he said. There was potential for an exhibition down the track. In the meantime, I was to do the monitoring. Then Noah gave me a lesson on sourcing information from the stock list on the computer. It was also a lesson for Noah, who had forgotten most of the steps.

'Jan really had this organised,' he explained. 'Shame she couldn't have trained you herself.'

'The convoy has headed off?'

'Yes,' he breathed. 'It was now or never.' Together, we worked out how codes were written on the back of each work in the stockroom. We also conquered printing out consignment reports and invoices. Before Noah raised himself from the chair, I asked, 'Do you know why this cupboard's locked?'

Noah leaned over to the printer and rattled the doors underneath it. 'No idea.'

'You wouldn't happen to know what's in it?'

'Stationery supplies, I suspect.' Noah shrugged. 'The key...Jan would have it. Blast. How she ran things at this end was up to her.' Noah stood up and collected his mobile and keys. 'If she calls, I'll ask.'

'Is she likely to call?'

'Hard to say,' he replied. 'If she doesn't, we'll work it out.' At that, he sprinted out the door, waving with his mobile. I waved at the air. It proved a fair exchange. The mobile was out of range all day.

Donned in my new olive-green suit, I rubbed my nose gently, the skin tender from all the blowing. At least it was drying, and I could smell again. At least I thought I could. There wasn't much to take in. The gallery had a faint dry smell to it. I wiffed my wrist, nothing exciting there. What possessed me to test my armpit next was anyone's guess but, while inhaling, something caught my eye. It was John, walking through the door. My head snapped up as I pulled my arm down. There was nothing in John's face that said, 'Caught you'. Instead, he stood before me with a four-metre- long plastic tube and an athlete's attitude, ignoring any fear of potential pain. In this case, rejection of his photography.

'Hi, John,' I said. I could have stood, but my new shoes were tight. And considering he was intending to force his work onto me prematurely, disappointment kept me anchored. 'This is a surprise.'

'You don't like surprises?' John said, his face impartial.

'We hadn't discussed delivery of your work, had we?'

'I know, but last night we did some more printouts. They came out really well. Today I got to borrow this truck for nothing. I was coming past this way anyway...' He moved his weight to the other foot and held onto the tube. 'Thought I could save you another haul to Paradise.'

I looked at him. I was feeling pushed. Sort of propelled, really. Maybe urged. Encouraged? I didn't know.

He held up his eyebrows in surrender. 'Look, I can take them away again. But I thought that maybe you would like to see them. It's up to you.' His eyebrows remained suspended, waiting for my decision to fall.

'I'll show them to Noah. But you may have to come back tomorrow and pick them up again.'

'Thanks, Anna. I really appreciate it,' he smiled. He seemed sincere. I felt used.

'I was just about to call you,' I said. 'I showed Noah your site this morning. He liked it, but we need to see how you develop over the next few months before committing to an exhibition.'

'Great, thanks.' John leaned the tube against a corner, then wandered around the gallery while I watched him from my desk.

'Nice show,' he said.

'Yes, it is.'

'This blurred effect is amazing.'

'I think so.'

'Sad paintings. Beautiful, but sad,' he said, wandering around the space. 'Looks like a lot of the works are finding homes.'

'We've sold a few.'

'Coffee?'

'Pardon?'

'I noticed a café a couple of doors down. I could bring us back some coffee.'

'Sure…thanks.' A caffeine peace pipe.

'Cappuccino? Latté? Black?'

'Latté, thanks.'

John disappeared before I could grab my purse. Maybe this was his way of paying me back. Or maybe he was buying me a coffee so I would sell his images. Or maybe he was just a nice guy. Eventually, he wandered back in with cups in hand. I was glad to be wearing the new suit. To feel attractive or to have more authority, I wasn't sure. Jamming my credit card with more activity on one night than it had experienced in its entire life felt, at that moment, worth it. I was also relieved to be sitting again. The new heels were much higher than my Docs. Ankle blisters were forming. John settled into one of the client chairs on the opposite side of my desk. While we blew lightly on the surface of our cups.

Thinking about John's molecules, his perfectly round dots, a question popped into my head. 'John, have you ever been to the Western Desert?'

'Once, when I was a little kid. Dad was pretty keen to climb to the top of Uluru. He was a big climber of all things. Mountains, corporate ladders, sacred sites. At some point along the way, I fell and grazed my knee. It can be pretty steep in parts,' he explained. 'Mum ended up taking me back down. I kicked up quite a sink about it. Screaming, crying, the works.'

'Thank god you can't do that now.'

'Have a tantrum?' he grinned. 'You bet I can.'

'No, I mean climb Uluru,' I laughed. 'You know how they finally officially banned it.'

'Which is good, isn't it? We've got no sensitivity to what the place really means. It's embarrassing,' he replied. 'But I do remember how amazing the place was.'

'How so?'

'I can't tell you exactly. It just has this…presence. You have to be there.' John was staring past me for a moment, then snapped his focus back on me. 'Meanwhile, back in Sydney, we have things like the gallery game. The buying, the selling. The profits and losses.'

'It does feel a bit like a game, doesn't it?'

'Well, for a select few. If we went to Pitt Street Mall,' John said, 'and asked ten people at random if they have ever bought an original work of art, I imagine we'd be looking at a small minority.' I cast my eye around his face while John spoke, spotting for clues. Clues for what, I wasn't sure.

'Must admit, I don't personally know that many people who actually buy art,' I admitted. 'My friend Simon calls it "The selling of dreams". He means it in a good way.' Then the heat distracted me. Must have been the coffee. Or perhaps the gallery heating was playing up again.

'The selling of dreams,' John nodded. 'Yeah, I know what he means. Maybe *sharing* might sound…' I automatically took my jacket off and John's smile went up a notch, but he kept talking. And then I remembered what I was wearing underneath. The semi-transparent top. The bra exposer. Jesus. I slid the jacket back on and buttoned up. '…so basically, the people who say, "I don't know much about art, but I know what I like" have probably got the industry by the balls.'

'Really?' I replied, wishing I was a less visual person. 'Well, maybe that depends.' I faltered, then got back on track. 'Yes, it depends on who's buying. And whether they actually buy what they like, or what they think they should like.'

'I've come across some people with a great eye from unlikely backgrounds,' he said. 'Blows me away sometimes, to see who gets it, you know?'

I nodded. God, he's a crumpet. Those eyes. 'What do you think gives someone a good eye?'

'Well…I don't know much about neurology -'

'But you know what you think?'

I knew what I liked to look at. But history indicated that, when it came to men, I knew nothing about ophthalmology. Looking back through my collection of past relationship disasters, Jamie (the first) who saw joint rolling as an origami art form, Greg who collected china chihuahuas, Richard who ended up preferring Liz (who preferred him for about twenty minutes while hammered on tequila – she has no recollection of the event). Then there was Mike. Mike was a great listener, translated duck conversations (so funny I peed my pants in the park) and owned a surprising number of Motown LPs. We grooved. Instant connection. I slept with Mike on our first date, holding back on showing him my doodles until our fourteenth. Then he thought I was strange and drifted away.

'Okay, here's what I reckon,' John said, tapping his finger on the desk. 'To me, the art has to be clever enough to capture someone successfully. But I guess the victim has to be a certain kind of person to get caught.'

'Maybe,' I said. He must have shaved this morning.

'So, you're not mad about me bringing the prints in, then?'

Growing tired of the game, I drank the last of my coffee. 'John, it doesn't matter how I feel about it.'

'What do you mean? Of course it matters.'

'As I told you yesterday, Noah decides.' I threw open my hands. 'I'm not exactly what you would call a controlling force.'

'Controlling forces are overrated,' he said, pulling a piece of paper from his jacket pocket. 'Here's a consignment list with titles and my prices. I'll email them through when I get back. Noah may decide that the work isn't suitable. That's okay, I won't mind coming back to pick them up.'

'Yes, you would. It's a drag to come all the way from Paradise.'

'Not if you're here.' John smiled, then threw our empty cups into the wastepaper bin. A few drops of coffee landed on the white wall behind. He glanced up. 'I'd better go. Let me know how you feel about it, okay?'

'Bye,' I called after him. Remaining seated behind the desk, unable to move, chosen and caught.

It could have been beginner's luck. Early that afternoon, I made a sale from the exhibition and two from the stockroom. Fifteen thousand in one hour, flying solo. That was seven hundred and fifty dollars in 'sweets' for me. Suddenly, the heavy debt on my credit card was looking lighter and fluffier.

I also had my fair share of irate telephone calls to field, meshed with sundry visitors. As the last wave of wanderers moved out the door, I sat down at the desk and prised off my painful Italian shoes. The blisters were getting worse. While toe twiddling, I realised that the air conditioning had remained constant the entire afternoon. Or so it had seemed. With all the distractions, it was possible not to have noticed the changes. Noah walked in, and I reluctantly slipped the shoes back on.

'Fifteen thousand?' he said, slapping his hands together. He looked so happy I could have been wearing my shoes on my ears. 'First week in and you're already a pro.'

I sat back, liberated from Liz-associated guilt. The day's sales collectively topped my flatmate's fictitious one.

'John Roebelling left these for you,' I said, pointing towards the tube in the corner. Though eager to see them, I had decided the prints were better kept in the tube for protection until Noah was ready. 'They're fresh off the press, well, fresh out of the mega-digi-printer. Do you want to have a look?' Sitting on the opposite side of my desk, he appeared distracted with papers in his briefcase.

'Huh?' He looked up and looked across at the tube. 'You decide,' he said before returning to his shambled contents.

'Me?'

'Yep. Put them on consignment if you like them,' he replied, pulling out that day's newspaper and throwing it on my desk.

'Crisis as Australian dollar weakens…' I read the front page upside down.

'You wouldn't know it from what you made today,' Noah said, walking towards his office.

After Noah disappeared into his private bastion, I slipped off my shoes again. Padding across the polished concrete floor with stockinged feet, I opened one end of John's tube and slipped out the three prints, each a substantial three by twelve metres. The sheets rolled out across the floor with relative ease. More of Paradise Shopping Centre, more of Candy incognito. I found some light weights in the desk draws – scissors, a screwdriver, metal ruler and a black notebook – holding the corners from curling. To understand the images and their micro-circle design, the prints really required wall magnets for proper viewing. It helped that I had already seen the images the day before on A4 printouts. But the new dimensions made all the difference. The prints were now spectacular in their quietness. Size, it seemed, did matter.

Each print had a white margin with John's signature in pencil at the lower right-hand side. The signature was small, contained, and barely legible. On the left-hand side was '1/15'. John had run an edition of fifteen at this size of each work, and this was the first of them. He may never print all fifteen. It depended on demand. But at least interested buyers would know that the edition is limited, therefore increasing its value. Fifteen was a lot for such a large work. I couldn't see a virtual unknown selling that many. Not at this size.

On the consignment form, John had asked for three thousand dollars per print. The gallery was to put its forty-five percent commission on top. Not knowing if this was reasonable, I decided to ask Noah. Tip-toeing my stockinged feet towards the office, I noticed the door was ajar. He was speaking to someone on the phone.

'No, I don't understand,' was the exasperated tone. 'I honestly don't know what you're talking about…I've never heard of it. The last time I had anything at all to do with…no one knows what they are looking at. This is exactly why I got out of it.'

I wanted to linger, but his eyes caught mine through the doorway. I held up my hand in acknowledgement of his privacy and closed the door behind me. I walked back to my desk for a soft lead pencil to write the new stockroom codes on the back of each print, but my mind was re-running Noah's side of the conversation. *No one knows what they are looking at. This is exactly why I got out of it.* My sentiments exactly. I really should reject Perry's intentions for my thesis. Dorothy Brown needs to be left alone.

I wrote the codes on each print, inserted them back in the tube, and stored them in the stockroom and completed the documentation at my desk. Noah strode from his office with his hands shoved deep into his trouser pockets, like he wanted to break through the stitching.

'I just wanted to show you John's work,' I said, 'but you seemed busy on the phone. They're in the storeroom now. Here's what's inside the tube.' I handed over the A4 printouts.

'Thanks.' He took the pages, though his mind seemed to be elsewhere.

'They are pretty amazing. Large scale, three-by-twelve.'

'Okay,' he nodded.

'I wasn't sure about the prices.'

Noah ran his eye over the page. 'Why not?' he said with a tired shrug. 'The artist is unknown, but the work looks pretty good. Worth a shot, I guess.'

'This contract okay to send to the artist?'

'What?' Noah asked. 'Oh, yes, that's fine. I'll sign them now, shall I?'

'Is there anything I can help you with?' I asked.

'Not really, but thanks.' He walked back into his office.

Looking down at the John Roebelling file on the desk, I called to let him know the good news. Waiting for pickup, I mumbled to myself, 'Be professional.' It went straight to voicemail.

'John, um, it's Anna. I just wanted to let you know Noah is happy to keep your work in the gallery storeroom on consignment. I'm emailing the contract to you now. But, um, if you are passing by, you can drop in and sign. Or whatever. Just if you want to, you know. Um, okay, bye.'

After hanging up, I wondered whether Noah would mind if I spent the rest of the afternoon researching how to hack another person's voicemail storage to delete left messages. Pain. The blisters on my feet were killing me. I retrieved the remaining three band-aids from the kitchen first aid kit. Covering my wounds, I pulled my stockings back up, gently moved my feet back in the shoes, and returned to the desk for seated activities. There were plenty of things to do. I just didn't know what they were. Jan obviously had her own schedule, so Noah wasn't used to delegating. Pretty soon, tasks would mount, I reasoned. In the meantime, it seemed prudent to understand where I was working. Tapping into the net, I searched for 'Noah Webster'. The official site appeared, as well as a number of gallery directories and art news critiques. On the second page were some sites referring to the Harrington's auction scandal. In one article, there was mention of a strong push for a dedicated label of authenticity, called The Indigenous Art Code, organised by The National Indigenous Arts Advocacy Association (NIAAA). The Code would assure buyers their purchase was the real deal, a genuine piece of Aboriginal culture for the living room or office. As the Indigenous specialist for Harrington's, Noah had his own point of view in an interview transcript:

'This Label of Authenticity has to be able to work in the commercial domain. Yet the NIAAA are behaving as if including commercial operators in any decision-making is like giving Dracula the keys to the blood bank.'

'Does this mean you support the label?' the interviewer asked.

'In principle, yes,' he replied. 'But the process concerns me deeply.'

The Indigenous Art Code eventually came into being – with commercial enterprises consulted in the process, according to the article.

At that point, a wave of tyre-kicking customers swept into the gallery. Tyre-kickers were lookers pretending to be buyers. Eva had referred to them as the worst creatures ever to crawl out of the slime and into an art gallery.

'But we walk around private art galleries looking interested, reading through the price list with no intention to buy,' I had pointed out. 'Doesn't that make us tyre-kickers?'

Eva had replied by eating her wedges and sour cream with her mouth open.

On that Saturday afternoon, I was feeling the irritation. While greeting everyone who came through the door with my best pasty smile, the idea of getting to my blistered feet was far too challenging. If they weren't buying, I wasn't standing. Ignoring potential signs of chitchat, I focused on the screen before me. But one woman, possibly in her early fifties, was bent on talking about some recent classes on abstract painting she had attended. Her many beads rattled as she spoke with flailing hand movements. 'The art world has not been the same since Kandinsky,' the woman announced. The reference was an obvious ploy to impress her friends standing nearby. A stupid comment really, considering the guy kicked-off abstraction. Of course, it hasn't been the same. And since the messy sandpit of abstraction, we had come full circle, trying to get some grasp on reality again. Reality TV was just the beginning. 'Kandinsky certainly turned heads,' was all I could muster. Unimpressed with my quippy response, the woman promptly corralled her friends towards the Philippa Cusacks, our realist exhibition.

I searched for Aboriginal+Art+Fakes, and several articles appeared. Again, Harrington's Auctions were mentioned in many of them. A separate drama happened in 2000 over a well-known Aboriginal artist who admitted to putting his name to works he had not painted himself. Then the artist retracted the statement. Then he retracted the retraction. It was confusing for all concerned.

An auctioneer from Harrington's was reported to have said, 'With this scenario, it's now a process of filming the artists painting the work to authenticate them – which sounds extreme but sadly necessary.'

'Would Caucasian artists ever be expected to do this?' the interviewer had asked.

'Not to my knowledge,' the auctioneer replied.

Another Aboriginal artist had pointed out fake paintings attributed to him in a Sydney gallery. Then it came out that he had painted them after all. Apparently, he called them forgeries to protect his 'exclusive' relationship with another gallery. '*The artist had become the breadwinner for his community,*' the article explained, '*giving the money earned to his family members, keeping none for himself. He had often painted for local non-Indigenous dealers in exchange for free food, so his paintings turned up in several exhibition spaces around the country, making his exclusive arrangement with his contracted Sydney gallery null and void.*'

'It's the void that is so captivating, isn't it?' The beaded woman was back at my desk. Her group, it seems, had finished their Cusack tour. 'The void of nature,' the woman explained for the benefit of all company. 'I'm glad you got so much out of the exhibition,' I smiled, wishing she were in a void. The woman nodded to her friends, then led them out the front door.

I clicked on another fake art article. It showed the photo of Dorothy Brown at Miles Porter Gallery Perry and I had spotted during our 'research period'. There Dorothy was, sitting on the floor painting while wearing the Road Runner t-shirt. I understood now, after my shopping experience with Liz, that if Dorothy wore that t-shirt today, she'd be considered at the height of fashion. 'Oh, my god!' I said out loud, then clamped my mouth with my hand. In the photo was a young Noah Webster with brown hair, also sitting on the floor, observing Dorothy in action. The photo was taken in 2005 – the same year as Whitlock's Dorothy Browns.

'Everything okay?' Present-day Noah Webster was standing in front of me, looking over the top of the screen.

'Ah, yes,' I said, thinking fast for an explanation. Noah was already craning his neck to see.

'Ah, you look so different…with dark hair.'

'Doing some research on me?' he said, staring at the screen, expressionless.

'Yes. I just googled your name, thought it would be a good idea to know more about the gallery's reputation online.' This was it. It was the time to strike, to throw myself on my sword and get Perry off my back. But I had to make it light. 'Noah, a small question. Probably not your favourite subject. Four Dorothy Browns were mentioned in a lecture the other day, now in London-'

'You are right, Anna, it's not my favourite subject. I don't comment on Aboriginal art of any kind. It's my rule.'

I threw my hands up in the air. 'Totally fine, excellent rule.'

He looked at his watch. 'I'm leaving now. Robert's nagging me to get home. We're off to the Hunter Valley for a couple of days,' he said, looking like he was ready to disappear completely into a bottle of grassy pinot gris.

'Sounds nice. Have fun,' I replied. 'See you Wednesday.'

Striding towards the door, Noah halted to let Simon pass. He smiled in acknowledgement, then strode towards the beige-coloured Audi on the street, looking back briefly.

'Now that man is definitely gay,' Simon said, thumbing behind him.

'That's my boss,' I explained.

'I know,' he replied with a grin.

'I don't really want to think about it,' I said. 'Better for bosses to be asexual, don't you think? Like parents?'

'No, parents are different. I've shagged my boss.'

'Really?' I asked. 'Surely sleeping with your boss is shameless, unprofessional behaviour.' I moved around the desk for a kiss on the cheek, taking on the shoe pain. 'So good to see you.'

A wave of alarm crossed Simon's face. 'There isn't anyone else here, is there?' he whispered.

'Don't worry,' I said. 'We're alone, your sexuality is safe.'

'It's not mine I'm worried about,' he replied. Turning to look at me, he said, 'My dear, something has definitely changed. It's not just having a new job, it's not the gorgeous new suit,' he said, stroking my sleeve. 'And those shoes are divine – Italian?' I nodded. '*Molto elegante,*' he exclaimed, while pinching at the air.

'*Molto* unbearable agony,' I replied, collapsing on my chair behind the desk.

Simon nodded. 'Just wear them around the apartment with socks. It'll break them in.' He took one last look at my shoes before returning to my face. 'There is something else about you that's changed...talking of sexuality...bosses...Perry...you and Perry,' A smile emerged. Cat-with-cream.

'Me and Perry?' I almost choked while laughing.

'Yes. That comment you made about bosses being like parents was a kinky red herring, wasn't it?' Lowering himself to where John Roebelling had been that morning, Simon placed his hands behind his head. 'You're having an affair with Professor Perry.'

'No, no, no,' I held up my hands. 'Don't confuse your fantasies with mine, Simon. Perry retrenched me, remember? Plus, he's bullish.' At that, Simon's eyes lit up like Christmas retail. I changed tack and lowered my voice. 'It's the shoes. My feet feel bound to breaking point,' I explained while slipping off the shoes. 'What you are seeing is that first flush of excruciating orthopaedic pain first discovered in China as a turn-on.'

'One night I'll take you to a couple of special, out-of-the-way clubs where you can learn all about that very topic.'

I could have told him about John, but I knew what the response would be. Simon would pull out the pompoms, give me tantric sex advice while planning the wedding. Time to change the topic.

'Have you ever taken Zed, Simon?' I asked. 'My flatmate says it's big in the gay clubs.'

'Zed?' Simon looked confused. Then his face changed. 'Oh, you mean Zee?'

'Yes, Zee,' I said, quietly recognising that Australia's English-informed alphabet was sounding its death rattle.

Simon shook his head. 'No, Zee is bad juju. No one knows how much to take. It gets out of control so easily.'

'Just wanted to make sure you were okay.' I shrugged.

'Sweetheart,' Simon said, giving my hand a kiss. 'I'm fine.'

'Hey, I sold fifteen thousand dollars' worth of art today.'

'Fifteen?' he exclaimed. 'So, it's the money that lights your fire, girlfriend?'

'I'm just feeling rather pleased with myself, that's all.'

'And so you should. That's quite a sum. Particularly in this climate.' Simon looked at his fingernails for a moment. 'But this shagging the boss thing...'

'Thankfully, not an issue here. Noah being gay.'

'I just remembered a bit of art gallery gossip. Noah and Miles Porter...'

'What do you mean?'

'Noah shagged the boss,' he answered frankly.

'Noah *worked* at Galerie Exotique?'

'Oh, yes. You didn't know?'

I swivelled my monitor so he could see the photo I was looking at.

'And there he is, looking gorgeous for the camera,' Simon said. 'What a loyal gallery manager.'

'And they were having a relationship?'

'Don't look so shocked, darling. Shagging the boss has been around for a while,' he said with a grin. 'Centuries, I'd say.'

'Simon, can we change the subject for a moment? Well, it's not completely off topic. I have a problem, one beyond podiatry.'

'What bothers you, my child?'

'Perry's pushing me to make the Dorothy Browns at Whitlock my thesis topic.'

'The fake ones?'

'Yet to be proven – by me, according to Perry,' I said. 'The authenticity certificates are from Galerie Exotique, signed by Miles Porter in 2005. But if Noah was there…'

'And later, the Harrington's fakes happened when Noah was there,' Simon added, rubbing his cheek.

'Still doesn't prove much. A few dots need to be connected.'

'I'll excuse the pun,' he smiled.

'I just asked Noah about them, but he refuses to discuss anything Aboriginal. It's his rule.'

'When were the Browns painted?' Simon asked.

'2005. Miles died in 2006, Noah worked at Harrington's when?'

'Not until 2013. And then left the following year.'

'So what did Noah do in between? It must have been significant, because I don't see Harrington's employing someone from a place called Galerie Exotique.'

'Noah went butch. I mean, bush,' Simon grinned.

'Noah was in the desert?'

'Oh yes. He hung out with Dale Spencer, our now resident Indigenous Art Specialist. Dale started as an anthropologist. Given enough time, anthropologists in Australia ultimately become Aboriginal art specialists.'

'Noah was shagging this Dale guy?'

'No, they were just mates. Dale's wife was out there, too,' Simon said. 'Anyway, Noah really earned his stripes with Dale. Dale was already doing work on a consultancy basis with Harrington's. Dale recommended Noah, and Noah got the job. Funny thing is, now Dale's got Noah's job – but not immediately. There was someone else after Noah at Harrington's...can't remember.'

'I wonder what Dale would think of the Whitlock Dorothy Browns.'

'If he says they're authentic, then Perry would get off your back, and you don't have to worry about digging around anymore where Noah Webster has been. Otherwise, it is all a bit awkward, isn't it? Being your boss.'

'Just as well I'm not shagging him, too,' I said.

'I've always liked this gallery,' Simon said, looking around.

'Me too.'

'All you have to do is email me the images and certificates of the Dorothys, and I'll forward them to Dale. He's up in the Pilbara at the moment. But he still checks his emails when he can tap in.'

'Brilliant. Thanks so much,' I said, imagining moving beyond Dorothy Brown to another London-inspired thesis topic, another early portrait artist perhaps. Something non-Aboriginal. Something safe. 'Simon?' I asked as he wandered around the Cusacks. I remained steadfast at my desk, luxuriating in shoelessness.

'Yes?'

'What happens if you don't shag the boss?'

'I don't know,' he replied, moving over to the paintings in the next room. 'You work, I suppose.'

'Hey, I just remembered,' I said. 'I already owe you a bottle of champagne. Remember when you said when I get a job, I can pay you back in bubbles? It's closing time now. Shall we go to that bar down the road?'

Simon appeared from around a white corner. 'Uh-oh, what's the time?'

'Five-twenty-seven and counting,' I replied.

'Sorry, can't. Have to go to a ballet premiere,' he groaned.

'Sounds rough.'

'It is, ballet performances are interminable. We are six rows from the front, in the centre.'

'Best seats in the house.'

'Impossible to escape.'

'Men in tights?'

Smiling, he said, 'There better be,' then leant across the desk to give me a kiss. 'Next time?'

'Of course.'


Before leaving, I dusted the desk area (white shows up everything). As I moved the keyboard aside, revealing a piece of cardboard with a list of 'End of day' EFTPOS processing steps. Noah's mobile was out of range, so I called the bank information line, checking if this was still the right procedure. The customer service representative did her best to be condescending and unhelpful, but it turned out the information on the card was correct.

Much to my representative's dismay, I kept her on the line while going through the steps to receive the final balance for the day.

'I must have done something wrong,' I said.

'Why?' the woman asked.

'It says here thirty-nine thousand. It should be fifteen.'

'Press clear and do it again,' she groaned. I did, telling her everything I was doing at every stage. 'Nope, still says thirty-nine thousand.'

'Well, you're richer than you think. Congratulations.'

'But -' I said.

'Just finish it off and go home, girl. It's the weekend. Go out and have some fun,' The woman hung up, leaving me staring at the twenty-four thousand discrepancy and an uneasy feeling no amount of red wine was going to be able to wash away.

# CHAPTER 13

Feeling wrecked, I locked up the gallery and hobbled to the bus stop. An assistant from a shoe store nearby was also closing, but she let me in out of sympathy. I promptly bought a pair of blinding white sandshoes and thick white socks and put them on immediately. Comfort was key. Walking down the street, I swung my expensive Italian high-heeled shoes in a cheap plastic bag and allowed my mind to oscillate from John to a big fat glass of red wine, to the twenty-four thousand discrepancy, back to John again, then to wine, then to the money mystery. This internal rollercoaster continued until after I got off the bus and arrived home to grab the bottle of Shiraz, half-full/empty, poured a decent portion and sat at my desk to email Simon the Dorothy Brown images and certificates to pass on to Dale in the Pilbara. Taking a gulp from my glass, I then messaged Noah explaining about the EFTPOS total and hovered over 'send', imagining him making his way to the Hunter Valley for a break. Then pressed it.

After which, I felt a soothing vibration. It was John on my mobile. On my mobile.

'Great news about the gallery keeping my prints, thanks.'

'No problem, Noah liked them.' I added, 'I've emailed you the contract, with Noah's signature already on it.'

'Great, thanks.'

'No problem.'

'So how has your day been?' John asked.

'My day? Good, made some sales…'

'Hot rookie.' *Hot rookie?*

'I think the art had something to do with it, too. How's your weekend been so far?'

'Had to help a friend move his afternoon.'

'Hard work, eh?'

'Borrowed the van again, did it all in one trip. A quiet night this end,' he yawned. 'I'm buggered.'

'And you can take it easy tomorrow.'

'Not really, got football.'

'You play?'

'No, I've got tickets. AFL, not rugby.'

My heart quickened its beat for a moment. Not for the reason John would suspect. 'You prefer AFL?'

'Yeah, I don't mind rugby, but I think AFL's better. Most of my mates don't agree, though. The friend I was going with just bailed on me. I'll still go. I've got the tickets. Probably can scalp the other, being a semi-final.'

'You probably could,' I agreed, paying more attention to his inflections than what was actually being said. Soft but still confident.

'Hey, you wouldn't happen to be into the footy?'

'Me?'

'It's okay if you're not.'

'You want me to buy your other ticket?'

'No, sorry,' he groaned. 'I'm crap with words. That sounded really bad. Let me try again. Anna, would you like to accompany me in the witnessing of the Swans thrashing the Hawks tomorrow?

My treat.'

'Swans thrashing Hawks,' I said, wondering what David Attenborough would think of it. 'And I'm assuming you're a Swans fan?'

'Indeed,' he said, then paused. 'Do you want to pay, like for your feminist independence? You don't have to come tomorrow if you don't want to. I just thought -'

'No...'

'No, you don't want to come?'

'No, I would like to go.' Not entirely true. But not a lie either.

'Can it be my treat?' he asked.

'Yes,' I said. 'That would be lovely.' *Lovely?*

'Can I pick you up on the bike?'

'Ah.' The helmet, the brains – as if I had any. I'm such a saucepan-head. 'Can we meet there?'

'Sure.'

It's happening. After swearing I'd never go to another game again.


I saw him first. In brown cargo pants and a grey fleece jacket, John was the only person not wearing colours of either team. Apart from me. I was sporting a black fitted coat, denim jeans and my comfortable Docs and camouflage green beanie. Leaning against a structural column, fingering the tickets, he spotted me. Gave that beautiful droopy smile with his eyes while straightening to greet me.

'I had this feeling you weren't going to come,' he said.

'What? And miss Swan Lake-of-Blood?'

John smiled and gestured towards the gates. The mob had us shuffling along towards our section, but we segued for sugar and fat (otherwise known as 'refreshments') before settling in. The trick was to push without appearing pushy and to slip through the gaps without getting a carefully placed thermos in your jaw. All this while balancing a full soft drink in a paper cup and sausage roll with tomato sauce seeping through the paper bag. We found our seats of red moulded plastic and collapsed there without spillage. The view of the ground was good with the benefit of being under cover. A waif-thin man at my left wore a red and white shirt, jumper, scarf and beanie. The face paint was probably being saved for the final. A fine day had been predicted, but clouds were gathering. I rubbed my cold toes together.

This was it. This was the competition. Whenever arts statistics were listed in newspaper articles, they were inevitably compared to sports. Attendance numbers, particularly. And the arts always came out looking like a wobbly-kneed old woman with chlamydia. Across the field, in the opposite stands, sat thousands of tiny moving colours, mostly red and white, but patches of brown and yellow. While galleries begged for hushed sounds, half the football crowd sang their anthem like nodulous blowflies. The rest yelled amongst themselves.

'When was the last time you went to a game?' John asked above the chorus of chaos.

'It's been a while,' I admitted loudly. 'So what are our chances?'

'Very good,' he said, grinning at me. I had my doubts. I knew nothing about the quality of these teams or any individual players. But I had my doubts.

A country and western radio station, one of many sponsors for the game, interrupted with rodeo music booming through the loudspeakers. Line dancers in western hats took their places on the grass and began to move like a crop on a windy day. The crowd cheered when a dust-free man on horseback arrived with yelping dogs and uninspired sheep. The dogs ignored their master's commands and, true to the workings of Australian middle management, enthusiastically moved the sheep right into the kicking legs of the line dancers.

Waif Man next to me used this period of sponsored extravaganza to plough his way to the kiosk. He returned laden with a beer, hamburger and hot chips as the last of the line dancers were herded into the changing rooms. The competition players then ran onto the field, warming up the crowd while they jogged laps and tossed balls to one another. When the Sydney Swans appeared, the home crowd cheered and anthem music blasted distortedly from the speakers.

Meanwhile, I worked through the rest of my sausage roll, wiping the sauce from my face and fingers with a serviette. John was a tidier eater, I noticed. Unusual for an artist. The game began, and the Waif Man spent the first quarter shouting surnames like a head teacher taking roll call. Every meaningless moniker was punctuated by bits of hamburger and puffs of cold air. John gestured to swap seats, but I smiled and gently refused. The running commentary made any conversation difficult. It became even more difficult when Hawks player Number Nine got a mark in front of goal.

'Go back to where you came from, you black bastard!' Waif Man yelled.

John swung around to face him. His eyes were now less empathetic-droopy, more downward-fire-arrow. 'Pull your head in for Christ's sake!' Then lowered his voice, 'Sorry, Anna.'

But Waif Man wasn't leaving it alone. 'What's ya problem, *mate*?'

'Your racism, mate. That's my problem. That and your complete lack of logic.'

'My what?'

'"Go back to where you came from?" He comes from here, you idiot. He's Aboriginal. It was our ancestors who came on a boat.'

Number Nine kicked a goal.

Waif man puffed up his chest. 'See? That's what happens when you support them, let them into the game – they screw ya.'

'You mean he plays well for his team?' John's eyes squinted, baffled by the insanity before him. We both were.

'Whichever way you want to see it, mate.'

John gave up at that point and apologised to me while insisting on swapping places. But it seemed strategically advantageous to stay between them. At least Waif Man had stopped his commentary for the time being. Sulking now took precedence.

'So do you work for Noah full-time?' John asked, changing the subject. Or at least he thought he was.

'No, part-time,' I replied. 'I'm studying at the moment. Pretending to, at least.'

'And what are you pretending to study?'

'Art history and theory.'

'Bachelor?'

'Masters,' I said.

John whistled, 'Thesis trauma?'

'You've got it.'

'What's your topic?'

I drew a breath. 'It was going to be about Vernon Jones -'

'Who?'

'Australia's most prolific nineteenth-century portrait painter. But Professor Perry, my supervisor and the faculty head, just changed it to…ah, Australian Aboriginal art.'

'He changed it?' John asked. 'Can they do that?'

'It's a long story.' *Of a young, passionless woman.*

'You must have a special interest in the topic, surely, for him to suggest it?'

'I used to have the interest,' I replied, 'and Perry's chosen to revive it.'

'So that's why, back at the gallery, you were asking if I'd been to the desert.'

'I've never been. Yet I find myself doing a thesis on an artist that comes from there,' I murmured into my cup.

'Who's the artist you're studying?'

'Dorothy Brown.'

'Dorothy Brown,' John nodded. 'She's amazing.'

I smiled, 'That she is.'

'Which means you need to go out there.'

'I do?' I was still in the phase of trying to get out of the trap Perry had put me in. Going to the desert would be like agreeing with Perry. Can't be done.

'To understand desert painting, you have to be there. Breathe and taste the place,' he said. 'No two ways about it.' I didn't reply. My mind began drifting to London. 'The other artists from Stumpy Downs,' John continued, 'the ones who have come through since Dorothy are pretty amazing too.'

'Yes, they are,' I agreed, 'but not quite Dorothy Brown.'

'No one else should even try to be Dorothy Brown.'

'Never a truer word spoken,' I said, wondering who was trying to be Dorothy in those four Whitlock paintings. 'You know what's really weird?'

'What?'

'The woman who used to work at the front desk of Noah Webster is out there right now. If it wasn't for me, she wouldn't be in the desert.'

'Freaky,' John agreed, taking a sip before shifting in his seat and saying, 'That would be the lady with the motherly smile, like she's just baked something for you. Her name's Jan, isn't it?'

'Yes,' I laughed, 'I've always thought of Cornish pasties when I saw that smile.'

'Exactly! It's a Cornish pasty smile,' he nodded. John gave brief, whispered updates on the history of the players as they held possession of the ball. My heart dropped when it became obvious by the end of the first quarter that the opposition was dominating the game and had every intention of staying that way. I automatically searched for the exits.

Midway through the second quarter, the crowd, tired of watching the Swans' lack of grace, coordinated themselves into multiple Mexican waves. The waves were successful until they hit against the hard rock of the members' stand. Waif Man also declined the Mexican wave. Instead, he buried his head in his hands for the vast majority of the second quarter. The commentary of names persevered as intermittent, muffled moans. At halftime, the teams huddled in their groups while the coach waved his arms about with the passion of a conductor for a heavy metal band. The players bent their heads. Meanwhile, selected 'under 12s' bounced onto the field in their little allocated jerseys. The accompanying 'under 12' cheerleaders pumped their fluorescent pompoms like irate puppets along to a recorded track by Tina Turner about high-quality intercourse.

John went to get beers. Waif Man turned to me. 'Your boyfriend, an Abo-lover or what?'

I could smell the alcohol on his breath. The air was cool, but it didn't stop my palms from starting to sweat. I began my attempt at reconciliation. 'He -'

But the man didn't let me continue. '*You have to breathe and taste the desert,*' he mimicked John.

'So you were listening to our conversation?'

'I'm fuckin' sitting right next to you, you dopey chick.'

'Hey!' I felt my anger surge.

The man held up his hands in surrender. 'Okay. I beg your pardon, Missy…miss…miss.'

I knew what arguing with drunk men caused. So did what I always do, ignored him and hoped for the best. John came back with the beers just as the third quarter began, along with light showers. We were under cover, but it was a different story on the ground. The ball became slippery and frustration built amongst both teams. Two players started a fistfight, leading to serious mud wrestling while the crowd in front laughed. As the red-faced referee arrived barking orders, the muddy players looked up from their respective headlocks like being sprung by a parent. One said something like 'he started it'. The referee walked away in disgust. Eventually, the rain let up, allowing better grip on the ball. It wasn't until a male streaker bounded merrily onto the field that the game really picked up.

'Classic,' John said, laughing.

'Bunch of poofs,' Waif Man said to no one in particular, then stared morbidly at the scoreboard. The streaker only had a few seconds to make his point. The police flocked to him and covered his flesh like vultures. Waif Man stumbled over my knees to buy a beer, spilling some of my own and blocking my view of the streaker's final moments. While he queued, the Swans kicked three goals in succession. I sipped at my beer. It was watery, but my spirits were picking up. Perhaps there was more alcohol in it than it tasted, I thought, peering suspiciously into the cup.

The home ground's mascot made its presence felt for the first time that day. The swan was a man in an enormous white top-heavy bird costume. He bounded around with as much movement as possible, given the restricted logistics. What the bird lacked in elegance, he made up in flapping and an original version of the twist.

Upon his return, Waif Man almost dropped his beer. Eyes clasped on the scoreboard, his mouth hung open like a fool at a solar eclipse.

'Shit! I missed it!'

The Swans moved toward goal once more and gave the supporters what they came for. The siren sounded. It was the end of the third quarter and the home team was only three goals down. The crowd waved jubilant ripples throughout the stadium. I gulped my beer excitedly while Waif Man calculated minutes remaining with goals required. Just before the next quarter started, Waif Man decided to buy some more beer. During his absence, the Swans kicked two goals. He arrived back and looked at the scoreboard.

'Shit!'

'You need to go to the kiosk more often,' a man behind us chuckled. The opposing team kicked another goal, keeping the game on its toes and the crowd along with it. As minutes passed, scoring pendulumed dramatically between teams. Points became even as the final siren blew, forcing the game into overtime. Euphoric pressure mounted as the players moved towards the centre.

In all the excitement, the team's gigantic mascot tripped over five cheerleaders and a protruding lens belonging to a sour-faced journalist. The bird was oblivious to the journalist's fury and the squealing women. Instead, he rolled around in different directions, trying frantically to become vertical without having to escape the costume and reveal his true identity.

Meanwhile, the umpire bounced the ball in the centre and players grasped madly like bridesmaids for a bouquet. Waif Man pulled out a stopwatch and clicked it as soon as the action commenced. Our team scored the first point. They were now in front, so they did everything to slow the game right down against the clock. One player was a fraction too confident and hand-balled the ball long. Interception. Goal to the other team. Bugger. The play slowed again, but this time at our expense. We were now behind. Tension built as nothing happened. It was like a documentary on grass growing, interrupted by last-day spring sale commercials. It was then when I realised it. Regardless of what the time was, we were going to lose. And the panic started. Palpitations, headache rolling in from the back of my head, the desire to turn into a pillar of salt. I stared at my hands and took deep breaths. The Swans tried for a nothing-to-lose long-range goal and missed by a mile. It was over. I was right. We lost, and the crowd groaned.

'Shit,' Waif Man spat, tipping the rest of his beer onto the ground. The majority around us hurried to the car park before the gridlock started. I didn't want to sit back and commiserate with Waif Man, nor did I want to rush into the throng either. More than anything, I didn't want a non-celebratory drink.

'Feel like a non-celebratory drink?' John asked. I told myself to grow up and nodded back to John. It would look strange to call it a day, even though that's exactly what I wanted to do. Close to the grounds was an old corner pub crammed with football supporters. We made our way in, found a couple of stools in the corner, and drank our pints in silence while listening to a speaker-fed *Hotel California*. The music merged with a small group's slurred version of the other team's victory song. They sang from the bar while nearby Swan fans glowered. Weighing up the room, misery outnumbered happiness. 'I don't understand why people put themselves through this,' I blurted, looking around. I couldn't see Waif Man, but there were plenty like him.

'It's great when we win.' John shrugged.

'Tell me you win,' I pleaded. 'That it does actually happen.'

'Sure, we won heaps this season. It's why we're in the semis.' John touched my elbow. 'Are you okay? More of a Swans fan than you like to let on?'

With the music, the singing and the moaning, our voices were almost inaudible.

'It's nothing,' I replied, shaking my head. 'I must be tired.'

John looked at me carefully and urged, 'Tell me.'

His eyes were clear, seemingly unaffected by the beer he had been drinking. Not that he had that much to begin with, I supposed. 'My father used to take me to the football every weekend when I was little. It was his way of bonding, I suppose. I'm an only child. I guess he decided it didn't matter if you were a daughter or son if introduced to football early enough.' John nodded, perhaps in agreement. 'Anyway, he took me to every weekend match. Our team, the Nagurra Galahs, are losers by tradition.'

'The Nagurra Galahs?'

'I'm afraid so.'

'They didn't call themselves the Great Galahs, did they?'

'No, but their fans did – after every game. Sarcasm became a staple beer snack,' I explained. 'Anyway, I remember the hopeful cheers in the first quarter, the worry at halftime, the lacklustre third and morbid fourth. And the anger that grew in the pub afterwards.' I looked around for a moment, but John's eyes remained fixed on me. 'It probably wasn't as bad to an adult, but I was only a little tacker. Seeing your dad get pissed and violent in the local pub after every match…

this was a country town, you see. You know everyone, and they know you. I'm sure he wasn't the only one. He wouldn't have been. But he seemed to stir up things the most. And I was watching him.'

'He was supposed to be protecting you.'

'Don't get me wrong,' I protested. 'Dad's great. He never laid a hand on me or even got angry with me after matches.'

'But he got angry,' John said.

'Let's say he's snapped a few pool cues in his time.' I took a sip of beer. 'How he did it, I still don't know. The place was packed after a game. You could hardly move. Puddles, that's the guy who owns the pub -'

'Puddles?'

'His real name's Graham. They call him Puddles because he owns the bar. Works behind it, too. He doesn't spill drinks or have incontinence or anything. I guess the name doesn't make much sense.'

'Yeah, it does.' John smiled before he looked concerned again. 'So what did Puddles do?'

'Well, he would be busy moving jugs and pints, but still found the time to spot me hiding under a barstool. He would put me on a chair behind the bar and give me a Coke.'

'So then you felt safe.'

'Not really,' I replied. 'Then I had fifty pissed men looking at me. Not in a lewd way, but it was weird. I generally slipped off the chair and found another place, usually next to the cigarette machine. Tried to keep out of sight until it was time to go home.'

'Where was your mum?'

'Home. By the time we walked through the front door, Dad collapsed in front of the TV and was asleep in seconds. Mum just thought he was knackered from all the cheering.'

'She didn't know he'd been drinking?'

'She knew, just not how bad. No one told her what happened at the pub, ever – it was sort of a boys' club back then.'

'Must have put you off the pub for life.'

'Oh no, we used to have great family lunches there,' I said, 'at the restaurant round the back. And when I was old enough, I would be at the front bar with friends because there wasn't really anywhere else to go.'

'And you kept going to matches with your dad?'

'As soon as I was old enough, I joined the local netball team – the Nagurra Possums,' I laughed, and John smiled but more out of sympathy. 'Our matches clashed with football. We lost just as badly, but the aftermath was different. Pizza, nail polish and bitching. I was only there for the distraction. To be honest, I didn't really like the game or the girls that much.'

'But you found safety in numbers.'

'I suppose I did,' I nodded. 'Sounds rather dramatic, more so than it needs to be.'

'It was dramatic,' he returned, 'for you.'

'But my dad's great, you know,' I said, 'for the rest of the time. I mean, we have a good relationship.'

'Have you talked to him about it?'

'To Dad? About this?' I stammered. 'God no.'

'Why not?'

'I guess it's water under the bridge,' I said.

'It's not water under the bridge, though, is it? We're talking about it now.'

'Must be the beer talking.' I smiled, hoping to shift the mood. This was terrible first date material. 'My childhood was a reasonably happy one, seriously. Except for Hannibal.'

'Hannibal?'

'Hannibal was a yabby at our local creek,' I explained. 'Picked him up when I was four. The pincers got me.'

'Ouch.'

'Bloody hurt. Refused to get back into the creek again. Or any body of water, for that matter. I blame Hannibal for my poor swimming skills.'

'When it gets a little warmer, I'd be happy to teach you,' John said. 'No Hannibals in my past, fortunately.'

'I know very little about you,' I said, frowning. 'Here I am whining about my dad and Hannibal -'

'You've seen my studio, my work, read my résumé, interrogated me about my age -'

'But that's the official you.'

'Seeing an artist's studio is very 'inside story', it's an extremely private space. You were a privileged visitor, don't you know?'

'But what about your family?' I asked. 'Are you close?'

'Well, they're Hawks fans. So we have a problem right there.' A small grin came to his face. 'Everyone's in Melbourne, my parents and sister. I don't see them that much.' John tilted his head and smiled. 'My family is close in some ways. But a little distance from the action isn't a bad thing.' He gazed around the room, looking at the moaning drunkards. 'Let's get out of here, eh?'

I placed my empty glass back on the round coaster, perfectly centred in the circle, feeling grateful. Making our way out to the street, John turned to ask if there was anywhere I would like to go.

'I'm actually feeling quite tired,' I replied reluctantly. My body was starting to ache. 'Think I might have to head home.'

'You okay?'

'It's been a big week, that's all.' I said, straightening up and smiling. 'Thanks so much for the ticket. And for listening.' The late afternoon sun finally broke through the shifting clouds.

'Why did you come to the football if it had all those bad memories?' he asked. 'I could have scalped both tickets, and we could have gone to a movie. I would have made a profit.'

'I wanted to get to know you. Talking in a movie means getting Fantails thrown in the back of your head.'

'A movie some other time, then. When we've run out of things to say.'

'Sure,' I smiled, unsure of when that might be, how long it might take, and whether he would wait that long.

The road was still wet from the rain. Rainbows of oil were glazing the asphalt, so there was no way in hell I was getting on that motorbike. We waited until my Uber arrived. I gave John a quick, firm hug, brushed my lips across his cheek and climbed into the warmth of the cabin. I felt good. And then I didn't. It could have been disloyalty to my father, or the possibility of boring John with my sob story. But it was neither of those things. The truth was, I had done a bit of soul-baring. And I was feeling bare. For the rest of the ride home, I stared out the window with my arms firmly crossed.

Opening the front door, I could hear groaning noises on the other side. Sprawled on the couch, Liz was watching MasterChef while pulling the cellophane off a cigarette box. Drawing her tired gaze from judges smacking their bountiful lips over poached barramundi, she said, 'Hi.'

'You're home…on the couch,' was all I could muster.

'Yes, I understand it comes as a shock.'

'Are you okay? You look a little pale.'

'I've just come down with a spot of the flu...or something.' She ripped off the foil, pulled out a cigarette, and lit it. Rolling had forfeited to pre-packaged. 'I'm kicking the sucker, though.'

'Good to hear,' I nodded in encouragement.

'Where have you been, madam?'

'Football semis with the artist.'

'Watching quality rough-and-tumble with The Younger Man,' Liz's eyebrows bounced suggestively. 'So how was it?'

'We lost,' I said, making my way to the bathroom, shedding coat and gloves on the way. All that beer. 'But I'm okay.' When it came time to return, I propped myself on the far arm of the couch and gazed at the television's flickering light. My face felt hot. 'I only had three beers, but they were big 'uns. I'm out of practice drinking pints.'

Liz glanced at me then, reaching for the remote, changed the channel to Bondi Rescue. 'He can't have been much muffin. You're sloshed, and you still came straight home.'

'No, he was wonderful,' I said. 'I'm just knackered.'

'Wonderful. That's a bit Mary Poppins, isn't it?' she asked while flicking back to MasterChef.

'He was hot flesh over writhing muscle,' I replied, walking towards the kitchen. 'I let down the side by piking.' I stopped and spun around. Something had changed. All the clothes on the floor had disappeared. Liz stayed focused on the screen, betraying nothing. Continuing my (clear) path to the kitchen, I turned on the kettle. A coffee wasn't what I wanted. It just seemed like the right thing to do, the comfort of urban ritual. Leaning on the bench, my phone received a text. It was Noah.

'Thx Anna. The extra $24k was sale from my priv.collection. Well done on the EFTPOS processing. Great initiative!' What a relief to discover that I wasn't the disaster I thought I was. And that everything has a reasonable explanation.

'Liiiiiz?' I yelled over the sound of multiple blenders.

'Yeeeees?' Liz screamed back, though her voice sounded like it was being wrapped in tissue paper. The kettle began to bubble noisily.

'Want a cuppa?' I asked, walking back into the lounge.

'No thanks.' Liz frowned at the television. I waited for a wisecrack about chocolate smears or balloon moulds inflated by the judges' anal wind emission. Nothing. Instead, there was Liz's head and her cigarette held up next to it. She looked so tired, so harmless. Not the kind of person who was about to lead me into criminal activity. But I should have known.

# CHAPTER 14

Liz was still asleep on the couch the next morning, surrounded by clumps of tissues, a soft aftermath of nighttime activity. Muted cartoons on the television fought in silence. When I clicked off the vision, Liz stirred, acknowledging the day with 'Doab... umb,' then turned over to sleep again.

Having already eaten breakfast, showered and dressed, I sat on the edge of the couch. It was a rare opportunity to see my flatmate still and close up, but it didn't engage me for long. The vulnerable feeling I had after the game yesterday had almost evaporated. My mind wandered to John. John painting, John taking photographs, John laughing, John living with me in London… It turned out that Liz was already half awake, but kept her eyes closed, knowing she was being watched and by whom. It was a practised ability developed through taking unnatural substances in public.

'Wha?' she asked eventually with a blocked nose.

'What?' I sat up, startled out of my thoughts.

Liz blew her nose and asked, 'Why are you staring at me?'

'Biding my time before going to uni.'

'You should be scary but you're not.' Liz felt her forehead. 'God, I feel shocking, where are my durries?'

'Here they are.' I found the half-empty packet of cigarettes wedged in the corner of the couch and handed them over.

'Where's my puffer?'

'Your puffer?' I asked. 'You have asthma, and you smoke?'

'Logic will get you from A to B,' she said. 'Imagination will get you everywhere.'

'Quoting Einstein will get you nowhere,' I replied, picking up the asthma pump near her feet and tossing it over. Cigarettes in one hand and asthma pump in the other, Liz looked like the landscape for a morning duel. I asked if she wanted a coffee.

'Only if it's a real one,' Liz replied.

Knowing what was in the kitchen, I could only offer 'instant or nothing.'

'Nothing then,' she groaned and stretched. 'I'll go...' she coughed, '...down later.'

'Down where?'

'Cat,' cough, 'Cat.'

'Cat Cat Café? That's three blocks away.'

Liz leaned across to look out the window. 'It's a beautiful day. The walk will do you good, I mean, me good.'

I left without answering. It was a beautiful day, granted. Returning with coffee and pastries, the apartment was empty. Cups and paper bags still in hand, I followed a trail of crumpled tissues up the building's stairs to the roof. Smoke greeted me as I caught my breath at the top. Upon a green banana lounge, a pale bikinied body was catching the first glimpses of spring (it takes one kind of person to make a swimsuit out of fake fur, another to wear it). Sunglasses were propped on Liz's small red nose. I decided not to lecture her about what being skin-bare would do for her cold. Balls of used tissues were rolling around underneath in the breeze. A boomerang ashtray sat under her smoking hand.

'Breakfast is served.' I put the coffee next to the lounge and one of the Danish bags on Liz's stomach. After thanking me lethargically through a stuffed nose, Liz put the bag beside her and lifted the lid off the coffee, took a sip, and reclined. Sitting in a deckchair close by, I sipped at my coffee. It was still too hot, so I moved on to the Danish.

'Second breakfast, Anna?'

'Early brunch,' I replied. My raised appetite may have been blamed on the cold weather, but it was probably the shackles of celibacy. 'Hey, don't you need to call work? Tell them you won't be coming in?'

'Maybe later,' she replied, ripping another tissue from the box. 'The boss is pretty relaxed about this sort of thing.' After blowing, Liz asked, 'How's Nora going, cranking sales?'

'Seems to be, but it happens out of the gallery or out of hours. When I'm not there.'

'To who?'

'Not sure, corporates I imagine,' I said.

'What's he selling?'

'Parts of his private collection, don't know what they are.'

'In financial difficulty, is he?'

'I don't think so. Not when he could have hired me on half the salary.' I sat back, feeling the morning sun on my face and the Danish in my belly. 'Suppose I'll hear more about it after he gets back.'

'Back from where?'

'The Hunter Valley,' I said, 'with his boyfriend for the weekend.'

'I love having dirty weekends. Shagging in some B&B on a Monday is my kind of civilised.'

'I really don't want to think about my boss doing such things.'

'Okay, so no one's at the gallery,' Liz mused, 'and you have the keys…'

'And?'

'Don't you want to know what Nora's so busy selling?'

'Not if it's going to cost me my job,' I replied. 'Plus I have lectures today.'

'You know, for a student, you suffer a severe lack of curiosity.' Liz then whispered, 'He's away, busy rogering Roger.'

'Robert.'

'Okay, bobbing for apples with Bob,' Liz smirked. 'He wouldn't even know anyone was in the gallery.'

'The alarm probably has some electronic history.'

'Call him on his mobile. Tell him you've forgotten something at the gallery. You're just going in there to pick it up. No surprises.'

'His mobile is constantly out of range. I'm generally on my own.'

'Every employee's dream,' she sighed. 'Let's text him and go play in his office.'

'He locks his office door.'

'He locks his door?'

'Customers could wander in there.'

'It's locked for a better reason than wandering customers,' Liz laughed. 'I bet it's good. And very, very bad.' After she sipped her coffee, she said, 'Shagged a police officer once. A pretty twisted guy, as it turned out. But one with a pick gun and torque wrench.'

'Pick gun and torque wrench?'

'Modern-day skeleton keys.'

'A policeman with skeleton keys?'

'Part of his private collection,' Liz laughed. 'He said he bought them on eBay, but more likely lifted them from the evidence room.

Anyway, he gave me a lesson by way of seduction.'

'Sounds like quite an evening.'

'I still have the kit.'

'He gave you his lock-picking tools?'

Liz's shoulder dropped as she searched the heavens for patience. 'Of course not, I stole them.'

'You stole skeleton keys from a cop?'

'They're tucked in between the top and bottom mattresses.'

'He must have been frantic looking for them.'

'Pleasantly distracted by my wiles. The panic started when he got home to his wife and discovered they weren't in his trusty pocket.'

'Did he come back and search your room?'

'He did. And searched me again, too, very thoroughly,' she replied. 'But they couldn't be found.'

'A policeman didn't think to look between your mattresses?' I licked the remaining pastry off my fingers. I wondered when Liz was going to eat hers.

'Yes, he did think of looking between my mattresses. He just didn't think to look between yours.'

'Mine?'

'Well, I wasn't going to have stolen goods – from a policeman – in my room, was I?'

'Jesus, Liz.' I shook my head in disbelief. 'I bet you'd put your mother on eBay.'

'Don't know what a seven-year-old corpse would fetch. And delivery might be tricky.'

'Sorry, I didn't know your mother had -'

'I'd actually forgotten all about the pick gun.' Liz interrupted. She sipped her coffee and stretched her shoulders. 'Now all you have to do is text Noah and off we go.'

'Oh, so you're willing to be an accomplice now?'

'I'm no accomplice,' she stated. 'I'm here to lead the mission.'

'You're not well, Liz. Possibly delirious,' I replied. 'Time for some rest, eh?'

'Why won't you do this?' Liz puffed. 'You afraid?'

'Afraid? What are you, six years old?'

'You are afraid, scaredy cat,' she said while blowing smoke. 'And I reckon Nora's up to something. I can feel it in my mucus.'

'There is something…it's to do with my thesis.'

'Not about the god-awful portrait painter?'

'No, I've changed my topic.'

'Thank Christ for that.'

'It's about some possibly faked Aboriginal paintings by an artist called Dorothy Brown. Noah used to manage the gallery that represented her early on.'

'I knew it!' Liz screeched. 'I knew there was something about that guy.'

'Not necessarily,' I explained. 'The certificates could be fake.'

'So how do you know the paintings are fake?'

I took a deep breath and promptly had a coughing fit from Liz's smoke. 'Because I just do. I can feel it,' I said, clearing my throat. 'Not very academic, I know.' I waited for the explosive cackle of condescension, but it didn't come.

'Gut feeling?'

'Yes, that's all I have at this stage.'

'Learned intuition.' Liz took a puff.

'Sorry?'

'I take it you know the artist's stuff pretty well.'

'Yes, I studied her work quite a bit in my undergrad years.' I wasn't going to go into the Marvin Brodie heckling story. 'Doesn't make me an expert.'

'Gut feeling's been around in the hallowed halls of academia for some time now. It is the meat in the rational sandwich. Some wankers with mortarboards stuck up their arses don't get it.' Liz took another puff. 'So you wangled your way into the job at this gallery to screw your boss?'

'I would never want to do that, Liz,' I said. 'Noah's gay.'

'I mean, fuck him *over*,' Liz clarified, punctuating her words with cigarette jabs in the air.

'No, when I took the job I didn't realise he was the manager of the Galerie Exotique at the time and -'

'Wait. Galerie *Exotique*? Sounds like a Vegas strip club.'

'I know,' I sighed.

'It's closed now.'

'I'm not surprised.'

'We definitely have to go to the gallery this morning. It's your chance to search for evidence.' Liz blew her nose. 'It's your duty to the artist and to me.'

'To you?'

Liz looked at me over her fan of white tissue and said, 'I need some fun.'

I gulped at the rest of my coffee. 'Okay,' I said after a moment of contemplation, 'on three conditions.'

'What?'

'That you pick up your used tissues and put them in the bin downstairs.' A gentle wind was pushing one light ball of sticky white towards the edge of the roof. 'And, once we're done, you come straight back here and spend the rest of the day in bed.'

'Alright,' Liz scrunched up her face in disgust. 'What's the third condition?'

'That if you have no intention of eating that pastry, I can have it.'

Liz dangled the bag in front of me with a mischievous chuckle, then threw it across onto my lap. After Liz picked up all her tissues, bar one that escaped over the edge, we returned to the apartment. I was certain we were about to do the wrong thing, albeit for the right reasons. Besides, all I wanted to do was keep to some routine and think about how John's cargo pants sat casually on his hips.

While I changed again (dressing in black for art gallery camouflage), I contemplated the strange advantage of having a flatmate who looked for the bad in people – for the pleasure of being a part of it. I then typed the codes of the Dorothy Brown paintings on the notepad of my phone.

Liz walked into my bedroom in blinding white trainers and fitted red tracksuit. The outfit only lacked a fluro orange balaclava with flashing lights.

'Can't find my car keys.'

'Again?' I asked, while feeling for the skeleton ones between my mattresses. My fingers hit metal, and I drew them out. A small handheld gun-shaped tool with a protruding metal spike rather than a barrel. Around the handle was a rubber band holding the small torque wrench, which looks a bit like an Allen key except flat. I couldn't believe I hadn't felt them before when lying down. Excellent choice of mattress, I nodded, patting the top of the bed. 'Okay,' I said calmly, walking into the lounge room, 'when did you last use them?'

'When I last opened the front door,' Liz said in moronic tempo.

I could remember seeing them myself not long ago. Scanning the lounge, they had become invisible. Liz hauled the couch seat cushions into the air, causing a crumpled tissue snowstorm. I reconned the kitchen. Nothing (except noodles). Returning to the lounge, I stopped. The keys were sitting on the bookshelf, next to my yellowing and dog-eared edition of *Shock of the New.*

'Got them.'

Liz took the keys off me and headed straight for the front door. 'Next search,' Liz yelled, 'Nora's dirty goods.' I followed, grabbing the tissue box on the way.

While Liz drove, I sent Noah a text explaining that I had forgotten something at the gallery. After pressing send, I stared at the screen, waiting to hear from Noah that it was fine to break into his office.

Being a Monday morning, the traffic was jammed. It took twenty minutes to reach the gallery. It would have taken thirty if Liz drove at the speed limit on the legal side of the road. I was pleased to get out of the car. Not so much because of the reckless speeding, more the sheer amount of food wrapper rubbish that was building up in there. I got out, scraping stray pickled ginger off the sole of my shoe.

'I haven't heard back from him, Liz,' I contended as we walked up to the door. 'Maybe we should wait.'

Liz took the keys out of my hands and entered the darkened gallery. I ran in after her to turn off the alarm before it sounded. Liz switched on all the lights.

'Shouldn't we keep them off?' I said in a hushed voice.

'Why are you whispering?' Liz asked as she walked through the space, looking again at the paintings.

Turning off the lights, I followed Liz to the office door. It was, as expected, locked. I hesitated before handing over the picklock pack. Liz began working her criminal magic. This involved clicking the gun, twiddling the torque, swearing, and then clicking the gun again.

'Do you remember how to do this?'

'It's coming back to me,' Liz replied. 'It would be easier if you got out of my light.'

I stepped back and looked towards the front door, expecting Noah to wander in. My bladder felt weak. After ten minutes and three toilet runs, I heard the gentle click of release. Liz blew on her curled knuckles in pride, then walked in and flicked on the light. It looked like someone had raided the place. Before we did. Papers were strewn in all directions. On the large black desk in the centre of the room were used polystyrene cups, takeaway wrappers, manila folders with contents precariously sliding out, note pads with scribbled notes with some (unoriginal) doodles, and business cards scattered like the end of a poker game. The paper chaos surrounded Noah's three most important items: a black computer monitor, a black leather office chair behind a black desk. My mother once told me that black was good for hiding dirt and stains, so perhaps Noah had good reason for his choice of décor.

'This guy's more of a pig than I am,' Liz said.

Breathing in the remnant smell of day-old greasy food, I had to agree. Noah always appeared so neat, so contained and tucked in. You would assume the tidiness would have carried through to his environment. At least there was art. On the wall behind the desk was a large painting of a yellow psychedelic boar. To the left, a window looked out onto a clump of black bamboo against a white wall. Noah's plush chair had its seat swivelled towards the door, beckoning me.

'This is a bad idea,' I said, retreating. But Liz was already rifling through the filing cabinets in the corner. 'Thank Christ he didn't lock these,' she said. 'What are we looking for again?

'I really think we should forget the whole thing. Let's go.'

'But what about the integrity of that artist, Dee Dee Brown?'

'Dorothy Brown.'

'This is for a good cause, Anna.'

Good causes were not integral to Liz's psyche. I doubted they were part of Perry's either, the other person who was making the same argument. Forcing myself behind the desk, I settled into Noah's chair and turned on the PC. 'Okay, we're looking for anything on Dorothy Brown, who is an Aboriginal artist from Stumpy Downs.' As the computer warmed into action, I sifted carefully through the papers on the desk. 'And anything with Galerie Exotique on it.'

'Dorothy Brown was represented by a business called Galerie Exotique,' Liz snorted. 'Well, that's a serious injustice against Aboriginal people right there.'

'We need to find information regarding the sale of a Dorothy Brown quadriptych -'

'Quad-what?'

'Quadriptych, four paintings to be viewed as one work. The title is *Country*, dated 2005.' I took out my phone and read out the codes. 'Maybe also look out for Harrington's Auctioneers. Noah worked there as an Indigenous specialist in 2013 and 2014.'

Liz began rummaging through the top drawer, wiping her nose with a bunch of tissues at intervals. Never had she been so industrious and so quiet in my presence. Pulling focus, I noticed to my left a wall of shelves holding an extensive fine art library: Asian, American, European, white Australian and Aboriginal, all covering a variety of eras. Two long rows of black cardboard catalogue holders contained auction and exhibition catalogues but nothing before the year 2015 and nothing Aboriginal.

Shuffling through the desk drawers of miscellaneous stationery and old, untitled CDs, I realised I didn't know who else had a key to the gallery, apart from Noah and me. And possibly Robert. Would Jan still have hers? Is she really on the road already?

The computer was finally awake, but with the obligatory password requirement. I felt relief, a reason to pack up and go home.

'Oh well, I don't know his password.'

'Try 1234,' Liz suggested, wiping her nose on a tissue and throwing it on the floor. 'It's the password for lazy people.'

Looking at the state of the room, Liz had a point. And it worked. There was no excuse but to go in. The only surprising thing about Noah's email correspondence was how little of it there was. What was there appeared brief, professional and legit. While looking up at the door every thirty seconds, convinced that Noah would be standing there, I managed to trawl through incoming and expense spreadsheets, images of artists' works, sponsorship pitches, catering details, travel arrangements to other capital cities, art freight invoices, packing material price lists, and artist and client correspondence. The clients were mostly from Sydney, some interstate, and a handful from America. Frank was there. None of the works of art discussed were Aboriginal. I then clicked on a final folder called 'n.webster_ priv collection'.

I heard Liz snort and turned to see her holding a pink, inflated puppy that looked like it was made out of long balloons. 'Hidden in the back of the bottom drawer. Now here's a kinky sex toy I am unfamiliar with.'

'Jeff Koons,' I replied.

'The puppy has a name?'

'The artist has a name. This is exhibition merchandise.' 'It's actually solid, made of some metal. Still, it could be useful for self-pleasure...' Liz said, putting it away. 'Buggered if I know where the dodgy stuff is,' she said, slamming the last drawer closed. 'Excuse the pun.'

'Thanks for trying.'

'It was worth a punt.' Liz waded through her used tissues, now covering the floor, and looked over my shoulder. 'Nora's private collection?' Liz asked. In the folder was a series of images titled: Rover Thomas, Clifford Possum Tjapaltjarri, Gloria Tamerre Petyarre, Tim Leurah Tjapaltjarri, Michael Jagamarra Nelson, Minnie Pwerle. All were well known Australian Aboriginal artists, many deceased. I clicked on each icon, and an image of the respective artist holding a painted canvas appeared. While their faces held little expression, each painting was museum-class. The final image was titled with a code rather than a name. I clicked on it and there was Dorothy, also expressionless, sitting cross-legged next to a large canvas of tiny red dots. She couldn't hold it up like the others had, as her canvas was at least four times the size. The red dots varied, almost verging into orange, pink or black. It was the most striking Dorothy Brown I had seen by far, yet it hadn't made it into the chopping block book at the art gallery store.

'It couldn't be,' I said.

'Oh, I bet it is,' Liz said defiantly before adding, 'What exactly?'

'If this is Noah's personal Aboriginal collection, or part of it, he really shouldn't be selling. These are incredible.'

'Maybe he needs to sell them to service his Harry Jones.'

'His what?'

'Hard core heroin addiction,' she said, eyes wide. 'It explains why he disappears for long periods of time.'

I stared at the Dorothy Brown, feeling her signature calm. 'One thing's for sure, they're all authentic – and very expensive.'

'Why are the artists photographed as well? They all look like they're holding up ID charts before being thrown into jail. I guess they haven't been taught to say "cheese" to the photographer yet,' Liz mused.

'Guess not,' I said, looking at Dorothy's painting. The expanse. The stillness. I then snapped out of it. 'Beautiful works, but they don't help me with my thesis.' I closed the files and shut down the computer. We both then looked at the carpet of crumpled tissues. 'I'm not picking them up,' I said. Liz pouted, then shoved them into her purse.

Meanwhile, I surveyed the room, ensuring everything appeared as we found it: Japanese tearoom meets downtown Baghdad. Fortunately, the door was easy to lock from the inside. No pick gun required. 'It's strange,' I said as we walked towards the front of the gallery. 'I would have expected Noah to have had the filing cabinets locked, considering he goes to all the trouble of locking the door all the time.'

'Yeah,' Liz nodded and sniffed. 'For a forger, it was a little too easy.'

'Faker,' I corrected. 'A forger is someone who duplicates from an original. A fake painting is one artist's style. Except Noah is possibly neither. Maybe he's the sort of guy who can't be bothered locking filing cabinets, so he locks his office door instead.'

'It's reasonable,' Liz permitted. 'Disappointingly boring, but reasonable.'

As we passed my desk, I looked at the locked cupboard. 'Liz, would you mind trying to open Jan's cupboard?'

'Who's Jan?'

'The woman who usually works here, Noah's surrogate mother. I'm keeping her seat warm. Noah said he couldn't remember what was in here and said he didn't have a key.'

'No key, eh?' Liz's eyebrows bounced.

'Jan's a very wholesome woman, looks like she sells Cornish pasties.'

'Yeah, right,' Liz said. Within seconds, Jan's locked cupboard sprung wide open to reveal Printer paper, toner, five boxes of red spot stickers (optimistic) and two archival boxes. Liz blew on her gun, and I offered silent applause. We sat on the carpet, pulled out a box each, and started going through the manila files inside.

'Liz?'

'Yep?'

'Thanks for doing this with me.'

'Hey, this isn't altruism, girl. I don't do charity. I do fun.'

The first few files were Noah Webster's financial documents from the previous five financial years – tax summaries and associated receipts. But then documents with Galerie Exotique letterhead surfaced. However, like the Noah Webster files, they appeared to be the sort of records kept for taxation purposes.

'You keep tax-related records for seven years, right?' I asked Liz. 'Galerie Exotique closed in 2006.'

'You're right there,' Liz agreed.

'So why keep the files now?'

'You wouldn't. Well, I wouldn't,' Liz reasoned. 'I'd have a big bonfire, make a party of it. But I don't think Jan sounds like the type to party up. Nora, on the other hand…'

'Noah could be nostalgic over these papers. Apparently, he was Miles Porter's lover.'

'Miles Porter, the director? I've seen his name on quite a bit of this,' Liz said, flipping some pages. 'So, Nora shagged the boss.'

'When in Rome.' I murmured.

'You wouldn't keep this stuff for nostalgia, Anna. It's much more likely that he wanted to profit from it in some way. Keep the contacts, maybe even use the letterhead to dumb up the certificates of authenticity, eh?'

'But Noah said he didn't know what was in the cupboard – he was going to ask Jan when she called.'

'Maybe he was faking it,' Liz replied. 'This *is* the arts industry.' Looking at a spreadsheet, she said, 'The figures were pretty bad during the financial year of '06. I guess that's why the gallery closed.'

'Miles died that year. Leukemia.'

'Really?' Liz looked up before flipping back and forth through the stack of pages on her lap. 'Haven't seen any certificates of authenticity, or anything on Dorothy Brown except as items sold on income generated.'

'Anything involving four *Country* paintings?'

'Dorothy had a thing for sand goannas. There are stacks of them listed here. Lots of numbers.'

'Sand goannas are her totem.'

Liz looked more closely at the page in her hand. 'What were those codes again?'

I read them out. Liz blew her nose and ran her finger down the pages. 'Bingo!' she said, spilling the file with her hand. *Country* quad… quadriptych. Sold in February 2005.'

'To who?'

'Er, doesn't say.'

At Liz's urging, I took a photo of the sale record with my phone. 'If the paintings were sold through the gallery to someone, the certificates are likely to have come from the gallery.'

'Does that mean the paintings aren't faked?' Liz asked mournfully.

'Not necessarily. They could still be fakes. If they are fakes, Miles or Noah might have been responsible – or they didn't know.

It depends on who in Stumpy Downs organised them. There doesn't seem to be any documents here about where any of the works originally came from.'

'Nope,' Liz said, shuffling through more files. 'Hey, wait.' She opened up a pale blue manila wallet folder. Out spilt a stack of Galerie Exotique certificates of authenticity. Photocopies. The originals usually travel with the paintings, as was the case for the Whitlocks. We quickly flipped through the pile and found the four *Country* documents, complete with photos of the paintings. But none with Dorothy holding up the works. Still, it looked like the same paintings now at Whitlock were sold by Galerie Exotique. I took photos of the certificates. We searched further for the original certificate of authenticity from the Stumpy Downs community, but none surfaced.

'That's it, we've gone through everything,' I said, looking over at Liz, whose nose was glowing while the rest of her body sagged. 'Okay, let's get out of here.' We put everything back, and while Liz was locking the cupboard, my phone beeped twice. It was a text from Noah: 'Thanx Anna. U don't need 2 let me know, I trust u.'

'He trusts you. Isn't that sweet?' Liz said with a laugh while slipping the pick gun into her bag. I looked around towards the front door. There was no one there.

# CHAPTER 15

I had become a criminal. Certainly, I had strayed from my moral compass and snooped on my highly respected boss to the extreme. But the Whitlock Dorothy Browns had gone through Galerie Exotique's books while Noah was manager. Whose moral compass was more off kilter? My next steps soon became clear. As smart criminals do, I resumed my daily routine. During that afternoon's lecture, I doodled while Perry circled the podium.

'Let's start with my favourite: the emotional value of art,' he said. 'Say the blue and green in an abstract painting make you feel peaceful. Or a painting depicting a soldier dying prompts feelings of sadness. Then there's the intellectual value of art. What's an example of that?'

I waited for Marvin, but his arm stayed limp. Eva spoke instead. 'Marcel Duchamp's urinal, exhibited in 1917 to challenge the meaning of art.'

'Ah, yes. *The Fountain.* Good, good. Another other way to value art?'

Simon came in with, 'Religious value, church icons.'

'Yes.'

Someone else said, 'Political value, Russian paintings of workers uniting.'

'Propaganda, yes,' Perry said, both fists in the air.

'Value for social status,' yelled another. 'An eighteenth-century landowner commissioning a painting of his property to show off to his guests.'

'Pre-camera, brilliant!' Perry's fists were shaking in triumph.

'Educational value,' someone spluttered. 'Can't think of an example.' The class laughed good-naturedly.

'Perhaps it is all educational, says the lecturer.' Perry laughed, dropping his arms. 'Good point though.'

'Cultural value,' another volunteered. 'Like an Aboriginal painting hanging in a city gallery.'

'Yes,' Perry confirmed. 'And that the origin of the imagery could be seen as an educational tool – amongst other things – to pass on the Dreaming stories down to the next generation. There's your educational example. Right, Lissam?'

Giving a half-hearted nod, I decided to shift topic. 'Financial value,' I said. 'Van Gogh's *Sunflowers* sold for $40 million at a London auction in 1987.'

Perry stood still before asking the class, 'Who else knows this story?' No one raised their hands. 'There were reams of press coverage at the time. $40 million, or £24.75 million to be exact, gets your attention. That's quite a figure, yes? But one must ask: Why so much?'

'Supply and demand,' I said.

'Yes, but what creates the demand in the first place?'

'The marketplace,' I replied.

'Why do they want to spend forty big ones on a van Gogh?'

'Because no one painted like van Gogh.'

'Except for Schuffenecker,' Perry said. The class was struck dumb, probably wondering how to spell it and, secondly, why they didn't recognise it. Perry milked the moment, wandering around the classroom, as if waiting for someone else to speak.

'Schuffenecker,' Perry began, 'never made it as a painter. He earned his crust teaching drawing in Paris and died in 1935 without recognition.' Perry paced around the room before saying, 'Imagine the dismay of the Japanese insurance company that purchased *The Sunflowers* for close to $40 million when they were told they had purchased, not a van Gough, but a Schuffenecker.' Perry wandered around some more, stopping in front of the podium.

I became tired of Perry's wandering pauses and found myself cutting to the chase. 'Schuffenecker copied *The Sunflowers* from the original van Gogh. Well, from one of the six he painted. The copy is believed to be twelve years older than the authentic original,' I explained.

'Well done, Lissam,' Perry confirmed. 'So how do we value Schuffenecker?'

'Schuffenecker has no value,' I stated.

'Why?'

'Because he was a thief, an artist so bitter about his lack of artistic success that he painted forgeries to prove that no one, not even the sharpest eye, could tell the difference.'

'Technician of the Year,' Simon piped up, amusing the class.

'I have a question, Dr Perry,' I continued. 'Who do you think is more tragic? Schuffenecker or van Gogh?'

He put his hands in his pockets and smiled up at me. 'The insurance company.'

***

'Stroke of genius, Anna, that Van Gogh example.'

'Thank you, Marvin,' I replied while packing up. Marvin continued to linger.

'Just wanted to ask if you ended up going to DAAOn with that artist.'

I grabbed the strap of my Freitag. 'Bloody hell, Marvin, what do you care? You've got artists up to your eyeballs, raking it in through your online shopping cart as we speak.'

'Not at the moment,' he said in a low tone. 'My business has hit a bit of a snag, and I could really use some new creative talent.'

'What kind of snag?' I had to hear this.

'Someone hacked the site, made a real mess of it. Took me ages to work it out and get it back up and running.'

'It was probably Perry.'

'Dr Perry?' Marvin's eyes widened. 'Why would he want to hack my site?'

'That was a joke,' I said, realising just how on edge Marvin was. 'The man's just crap at tech.'

'Some of my artists went across to DAAOn. Well, most actually. To confess, I think the crash was just a last straw for them. I'm rethinking how I support my artists better, take more time with them. Even give them a bigger percentage.' Looking hard at Marvin, assessing his body language and inflections, the knob seemed genuine. 'Anna, I realise that, from time to time, I've been a bit of an arsehole. Sorry about that. Anyway,' Marvin looked like he was going to add something, then thought better of it. Instead, he walked back down to the front, picked up his bag, and made his way to the door. Perry called out to him, but Marvin didn't seem to hear.

'Hey, you,' Simon said as I walked towards him.

'So how was the ballet? Not as painful as expected, I hope.'

'The performance was very Swan Lake,' he explained. 'But the after party was more Cirque du Soleil.'

'Sounds athletic.'

'Hey, how did you know about that van Gogh rubbernecker?'

'Schuffenecker? Read it somewhere, can't remember.' I shrugged. 'I need coffee. You want some?'

'That would be great, except I've really got to go back to work,' he started, then clicked his fingers. 'Forgot to mention, Dale's back in contact. He rang earlier this morning.'

'What did he say? Did he look at the Dorothy images? Had you sent them yet?'

'Yes, yes.' Simon placed his hand on my arm. 'I forwarded them yesterday. But he didn't talk to me. He was too busy freaking out at my boss over the federal government's export ban on some Aboriginal paintings listed for the next sale.'

'Export ban?' I probed. 'Is that to keep certain artworks in Australia for preservation?'

'Yep, the Moveable Cultural Heritage Act has become a thorn in our side. The government has experts to assess whether Aboriginal works should remain in Australia. The beauty of it was that the stingy government only has three expert examiners for Indigenous objects.'

'Only three people?'

'Well, they say there's eleven on the committee, but only three know anything about the Aboriginal side of things. And being so overworked, they could only look at about a quarter of what was presented and had to wave off the rest. But now there's a new kid on the block and, despite the workload, this guy's a hoarder.'

We made our way down the lecture room aisle. As Perry was picking up his satchel and walking towards the door, his free hand moved to his chest. Face red and teeth clenched, took some breaths and walked out.

'One day he's going to be talking about Hirst's diamond skull, then drop dead right in front of us.'

'For the love of god, Anna,' Simon whispered, staring at the man walking away from us. 'I appreciate the thesis isn't going as planned, but to wish the man dead?'

'No, I don't wish him dead.' Then I thought about it. No, I didn't really wish him dead. 'Haven't you noticed? He has some kind of heart condition, turns him into a sunburnt blowfish, but then seems to recover.'

'Really? No, I hadn't noticed. Poor thing.'

'You didn't hear it from me. He doesn't like to talk about it.' We made our way out. 'Australians still buy Aboriginal paintings from Harrington's, right?'

'Sure, but the big money's overseas,' he explained. 'And, get this, the Federal Arts Minister accused *us* of self-interest. Can't wait to see that idiot go down in the next election.'

'But isn't that sort of true?'

'Of course it's true,' Simon replied. 'The paintings are valued at more than $800,000, and so if we get the price, we earn about $200,000 in buyers' and sellers' fees. That's a lot of spondulicks, m'dear.'

'And I suppose Dale Spencer gets a nice Christmas bonus out of all those spondulicks?'

'Dale? I guess,' he mused, 'But Dale wouldn't just pass anything through for sale. He's a good guy. He takes his work seriously. Why don't you come with me? We'll try him from the office.'

'That would be great.' I faltered. 'Do you have coffee at your office? I mean, real coffee?'

'Honey, we have an espresso machine that will fuel your nervous system like a bowser. Now that machine is something worth protecting.' Then he asked, 'Can I poach your notes from this morning?'

'Sorry, I wasn't here either. I was hoping to poach yours.'

'Hey Simon,' Eva said as she joined us down the corridor. 'Slugger,' she said, looking at me.

'Did you make it to this morning's lectures?' Simon asked.

'Yes, I did, you two slack arses.'

'Can we have your notes?'

'In exchange for?'

'Come to Harrington's and have a caffeine experience that will change your life.'

'When I'm looking for beans to change my life, I'll call you,' Eva replied.

'But thems is magic beans, Eva,' Simon smiled.

'Later, Jack,' she said. 'Anna, if you find your boss is trading in work other than what's on display...'

'Other than our exhibitions? Well, there are some paintings in the storeroom.'

'Perhaps Aboriginal works for those special American clients he's shacked up with?'

'He doesn't touch Aboriginal stuff,' I replied a little too quickly. 'Remember?'

'Chill, slugger. I'm just winding you up. I'll email my notes through tonight.'

Walking out, we shielded our eyes from the sinking sun. Crossing the courtyard, I wondered how three people decide what to protect, what 'things' future Australians need to see to understand what has possibly already gone.

The foyer of Harrington's was like that of a nineteenth-century mansion. Expansive stairs with an ornately carved wooden bannister that swirled downwards to greet collectors. Red carpet led up to another foyer, offering a choice of various entrances to the enormous saleroom, which I glimpsed through some open doors. Rows of chairs faced the stage where a large burgundy velvet curtain hung behind the pillar-like wooden rostrum. It looked a bit like an old theatre from a once glorious age.

Simon had a different interpretation. 'When the room is full,' he explained, 'the competitive energy can get pretty hot. Art auctions are the closest thing we have to sport.'

Simon had already shown me 'backstage' of Harrington's on a previous visit. It made the saleroom look like a nook. Rooms upon rooms for sculpture and furniture. Racks upon racks of paintings. Shelves upon shelves of vases, platters and other ephemera. Harrington's staff, with white protective gloves and great purpose, were cataloguing it, wrapping it or moving it. Order abounded. There was no place for creative licence here.

Offices rimmed the saleroom, and Simon led me to a one near the back, close to the storage area. Here, space and ostentation ended. This was not a place to bring clients. Recalling Simon's earlier reference to their overseas buyers, I understood clients were increasingly 'virtual'. The size of Simon's working space was much like my old image library office. But, I noted, it did have a window. The view looked out onto the adjacent concrete building. More specifically, a rusted air-conditioning vent with leak stains down the wall.

Simon squeezed behind the laminated desk and picked up the phone to make an internal call. I sat in front of the desk, wondering where the promised coffee machine was secreted.

'Dale is still on the same number? Great...no, I need to call him about something else...yes, I know...I'll give it a shot anyway, thanks.'

Simon dialled again, this time a Western Australian number. The tone of Simon's voice dropped to a lower pitch. 'Good afternoon. This is Simon Murray from Harrington's in Sydney. I was wondering if I could speak with...that's right, Dale Spencer... thank you....(pitch lifts). Dale, hi. Yes, I know...I can't believe it either...' At that point, Simon pulled the telephone away from his head. I could hear the expletives from where I was sitting. Simon rolled his eyes back at me. After a time, he was able to resume, 'Look Dale...yes, I'm sure the government is probably wanting to look culturally responsible...Well, the buyers affected aren't voters, are they? I suppose you're right, they could pressure...But, I don't think it's a big enough issue...not exactly affecting coal prices... Dale, on another matter...' Simon laughed. 'Yes, Dale, there are other matters...well, yes...the Dorothy Brown images I forwarded to you...email, yes...did you get them? What did you think? I think they're lovely too, Dale. But that's not what I'm asking.'

*Lovely*, I thought, forgetting the coffee. Simon looked over at me, now crossing his eyes 'Certificate of authenticity? I thought it was strange that they are on gallery letterhead, not the art centre, and no photo of Dorothy holding up the painting...True....Well, that's tricky because they're in London. Yes...no, don't move to London, Dale...everything will be fine, I promise...Back to the Browns, Dale....Dorothy Brown...the certificates...do you think they are enough to authenticate the paintings? Hard to say? Right. The client's in London, too. The paintings were a gift from some pharmaceutical company. But, not being art lovers, they don't know much about the provenance. Pearls before swine, yes...' Simon let out a laugh as authentic as the paintings they were discussing. I checked myself. His laughter was for my benefit.

'Well, we know we can't talk to Noah Webster about it...' he continued. 'Or the artist, for that matter ...' I watched closely. 'Bugger, isn't it? Small fortune...well, if they were genuine. No, London office doesn't know a thing about it – and don't tell them, Dale,' Simon laughed again. 'No, don't book the flight just yet. Thanks so much anyway...yes, I will. Are you coming back soon? Dale, you have to come back sometime...we miss you (chuckle)... okay, thanks again...cheers...bye.'

Simon hung up and turned to me. 'He doesn't know.'

'What makes him doubt they are Dorothy's?'

'History,' Simon said. 'The history of fakes running around the marketplace. Dale's very careful, doesn't jump to conclusions. He thinks they could be genuine, but the digital images are not the best quality.'

'The images?'

'They're not bad, mind you, but...you know...for Dale to be absolutely sure, they have to be pinpoint clear. Print publishable quality. Well, that's what he says. He wants to see the paintings properly. As we know, this isn't possible.'

'You said that the certificates should be from the art centre?'

'Dale agreed, but then said sometimes the art centre stuffs up and the gallery steps in – if the relationship is a good one.'

'Thanks so much, Simon.'

'This job's getting a little dull,' he confessed. 'Nice to have something interesting to help out on.'

'Well, it's a great help to me. Might get me off the hook. I'm seeing Perry tomorrow. I'll tell him what Dale said, that it is too hard without seeing the paintings themselves.'

'Another thesis meeting?'

'Every Tuesday until he says otherwise.'

'Talk about close supervision,' Simon said, clasping his hands behind his head. 'I'm jealous.'

'Don't be,' I replied. 'It's a strange experience.'

Simon stared out onto his piece of concrete wall, deep in thought. 'You could send the Dorothy Brown images to other people, curator of Australian Indigenous art at the gallery and the like. But I suspect you'll get the same response. I've found that with Dale. He is a very accurate barometer for the industry.'

'Good to know,' I nodded. 'And thanks for giving the impression that the paintings may be for sale…but not quite.'

'It's all part of the service,' Simon grinned. 'And, let's face it, Dorothy Brown is special. If I can assist with uncovering someone trying to rip her off, I'll feel a warm glow.'

'Simon, you already have a warm glow. It's a permanent feature.'

'It must be from the coffee here,' he said, then sat up straight. 'Coffee! I forgot, want some?'

I smiled, 'Thought you'd never ask.'

The coffee from Harrington's espresso machine didn't create a warm glow. After half a cup, my heart was about to rocket out through my ribcage and ricochet around the saleroom. I held onto the furniture for a while. But by the time I walked out through the double glass doors and into the late twilight, I felt ready to do something – anything, as long as it was big.

I pulled out my phone to text John and it rang. It was John. 'Hey Anna,' he said. 'I know it's only Monday, but I had a good time yesterday and was wondering if you wanted to catch up again sometime?'

'Yes.' It was a small word for such a large emotion. Urgency hammered at my brain. 'Where are you?'

'Now?'

'Now.'

Then I waited. Thank god John was coming from Newtown and not Paradise. Biding my time, I decided to call home. I tapped my foot, waiting for a response.

A croaky voice was heard to whisper, 'Hell...hello...'

'Liz, it's me.'

'Who?'

'Anna, the person you live with...sometimes.'

'My assistant in crime,' Liz corrected, her voice clearing.

'Just wanted to check that you were okay.'

'Stop right there.'

'Sorry?'

'There's one thing worse than being trapped in this apartment with a head that's trying to hold in the fucking Pacific Ocean, and that is being fussed over. If you continue, you'll have something worse under your mattress than a pick gun.'

'Okay, bugger you then,' I said. 'And I might not be home tonight either.'

'Finally,' Liz said and hung up.

I paced back and forth outside Harrington's, looking in adjacent shop windows at nothing in particular. The streetlights were on and natural light was fast fading, but I caught my reflection in a mirror on display in an antique store. I was looking a little wired, granted, but okay. I rummaged through my Freitag looking for lipstick, but John's Triumph appeared in the reflection of the shopfront window.

Donning the helmet, I didn't think about safety. Instead, I felt a quiet freedom humming inside.

'Where do you want to eat?' he asked. I wasn't feeling particularly hungry. Not for food, anyway, more for air. 'Let's try somewhere around your neck of the woods,' I suggested. I wanted to ride forever, and Paradise seemed that far.

'Want to see how the other half eat, eh?' John grinned before putting on his helmet.

'Other half of what?' I asked, and he laughed behind the visor. But the question was sincere. Just because I lived inner city, didn't mean I related to the people who owned property there, the ones who could afford to buy art from galleries like Noah Webster. I was a collector of instant noodles. They didn't last long.

Riding pillion to the outer suburbs, I wondered about Candy, the ordinary star in all of John's photographs. Candy was flexible. She could be anything John wanted. But as I became hypnotised by the buildings, strip shops and houses that passed, my insecurity seemed to roll off the visor like a wayward blowfly. Holding on, I closed my eyes and felt the stillness.

Paradise presented itself as an edible United Nations. An American-style burger joint was flanked by Balkan and Vietnamese eateries. French crêpes were joined to English-style fish 'n chips, adjacent to an Indian curry house. Vegetarian was nestled next to a Chinese restaurant with ducks hanging from hooks in the window. Choosing Australian required eating at all of them. John had certainly tried. For a struggling artist, he still seemed to have a reasonable dining out budget. Not that anywhere looked expensive. We ended up eating at Tuck-In Thai. I was impressed when John pulled out a bottle from his pannier.

'Took the liberty of picking this up before…Thought you might be a red wine drinker, but if you're not, I can -'

It was a Grant Burge Shiraz, Barossa Valley. Not bad. 'I love red,' I said, almost taking the bottle by accident. I don't know what I was thinking, but he took my outstretched hand with his free one, and we walked towards the fluorescent gleam of the restaurant.

A paper screen with an ornate blossom tree motif divided the front desk from the restaurant area. With a phone wedged between her neck and shoulder, a large woman wearing a red Suzy Wong number at least two sizes too small smiled and nodded at us while jotting down an order. The tiny entry area had four people sitting on plastic chairs along its perimeter, as if waiting for a doctor's appointment. The woman got off the phone and yelled something in a language other than English towards the kitchen. Turning to us, John anticipated the woman's question with 'Eating here'. She led us around the partition to a vision of vinyl and laminate. Every table provided its standard collection of soy bottle, paper serviette dispenser and a large supply of balsa chopsticks. No surprises, which helped in a way. I was starting to feel a little nervous. Maybe it was the second stage jitters from Simon's cop-this caffeine.

'One of the area's more salubrious establishments,' John whispered after the waitress had passed out the laminated menus and left us for wine glasses.

'Excellent choice,' I said, and meant it. I was famished. We worked our way through dishes that sounded like exclamations from a fight scene in a comic strip: *Phick khing! Kaeng dang! Kaprow! Kao prow!* I chose not to share this with John, given the childish-slash-racist nature of the observation. True to the sound of their names, each dish was delicious and then very hot. By the time we finished what we could, the Shiraz had made our chillied lips purple and wet.

'This is going to sound like quite a claim,' I said. 'But I think that was the best Thai I've ever had,' I said. 'Admittedly, I wouldn't know what authentic Thai food is, having never been there.' Sitting back in my chair, I wondered if it was too early to admit I had never been on a plane. Probably.

John shrugged. 'I haven't been to Thailand either.'

'I've never been on a plane. Ever.' Bloody wine.

'Never?' John asked, though polite enough not to look too shocked. 'Well, there's an adventure waiting for you. Unless you have a fear of flying?'

'No. Just haven't had the opportunity yet.'

'People seem to like complaining about flying, particularly the food.' He leant in. 'But I still like it when the meal trays come out. And you have to be dead not to feel some kind of buzz at take-off and landing. No one wants to admit that.'

So enthralled by his endearing admission, I accidentally burped. 'Dreadfully sorry. I probably ate too much.'

'Not enough,' John said before a well-timed burp, taking etiquette belching to new heights. 'Look, we didn't even finish it all.'

It was true. There was probably enough left over to feed a small army with a penchant for chilli. 'Those little aluminium serving bowls really trick the eye.' Was it too early in the evening to start unbuttoning my jeans? Probably.

We sat in silence for a moment. It was almost a comfortable silence. Looking out through the window onto the car park and industrial bins, I said, 'You're a liar.'

'What?' John asked, startled. 'A liar?'

'You said that you weren't good with words.'

John relaxed back and turned the stem of his empty wineglass. 'But I'm not, I'm hopeless.'

'Well, that means I'm crap with words, too. I've enjoyed our conversations so far.'

'I don't know. I guess I feel comfortable with you.'

Ironically, we then sat with an awkward pause between us. 'The words on your website were good too,' I added. 'Surprisingly good.'

'Ben, a friend of mine, is a freelance copywriter. He's helping me with the site a bit. Well, nagging me, actually. He's trying to get me to write the text, so I learn how to do it.'

'Have to say I really liked the words. And I rarely think about text on artist websites. Or any websites.'

'That's great, but don't tell him how much you like it. It'll just encourage him. Between you and me, I think Ben just enjoys telling people what to do. I told him he should buy a video camera. He would be a great arsehole director.'

Both feeling parched, and our little water carafe drained, we looked around for the waitress across the landscape of busy eaters. She had disappeared. I remembered my water bottle in my Freitag, which of course was at the bottom, so I pulled out my notebook and threw it onto the table, wrestling it out from a cacophony of gloves, scarf, purse, phone, sunglasses, tissue pack…'Got it!' I said. 'My bottle is clean. Just hasn't been open since last autumn…' I pulled up my body to the table to notice John was on his feet, looking down at my notebook. My open notebook, my doodles.

'Anna, these are great,' he said, beaming, then looked apologetic. 'It was open, I promise. You'd flung it on the table in such a way…it fell open. I would never-'

'You like my doodles?' I said, staring at him, numb.

'These aren't doodles. This…,' he said, scanning the page. 'This is art.'

'I'd like them to be doodles,' I said, feeling shy all of a sudden.

'That's okay. The name doesn't matter,' he said, shaking his head while staring at the page. 'How they feel is what matters. May I look closer? Is there more on the other pages?' I nodded and handed the notebook over to him, daring myself not to feel anything at this moment.

I couldn't believe an artist would accuse me of having an overactive imagination. Following John into the dark studio, I grabbed at the back of his belt so that I could be led inside without red wine injury.

'You thought I was flirting with you to get to Noah?'

'Technically, that would mean you prefer to sleep with men.'

'Well, that's not true,' he replied.

'I hoped not. Anyway, what I mean…what I meant…'

'What did you meant?'

'How could I be so…light-headed after half a bottle of wine?' I asked, knowing I was light-headed by John, his response to my doodles – his face said it all – and, yes, the wine.

'You're out of practise?' It was still dark in the studio. I wondered whether the lights only worked in the day, being solar powered.

'The wine seems to be doing strange things to my system,' I said.

'I was hoping to do some strange things to your system, actually.'

'Strange things?'

'Things that you are possibly unfamiliar with. Good strange things.'

'I'm all for good strange things.'

'Good.'

'But how do you know what I'm familiar with? Isn't that a little pre…pre…sumpchus?'

'Yes, I would like to be sumptuous as well,' he replied. 'But, believe me when I say this…' John turned around. Still holding onto the back of his belt, I swung around, remaining behind him. He straightened up again and continued walking. 'I don't know what you're familiar with. I intend to find out first, you see?'

'I see, research,' I said, stumbling behind him in the dark. 'Then what?'

'I want to give you something different. It may involve being creative.'

'But you're an artist,' I exasperated. 'Being creative…that's no challenge.'

'Being creative is always a challenge.' John stopped. He took the hand that was holding onto his belt and led my body to his. In the dark, he found my lips by first kissing my forehead, ear, cheek, nose. The scenic route.

After a few more steps, we reached the unusually located light switches. They worked. His friend's naïve paintings greeted us. Not much development had occurred there since my last visit. Roll on adolescence. I unhooked myself from the belt, and we walked through to John's darkened studio. He switched on a lamp in the corner, lighting up his gentle profile and a three-metre radius. I looked around as if I hadn't seen the space before. Easels, cameras, rolled up prints, and stacked paintings took what little light there was to create more shadows.

The bed in the corner of the studio was still unmade. He smoothed it out a little while I stood, needing something to do. It was too dark to look at the paintings again. A collection of vinyl records lined a small section of the nearby wall. I could just make out the word 'Blur' on the first cover. A pile of paperback books sat in the shadows, as if they knew life was going to be hard from here on. The tragedy of not being a touch screen. John sat on the bed and turned on a small bar heater nearby.

'Come,' he patted the mattress beside him as a soft command.

'Um, right.' I walked a Modrian-line to the bed. Straight from a distance, but on closer inspection, a little rough around the edges. He looked up at me. 'Have you ever been painted?' he asked. I wondered if it was a line. It was natural in romance, if this was romance, to want the original. That nothing should be the same as some other woman's experience. Reproduction meant death.

'Um, no,' I replied. 'My mum once had her portrait done… by a priest, would you believe…she was quite young, but….' I stopped when I realised I had just brought my mother into the conversation.

'But not you,' he said. John shifted his position slightly and then launched into what was the biggest art cliché pick-up line ever. 'I want to paint you,' he said solemnly.

'Okay,' I nodded slowly, struggling to pull down my eyebrows in seriousness. 'Um, when?'

'Now.'

'Now?'

'Yes.'

'On canvas, or are we just talking a quick five-minute study on paper?'

'On you,' he said quietly.

The suggestion, being the second biggest art cliché pick up ever, was unexpected. I had never imagined that a sexual art cliché would manifest into life, a cliché intended to be feared or create a thrill. But I was neither scared nor thrilled. Instead, I stared after him in horror as my date, the artist – the performer – walked over to a stack of paints and brushes. Props, I thought. John selected a medium-sized brush and a pot of acrylic cobalt blue. He may as well have been selecting a syringe. He walked towards me. I couldn't watch.

My shirt was unbuttoned. I opened one eye briefly and saw the dripping brush in his other hand. I was still life. I was being arranged. He reached behind me and leaned towards me. I smelled him – a surprise considering how often my sense of smell failed me – the plastic aroma of acrylic paint and some sort of musky aftershave. My ear was kissed, just under it. My shoulders moved back and my bra unhooked. The brush was on my skin. The paintbrush did not run a line, as expected, but a series of dots. Slow dots about my neck, like kisses. The paint felt cold and almost tickled. I tried not to laugh. The dots continued past the shoulder blades and around the outskirts of my breast and belly. He laid my body down. Jeans were unbuttoned (finally) and unzipped. I was undone and unaware that I was the one who had done it. He had watched, head to the side, and then rested the brush for a moment in my belly's waterhole.

The touch of the brush disappeared. I opened my eyes, wondering where it was headed next. He was taking off his t-shirt, arms raised and eyes covered. I grabbed the bristled toy from its pot and approached the flat, hairless chest with initial bravado. Without guidelines, I hesitated, unsure where to start. I thought of just throwing the paint at him from the pot, hoping he would appreciate the Pollack influence. But then, as the t-shirt was flung onto a pile of old egg sketches, I worked the brush around shoulders and arm muscles, in and out of ribcage valleys and underarm caverns. The purely aesthetic nipples were circled, and one strong stroke travelled to the button on his jeans.

He took the brush from me and held my hand to his chest. The cool paint had not yet dried. My hand smeared his, his smeared mine. Before long, we were a mess.

# CHAPTER 16

'John, there's something I need to know.'

It was a natural declaration, though spoken in a low-toned whisper. He didn't hear it. The night before, we fell asleep into a paradise suburban developers knew nothing of. The morning, however, had brought panic. Looking around the studio, I felt in foreign territory. Getting home under my own steam meant a treacherous journey. I stuck my foot out from under the covers into the cold and drew it back in. Lifting the blankets a little, I looked down to see my body covered in crackled blue paint. There was a curly-topped lump next to me, and the inevitable question came: Who was this guy, anyway?

While John slept, I sat up and scrutinised the place for signs of interest beyond art, a personal history précis rather than the professional one. There were no family snaps on display. I wondered if John's father was as bad at photography as mine. The paperbacks were mostly art books and journals, serving as a stand for a red coffee mug. He wasn't much of a reader. The clothes on an open rack were fairly monochromatic. A pizza menu was on the fridge with two plastic alphabet magnets, 'H' and 'w'.

Women were better at this, I thought. Curating objects in the home to communicate aspects of ourselves, or at least aspects desired. A female's residence was a personal and delicate one-woman exhibition. And was unfortunately interpreted more readily by a female stranger than a male lover.

'Did you say something?' John cracked his eyes open like an old trumpet case.

'No,' I lied. Shimmying down under the covers, more blue flakes fell into the sheets. I kissed him lightly on the lips. 'Last night was…very good. Thank you.' I kissed him again. Just as light, just as gentle.

'Good?' he said. 'That's an unusual word to use…'

'I said "Very good".'

Waking up a little, he then asked, 'But was it strange?'

'The first time with someone is always strange.'

'But good strange?'

'Well, I thought so. Quite possibly excellent-strange, but I'm only fifty percent. What did you think?'

'I thought it was exceptionally excellent strange.' He kissed me back, a little harder, after more flakes of blue fell in between the sheets.

'I'm glad you don't paint with oils,' I said.

'Then I'd have to douse you in metho and rub you all over.'

'That could cause a fire, John.'

'It would most definitely cause a fire.'

I studied his face for familiar signs. I had seen his face before, but couldn't say I was feeling familiar with it.

'Crap,' I said with a start. 'What's the time?'

John looked across at his mobile phone. 'Seven-eighteen, why?'

'I have lectures this morning. Got to be in the city by nine. Charlotte Armstrong is giving a lecture on museums and the changing rhetoric of display.'

'I guess someone has to do it.'

'And I have to be there. I've missed a few lectures lately.'

'No problem, I'll drop you off. Can't let you go without a coffee first.'

'And a shower,' I said, examining my bespeckled body.

He got up and filled the kettle with water, his bare bottom with blue dots wobbling its way around the kitchenette. The water poured sideways. This was because my head was lying on the pillow as I watched. I hugged the blanket to my chest and wished I could look as good as he did in the mornings.

John brought the coffees across to the bed, long fingers cupping both mugs before putting them down. His warmed hands made their way under the blanket, finding the right pressure point to open my nostrils, among other things.


We could have got a speeding ticket. The risk was, in one way, a sizeable declaration of love for an artist in the garrets of Paradise. But I felt safer riding on the back than ever before. Arriving at the uni without incident, I pulled off my helmet and kissed his nose through the visor hole. 'Blue will never be blue again,' I added with a broad smile before dodging a skateboarder and running through the double doors towards the lecture theatre. The room had been darkened for a PowerPoint. Feeling my way, I settled near the door at the side. Perry's spectacles shone in my direction from the front row, held long enough for me to notice. I was surprised to see him there. This wasn't his lecture. Marvin sat next to Perry. I could tell by the strange shape of his head. He had been looking in my direction as well, like a puppet.

Turning to the screen, I let out a small, high-pitched sound. A magnificent painting by Dorothy Brown had glowed and then, in seconds, disappeared. A crosshatched bark painting by a different Aboriginal painter flashed onto the screen instead. This was not a lecture on museums and the changing rhetoric of display.

'But enough about Dorothy Brown,' the speaker said in a broad Australian accent. It was not Charlotte Armstrong but an Aboriginal male. In the dark, I could only see his teeth. 'Now from the Western Desert we go to the Top End, the very north of Australia…'

'Noooo…,' I said under my breath. The speaker explained how trees and reeds can make all the difference in Top End Aboriginal art. An Aboriginal guest speaker had not been listed anywhere on the lecture calendar. I turned back to Perry, whose glasses were now shining toward the direction of the screen.

The rest of the lecture was interesting and torturously unhelpful. When Marvin, as self-appointed class schmoozer, turned the lights on and pulled up the blinds, I sat back and adjusted my eyes on the blank pad before me. Perry stood, ending the talk with a humble admission. 'As an Englishman, I cannot pretend to be an expert on this very important topic. I am grateful to Albert, who fitted us into his busy schedule. Your lecture, Albert, has given us a refreshing view, bringing us back in touch with the land upon which we stand…'

Albert was a middle-aged, dark-skinned man wearing a simple, chequered flannel shirt and black jeans. As Perry spoke, Albert unplugged his laptop and sat in the front row, staring out through the partially open door. It was hard to tell if he was listening. After Perry finished his speech, I rushed up to Albert and attempted to converse about his relationship with Dorothy Brown. My questions were phrased to avoid letting on that I had missed the first third of his talk. I received a series of grunts in return, the sort of grunt that failed to indicate a yes or a no. The experience had made me feel like a crass fool. Learning nothing, I thanked him all the same. He smiled in return, a smile absent of mockery.

I walked up to Simon, who anticipated my thoughts. 'Don't worry about missing the Dorothy Brown stuff,' he comforted, 'there wasn't anything that you couldn't get from Google.'

Eva nodded. 'Boring as a waiting room in a coma ward.'

I nodded back, wondering what they missed that I might have caught. We watched Albert attempt to extract himself from Perry's hospitable grip, insisting he could find his own way. Once free, Albert shot out the door. I followed Perry, given my thesis meeting was next.

'You didn't say he was coming...that Albert,' I stammered.

'The department is not obliged to announce when guest lecturers will be present,' he said, walking down the hallway at a brisk pace. 'You are expected to be there, regardless.'

'But wasn't Charlotte Armstrong supposed to be giving a lecture on the changing rhetoric of display?'

'She was flexible.'

'I thought you were giving the Aboriginal art lectures. You said the budget was blown.'

'The government loosened the purse strings for Albert, not Prescott. He organised the grant himself for the speaking tour. It was a last-minute opportunity.'

'I'm not familiar with Albert,' I said. We were out the door and crossing the courtyard, heading for his office. 'Who, may I ask, is he exactly?'

'A man who was stolen as a boy, worked on properties around the Northern Territory, then traced himself back to the remnants of his tribe.'

'Community,' I said. 'They seem to prefer the word community.'

'Albert used the word 'mob' a bit in his presentation -'

'They can use it.'

'But we can't? It's an English word, for goodness' sake.'

'Dr Perry, is Albert an artist?'

'That depends on your definition.' Perry entered the building and opted for the lift. 'Someone gave him a paintbrush about five years ago. He does Honey Ant Dreamings. Awful purple and orange, scratchy things. But people insist on paying him several hundred dollars a pop. Maybe he knows he's talentless, and that's why he prefers talking about his friend's paintings. Albert's no Dorothy Brown.' We walked into the lift and Perry continued, 'I noticed you tried to talk to him after the lecture.'

'Yes, I tried.'

'Turn the lights out, the PowerPoint on, and the guy can rabbit on like nobody's business. Turn on the lights, attempt a one-to-one, and he clams up completely. Wouldn't take it personally.' The doors opened, and we walked out into the corridor.

'But he knows Dorothy personally?'

'Apparently.'

'What did he say about her? Anything significant?'

Sharon emerged from her office. 'Hi Anna,' she said. 'Dr Perry, I have papers for you to sign.'

'I'll do that quickly now, shall I?' he answered while unlocking his office door.

Once settled at his desk, there was reverent silence while Perry scribbled his signature, his autograph, his mark. *Ordering staples?* I wanted to ask.

'How's Rupert and Grace?' I asked instead.

'Fine,' Sharon replied. Once Perry was done, she took the pages back and walked out without another word.

'Now, where were we?' Perry asked.

'You were about to tell me what Albert said about Dorothy Brown.'

'Yes, that was it,' he said, settling into his chair. I settled into mine. 'Albert said nothing that you couldn't find out on your own.' Perry swivelled mischievously.

'Dr Perry, I took the liberty of showing the Whitlock images to Indigenous specialist Dale Spenser at Harrington's Auction House. He said he couldn't determine their authenticity without seeing the paintings in the flesh.'

'So?'

'So if he can't authenticate them, I doubt I can.'

'You can, Lissam.'

'I can't -'

'You can,' he persisted. 'You have scads more time than this Dale person has to find the answer. He needs to make decisions quickly, under commercial pressure and all that. You have the benefit of academia.'

I then attempted Plan B. 'Anyway, there's a conflict of interest,' I said.

'How so?'

'Noah Webster was working at Galerie Exotique at the time the certificates were signed. And now Noah Webster is my employer.'

'Noah Webster worked at Galerie Exotique…interesting,' he admitted. 'Hold on…didn't you say the certificates could be fake?'

'I happened upon some Galerie Exotique records at the gallery. The gallery copies of the certificates were in one of the files, which means the paintings – fake or genuine – did come from Galerie

Exotique. I shouldn't have seen these files, so I can't tell Noah that I've seen them. Or anyone for that matter.'

Perry was grinning. 'You think your employer may have orchestrated these fake Dorothy Browns. That's an extraordinary coincidence, wouldn't you say?'

'If they are fake,' I replied. 'Yes, it is a coincidence. I had no idea he worked for Miles Porter until this last Saturday.'

'An extraordinary coincidence,' he repeated. 'One could almost say that it is fate, Ms Lissam. Fate, I believe, has taken its hand here. Fate is taking you to the answer.'

'Or to a lawyer,' I replied. 'I signed a confidentiality agreement when I started working at the gallery.'

'But you don't have to use any information directly in your thesis. Just use the information as an informal guide. Sometimes research can take us to awkward places, but that's often where the treasure is buried. Just tread carefully on your way there.'

I must have looked pretty jaded by this stage. All my blue paint had definitely peeled off. And it was the first time that morning I realised I had a hangover.

'I know about the penalties that come with having principles, Lissam,' Perry said, leaning forward. 'Let me tell you why I left Whitlock.' He had my attention and knew it. Which was probably why he held back for a few Shakespearean seconds before continuing. 'The Vice-Chancellor of Whitlock, Reginald Hook, has a son called Christopher. Young Christopher happens to paint unconventional portraits of his friends.'

'Christopher Hook?' I saw his work while researching the National Portrait Gallery collection online (before my Perry-propelled Armageddon). Hook's paintings were usually of two people holding each other's naked body parts. A little odd, granted, but his cool colour tones were convincing. Never had sexuality looked more like a frozen dinner.

'Yes, Christopher Hook.' Perry let out a sigh. 'Anyway, little Christopher wanted to become a Trustee of the National Portrait Gallery. And with his daddy's help, he made it. During that time, he won all kinds of prestigious awards and major acquisitions. More than one of which happened to be through the NPG. A conflict of interest, if ever there was one. I'd had it with the London boys' club. So I dropped a hint about the NPG into the Charity Commission, who are now carrying out their investigation, as are the National Audit Office. It's created quite a stir and will be in the papers soon enough. I did my best to be anonymous, but Reginald was like a bloody dog with a bone and found me out.'

That was the clincher. Perry was hated by the National Portrait Gallery. No wonder he was less than impressed when I mentioned it at our first meeting. Perry moves London further away from me, not closer. Just my luck.

'And so that's why you left Whitlock?' I asked, unsure if I could be bothered continuing the conversation.

'Ol' Reggie couldn't sack me for that now, could he? But he threatened to soil my reputation on the basis of racism.'

'Racism?'

'A load of hoo-hah. I had challenged my students to a debate series. And the first was to argue that English culture is more valuable than Asian culture. One student had complained to the administration that I was anti-Asian. Another complained I was anti-multicultural. They completely missed the point, of course. Students are getting stupider by the second.' Perry had forgotten he was talking to one. 'But when Reginald found out about it,' he continued, 'and he was actively sniffing around for anything incriminating, that was that.'

'I don't remember reading about it when I…ah…researched you.'

'It's perfectly fine to research me, Lissam. Sensible, in fact. But the university didn't want bad press about a racist lecturer if they could help it. I was given a handsome payout, and it appears to all and sundry that I left of my own accord. Off the hook, as it were,' he chuckled to himself. 'To be honest, I was quite relieved to be shut of the place. It was getting dusty. Much more interesting things are going on out here.'

'In Australia?'

'In the desert.'

'The desert's pretty dusty, Dr Perry.'

'As I said, sometimes research can take us to awkward places, but that's often where the treasure is buried.'

'A proper research assistant is obviously required here to support your academic focus. Not me.'

'Can't afford one. Prescott's doing it tough, as you may recall from your retrenchment. Besides, you are by far the best student here. You have something the others don't.'

'I have? What's that?'

'Sharp learned instinct.'

'How do you know that when I haven't proven the Browns to be fakes?'

'Because it takes one to know one,' Perry smiled. 'I, too, have a sharp learned instinct, my dear. Plus, you know and care more about Dorothy Brown than you let on. And what if you are right about these paintings? Don't let the boys' club win, Lissam. Whoever they are.'

I looked at Perry, more unenthused than ever before.

'While you are contemplating, Lissam, you might want to know that a new Director is about to be announced at the NPG – just before the announcement about the Trust's conflict of interest. His name is Adam Buckley, who happens to be an old friend of mine. Not information the Trust is privy to, mind you. Adam thinks it's a cackle,' Perry snorted. 'The identities of Western Desert Aboriginal artists are so integrated with their country that a landscape may also be considered a portrait, can it not? Particularly paintings of landscapes with, say, their totem? I read somewhere that Aboriginal people don't *have* totems. They are their totems.'

London's National Portrait Gallery was back in the picture. And again, Perry knew it. Despite his yen for blundering tactlessness, the man was irritatingly adept at political one-upmanship. I considered my next move.

'If I am to continue with this thesis topic,' I said, 'I would like to request an additional supervisor. You said yourself that you can't pretend to be an expert on this subject. No offence intended, Dr Perry, but I need someone who is an expert.'

'Like Albert?' Perry giggled. The giggle was filled with mockery.

'Someone who is prepared to speak to me, who has academic qualifications as well as knowledge of Western Desert painting.'

'You need someone who is prepared to be open to your gift. I am.' At that, Perry's hands came down and rested on the desk. He leaned forward and said firmly, 'Consider yourself lucky, Lissam.'

'But -'

'Not a chance,' he interjected. 'If you're doing a PhD, we would, of course, consider it. However, this is not a PhD, and we have no funds to invest in an additional supervisor.'

'But -'

'You can do this, Lissam.' Perry wasn't saving his supervisor's ego from being damaged. It would take quite a blow to injure something so large.

'Professor Perry, Galerie Exotique is closed, Miles Porter is dead, Noah refuses to talk about anything Aboriginal,' I said, listing the brick walls on my fingers. 'Dale Spenser, Sydney's premier Indigenous art specialist, won't comment without seeing the paintings first-hand, and the paintings are in London.'

'That's a shame about Webster,' Perry sagged. 'But don't give up on him just yet. In the meantime, try Stumpy Downs again. Go back to the source.' My chest deflated like a jellyfish hitting dry sand. 'This is important,' Perry said with a surprising intensity. Breathing heavily, his face flushed and then paled. As his hand rose to his chest, he puffed, 'I'm fine.'

'I'll call the campus medical clinic,' I said, reaching for the phone.

Perry slapped his hand on top of mine. 'Don't. Please, I'm fine. Now go. We'll…we'll meet next week. Next Tuesday.' His breathing eased and colour returned to his face. 'Another thing. That little story about the Hooks stays in this room, Lissam. Understood?'

'Yes, Dr Perry.' I walked towards the door, then turned back. Wiping water from his eyes, Perry grinned from his desk and waved me on. 'Go forth and discover,' he yelled like a young mother on the first day of school. I walked down the corridor and stopped at Sharon's door to let her know of Perry's apparent condition.

'He won't talk to me about it,' I explained.

'He won't talk to me about it either,' Sharon said, while continuing to type.

'Is anyone using my office yet?'

Sharon shook her head and said, in her usual scattergun delivery, 'No nothing's changed there the computer still has your password.'

'Can I use it to make an interstate call? It's for my thesis. Perry wants me to call the Northern Territory.'

'Sure why not here's the keys,' Sharon said, pulling the keys out of a drawer, handing them over and fast resuming her typing.

It was odd being back, looking just how I left it. I warmed up the computer and found the number again. The phone rang out several times. I could anticipate Perry's response if I left my efforts at this. Besides, London's NPG was back in the game.

I rang the Alice Springs tourist bureau, which forwarded me to the Araluen Arts Centre, also in Alice Springs. I doubted I was going to dig up much information, but the assistant was helpful. She said there was a fire out at Stumpy Downs about a week ago.

'How bad was the fire?'

'Pretty devastating. Their art centre's gone. Everything inside went with it, including hundreds of paintings. They saved the houses around it, though,' she said.

'I'm not quite sure how this art centre fire started. The electronics aren't too flash around the settlements, so fires aren't that unusual. Sometimes the young blokes get drunk and start a fire for fun, although there's not supposed to be any alcohol at Stumpy. The community manages to keep the grog mostly at bay.'

'Was anyone hurt?'

'I don't think so.'

'That's a relief,' I said. 'When I call the art centre number, it still rings.'

'It's been diverted to the coordinator's home. It was supposed to be diverted to her mobile, but there was some technical glitch, which is irritating because she's now away a lot, levering for more money to set up again. Up to Darwin and down to Adelaide, talking to any government department that will listen.'

'Explains why I couldn't get through.'

'Distance, technology and bureaucracy. Our holy trinity of outback blockage.'

'Is Brenda Wood still around?'

'Who's Brenda Wood?'

'She used to be the art coordinator at Stumpy Downs in the nineties.'

'No, she's long gone. It's Helen now. Helen someone…they change quite a bit, you see. It's hard work in tough conditions. The pay's not that great. Not that there's anywhere to spend it,' she said.

'So not a great job then?'

'It can be, depends on what career move you're after. But if the art coordinator stays too long, they build all kinds of relationships both inside and out of the community. So that person can…how do I put this? They can become highly influential. It's easier for the community if the coordinators come and go.'

'Sounds like you've been around a while.'

'I was born here. But it's different in town to the settlements.'

'Do you go out to Stumpy Downs to visit?'

'Me? Not to Stumpy, but my uncle does sometimes. He runs cattle nearby. You need a permit through the Central Lands Council just to go there.'

'Is it easy to get a permit?'

'Unless they know you well, it can take months. It helps to know people.'

'How does your uncle run cattle in the desert?' I asked. 'What on earth do the cows eat out there?'

'Well, they eat pretty much whatever is on the earth.' The assistant laughed at my unintentional pun. 'It's not the Sahara. There is growth…spinifex. A lot of spinifex. I take it you haven't been here?'

'No, but I hope to someday.' *Maybe after London.* 'What about the historical documentation of the paintings at the Stumpy Downs art centre? Was it kept on a cloud?'

'No, the internet's terrible,' she replied. 'I heard it's all gone, too. Helen was trying to get archive funding before, and better internet. Not in time, unfortunately.'

'Was there much happening at the centre before the fire?'

'The women had an exhibition lined up in Adelaide, but that's now toast.'

'How is Dorothy?' I asked. 'Do you ever see her?'

'Nah, she pretty much keeps to herself. Doesn't talk to anyone much, except those at Stumpy. Others have tried – god, have they tried – but she won't crack.' The assistant laughed. 'On a day when she's feeling polite, Dorothy will pretend she's deaf. Otherwise, you'll just get the cold shoulder. At least that's what my uncle says.'

'And she's still not painting?'

'Nah, hasn't touched a brush in years.'

I pictured the destroyed art centre as a blackened shell and wondered what was left to ask. 'You've been very helpful, thank you.'

'All part of the service,' the assistant chirped. 'Good luck with the thesis. Pop across and visit sometime.'

'I'll try,' I replied, wondering what was left to see.


Hanging my head around Perry's doorway, I gave the news. 'Devastating fire at Stumpy Downs art centre three months ago. Everything destroyed, including all records.'

'A fire,' Perry pondered. 'The whole art centre gone, you say?'

'Yes,' I replied.

'Interesting,' he said, swivelling to stare out the window.

After sixty seconds of silence, I broke his meditation. 'Why is it interesting, Dr Perry?'

Perry swivelled back. 'Here's Prescott's chance to help the community. Come to their aid in the form of funding. We can't get any funding for ourselves, but project investment – private and public – for Indigenous cultural development is there for the taking. This could be it, Lissam.'

'It?'

'It,' he replied, staring out the window.


After two more unhelpful lectures, I made my way home. John had left a message on my mobile, one that was both hot and blue. I rang back, leaving a message attempting similar colours. Entering my dark apartment, I turned on the lamp and noticed that Liz's bedroom door was closed. It was only six-thirty. Deciding not to disturb, I sifted through the mail (take-away menus, real estate agent flyers and a letter from my mother who considered email unnatural). Walking into the kitchen to make a cup of tea, I read about how my father was fully recovered from the hip replacement, but kept insisting he wasn't. It seemed there was power in being disempowered. Mum was having none of it. Puddles from the pub had helped to raise almost seven hundred dollars for the Historical Society through a series of well-timed sausage sizzles over winter. Enclosed was a clipping from the local newspaper to prove it. I had no recollection of the Historical Society discussing or exhibiting anything about the original inhabitants of Nagurra. Would Puddles know anything? Country hotel owners were usually the best oral history sources, not local historical societies. But they were also the best secret keepers.

As the kettle began its rumble, I wandered back into the lounge and flopped onto the sofa just as Liz barged through the front door, blowing her nose as extravagantly as possible while trying to untangle herself from a knee-length apricot and electric blue jacket.

'Where have you been?' I asked. 'I thought you were in bed. You know you're not supposed to be out in your condi- '

'Shut up,' was the croaky reply. Apparently, during the day, Liz had lost the ability to speak completely. I was disappointed I had missed it. 'It's okay,' she said, her voice moving from croaky to husky. 'I went to the medical centre for a prescription. They don't make house calls anymore.' While Liz was rummaging through her 3.1 Phillip Lim handbag for legal drugs, her mobile rang. Looking at the screen as if it had sneezed, Liz decided to receive the call. 'Dad? Hi, this is a surprise...Yeah, I'm okay. Yourself?...Good... No....I didn't expec...I know that you've been busy. You've just caught *me*... Yes...I was on my way -'. Her voice rose in agitation. 'Just home to change…what?' Liz sat down and slowly moved her index finger up and down the bridge of her nose. 'Yeah, well, maybe we should. It's been a while since we've- ' She moved her hand from her nose and held her throat. 'Yeah...Listen...Dad, to be honest, I haven't been feeling-'. She looked up in the air. 'Really? That's great...yeah... okay....no, it's okay. I guess we can catch up sometime later. No big deal. Call me when you...Okay...whenever. Alright, bye.'

She hung up and looked at me. 'Wow, what a cack. The old man…shit...' she said with a half laugh.

'You're going to see him sometime?'

'Unlikely.' She stood and headed towards the bathroom. 'He really pisses me off sometimes, when I think of how he treated Mum.' The door closed while I watched, cup of tea forgotten. A few seconds later, the bathroom door opened again, but Liz didn't emerge. Instead, there was an odd thump.

'Liz?' As I leapt to my feet, Liz began crawling out of the bathroom with an expression of concentrated terror.

'What's wrong?' I asked, dropping to the floor. 'What do you need?'

Liz looked up, pale-faced and gasping for air. She leant forward and continued to stare at the floor, her shoulders pumping up and down. I grabbed her handbag and emptied the contents on the carpet. Purse, sunglasses, dog collar, sample sachet of Manuka honey, St Patrick's Day novelty condom (luck of the Irish), hotel room swipe card, plastic statuette of a dancing Shiva, goggles. The asthma puffer wasn't there.

'Your puffer, Liz? Where is it?'

Liz lifted a finger towards the bookshelves, then lay down completely. I spotted the puffer lying in front of *Zen And The Art of Motorcycle Maintenance*. After spending a millisecond wondering if John had read it, I sat Liz up and placed the puffer into her mouth, squeezing the little plastic and metal lung into motion while trying not to shake from fear. If Liz's life wasn't flashing before her, my imagination played it instead. I could have watched the sequel, as it seemed an eternity before Liz could utter a word.

'Hos..hos..pit..al,' was all she could muster.

'Ambulance,' I said, standing up with fake confidence.

Liz shook her downward head, croaked 'Cab,' and gasped. She was right, of course. Perhaps if the city traffic responded to wailing sirens, it would have been different. But taxis, fuelled and focused on their precious destinations, paid little heed to even authoritarian urgency. Better than rule-compliant Uber and faster than any overgrown virgin white ambulance could be. Except when the driver doesn't speak English.

'Homeboosh?'

'No, hospital,' I yelled over 'By The Rivers of Babylon' coming through the speakers.

'Liverpool?'

'No, *hospital.*' As my cheeks became redder, Liz's lips turned blue. 'Just go up this street here and turn left. Now!' I felt like pulling at his gold neck chain to restrict his air passages, purely as an interactive demonstration. Liz was leaning on my shoulder. Through a process of life-threatening experimentation, we discovered that lying down had made it harder for Liz to breathe. Still gasping, Liz turned paler by the second. The city lights flashed rudely onto her complexion. Her eyes were rolling upwards. Whether this was because she was becoming unconscious or because she was reacting to the driver's limitations was unclear.

'You tell me,' the driver said. He looked back at us and smiled.

'Just go! Go, go, *go.*'

'Okay.' He pushed the accelerator hard, flattening us against the back seat. At the end of the street, we discovered he had the same touch with braking. Liz rolled onto the floor, groaning, while I hung over the front seat. I moved back, strapped Liz in, and then climbed into the front.

'Left,' I ordered. The driver put on the right-hand indicator. I leaned over, flicked the indicator to the left and began to turn the steering wheel. 'Now go.' The driver nodded, delighted with the arrangement. I continued to steer and indicate while the driver peddled on command. Vehicles blocked as Liz's internal passageways constricted. I swore. Liz gasped. Speeding down the hospital entrance ramp, we almost collided with a parked Tesla in front. I fell back into my seat.

'Forty dollar.'

'Forty dollars? Are you kidding me?'

'Forty dollar,' he said, determinedly and thumped his fist on the steering wheel. The horn blew, and his safety air bag blew out. Liz started to crawl out of the vehicle.

'Here's twenty,' I yelled as I headed out to help Liz.

'Thirty! Thirty dollar!' the driver fought the bag and got out of the car to follow us into casualty, chanting his price until he became distracted by a vending machine. Once the nurse had Liz on the nebuliser, I collapsed into a chair. After a few minutes, I began to breathe more regularly myself. I stared at the wall opposite, where a framed poster of a tropical island hung. It was a little faded, and the yellow sand had become a little too yellow. The illusion had been lost. Meanwhile, our driver was attacking the vending machine with his fists. The nurse, who had seen it all before, returned to the desk to organise paperwork. A deadening aspect to saving life. I turned back to Liz, who was feeling her pockets for cigarettes.

# PART 3
# HEAT & COOLING

# CHAPTER 17

The next morning, Liz was sitting up in bed, her expression as serious as a judge with vertigo. She had lost her voice again the night before, though both lungs remained in reasonable working order.

'How are you feeling?' I asked her from her bedroom door. 'Sleep okay?'

'Yes,' she replied huskily. 'Hey, I can spea!' The rest of the word was mimed, but the lost letters waved from the scenic deck of her eyes. She started to climb out of bed.

'No moving about until you finish your sentences.' I said, before walking out. A squeaked noise in the shape of my name drew me back to the door.

Liz was still sitting up, looking ahead at nothing in particular. 'Thanks for la ni.'

'That's okay.' I turned away, but turned back again. It was worth a try. 'So you're going to stop smoking now?' An empty tissue box flew towards the doorway but fell short, landing at my feet.

On the way to the bus stop, green buds were forming on hedge-lined fences. Neighbourhood sparrows ceaselessly bounced around on the footpath. They looked happy, but they might have just been hungry. One started nibbling on a small piece of plastic. I walked past, making a mental note to carry organic trail mix.

While at the gallery, I toyed with the urge to call John. It would have been easy. Noah wasn't in, and visitors to the exhibition were lightly sprinkled. No buyers today so far. But then a middle-aged gent walked in and stood in front of an unsold Cusack. 'Good morning,' I said, gritting my teeth against the pain of my Italian shoes as I walked towards him. I noticed his clothes were 'carefully casual'. In other words, money was possible. The Merc key chain meant money was likely. 'Morning,' he said, still looking at the field. It was a field without the obvious threat of concrete, just wispy grass against a pale blue sky. Many visitors had commented on the charm of the work, but couldn't imagine living with it. The painting lacked tension.

'I noticed you walked directly to this one,' I said, angling my head at the wisps.

'It reminds me of home,' he replied.

'It does the same for the artist,' I nodded.

'Is the artist available to talk to?'

'Unfortunately, not at the moment she's in…' I was about to say Hong Kong, but came out with, '…Tasmania. Pastoral research for the next series. Doesn't answer her phone, very focused. So where's home for you?'

'It was…' he drifted off, staring at the painting, 'just like this.'

I joined him in his drifting as best I could. Ten whole seconds. Then asked, 'Would you like a price list?'

After selling the field – two hundred sweets for me – I realised I had left my lunch at home. Takeaway was in order, I reasoned, to celebrate another sale. Slipping out of my painful shoes into the sneakers, I slapped a 'Back in 10 mins' sign on the door, locked up and headed for the chicken wrap waiting for me at Sassa Café close by.

The day was warming. Prime weather for drinking a crisp white wine in a courtyard, I thought. But this was not my fate today. Plus, Sassa was out of wraps, and the chicken baguette would be more fattening. Not a great time to put on weight, with new clothes and new… I negotiated a middle ground: a multigrain salad roll and black coffee. Returning with my lunch, I pulled out my keys. Then noticed the gallery was already open.

Robert was sitting in the client's chair at my desk, flipping through an art magazine while sipping on a takeaway latte. Robert's greeting was less Cornish pasty, more Mardi Gras float.

'I was in the area. Thought I'd drop by, see how you're settling in.'

'Noah's not here?'

'No, not sure where he is.'

'Did you have a nice weekend away?' I asked.

'Delightful,' he beamed. 'Coming back to this warm weather is even better. Aren't you just loving it?'

'Oh yes,' I agreed, settling into my chair and slipping back into the Italian shoes. Some softening had begun. I moved to put the roll in my desk drawer for eating discreetly later, but Robert intercepted.

'No, don't let me stop you from your lunch. I just had mine.'

'But I probably shouldn't be eating at the front desk.'

'No one's here,' Robert whispered. 'I won't tell.'

I munched while Robert explained to me his line of work. 'The jack-of-all-trades-master-of-none variety,' he replied. 'Management consultant,' he added by way of explanation.

'You're multi-skilled, then?' I asked.

Robert raised his eyebrows. 'Suppose so. One must be to survive these days.'

'Being a management consultant requires some creativity, doesn't it?'

'Creativity?' he asked. 'It depends. I may create opportunities, but I don't create like Ms Cusack or the masterful John Roebelling.' Robert pursed his lips in amusement before asking, 'Is Mr Rosebelling still being masterful?'

'Indeed, he is,' I grinned before shyly burrowing my nose into my coffee.

'Wonderful,' he enthused before glancing at his watch. 'Ooops, got to dash.' After giving me a hug, he bent into a whisper, 'About John, couldn't happen to a nicer gallery hostess.'

'Gallery hostess,' I laughed. 'Sounds quaint, but I think I like it.'

'Perhaps I should become a match-making master, set up a shop called "The Hook-Up Hang-Out" or maybe "Aphrodite's Aphrodisiac"?'

'Maybe,' I grinned. 'How about "Just the Three of Us?"'

'That's it,' he clicked his fingers.

'If you speak with Noah, let him know we sold another Cusack this morning.'

Robert's eyebrows raised, 'Excellent work, Hostess. Which one?'

'Wispy field,' I said, pointing to the new red dot.

'A triumphant sale. Noah and I had doubts that one would move,' he said, before gasping at his watch. 'Best dash.' Instead of running out the door, he bowed with theatrical flair and strode out into the street. It was easy to hear the make-believe bugles, the cheers and the flapping of flags that followed him. Never had a jack-of-all-trades looked so extraordinary.

As I gazed through the front window while talking to the caterer about appetisers for the next opening, I noticed a short man with grey hair making his way towards the gallery. 'But don't we normally have the standard antipasto platters? The Brie rounds, caper berries, stuffed olives, that kind of thing?' I asked, recalling the Cusack opening. 'American caviar? No, I don't think so,' I replied. Say yes to caviar, then landslide to truffled quail foie gras.

A man walked in. I held up my hand, indicating I was on the phone but would be with him in shortly. It's amazing how sign language pares down to one simple gesture everyone understands. Well, almost everyone. The man waved and promptly walked out of the gallery.

He had looked Chinese. I could sometimes distinguish a Japanese from a Chinese person. Whether he was Chinese from China, Taiwan, Korea, Malaysia or Singapore, I was a poor judge. He was possibly sixty years of age, unless he was one of those people who did tai chi at Centennial Park, in which case he was likely to be one hundred and seventy.

'Buffalo's balls? You're kidding, right?' The caterer then clarified the suggestion, but not without the sneer that belonged only to chefs. 'Oh, *mozzarella* buffalo balls. Sure, add those to the platters.'

After hanging up, I noticed the man was standing outside. 'Can I help you?' I asked from the doorway.

'Good afternoon,' the man said, slight accent only. Accent of Cantonese or Mandarin, I wouldn't know.

'Would you like to come inside?'

The man had the polite but focused gaze of a hypnotherapist. 'I'm Huojin Cheng. My grandson, Ho Wei Huojin, is an artist.' Here we go, I thought. Another pitch for an exhibition. Still, getting your grandfather to do it was a novel approach.

'Ho Wei Huojin?' I asked. 'I'm not familiar with the name.'

'Not Ho Wei,' the old man corrected. 'Howie as in Howard.' He made a concerted effort with sounding the 'd'. 'It would be best if Howie did not exhibit here.'

'Hold on, you *don't* want your grandson's work exhibited here? That's…unusual.' And then it hit me. The embarrassingly bad paintings for the clubs, shameful for the family. Of all generations. 'Are Howard's subjects people holding flowers painted with glow-in-the-dark paint?'

Mr Huojin appeared shocked and shook his head. 'No, nothing like that. I just came to say Howie has done some bad things to be exhibited here. It's not right and has to end. I've told Howie, and now I must tell you.'

The phone rang inside. It was probably the caterer, wanting to push some Moreton Bay bugs. 'Bad things? Please come inside,' I urged. 'We can talk about this.'

'No, thank you.' The grandfather's voice was so quiet it sounded like a breeze wrapped in newspaper. At that moment, a burly, thickset man forced his way down the street towards us. Nothing was stopping him. It was just the way he moved. His head was shaved bald, and he wore a tight black t-shirt with purple leather pants. Despite the pants, he looked like the kind of guy who uses people for scales to stand on in order to measure his own weight.

Mr Huojin had already made off in the opposite direction. His orderly movements left the powerful impression that tai chi was indeed part of the old man's program. While the purple-panted man was moving less fluidly, he was picking up speed towards the gallery. I made my way inside to grab the phone before it rang out. The caller hung up just as I answered. Puffing a little from the strain of my heels, I shrieked when I saw the purple pants right behind me. As awful as they were, it was easier to look at them than at the face of fury towering above them, symbolised by the large tattooed cross on his Adam's apple.

'Noah,' the man demanded, his presence like landfill.

I moved around to my side of the desk, bunkered by its flimsy laminated chipboard and bone-thin chrome legs. 'Sorry, he's not in at the moment.' The purple pants appeared unsatisfied. I offered to try Noah on the mobile. Fumbling with the handset, I dialled, but I knew it was useless. Using my phone, I texted him but no response. 'Sorry. Can I help you at all?'

The man's plump knuckles landed on my desk, holding his massive volume while leaning across. His breath smelled of chicken pesto. I spotted some green souvenirs between his yellowed teeth. Definitely pesto.

'Noah is supposed to be here,' he said.

'Perhaps I can be of assistance?'

The man shook his head and laughed in an irritated manner. 'Well, Miss-Of-Assistance, I'm upset.' He squeezed into the chair opposite me and glared. My mind scrambled through the options of what to do. At least that was what I hoped it was doing, being too paralysed by fear to tell. He spoke again, breaking the ice with a large pick. 'My name is Kevin. I'm a sculptor. Does that mean anything to you? I think it should.' I now understood why Noah took on this guy's work. He had been handcuffed by Kevin's teeth.

'You are Robert's friend,' I nodded, wondering if this man was capable of such a role with anyone. 'You'll be exhibiting your sculpture with us next week. I'm looking forward to seeing your work.'

'Well, I'm glad you are, sweet pea. Noah has promised to come to the studio three times in the last two weeks. Take a guess how many times he showed.'

I took a deep breath before answering the obvious. 'None?'

'Bingo!' Kevin laughed again without merriment.

'He's been particularly busy at the moment.'

'Gathering interest in my show, I hope,' he said. 'Noah said he needed twenty pieces and I only have twelve. I was holding back production for his guidance, but...' At that point, Kevin looked like his rage may turn to tears.

'I'll try him on the mobile again,' I said, hitting redial. Miraculously, Noah picked up. 'Noah, I have Kevin here.'

'Oh boy.'

'Are you on your way to the gallery?'

'I can't, I'm stuck here trying to... Tell him to see me next Wednesday.'

'That's the day before his opening.' I looked across at Kevin, who was still leaning towards me, unintentionally impersonating one of his sculptures.

'Tell him I'm trying to sell his work internationally. Kevin will like that.'

'Ah, Kevin,' I said. 'Noah just informed me he's currently trying to sell your work internationally.'

It didn't seem to please him. 'I only have twelve pieces for the show,' he replied, his voice now flexing into a whine.

I returned to the phone. 'Kevin only has twelve pieces for the show.'

'He promised at least twenty.'

'He was waiting for your visit to the studio.'

'It's too late now, even if I visited the garage today,' Noah muttered.

'Studio, you mean? Kevin's studio?' I asked.

'His studio is in his garage. Kevin's a mechanic. Just as well he has a second income. Okay, we need another artist to exhibit with him. Someone with work ready, who doesn't mind not having any lead-up publicity…'

'How about John Roebelling?' I asked. It was worth a shot.

'Can't see the eggs or the shopping centre pieces matching up with the sculpture,' Noah replied with a laugh, but the laugh had the edge of rising hysteria. 'And it's important that Kevin feels happy with whoever he's exhibiting with.' Then it was my turn to laugh. I looked across at Kevin, whose facial expression was now the Mona Lisa with constipation. 'The battery's going, I'm on another call, and I'm just about to drive under the bridge.' Noah's voice went dead. Turning back to Kevin, I felt a moment of truth was near and wished it didn't have to come from me.

'He's stuck. Some accident happened and it's blocking traffic. I'm so sorry.' Kevin sat, vibrating quietly with rage. 'We need another artist to complement your exhibition and fill the gap. Any suggestions?'

Kevin stopped shaking for a moment. He rose and leaned on the desk as he had done before. 'Tell Noah I'll be seeking personal contact with him,' he whispered. 'No mobiles out of range, no cheques in the e-mail. Next time we make contact, it will be in the flesh, so to speak.' He turned, pushing his way out of the gallery and onto the street. I sat alone, listening to the faint ticking of metal cooling.

# CHAPTER 18

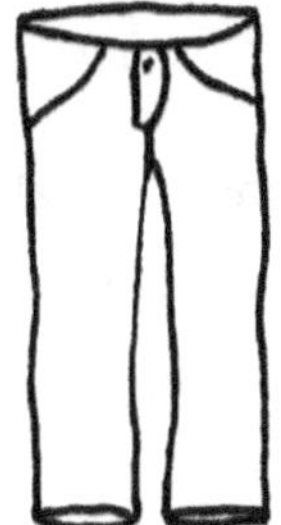

'I've just had a scary artist in the gallery.'

'We're not scary, Anna, just over-sensitive,' he replied over the phone.

'Seriously, John. This guy really freaked me out. He was like a tall Hannibal, with pants.'

'Hannibal, the yabbie?' John asked.

'It was Kevin Bradley. Know him? He has a cross tattooed on his throat, but the symbolism seems to have escaped him.'

'What happened? I'm coming over right now.' His response was more than I expected.

'Thanks so much, but he's left. I'm fine now, just…processing,' I said. But was I fine? My feet were still dying a slow and torturous death in the new shoes.

'Kevin Bradley,' John repeated. 'Doesn't ring a bell, should it?'

'No, I don't think anyone knows him. Which is okay. Noah is known for his unknowns. But it seems like this exhibition is a favour, which is a shame. His work isn't bad. Well, it looks okay from the one photo that I've seen. Anyway, he was pissed off because Noah was supposed to visit his studio ages ago. Noah didn't get around to it. Kevin's held off on some work because he wanted to discuss it with Noah, and now we're short on pieces for what was supposed to be a solo exhibition. Kevin's furious, and I was the bunny sitting behind the desk,' I said. Feeling calmer, I added, 'I'm sure his bark is worse than his pants.'

'Pants?'

'Purple,' I said. 'The thing is, Noah needs a second artist from the show. I mentioned your name, but he doesn't think that it matches up with the style of Kevin's work.'

'Thanks for trying.'

Then I got an idea. It was genius. 'Are you at the studio?' I asked. 'Can you open up the gallery website?'

'Yeah, sure.' There was the tapping of keys, then 'Okay, I see the Bradley image. Yeah, not bad...'

'Imagine three Roebelling digital prints. One in each gallery room opposite the Bradley sculptures.'

'But Noah said the shopping centre ones won't fit with the sculpture,' John replied.

'Garage images. A new series, with mechanics, a receptionist turning away from a supplier maybe. A client...a woman...with a child...the woman's arguing with the mechanic, or something like that.' Once out of my mouth, I realised the idea was insane. 'Sorry, bad idea. Rush your work to save the arse of an artist who's an arsehole.'

'Picasso was an arsehole,' he said.

'Kevin's not Picasso.'

'I see here on the site that the show starts next Thursday, Anna. That's like no time.'

'Madness,' I replied, waving at the air. 'Forget I said anything.'

'Wait,' he said. I sat on the phone listening to John thinking. And thinking. 'It could work,' he said. 'Juxtaposition of blokes working in metal, Candy as a female client, and the gentle freeze-frame thing could bring about some nice tension.' Then John halted his musings. 'We'll need a garage.'

'Kevin might let us use his garage. Noah says he's a mechanic. Kevin's business gets some free exposure. A win-win for Kevin.'

'Yeah, maybe,' John pondered. 'There is one problem. I'm no longer considered a curious guinea pig by the guys at the tech park. They'll start charging.'

'Maybe I could try to get Noah to rustle up some money as a kind of sponsor. Sales have been good lately.' I could feel blood pumping through my body. Except to my feet.

'Okay, bun buster,' he said. 'I'll do some concept sketches now and email them to you. I'll chase the printer for costs and send through proposed artist prices. Show Noah, and if he approves them today, we'll give it a shot.'

'Snap,' I said, high on adrenal buzz.

'This is nuts.' John's laugh was without a hint of hysteria.

'You're right,' I quickly sobered. 'Let's forget it.'

'Too late. I can see the work. It's as clear as day.'

'I don't want you to contort yourself for a purple-panted moron on a crazy deadline.'

'I can feel that mojo rising....'

There was some rustling in the background. 'What are you doing?'

'The concept drawings. Pretty basic, but it's all coming out. Artists can inspire each other, this is what this is.'

'Don't do it, John. Or at least do it in your own time.'

'All.....is.....coolio,' he said slowly as he drew. 'I won't be able to.....convert the images.....to faux printing dots.......due to said.....insane......timeframe.'

'Another reason we shouldn't be doing this. Your work is already being compromised.'

'Noooo….it…is…..fine.' John was obviously still drawing.

'Sacrificing molecules for a deadline? Not fine, John.'

There was a pause on the phone. Eventually, he asked, 'Can we call my exhibition *Molecules*?'

'Ah, sure,' I said.

'If Noah goes for it, that is. These sketches are wild. I'll scan these babies and send them across to you.'

'Okay,' I said, resigned. Noah probably won't go for it anyway.

'Speak soon.' He said, hanging up.

I was about to ring Noah, urging him to come to the gallery by the close of business. And to let him know the coast was clear, that Kevin had left. But calling was probably futile, so I texted instead. A reply came through almost immediately, saying he was on his way and would be there soon. The speed of communication was historic.

Then I remembered Huojin Cheng and carried out a quick search for his grandson, Howard, through the files on the computer. Nothing came up. So I searched through the artist manila files in Jan's filing cabinet, but no artist file with his name was found. Going online, I typed in Howard Huojin. No matches. Howie Huojin, again with no results. I then searched Huojin+Cheng, in case the grandfather was the Master, guiding his grandson in the way of art. A site about a famous explosives engineer from Beijing topped the list. I looked hard at the old black and white photo of a young, well-dressed man in a suit and glasses calmly sitting at a lab table, about to light an explosive fuse. He didn't look like the man I had just met, but it was hard to say for sure, and the text referred to Cheng Huojin. Not Huojin Cheng. When clicking into the white pages, no 'Huojin' appeared in the New South Wales listings.

'Everything in its rightful place when you arrived today, Anna?' Noah asked as he walked into the gallery. Reality hit me like a bucket of bricks. Did he know about us breaking into the office? I could feel my face flush and a thick band of guilt tightening around my throat.

'Yes,' I stammered, 'I believe so. Why?'

'Well, with Robert holding fort for you, anything was possible.' A flicker of a grin ran across his face.

'Oh right,' I smiled, feeling as honourable as a rhino with diarrhoea.

'Jan called,' he said, reading my mind. 'She's having a great time. And she reminded me that the cupboard key was with her gallery keys, which are in my office. I'll just get them before I forget that too.'

'Noah, I need to talk with you about Kevin's show,' I said, calling out after him.

'Yes, we must find that second artist,' Noah yelled as he disappeared.

'Well, think I have a solution,' I said when he returned to my desk, passing over the cupboard key. I took it, feeling beetroot shame, then turned to check my emails. Nothing had come through from John yet. 'But, first, on a different matter,' I said, 'A Mr Huojin Cheng visited today. He said his grandson, Howie Huojin, exhibits here, or is going to, though I haven't seen a file.'

'Howie Who?' Noah asked.

'Howie Huojin's the artist. Grandfather Huojin requested not to exhibit Howie's work in this gallery as it is causing trouble for him. His grandson, that is. Odd message, I know. He didn't want to talk further about it, just took off down the road.'

'This guy must have the galleries mixed up,' Noah ruminated. 'Never heard of either of them.' He shrugged. 'This sort of thing happens from time to time, having so many galleries on one strip. People get confused. Now,' Noah clapped his hands together, 'Kevin Bradley's new dancing partner.'

I held up my finger while checking the inbox again. John sent through three concept drawings. 'Just let me print these out.' Considering the timeframe, the drawings were extraordinarily detailed and depicted clearly how each image was going to look. One drawing had a worried female client, with a distracted child, talking with a mechanic. Another depicted the receptionist about to answer the phone in the office to one side of the frame and a mechanic under a car on the other side, each in their own world. The third continued the theme of the mechanic absorbed in his work while a supplier nearby was laughing with a young male assistant. The beauty and tension in each work were already apparent. 'One Roebelling print in each gallery, each taking up almost the entire wall,' I explained, handing over the printouts. 'Kevin's sculptures are opposite, viewed against a white wall.'

'These are incredible,' Noah nodded, shuffling from one page to the next.

'The timeframe's pretty tight, of course,' I warned. 'These are brand new works.'

'But John thinks he can do it?'

'Unfortunately, there isn't time to convert the photographs to faux printing dots.'

'But John's okay with that?'

'Yes, as long as we call his exhibition *Molecules*.'

'He can call it dog's bollocks if he wants to. But we have one problem.'

Here's the snag. 'What's that?' I asked.

'These images…their dimensions, let alone the subject matter…will be so prominent it would make Kevin's work look like the second exhibition.'

'That is a sticky one,' I agreed. 'Maybe there's another artist we could try instead, who already has -' I began to suggest, feeling the blisters on my feet.

'Let's just show these to Kevin, see what he says,' Noah said, staring at the sketches. 'We can email them through.'

'You really need to go to his studio. Kevin's demanding a face-to-face.'

'Okay, it's closing time now,' he said, looking at his watch. 'You're coming with me. I'm not visiting that lunatic on my own.'

'Okay,' I said. 'But there's one other thing.'

'What's that?'

'John needs extra funds in order to pay for the prints. The R&D period is over. The printer is charging more now. And the fast turnaround costs even more.'

'How much?'

I read through the email message. 'He says here that they will be three thousand each just to print onto archival quality paper at these dimensions.'

Noah started rubbing his forehead. 'It's a bit of a stretch for me right now.' I stared at the EFTPOS machine, contemplating all our recent transactions combined. Nothing made sense anymore. 'Frank,' he said, smiling. 'Frank could sponsor the show.'

'The car guy from Michigan?'

'It's $9,000. Doable for him, I guess. It's under six grand US'

'My thoughts exactly.'

'It's worth a try,' Noah said, switching off the gallery lights. 'Let's see what Kevin has to say first.' I grabbed my bag from the back, switched on the alarm and followed Noah out onto the street.

The air was cooling, and the day's light was almost gone by the time Noah's Audi reached Kevin's garage. We had travelled twenty minutes south to Heffron, a suburb I'd never heard of. Noah pulled up to an old shed with a rusted sign promoting 'General Service & Panel-Beating'. The neighbouring shops (shoemaker, dry cleaner and chiropractor) were closed, dark and quiet. A beam of light shone around the partly open door to the garage. Walking in, I could smell a blend of motor oil and curry. The remnants of Kevin's lunch lay in a takeaway container at my feet. Scrap metal lined the walls. Piles of damaged mufflers and bumper bars lay on the concrete floor like old furniture. Dusty bands of fluorescent light from above revealed the place for what it was, warts and all. Six sculptures stood in the middle of the space in various stages of completion. Kevin moved out from behind one of his larger pieces at the back. He had replaced the purple pants with a mechanic's blue jumpsuit covered in black grease stains. Kevin squinted hard at us through his welding goggles.

'Noah, you came,' he said, dropping the welder and whipping off his goggles. Kevin's sprint across the room, deftly missing piles of debris, was like watching Godzilla playing hopscotch. When he made it, Noah 's suit copped an oily hug.

'I heard you were upset, quite rightly,' Noah said, untangling himself and staggering back into a pile of fan belts. 'I've come to apologise and make it up to you.'

'Apology accepted,' Kevin replied, beaming from ear to ear.

'These look great,' Noah said as he wandered further to the back where the finished pieces stood. They were all different heights and forms. Two were a wave similar to the image in the invitation, one curved almost to a circle, and three had different bits of metal weaving into others. I could see Noah's relief with the standard and variety better than expected.

'We think we've found a solution to your quantity problem,' Noah said.

'Really? That's wonderful,' the artist smiled back at us. I stood by, wondering how many personalities Kevin had and how often they changed batons.

'Remember, this is still your show. The invitation has only your work promoted.'

'Right,' Kevin nodded.

'There's a dynamic new Sydney artist called John Roebelling,' Noah began. 'He is planning some large digital photographic prints of people in a garage, much like this one.' (Exactly this one) 'It's kind of a freeze-frame effect. Here are some sketches John has emailed us, works in progress.' Noah handed over the printouts. 'There are three prints, quite large, about twelve by three metres. One for each gallery room. We will place your work near the white walls opposite each of the prints. The exhibition will be a conversation between reality and abstraction, and between two and three dimensions. What do you think?'

We watched Kevin pore over the pages. I had also printed out one of the shopping centre images to give Kevin an idea of the quality and feeling of the end product.

'John is open to using your garage as the site for his work,' I added, 'giving the show a collaborative feel, and your garage some free publicity. If that offer is attractive to you.'

Kevin said nothing as he held each page up, then looked across at Noah. Noah's hands rose in surrender pose, 'It's still your show though, Kev. First billing.'

'Kevin,' he corrected.

'Kevin,' Noah repeated.

'Okay.'

'Okay?' Noah replied, disbelieving.

'Yes, I can see the relationship. The juxtaposition will be harmonious. Thank you for your considered solution. John has my permission to use the garage for the location if he wishes. I'll be closing it for the next few days anyway, so I can prepare for the show.' Noah received another embrace from Kevin. Noah seemed to even hug him back for a moment before stumbling over a piece of corrugated iron and falling flat into a pile of headlights. Kevin and I helped him up and towards the door. With blackened suit and bruised shin, Noah winked at me while Kevin hauled him over the threshold.

While the Audi sped towards my Surry Hills apartment, Noah called Frank via the dashboard monitor. It was good timing. Frank had just finished scuba diving in the Barrier Reef. The American seemed to have more to say about the poor mechanics of the boat than about the colours of tropical fish. Noah eventually steered him towards the subject of art. Frank liked the idea of sponsoring the show. 'Okay, here's an opportunity to teach Australians about philanthropy,' I could hear Frank yelling through Noah's mobile. 'You guys are crap at it. America is so public-spirited, you wouldn't believe it.' But Frank wanted to see the sketches before making a final decision.

'I'll email them to you first thing tonight.'

'Tomorrow I've got some butterfly park tour thing, but that's scheduled for lunchtime. Hope we're not supposed to eat the critters. Don't really get off on bush tucker, if you know what I mean,' Frank ended with a long chortle.

'Thanks, Frank,' Noah replied.

'Love ya, Noah.'

With the end of the call, Noah turned to me and smiled. 'Anna Lissam: Fastest curator in the west.'

'In the east,' I corrected before noticing something in the corner of my eye. 'Watch out!'

Noah swerved the car, missing a meandering possum by seconds, but had us heading straight for a speed hump sign. I gripped onto my seat belt as Noah braked hard and swung the car back into the lane, which flew us over the speed hump, narrowly missing an oncoming Range Rover.

'Jesus mother of god, that was close,' he said under his breath. 'Body repairs on this baby cost a fortune. Still, after tonight, ol' Kev would have done me a deal.' Noah's phone rang through the dashboard monitor. It was Robert. 'We just saw your mate, Kevin,' he said. 'Yes, I know. But better late than never, right? So what are you cooking me for dinner?' As Noah discussed the dubious pleasure quotient of lettuce soup, I kept my eyes peeled to the road. One of us had to.

# CHAPTER 19

The apartment was empty. There was no note. Or maybe the dressing gown on the floor was the note. I flopped on the couch and prised my heels off, knowing I should take Simon's advice and walk around the apartment in them with socks. But I was exhausted, and the rest of the week didn't look like letting up. On the way home, Noah had already talked me into missing lectures the next day. My mission was to promote John's last-minute exhibition. While driving, Noah risked our lives further by texting John about the project (green light on all fronts of the project, assuming Frank signs on the dotted line tomorrow) and included Kevin's garage address. Already seeing a range of ways Kevin could disrupt John's shoot, I hoped John knew how to use a crowbar.

'It's time to paint the town,' Noah announced the next day. 'The monthly glossies already received Kevin's information before Jan left, too late for John. So now we're down to the weekly and daily media. And social media, of course. John's photography would be great for that.'

'Social media?' I asked.

'Yes, Facebook, Instagram, Twitter and all that stuff. Jan and I knew nothing about it, being aged. Fortunately, we now have you on board.'

'Me?'

'Yes, social media is a second language for people your age, isn't it?' It wasn't. I just wasn't a poking, liking, tweeting, pinning kinda gal. Noah was gobsmacked.

'But I'll give it my best shot,' I offered. 'Can't be too hard.'

Noah's relief was palpable. 'And we need to send out another e-news to our list about John. You know MailChimp, don't you?'

'MailChimp?'

Frank approved the sponsorship deal prior to the butterfly tour, agreeing to the full amount. 'In fact, he's emailing you the company logo so we can plaster Sydney with it on his behalf.' Noah disappeared into his office while I called John with the good news. He was already at Kevin's garage and couldn't talk for long.

'Just quickly, do you know social media – Facebook, Twitter and stuff like that?'

'Sure, I hop on from time to time.'

'I know you have no time at all, but if you could tell your followers and likers about *Molecules* and the sponsorship deal.'

'I'll try. And I'll tell everyone here to do it too.'

'Great. Don't work too hard.'

'Ha ha,' he said. 'Hey Jason, that's not going to work there, mate – could you shift it…yeah…no, over there…closer….'

'I'll let you go.'

'Sorry, Anna…yeah…okay, bye.'

My shoes rubbed when I headed for the kitchen for a caffeine booster. I figured Noah could use one, too. Holding a cup in each hand like floaties, I worked my way, step by painful step, towards his office. My shoes rubbed back to raw, half-repaired blisters, and I let out an involuntary groan. Noah paused from a telephone conversation and yelled, 'Are you alright, Anna?'

'Yes, fine. Thanks,' I yelled a little too loudly as I bent over to inspect the damage. 'Sorry to disturb,' I said, appearing as if I was apologising to my feet.

The front desk telephone rang. 'Bugger,' I said, holding the mugs as steadily as possible and groaning quietly all the way to the front. A young gothic couple dressed entirely in black had arrived while I was in the kitchen. They wandered out from a blind spot around the corner, possibly curious who was walking so loudly. I only had eyes for their footwear, black Doc Martens.

'Very sensible shoes,' I said to them, placing the mugs on the desk and reaching to pick up the phone. 'Fashion need not be about self-inflicted pain.' It was only then that I noticed their abundant adornment of piercings and tattoos. The couple nodded in agreement and continued to walk about the fields.

The phone stopped ringing just as I was about to answer. 'You've got to be kidding.' I made my way back to Noah's office, mug in hand, grunting in whispered tones. He was talking on the phone, so I lightly knocked on the partly open door and crept in. The office looked the same as when Liz and I had found it two days before. A space had to be cleared amongst the disarray of papers before placing the cup down on the desk. Noah gave me the thumbs up, and I crept out again.

Attempting the gallery hostess persona, I asked the sure-footed couple if they needed any help. They shook their heads and mumbled 'fine'.

'Excellent,' I breathed before heading back to the desk. The visitors soon made their way to the front door exit. 'Enjoyed the exhibition?' I asked. Addressing the question involved leaning over to hook eye contact and give a best-in-show pasty smile. The woman turned and nodded glumly before following the man who was already shuffling out the door. It was too late to fold up the Kevin invitation like a paper plane and fly it in their direction, so I resumed my promotional tasks in the world of digital banter. Noah and I had realised earlier that day that not having any images to promote John's exhibition might be a problem.

'We'll have to use the sketches and past work as tasters,' Noah shrugged, 'like we did for Kevin.'

'Or we could promote it as a mystery thing, a real opening,' I suggested.

'What do you mean?'

'Deliberately not showing any images of the work until the opening. A true unveiling. No one, not even the most pivotal critics, will see the work until the day of the opening.'

'But who would care?' Noah asked. 'No one's heard of him.'

'That's true, but we use words rather than images. And we beat it up as if they should've heard of him already.'

'Which words should we use?'

He had me there. And then it came to me. 'I know of a good freelance copywriter who could help us with some headlines to hook interest.'

'Okay.' Noah sucked air through his teeth. 'But I can't pay through the nose for this.' He clicked his fingers. 'We'll give him free exposure through the campaign. Won't have to pay a cent.'

I remembered seeing a video of a guy asking for free service from a cafe, personal trainer, architect, picture framer and others on the premise of "If I like it, I'll tell other people and might come back and pay next time. It's great exposure, but I'll also own your intellectual property," All interviewed just laughed in his face. The point was, for creatives, this very situation never seems to end.

'Ben's just freelance. He won't be charging the big firm fees. But we must pay him properly.'

'Okay, check him out.'

I rang John again. 'Good news,' I blurted before he even had time to answer. 'I have a writing opportunity for Ben.'

'You do? That's *brilliant*.'

'Is this John?'

'No, it's Ben. John's taking shots. I'm his right-hand man on set.'

'You're my best boy,' John yelled from the background.

'I'm helping the guy for free, and he insists on calling me his best boy. One more time and I'm- '

'BEST BOY!' was yelled from the background by the entire crew from the sound of it. I explained the campaign concept to Ben. And the urgency.

'You mean I have to leave here right away to work on an art exhibition campaign for the prestigious Noah Webster Gallery?'

'We may be prestigious, but we don't have a huge budget for copywriting. We can pay you, of course,' I explained. It was awkward.

'You're a special friend of John's, so let's not worry about money. Maybe some exposure -'

'You will be paid whatever you usually charge. And you will have exposure.' If all else fails, I figured I could supplement what Noah was prepared to spend through my sweets.

'Wow, thanks,' he replied. 'I'll be there as fast as my 1992 Nissan can carry me.'

While Ben made his way, I watched some short online social media tutorials and managed to create a LinkedIn profile, a Twitter account and a Facebook page for the gallery. Somewhere in between creating an Instagram profile and a Pinterest account, I got a text from Ben saying he had an idea and would be a little late.

It was close to two hours before a tall guy wearing black, classic-framed glasses, jeans and sweatshirt (green Crumpler messenger bag slung across his body) walked through the door. His smile was his nametag.

'Ben.'

'Anna? Hi. Just letting you know, we're doing a promotional video for John.'

'We are?'

'Thirty seconds. Short but very sweet.' During the drive, Ben had moved up from best boy to director. 'We can upload it on Vimeo…I guess we should do YouTube too…then feed it through all your online profiles. I'll show you what we've done. It's why I'm late, I was creating it on site.' Ben pulled out his laptop and began warming it up.

'Like a coffee?' I asked.

'Have any herbal tea? Peppermint?'

'I think we only have black tea, Liptons.'

'Don't worry, I think I have…' he fumbled in his Crumpler, 'yes, here you go.' He handed me a box of peppermint tea, organic. 'Try some. It's soothing and excellent for digestion.' He then turned back to his screen and started typing in his password.

Throwing off the shoes, I went to the kitchen and tested out the tea before committing (not bad). I asked Noah if he wanted some. 'Sure,' he replied, distracted by his computer. I dropped his off on the way through to the front, where Ben was still tapping away.

'Okay, here's one approach we could take,' Ben said, clicking on a button and showing me his screen.

'Hey, this is herbal tea,' Noah said, striding out of his office with a perplexed expression. He stopped when the screen caught his eye. *What does it take to make art?* appeared, along with the sound of people chatter. And then filmed snippets – close up, black and white – were played from what was obviously John's team of people at Kevin's garage. Hands handling lighting equipment, then feet moving around on broken up asphalt, Kevin laughing (he was supposed to be working on his sculptures). *It can take a group of special people* moved through and over Candy's head while she talks to someone out of frame, then John calling out 'best boy' and laughing, someone's hands working on a car engine. *And half-decent equipment helps.* A guy I didn't recognise was talking on his phone, saying 'Yeah, you can see it on my page…', then we saw John taking photos while saying 'We're calling the exhibition molecules.' Then you hear a murmur from someone off camera. *Why molecules?* appears around John's ears. John lowers the camera and says, 'I'll tell you when you come to the exhibition'. John fades to text on dark grey again:

*Most of all, for art to be art, it needs you to come and see it.*
*(New frame):*
***Molecules***
*New Work by John Roebelling, photographer*
*(New frame):*
*Exhibition Opening: Thursday 13th @ 6pm*
*www.NoahWebsterGallery.com.au*
*Video by Ben Mitchum (appearing in subtle mid-tone grey)*

'Amazing,' Noah said, taking a swig of his tea without thinking.

'You did that in the last two hours?' I asked, 'That's incredible.'

Ben looked suitably humbled and rather pleased. 'John thinks it's okay.'

'I like the end,' I said. 'It's like that Ansel Adams quote. What is it?'

Noah remembered it. 'There are always two people in every picture. The photographer and the viewer.'

'That's it. And you can't appreciate it online, not John's work anyway. You have to come and see it,' I said. 'And this video takes the idea to a new level. Involving a group to make art. And the quality is top end, Ben,' I pointed out.

'I bought a decent video camera recently,' Ben said. 'John suggested it, actually. Spent most of my money, but I'm glad I did. It was either that or having to go to counselling.'

'One small thing,' I said, turning to Noah. 'Are you okay for the opening to be open house?'

'Why not?' Noah shrugged. 'People can stand on the street, they usually do anyway.'

'Ben, is it okay to give out your number to people interested in your work?'

'That would be great,' Ben said, almost coy, as he began creating a Vimeo account for the gallery. We posted the video on the gallery's website and new social media profiles. Meanwhile, Noah hit the phones, telling contacts about the video and to check it out. We then worked off the active client list and the gallery media list to get connections going. Ben helped me with the MailChimp e-news, sending out the video along with a reminder about Kevin's show. The e-news now had social media icons for people to connect directly there. The hum had begun.

On Saturday, Sydney's least prolific but most deeply respected freelance arts writer wandered into the gallery. Rosalind Waters. Publishing infrequently meant that when her appraisals were published, the city's cultural set landed on them like a diabetic on a box of Lindt. I recognised the woman instantly. Rosalind had stuck to her trademark Cleopatra haircut and tangerine orange lipstick, which at least gave me a few seconds' warning. This visit was likely to determine Noah Webster Gallery's future reputation. But Rosalind also happened to be the daughter of the woman ditched by Frank, our exhibition sponsor. The future did not bode well.

As usual, Noah was nowhere to be found. It took all of my will not to hide amongst the glow-in-the-dark paintings in the stockroom. Instead, I prised myself out of my chair and stared stupidly at the tangerine lips pointing in my direction.

'This is the space,' the lips said.

'Welcome, Ms Waters.' I held out my hand and raised my gaze to somewhere between Rosalind's eyes. Her shake was surprisingly limp. 'Wanting a last look at the Cusack show?' I asked.

'No,' she said flatly. 'Frank told me to come about the Roebellings.'

It was hard to imagine anyone telling Rosalind Waters to do anything. 'American Frank?'

'Well, I'm not talking about Anne Frank, darling,' the woman snapped. 'The guy has my mother wrapped around his little finger. It's tragic.'

'They're back together?' I asked, my heart lifting.

'Oh yes,' Rosalind said, taking a deep breath. 'Scaring fish in the Barrier Reef, no doubt. Now,' she said, clapping her hands, 'Roebelling.'

'The photographs for the forthcoming exhibition are yet to be delivered to the gallery,' I faltered, 'but I have some of his recent work that is similar, if you would like to see those.'

'Yes, I saw them on the site last night. And now I would like to view Roebelling's mall in its full splendour.'

'I'll get them,' I said. The American term "mall" was Rosalind's. Maybe I should have suggested to John to use that instead of "shopping centre".

Negotiating the tube out of the stockroom, I unrolled the photographs on the floor and hoped the process had a red carpet effect. Using rulers and staplers to weigh down the corners detracted from the attempted ambience, but they didn't stop Rosalind staring at the work for a good ten minutes a piece. A good sign? Who knew? In the meantime, I was busy moving other gallery visitors around the photographs like a sheepdog.

'When will the exhibition work be delivered?' Rosalind asked.

'Not sure yet,' I admitted.

'I need to see them immediately.'

'That might be tricky...'

'Why?' Rosalind said, insulted.

'Er, because the artist is still working on them.' I drew a sharp breath. Was I supposed to say that? Bugger, crap, fuck.

'Still working on them?' she baulked. 'Cutting it fine, isn't it?'

'The artist is a... a perfectionist.' I showed John's concept drawings.

'Scribbles won't cut it,' she snapped. 'The video was cute, but it doesn't help me either. Okay, so why is this collection called *Molecules*?'

'Because,' I stammered, 'because it's about our physical essence.' The critic shrugged in acceptance, so I pushed on. I attempted to describe the tension that exists between gentle human expression and the mechanical. Words continued to stumble out of my mouth, filling up the air between us. The word 'welding' was thrown in somewhere as a metaphor, but I wasn't sure if it made sense.

'My mechanic is anything but gentle,' Rosalind stated. 'Last time I saw him, he tried to screw my wallet to the wall with a CV shaft and timing belt.' I nodded sympathetically. 'Get him on the phone.'

'Your mechanic?'

'Roebelling,' she said, still staring at the prints on the floor. 'I want to interview him. Right now.'

Knowing John would still be shooting at Kevin's garage, I rang his mobile. It involved ringing three times before he answered.

'Rosalind Waters wants to interview you,' I said before he had a chance to speak.

'Wow, that's great,' he said. 'When?'

'Now. On the phone, I think.'

'Now?' he spluttered. 'Jesus, okay.'

I only caught fragments of Rosalind's inquiry, as gallery visitors were milling around the Robelling prints, talking animatedly amongst themselves.

'I swear there's god in this,' one elderly man said. 'And I'm an atheist.'

'Yeah,' replied a young man, 'it's captured space and time in a really awesome way.'

'You know,' the elderly man replied, 'that's the first time I've heard a young person use the word awesome in its correct context.'

'Who's the photographer?' a girl asked.

'John Roebelling,' I replied. 'Sydney artist. His new work will be unveiled on Thursday night, along with Kevin Bradley's sculptures.'

'I see he's got editions of fifteen for the Mall Series,' Rosalind said, hanging up the phone. 'Will it be the same edition number for his new work?' Her tangerine lips were staring straight at me again.

'I'm not sure,' I stammered. I couldn't remember. Had we discussed it? I don't think we had. How could we not have talked about it? Where the hell is Noah?

'The artist didn't know either,' Rosalind replied. 'You'd better sort it out.'

'I'll have Noah call you about that.'

'Fine,' she said. 'Here's my card with my email and private mobile. Don't share it around like you do your opening invitations,' she said, nodding to the wandering visitors.

'Absolutely,' I replied. 'The number of prints…Noah would already have thought about the edition size. But, just out of interest, what number of prints would you recommend?'

'Look, normally, with work like this, you would just have one. Treat it like a painting. But something tells me you should consider an artist proof and maybe six,' she replied. 'He's an unknown, but you don't need to be too shy about the price. Having a short run gives you that opportunity to make the most of it. Just exhibit the artist proof and take orders. But you need to establish your limit publicly from the start.' Rosalind dropped her voice further. 'Big picture – excuse the pun – this guy's going places.'

'I'm so glad you think so,' I smiled. 'What is it in particular that draws you to this conclusion?' I figured I might be able to lift her précis, reword it a bit, and spread it on Facebook.

'It's my little toe.'

'Your little toe?'

'My little toe twitches when I see something good,' she said, nodding. 'And that, sister, is more secret than my private mobile.'

'I understand,' I replied, wondering whether Rosalind's little toe was somehow connected to Frank's wallet or her mother's carnal desires for American car salesmen. But the woman had her reputation as well as a trigger-happy toe.

'I'm not doing this for Frank,' Rosalind said, as if her journalistic prowess extended to reading minds as well as toes. 'Coming here, admittedly, I did for Frank. And some peace from my mother. The rest is my decision and my decision entirely.'

'Excellent.' My shoulders sagged in relief, while my eyes dropped to Rosalind's tangerine-painted toenails peeping out from her sandals. It was uncertain as to whether it was the little toe on the left or the right that closed two galleries in Paddington, one in Newtown and five on the North Shore over the last three years.

'I'll need to hear from you or Noah about the edition number today. Also, email me high-resolution images of the Mall Series and one of John himself.'

'No problem,' I said to Rosalind, who was, along with her little toes, already out the door. There was a problem, of course. Noah was elusive all afternoon, even with my SMS efforts. John and I took Rosalind's advice to have an edition of six. I texted Noah the decision and heard back within seconds. '6 is fine, gr8 about roz'. I immediately rang the number through to Rosalind, who was already writing the review. Later that day, John emailed me the high-resolution shopping centre images, as well as a couple of professional images of himself. One was the shadowy artistic shot from his website, the other was similar but with all features revealed, the way I saw him from the start. No surprises.

Surprises. It occurred to me that Rosalind Waters could be one. The woman was a journalist, after all. She could have been using 'comfort tactics' to tear John apart. In the dog-eat-dog world of digital media, journalists are baring their teeth all over the place just to get noticed. When Rosalind said that John was 'going places', she could have meant a TAFE course in real estate sales. His artistic career could be over before it began.

# CHAPTER 20

'Don't poke the bear.' It was Eva's warning. Not that we needed it. As soon as Perry entered the lecture room on Monday, it was clear someone had taken his jowls and stretched them to the floor without his permission. It possibly explained the nature of his correspondence with me earlier that day. I had sent Perry an email via my phone requesting deferral of our Tuesday thesis meeting, citing the preparation for the forthcoming exhibition opening that Thursday night as the reason. In the email to Perry, I included an invitation to come along, hoping it would work as a possible softening agent. It didn't. Perry RSVP'd immediately, demanding that we talk after the lecture. That he made no mention of the exhibition indicated a lack of interest. But I was wrong on that, too.

Sitting alone up the back, I saw Gordon from IT walk in with a laptop. He methodically set it up on the table next to the rostrum and twiddled about until he gave Perry the instruction to kill the lights. At first, this irritated me. It's hard to doodle in the dark. But when I heard the recorded sound of people talking, I felt a twinge of panic. *What does it take to make art?* came up on the screen. Simple white text on a dark grey background. All very familiar. It was Ben's video on John's exhibition. Perry already knew he could come to the exhibition. My invitation had backfired. The video ended thirty seconds later. My attention had been fixed on the screen. I hadn't even noticed someone had snuck in late and sat next to me. I almost jumped out of my skin when I saw it was Barack Obama. 'Simon, please take the mask off.'

Simon was fond of his novelty façade and refused to comply. 'Just came from the most amazing political art flash mob. 'Reagan and George W were brilliant.'

'I find that hard to believe.'

Ben's video deserved applause, I felt, but the class sat in silence. They were all waiting for Perry's opinion before launching their own. Cowards. The lights were turned back on. I expected Marvin at the switch, but it was another student. Marvin wasn't in the front row either. Or anywhere else in the room.

'Now that you've seen the promotional video,' Perry asked, 'are you going to go?' The class remained quiet, wondering if the question was rhetorical. It wasn't. 'Anyone?'

'Yes,' Barack Obama said.

'Why?' Perry asked, unfazed by Simon's plasticised persona.

'Because Anna invited me. She works there.'

'You're not going because of the video?'

'I got the invitation first, but the video makes me want to go even more. I think it deserves a round of applause.' Bless him.

But Perry stopped Simon's attempt to gee up the audience with the flat question, 'Why is that?'

'Apart from being beautifully made, it looks like a fun group of people got involved. The opening is likely to be the same.'

'Interesting observation,' Perry replied. 'The video bypasses the usual notions of the artist as lonely painter or sculptor in a morbidly lit studio. Here we have a group of people, well-lit, in a commercial garage. Quite noisy by the sound of it.' The class tittered. I wanted to smack them. 'What we see is a group of people. A community, if you will. The saying "It takes a village to raise a child" can apply to art, in some instances,' he added. 'But the *Molecules* exhibition is not attributed to the group but to one artist, John Roebelling. Anything wrong with this?' The class sat silent, again unsure if the question was rhetorical. 'Anyone?'

'No,' I replied. 'Unless Andy Warhol should be strung up for his factory or Rembrandt should have closed down his school.'

Perry nodded. 'Yes, we've seen this before. Of course, we don't see the hours of quiet labouring by John Roebelling as he develops his visual concepts.' (in this case, seconds) 'So we assume he has earned his stripes as The Artist.' Perry began pacing the room. 'But we can't say that for certain. What if the ideas were not his own, that he just points and shoots? We can't believe that, can we?' Perry stopped pacing, looking at us as if we were the biggest disappointment of his career. '*Can we?*'

'No,' the class mumbled.

'*Why?*' Perry clenched his fists, his face turning red.

'Because the person with the ideas would want the world to know,' Eva offered from the far left of the room. 'They could hire their own technicians and get the glory. It would come out somehow.'

I whispered to Obama, 'He's getting that heart problem thing again.'

'Is he?' Simon peered across the room. Meanwhile, Perry pushed on, the colour of his face now well beyond that of a baboon's bottom. 'What if the gallery director, Noah Webster, came up with the ideas? Or your esteemed colleague Anna Lissam? They both benefit financially from a successful exhibition.'

The room remained quiet, except for Obama, who whispered, 'He's just being a drama queen to make a point. Don't take it personally.'

Perry's face began to look a little pale, as did mine. It was only then that I realised John had taken some of my blurted out suggestions and converted them into concepts. Had I interfered too much? Meanwhile, Perry's hand pressed on his chest as he stared at Eleanor sitting in the first row (her specialty: tea cosies in conceptual art), though he might have been focusing on staying alive.

'But people still want acknowledgement of their own ideas,' she ventured.

Perry took in a deep breath, which made him appear contemplative rather than in recovery. He took on the part with conviction. 'So even though there's no evidence the Roebelling concepts are his own,' he said to the student and then to the class, 'you are all assuming as much due to one simple three-letter word: ego.' Perry started pacing again. 'Are you?'

'Yes,' the class responded, though their timing was far from uniform. Not one student could be completely certain of artistic authenticity, their own opinion or which of Perry's questions were rhetorical.

'We haven't seen John Roebelling's photographs for *Molecules* yet. But we can take a gander at his shopping centre series, currently on Webster's site. You will see that Roebelling has developed his own style.' Perry clicked on the laptop keyboard several times. He then scanned the room for support, but Gordon had left. After trying a few other buttons, John's images came up. 'Voila! Here is his previous work, possibly inspired by the styles of others such as Edward Hopper, Robert Frank – look Frank up if you're not familiar – and George Segal. Perhaps there's even some Jeffrey Smart in there.'

A clever Australian reference. Perry does it again. 'John may have expanded on ideas given by others close to him. This makes him no less an artist. All artists appropriate, all artists *take*.' Perry began pacing again while I felt my body relax. 'Earlier in this lecture, I said, "point and click". But we know there's more to photography than that. Annie Leibovitz would have my guts for garters for saying point and click. I noticed no one here contested me. Did it occur to any of you to do so?' Perry grinned, but didn't wait for an answer. Instead, he continued the photographic theme, staying on the solid ground of safe history rather than potential fraud.

'John looks cute from the video,' Obama nudged. 'Even better in 3D?'

I did my best to look appalled. Simon let out a squeal. stopping Perry halfway through the definition of 'latent image'. His jowls seemed to tighten prior to continuing.


'Lissam!' Perry yelled across the room after the lecture.

'Yes, Dr Perry?' I walked reluctantly towards him, Freitag slung across my body.

'I can't talk now,' he said. It was more of a declaration.

'Okay,' I said, relieved.

'We'll meet again next week to discuss options.'

'Absolutely,' I said, backing away towards the door.

As I reached the hallway, I thought I heard him say, 'It doesn't end here. It just can't.'


The exhibition installation was a day of people pointing and others dropping things. A thousand details needed to be attended to, so John and I had barely talked to each other. I spent most of the day shuttling from the installation to answering the phone. There was a surge of interest from the media, both on and offline. A few people who had seen the video rang to find out more about Ben and how to contact him. Potential clients rang to check whether they could see John's work prior to the opening. The answer was 'not this time', which just geed them up all the more.

All Cusack's works were packed safely and delivered to new homes or stored for future sales. Caterers delivered glasses, platters and cases of wine bottles. Kevin's temper blew out on three occasions during the installation of his sculptures. The plinths were too small, then they were too big. Then he was just angry because he was tired and needed something to eat. I collected lunch orders and sent Kevin down the street for sandwiches. Installing John's work required calm and focus. It was supposed to happen the day before, but there had been a technical glitch with the printing (glitch: a cute word meaning something that causes deep emotional stress), and so installation was the day of the opening. Not ideal.

Large flat aluminium frames, all spray-painted white, were the exact dimensions of each of John's prints as backing to be affixed to the wall (high, à la billboard). Special brackets had been created to attach the print to the frame temporarily without damaging the paper. This meant that the print could be removed, rolled up and packaged in a tube ready to be sent anywhere required. The system hadn't been used before, so it was a nail-to-cuticle biting experience.

We did not lose our cuticles in vain. The installation was a success. Toasting with strong cups of coffee, we stood and admired the feeling that John had captured in each work. The gentleness of the mechanics and their clients, amongst the grease, concrete and metal. Candy was only in one of the works this time, as the young male mechanic, not the receptionist. This didn't stop me wrestling with jealousy around something that probably didn't exist, involving someone I've never met.

It took a moment to notice that Kevin was in all three images, working on a car in the background. 'He demanded to be in them,' John whispered to me. 'I figured, what's the harm? A real mechanic among actors. Rosalind Waters saw it as an interplay of reality and construct…or something like that. Apparently, interplay is a good thing.'

'If Rosalind likes it, we love it,' I whispered back.

Under directed gallery lighting, Kevin's juxtaposition of smooth, gleaming surfaces with rough textured ones came to life. The sculpture's shadows flowed and halted against the white of the walls. And, as planned, they faced John's prints across each of the three large spaces. Two-dimensions opposite three-dimensions, realism opposite the abstract (grounded emotional maturity opposite a man-child). The two artists complemented each other perfectly.

Rosalind came as soon as Noah called. She had demanded to see the works installed before applying the final touches to her work. I zipped and emailed high-resolution images of the garage work to her that morning. Her critical eye looked over the prints carefully for over half an hour, standing close, then back to full view, then close again. The rest of us munched on our sandwiches, pretending to be relaxed while watching the critic dosey doe. Tortured by Rosalind ignoring his work completely, Kevin disrupted her gaze and began vying for attention. Noah quickly curbed him away and sent him down the street for Danish pastries.

'Rosalind likes apricot,' he whispered in Kevin's ear.

Meanwhile, I stared in dismay at Rosalind's boots, wondering what her little toes were up to. The boots gave nothing away.

Rosalind gave a sharp nod to Noah and John before leaving, well before Kevin's return.

John went home and arrived back at five o'clock. The opening began at six. He was wearing a brown suit without a tie and looked more than a little uncomfortable. But the expression changed when he saw me in my black 'free cocktail' dress I had bought with Liz. 'You are a sight for sore eyes,' he said, kissing me lightly on the lips. It was an accurate comment as John's eyes were a shade of piglet from working around the clock.

Noah and Robert walked into the gallery, both dressed in their freshly pressed opening attire. The whites of their eyes were clearly visible, sales-ready. Robert spotted me first. 'Gallery hostess, you look gorgeous,' he said, though his eyes did flicker towards John. 'May I get you a drink?'

'You certainly may,' I said, 'after work.'

'No drinking on the job, eh? We've never managed that.' Robert winked at Noah. 'But I bet our photographic star could use one about now.'

'One glass might calm the nerves,' John admitted. Robert was already making his way to the kitchen and, in no time, produced three flutes of sparkling wine and one of sparkling water for me.

The waiters arrived at five-thirty and began tending to the early comers – one of whom was Ben in top-to-toe filmmaker black, and a slightly older guy wearing a red t-shirt that said *Boat People* on the front. 'Dude!' he said, passing me and walking up to John. On the back, the t-shirt had *Rock*. Meanwhile, Noah and Robert disappeared into the office.

'Anna, this is Eden, who owns the studio,' John said. 'And you've met our resident master of film, who has received several new clients since the video launched.' He gestured towards Ben, who was distracted by the exhibition.

'Great to meet you,' Eden said, pumping my hand heartily. 'Killer dress.'

'Thanks,' I replied, working my shoulder back into place.

'Getting John's work finally out of the studio and into the community was a major score. I thought those Botticelli eggs were going to go places. But these photos, man, they're way wicked.'

'I've seen your work, too,' I said. 'At the studio.'

'Yeah? Well, I'm just playin'.'

'At what, exactly?' Ben asked with a grin.

'Benji, don't be cruel, man.'

'Calling me Benji is cruel, man,' he replied, before wandering off to look closer at the first print. We followed.

'I have to admit, dude, your work looks incredible in this space,' Eden said.

'I feel like I'm discovering my inner mechanic,' Ben pondered. 'And I can't even change a tyre.'

'Man, you have trouble enough changing lanes,' Eden replied. 'But you're right, these photos have captured the Zen of the grease-monkey.'

'Perhaps I should've put that in the media release,' I whispered to John with a smile. But he was looking over my shoulder towards the door. I turned and saw a blonde, tanned young woman entering the gallery, wearing a fitted satin dress in flamingo pink and matching stilettos. I recognised the wide-set eyes instantly (the ones fixed on John). Candy glided across the floor and planted a kiss directly on his lips.

'Hello, sweetheart.' She said. 'Congratulations.'

'Hey,' he smiled. 'I'd like to introduce you to Anna. Anna was the one who made all this happen.'

'Quite a feat in such a short space of time,' she said.

'Well, John stepped up to the crazy deadline.'

'Crazy,' she nodded. 'But he did it.' She squeezed John's arm before dragging him towards the nearest print. It happened to be the one with her in it. 'This is amazing! You must be so happy, babe.' There was no time to contemplate this disturbing scene further. Kevin arrived, donned in his signature purple pants, sporting a slab of Guinness on his right shoulder. Nodding to Noah and Robert, he walked over and shook John's hand, checked Candy over, and said nothing to me. After which he stood in the middle of the gallery and stared at people looking at his work, still with the slab on his shoulder. The place was already starting to fill. Robert flapped around him as an attempt to distract his inhibiting eye, but it was Noah who managed to lure the beers' descent. Extracting one tin for Kevin, the rest was passed to the waiter. Robert then escorted Kevin outside for 'smoko'.

I anchored myself at the front desk, ready to answer questions and process sales. But I couldn't help looking across at John and Candy walking around the gallery, talking and laughing. About what, I wasn't sure. It was impossible to hear them at that distance, but to me they were deafening. I shifted my attention to Noah, who was busy kissing cheeks and appearing more like an esteemed philanthropist than an art dealer. As the space became more crowded, everyone's hand gestures became smaller, and voices became louder. Surrounding indicated that Ben's video had hit the mark, and our presence on Instagram and Facebook had ramped up some fresh interest. Word had it that a throng was gathering outside, but I couldn't see through the front door for the people.

Then Frank arrived, hand gestures aplenty, but without Penny or Rosalind Waters.

'Penny couldn't make it?' I asked.

'She's got a bad back from our Queensland sojourn,' he replied, eyebrows bouncing. 'FYI: her daughter's written a big article about John. It's a whopper,' Frank added before grabbing a red wine from the passing waiter and hurrying across the room to cuddle Noah.

The news came as no surprise. Rosalind's articles were always lengthy, but that didn't mean they were positive. The last artist she ripped to shreds took a good six pages in *Australian Art Collections* magazine. One never knew which way it was going to end until the fat article sang.

I continued to stand at my desk, handling enquiries, answering the phone and touching wood (more accurately, laminated chipboard). I also kept a wary eye out for Perry. There was every possibility he would charge through the door, climb onto my desk and body surf through the exhibition. By quarter past six, the gallery was packed. Crowded openings make it difficult to see the artworks from any reasonable distance, which tends to put a handbrake on sales. But as John's prints were closer to the ceiling than normal for billboard simulation, everyone could still see them. Then another kind of handbrake arrived in the form of Kevin's friends. They were a rowdy, unkempt bunch that gathered near the kitchen doorway in order to filter the finger food as it emerged, and duck into the kitchen to nab another Guinness as required. There was little I could do from up the front, so I focused my attention on potential clients gathering at my end, quietly praying that Kevin's group would run out of Guinness and leave before things got out of control. I also did my best to stop looking for John and Candy in the crowd. But Simon was busy doing that on my behalf, as he and Eva hung around the front desk to keep me company.

'Lollypop is working hard for John's special attention,' Simon monitored, 'but he's not picking up her cues. Nope, he's hopping into the red wine instead...' Meanwhile, Eva was busy following the hors d'oeurvres (with the caviar I didn't order). And then I spotted him. Perry, drinking Guinness at the back of the gallery with Kevin's mates. He had somehow slipped past my surveillance.

'Englishman abroad,' Simon said, following my gaze. Perry's beer-free hand was waving around enthusiastically like a conductor, punctuating his points. When his fingers starfished, everyone around him laughed.

'I might see what all the fuss is about,' Simon added. 'Shall report back presently.'

'Just don't mention the word "thesis", will you?'

'Don't worry, darling. He knows it would be poor form to bother you with that tonight.'

I nodded, but with hesitation.

'Hey, where did he go?' Simon said, peering across the gallery. Kevin's friends were busy attacking a tray of buffalo balls, and Perry was nowhere to be seen.

'You've got to be quick,' I said, frantically scanning the room. 'He's a slippery sucker.' But Simon saw someone he knew and had begun moving his way through the crowd, passing John, who was shimmying his way towards my desk. He was alone, looking tired, but also relieved. Or maybe a little drunk. Then Perry appeared, shook his hand, and started talking. John nodded intently while staring hard at Perry's tie.

Maggie and Ruben emerged from the hoard. Maggie wore a stunning emerald green silk shirt I hadn't seen before, and Ruben wore the dark grey suit and red tie I knew was reserved for special occasions. I turned to introduce them to John. But Noah intercepted the meeting, hauling the bleary-eyed photographer-of-the-moment towards Frank's corporate colleagues.

Half of Kevin's exhibition had sold by the time speeches began. Eva accused our clients of being a little slow in interpreting the economy. 'Their ignorance, our bliss,' I whispered, placing a red sticker spot on yet another of Kevin's pieces before resuming my post at the front desk. Noah gave the main speech, which mostly involved thanking people in a polite and tedious manner. Then Frank, as sponsor, plugged his business for the allocated three minutes while simultaneously promoting the importance of charity.

Despite Kevin's sales activity, there was no doubt that the focal point of interest was John's photographic prints. Being so large, they were difficult to sell to private buyers looking for something over the mantelpiece. Noah hadn't expected sales for John that evening, seeing it more of an opportunity to attract interest from public art museums, the corporate with a penchant for art, and big-time private collectors. Sales would happen later. However, much to the surprise of both Noah and John, one had sold early that evening to a colleague of Frank's, who left as soon as the deal was done. Frank was determined to buy one, but was still choosing which.

At one point, I spotted Perry talking to Noah. They were both smiling, looking genuinely relaxed. But at that moment I realised Perry could – at any time – introduce my thesis into the conversation. About Dorothy Brown, about Aboriginal art fakes. Shit. They both turned their heads towards me, smiling. Perry sent a wave across the room. Teeth clenched, I waved back. Then Noah was interrupted by another, and Perry was promptly swallowed up by the crowd. Saved.

As the evening went on, John's reputation rose. And as John's reputation rose, sales climbed. As the sales climbed, the artist himself sank. Between EFTPOS transactions, I noticed waiters topping up John's glass. At one point, John turned when hearing his name called, knocking one of Kevin's sculptures off a plinth. A nearby guest with dexterous hands caught it, holding up the piece like a trophy. The surrounding crowd cheered. Noah thanked the man, quickly returning the sculpture to its rightful place. John looked on in mild confusion.

'Darling,' Simon said. 'Why don't I hold the fort and you take that poor boy photographer out for a breath of fresh air?'

'You're a gem.' I hugged him before heading over. My stomach growled, and I had a sudden desire to eat a horse. The roaming antipasto platters were all at far points of the gallery. John had eaten something during the evening, but now it looked like he might return it. Taking his hand, I steered him towards the front door. Eva, Candy, Ben and Eden formed a phalanx around us.

'I see a grim loneliness to your work,' Eva offered John. 'The powerful isolation of our mundane existence.'

'Ta,' John replied with a smile, almost tripping over himself.

At that moment, Liz glided into the gallery in a red sequin dress with a miniature pineapple affixed to the side of her head. A tropicana fascinator. Everyone had eyes for Liz except for two people. The musclebound man she was with – he only had eyes for Kevin's sculptures – and Eva. But then that changed when Eva's eyes lifted and met Liz's. There was some kind of recognition.

'Do you two know each other?' I asked. They shook their heads, but slowly. 'Eva, this is Liz, my flatmate. Liz, this is Eva, who is also writing a thesis. Well, she has one that actually exists …'

Our star artist burped, so we kept moving. Once out on the footpath and down the road beyond the bulk of bystanders, John turned to me and slurred, 'You are the darkest night.' I frowned, wondering if he thought I was Eva. He kissed me and added, 'You are where dreams are born.' At that point, he threw up in the bushes.

'Eww,' Candy said.

With hands carefully splayed, John lowered his bottom onto the footpath. I helped settle him down. And, like a mother unfazed by a messy nappy, food was still on my mind.

'He'll be right,' Eden said. 'I'm always better after I chuck. Still, I'd better go get him a glass of water.' As Eden disappeared back inside, I squatted while holding John's wobbling body up from collapsing completely. It was then that I noticed an older Asian man was holding up John's other side.

'Mr Huojin?' I asked.

'Hi there,' he replied, before jerking his head to the side. 'This is Howie.' A teenage version of the old man stood nearby in jeans and a hooded sweatshirt. Howie nodded, but stayed silent. Guests standing nearby were locked in a conversation about the sinking stock market and the demise of real estate, unaware of what was happening around them.

I looked up and noticed a woman and young girl standing nearby with three boxes and a suitcase. Cheng explained, 'This is my daughter, Lan,' he said, pointing to a woman with a smart pixie-style haircut, fitted black trousers and well-pressed blue cotton shirt. Still, the neatitude didn't stop the woman from looking frayed. 'And this is my granddaughter, Amy,' Cheng added. Amy must have been all of six, dressed in a white long-sleeved t-shirt under a red pinafore. Her black hair was reminiscent of the Princess Leia earmuff style. She could have been mistaken for an innocent, except for the dark eyes that seemed unimpressed by everything before her. It was possible this bundle of joy was the reason her mother looked so spent.

'Are these pieces for the gallery?' I glanced back at the boxes.

'Ah, no,' Cheng replied. I was on the verge of asking if he had a packet of chips or some chocolate in his stash, but he said, 'We need to speak with Kevin Bradley.'

'He is rather busy at the moment, because of the opening. Maybe I can have him call you tomorrow?'

Cheng's face remained passive while Howard looked like he wanted to disappear into the vomit-decorated foliage behind him. Ben and Candy shifted their feet awkwardly. And then came the icing on the cake. Kevin emerged, striding directly toward the group. By the confident footsteps, he appeared to hold his liquor better than John. I caught sight of Robert at the entrance. He looked irritated, then retreated into the gallery.

The breeze picked up. 'You better move on,' Kevin yelled. The stock-and-real-estate people stopped talking. Taking one look at Kevin, they promptly moved their conversation back into the well-heeled safety of the gallery. 'I didn't mean you,' Kevin shouted after them.

'Congratulations on your opening,' Cheng said. 'We haven't come to make trouble. We just want our home back.'

'Australia's not really your home, now is it?' Kevin replied. 'Go back from where you came from.'

'If it wasn't for you, we would still have a home,' Amy screamed at Kevin in defiance, her dress serving as a red flag to a purple-panted bull. Lan pulled her daughter back under with one arm while awkwardly lifting a box with the other in preparation to leave.

Then Eden appeared with the glass of water for John. Kevin first saw the front of his t-shirt, 'Boat people' and, as Eden passed Kevin to get to John, the purple pants almost exploded. Kevin took a swipe at Eden's shoulder, knocking the glass out of his hand. Glass smashed onto the footpath near John and Howard's feet.

Eden turned to Kevin. 'What was that, man?' he asked.

'I take issue with your attire,' he replied.

'Really? I wasn't going to say anything, Kev mate, but those pants are a bit Jefferson Starship.' That gave Kevin pause. 'Well,' Eden continued, 'I'd better go get a dustpan and broom before anyone hurts themselves on this glass.' Eden wandered back towards the gallery, passing Maggie and Ruben on the way.

'Maybe I should get Noah,' I said, but Kevin's hard grip caught my arm.

'Hey, hands off,' John said, unable to move.

'Noah won't be necessary,' Kevin snarled, still holding my arm. 'The gate crashers were just leaving.'

'Firstly, tonight had an open invitation, so there are no gate crashers,' I said, pulling free. 'Secondly, it sounds like they have nowhere to go.'

'He promised Howie an exhibition,' Amy yelled. 'All Howie had to do was–'

'That's enough storytelling for one evening, you little runt,' Kevin's spittle hit the concrete. Howard studied the cracks in the footpath. They must have been fascinating. He couldn't keep his eyes off them.

'But it's true,' Amy mumbled back.

'Aren't you people supposed to be following the one-child policy?' Kevin shot a glance at Lan before approaching the little girl with clenched fists. 'Let me help you with that.'

'Do you have friends to stay with tonight?' Maggie asked, crossing Kevin's path. Her swift move diffused the situation, but only momentarily.

'That's it.' Kevin glared at Howie and then back at Cheng, as if weighing up whose face should be broken first. 'I'm getting the lads. We'll be more than happy to help you find your place.' With that, Kevin disappeared back into the gallery.

'We don't know many people here.' Cheng rubbed at his face. Fear and embarrassment were taking their toll.

'Ruben, will you get the car, please?' Nodding, Ruben trotted quickly down the street.

Maggie said to Lan and Cheng, 'You and your family can come and stay with us for the night. We have plenty of room.'

'That's a very generous offer,' Cheng said. 'But we can't possibly accept.'

'Yes, you can.' Maggie smiled softly. 'And I think you'd better.'

'You'll be safe with Maggie and Ruben,' I said. 'They're good people.' But everyone's eyes were on the gallery entrance, waiting for Kevin's posse to arrive.

# CHAPTER 21

Kevin reappeared with his four mates and a case of wine lifted from the gallery kitchen. There was one small blessing. Perry wasn't with them. As the group had been drinking heavily, their movements were sluggish. Assessment of the situation was ponderous. Decision-making had become challenging. 'What shall be the fate of these infidels?' a more histrionic member of the group proclaimed. A glowering competition followed.

This fundamental lack of coordination gave Ruben time to drive up, and for me and Maggie to load the SUV with the boxes and suitcase. Meanwhile, Ben ushered the family into the back seat. Before the thugs knew it, Maggie was waving through the window as they disappeared down the street.

John turned to me and said, 'They seemed nice.'

Kevin glared at me before walking up the street with his bedraggled gang. Candy and Ben went back inside to see what happened with Eden and the broom. Robert passed them on his way out.

'Are you okay?' he asked while I crouched down to inspect John's condition.

'Okay?' I retorted. 'Kevin just bullied those poor people off this street. He threatened a minor with physical abuse. And that...thug... is a friend of yours?'

Robert held his hands up in placation. 'Whoa there.' John copied the gesture in fascination while Robert continued, 'I didn't know Kevin was going to be out of hand. Must have been the alcohol. It changes people.'

'Or maybe Kevin's just a bully. He bullied me at the gallery a couple of weeks ago.'

'Really? He may have been drinking then, too,' Robert shrugged. 'He was feeling very stressed about the exhibition.'

I shook my head. 'There was only pesto on his breath. And in his teeth.'

'Look,' Robert replied, 'there are reasons for everything. You may not know the whole story. Do you know about that family? Those strangers who took a ride with your friends?'

'You saw that, did you?' I felt my cheeks flush. 'I know that the trouble has something to do with Howard working for Kevin. Cheng has the impression that his grandson was exhibiting here at this gallery. Why would he think that?'

'I have no idea,' he said, hooking his arm under John's and standing him up. 'Looks like it's time for this guy to head home. I'll order an Uber.'

Noah came out, asking 'Everything alright?' shocked to see John leaning on Robert's shoulder while Robert was using his free thumb to tap on the Uber app. 'Goodness, our artist looks a little worse for wear.'

'It's 'cause he hasn't slept for the last few nights,' John explained with focus and effort. 'The alcohol…I'm so tired…sorry.'

'That's okay, champ,' Noah said, taking John's other arm to steady him. 'You did well, but it's time to go home now.' Robert dropped John's arm. 'You've done a brilliant job tonight, too, Anna,' Noah said. 'Perhaps you wouldn't mind escorting our successful artist home? Your friend Simon has been a great help inside, but it's all quieting down now. Everyone's leaving. I can take it from here.'

'Okay,' I sighed, feeling the ache in my feet for the first time. 'I'll just go get my bag from the back.' The gallery was indeed emptying, and Perry was nowhere to be seen. But Liz and Eva were in what looked like an intense discussion. I bypassed them to hurry back to the footpath. Simon was in tow, and many followed. It was almost eight. Witching hour for the art crowd. Guests had restaurant reservations to keep.

'A brilliant opening,' Simon said before leaving. 'You should be very proud. As should you, John,' he added gently to the man hanging on Robert's shoulder. 'You sold nine prints tonight.' Simon held up nine fingers to demonstrate. John smiled back. It was all he could muster.

Noah returned to the gallery to farewell clients. Our ride pulled in, and Robert assisted John into the back. 'I guess I'm going to have to get you a drink some other time, hostess,' he said with a smile.

'Thanks for organising the ride, Robert,' I replied, wondering if I'd been too harsh on him. I was tired too. And, with the success of the opening, relief brought a wave of fatigue. I smiled weakly before moving in next to John and closing the door. Robert sauntered back into the gallery.

'You going already, piker?'

I looked around to see who was yelling through the window. It was Liz, in all her scarlet glory. The pineapple had disappeared.

'Liz,' I said, winding down the window. 'I'm taking John home to our place.'

'Thatta girl,' Liz smiled and cocked her head towards John. 'You must be the overnight sensation.'

John smiled and waved before closing his eyes and began snoring. 'My god, he's gorgeous even when pissed,' Liz said. 'Well, I'm going back in to say hi to Nora.'

'They're closing up, so it'll have to be brief, I'm afraid.'

'That's a shame. We had so much to talk about. His filing system for a start.' She winked before making her way up the steps, lighting a cigarette before entering the gallery.

There was no point in driving out to Paradise. It was a short drive to my apartment and a quiet one in terms of conversation. John slept all the way, but roused when the car finally came to a stop.

He opened his eyes and smiled. 'Nine,' he said, 'nine.'

We made it up the terrazzo stairs and into the apartment. John got his feet caught up in Liz's multi-coloured boa on the way to my room and collapsed on the bed, fully clothed. My stomach went head-to-head with John's snoring, like a faulty dishwasher competing with a malfunctioning vacuum cleaner. I left John for the kitchen. Opening up the pantry cupboard door, I thought about the Huojins and felt gratitude for this pokey place I called home. How strange it must be to move across the world and attempt a life in a completely foreign land, a country so different from your own. My stomach grumbled as I pulled out the noodles. Thank god for comfort food.

I woke at eight the next morning, praising my restraint from drinking the night before. John remained fast asleep, though his mouth was wide open, as if ready to suggest something. I showered, dressed and made coffee. A fresh pack of Fair Trade Breakfast Blend was sitting in the cupboard. Liz must have bought it, but it was not her usual brand. It was mine. Returning to the bedroom,

I found John awake, holding his head and mumbling, 'Naughty John, naughty John.'

I handed over a glass of water and some aspirin, which he took dutifully. Then a mug of long black and a cheese toastie. Hangover food.

'You are a goddess,' John said before taking a gentle sip. 'This coffee is so beautiful it deserves a frame.'

'Wish I could stay, but I have to go to work.'

'I'd better get up, go with you,' he said, attempting to raise his body, but then rested back down again. 'Sorry about last night. I can usually hold my liquor better than that. Much better.'

'You were exhausted,' I said, 'and you still are. Maybe you should try to sleep some more?'

'I was bad last night, wasn't I?" he said, his face clouding.

'In many ways, you were wonderful.'

'I was horribly drunk.'

'I've seen a lot worse,' I said. 'And it didn't matter anyway. You are Sydney's new star photographic artist.' John looked dubious. 'You worked so hard under ridiculous time pressure and produced a brilliant exhibition. Noah and I are very grateful.' He still failed to be comforted by the news. 'And I still think you're cute,' I added.

'That's a relief.' His face brightened despite itself.

'Come to the gallery when you're ready. Just pull the front door when you leave.'

'Sage,' he replied, lying down. 'But it won't be the same without you,' he added with a grin.

'By the look in your eyes, it probably will. Sleep tight.'

I left for work feeling strange that John was in my bed without me. Liz wasn't home, but I left a note for her on the front door: 'Sleeping artist in my bed. Do NOT fondle.'

Noah was already at the gallery, looking like a four-year-old finally entrusted with all three primary colours of play doh. 'Rosalind's article is out,' he beamed.

'Already?' I gasped, dropping my handbag. 'How?'

Noah thrust that morning's edition of the *Sydney Morning Herald* in my direction. 'The *Herald*? Rosalind hasn't done newspaper in ages.'

'I know. I couldn't believe our luck,' Noah replied. The cover of the arts section, titled *Moments of Our Lives,* featured the first page of her article, with the full story to appear in the Saturday edition. Images from both the shopping centre and the garage series broke up the text, as well as the shadowy photograph of the artist himself. The article had restraint, as per Rosalind's style, but there was no doubt about John's significance in her eyes.

'This is amazing.'

'Isn't it?' Noah replied. 'Last night was quite a success, don't you think?'

'Indeed, it was,' I smiled, stopping myself from calling John. He'd better sleep. The news won't run away.

'Your friend, the colourful and dynamic Liz Calder, visited after you left.'

'Yes,' I released a small groan, 'I saw her when we were leaving.'

'Hard to miss.'

'Hope she didn't give you any trouble. Or say anything, ah, disturbing,' I hedged.

'Disturbing?' Noah asked. 'Not at all, the fella she brought purchased two of Kevin's sculptures.'

'That muscled guy bought two sculptures?'

'Yes, he did.'

'Incredible.' I let out a breath. But it was time to move on to more sobering matters. 'Shame about those poor people outside the gallery.'

Noah looked shocked. 'Poor people were here?'

'The homeless Huojin family,' I explained. 'Didn't Robert tell you?'

'No, but the name's familiar,' Noah pondered. 'Who was he again?'

'Remember Huojin Cheng had come by about a week ago, asking us not to exhibit his grandson's work? Howard Huojin?'

'Oh yes, he had got the galleries mixed up. Goodness, is he persisting with this?'

'He didn't get the galleries mixed up. It looks like Howard was working for Kevin, who had promised an exhibition at this gallery.'

'*Kevin* promised an exhibition *here*?' Noah's upbeat groove sapped.

'It was a white lie,' I said. 'A hook to lure Howard in.'

'To what?'

'The details are still a little vague,' I said. 'Kevin somehow made the entire family homeless. His behaviour was pretty offensive out on the street. My friend ended up offering her house as a refuge. We had to get them away from Kevin and his…guests.'

'Your friend already knows this family?'

'No, she's just one of the good guys.'

'I'm humbled,' Noah said, lowering himself down at my desk.

'Huojin Cheng seems like a pretty reasonable person, too, Noah. I think Kevin's been up to something dodgy.' I paused a moment before suggesting the obvious. 'It might be worth asking Robert about this.'

'Robert?' Noah asked. 'He knows about this?'

My gut feeling said 'yes', but my employment security said: 'I'm not sure.'

Two men from the glass hire company arrived with a trolley and headed towards the kitchen. Noah followed them to make sure that they didn't confuse their glasses with his Norwegian ones. It had happened before, apparently. I pulled out my phone to check up on Maggie.

'Thanks so much for being my caped crusader last night, Maggs,' I said as soon as she answered.

'Absolutely no problem.'

'Hey, aren't you supposed to be at work?'

'Pattie offered to fill in for me today. I explained I had unexpected guests from out of town.'

'That's one way of putting it.'

'It's been quite fun, like a slumber party.' Maggie's voice sounded relaxed, almost giggly. 'Lan made the most amazing breakfast with rice, eggs and some vegetables. Quite delicious. And it turns out Cheng's batty about orchids. Ruben's pulled a sickie, and they've both disappeared to the greenhouse.'

'Ruben pulled a sickie?' Under normal circumstances, Ruben would have to have plague before being extracted from his office chair for fear of it being removed in his absence.

'I'm just pleased they haven't been a bother, considering we don't even know these people.'

'They're great, just in a new country trying to find their feet.'

I felt my shoulders relax for the first time in a week. 'Any mention of what Kevin and Howard have been up to?' I saw Noah emerge from the kitchen, then disappear into his office. The caterers rumbled past with boxes on trolleys to their van outside.

'Not really,' she replied. 'I thought it best just to let them settle in, help them feel at home.'

'Maggie, they're only supposed to stay one night.'

'Well, Ruben and I talked about it this morning. They are so nice and deserve a break. A few days at least. Howard's still looking a little hunted. The truth about all this will rise to the surface naturally.'

Robert's warning the night before about not knowing the full story rang in my ears. 'But we don't know them.'

'We're getting to know them.'

'What if they're caught up in something illegal? You could be harbouring criminals. I did a web search and there was a Houjin Cheng, or was it Cheng Houjin? I can't remember. Anyway, he was an explosives expert in China. Not sure if it's the same guy though.'

'They're great people, honestly,' she said. It seemed nothing was going to mess with Maggie's good mood. 'Did John get home okay?'

'I took him back to my place. He's still sleeping it off.'

'Would you both like to join us for dinner tonight? Looks like we'll be cooking large quantities.'

'John might want a quiet one, but-.' At that moment, a loud crash came from the other end of the phone. 'What was that? Maggie, are you alright?'

'Gotta go,' she said. The line went dead.

# CHAPTER 22

A gaggle of journalists descended on the gallery. Cameras on flash and smartphones on record were coming at me from all directions. Rosalind's article, with the promise of a sequel, had got the gossip ball rolling. Everyone wanted to know about John Roebelling.

'What kind of name is Roebelling?' a guy from Splodge art magazine asked. And the inanity continued from there. Noah stood in to field the questions while I copied high-resolution images onto flash drives for the journalists and rang John, hoping to wake him. No luck.

'I have to go,' Noah said, looking at his watch. 'I'm already half an hour late for an important meeting.'

'More important than this?' I implored above the hubbub.

'I'm afraid so,' he said. 'But you are doing wonderfully, and you can always call me on the mobile.'

'That's a comfort,' I said as Noah ran out the door.

Five minutes later, Kevin walked in, still wearing his purple pants. I wondered if he had welded them on.

'What's all this, then?' he asked.

'Media. Not for you.' I glared while waiting again for John to pick up.

Kevin moved towards the journalists, introducing himself. They asked if he knew what time John would arrive at the gallery.

'Don't know, he was pretty pissed last night,' Kevin chuckled while curbing one young woman with a lapel microphone towards his most expensive sculptural piece.

'What's John's favourite drink?' the Splodge journo asked Kevin, who replied with a snigger, 'a Shirley Temple.' Then the gallery phone rang. It was John.

'Sorry I missed you,' he said, his voice still groggy from sleep. 'Though I'm not sorry I miss you.'

'I miss you, too,' I replied, 'as do about twenty journalists who are here in the gallery hoping to speak with you. And some photographers. TV, newspapers, magazines, some digital, even radio. They've all read the glowing piece on you Rosalind wrote in today's *Herald*.'

'That was fast,' he said. 'What about Kevin? Is he there?'

'He just showed up,' I dropped to a whisper, 'but they want to see you.'

'They already have. I'm up on the walls.'

'I know, but…'

'Just ribbing, I'll be there in a jiff.'

'I'll organise an Uber.'

'Thanks,' he replied. 'But I need a shower first.'

'Just do your teeth. The rest is artist-as-rock star.'

'My suit is all creased, and there's vomit on the left sleeve.'

'I believe that will count towards you.'

Much to Kevin's disdain, I announced John's pending arrival to the impatient group and began serving placation coffees. John arrived within fifteen minutes. Noticing his complexion was much like that of a kabuki performer. I handed a cup over and hoped for colour. He sculled the coffee and burnt a sizable portion of his mouth, but at least some skin colour came back. John gave articulate answers to the disorderly panel of journalists, never once betraying the rushed timeline for his artistic output. And as far as the media was concerned, Kevin might as well have been a farting fox terrier. Despite John attempting to draw Kevin into the interview, all lenses were on the photographer.

Ben and I had plastered the internet with details about John's show. But a good portion of the public still use the phone to actually speak to a person. The calls did not let up. Even more descended upon the space to see the work in the flesh. Media photographers snapped John standing next to one of his depicted mechanics. Kevin mentioned he was the real mechanic. 'A three-dimensional one,' he said, but no one seemed to notice. Reality was out. Abstraction was also out. It was a contrived reality that the people rallied for. One without obvious molecules was fine.

After the media had left, John sat in a corner scribbling concepts on some photocopy paper for a buyer interested in a commissioned work. A suburban bank branch with staff and customers expressing a range of emotions. I didn't have time for emotion, swiping credit cards through the EFTPOS machine as I processed sale upon sale. All three editions sold out, which meant moving onto the 'Mall' series, which had to be rolled out onto the floor. I put gaffa tape on the concrete floor around them to keep people from stepping too close. They promptly started selling as well. Kevin left by lunchtime, steaming at the lack of interest in his sculpture despite the sales from the night before. The action wound down over the afternoon.

John had settled into the chair in front of my desk. 'You're going to have to think about what to do with all that money you've just earned.'

'It won't be so much,' he shrugged.

'What do you mean? You're going to be loaded.'

'Well, my commission gets split evenly amongst the team. We had an agreement before starting the project. There's one person I didn't tell, but she's on the contract.'

'Candy?'

'No, silly moo,' he smiled. 'You.'

'But the whole thing was your idea. None of us should get anything.'

'Actually, it was kinda your idea...'

'Directly inspired by the shopping centre series. Not a big leap. Plus, I'm already earning my sweets from the sales,' I said. 'Whatever you had in mind for me goes straight back to you so you can create more. The world needs more John Roebelling. As do I,' I added with a cheeky grin.

His eyebrows lifted, then dropped. 'Stupidly, I'm going to hit the road. Now that I have just enough caffeine to power me home so I can hit the hay.' John stretched and leaned over to kiss me.

'Thanks for today,' I said. 'You're amazing.'

'You have just made my career, my love, so thank you,' he grinned. His eyes were a little wired from the coffee. 'Feel sorry for ol' Kev though.'

'He did pretty well last night. No need to feel bad for him.'

'Guess not,' he said, stifling a yawn.

'Maggie,' I gasped, remembering the crashing sound before she hung up. 'Better make sure she's okay.' John looked concerned. 'But you go,' I added, 'you still look knackered.'

'I've never been happier.' He leaned over and kissed me again before taking his helmet from under the desk. Walking out onto the street, the sunlight and leaves seemed to take pleasure in mottling him.

'Ponty knocked a vase over,' Maggie explained. 'No, the real drama was when Cheng found a substantial amount of money in Howard's wallet, hundreds of dollars. Cheng was furious, obviously wondering where the money came from.'

'I bet he was,' I replied. 'They could have stayed overnight at the InterContinental.'

'Howard then yelled something in Chinese and stormed out. Everyone thought he was just letting off steam out the front, but we haven't seen him since. Ruben and Cheng drove around the neighbourhood, but no luck. They said when Howard returns, they will move on. Cheng said they're too much trouble. Untrue, of course.'

'Where did the money come from?'

'Howard worked for Kevin,' Maggie replied. 'Something about importing a cleaning product from China.'

'A cleaning product?'

'Strange, isn't it?' Maggie said. 'Anyway, the story to date is that their landlord knew Howie was an artist, and that Kevin was an artist. Thought he was doing a good deed by introducing them to each other. Kevin said he had some work for Howie, for a bit of pocket money, and could get him a show at Noah Webster Gallery. Then Cheng put a stop to it. Kevin got angry and had the landlord oust the family.'

'But what did Kevin do to get Cheng hot under the collar in the first place?'

'I don't know. I asked, but he doesn't want to bother us with their problems.'

'And now everyone is waiting for Howard to return?'

'Ruben says it's too early to file a missing person report. Cheng agrees. I'm sure it'll all be okay.'

'Where's the father in all this?'

When Maggie told the story, the sadness of this family hit a low I couldn't even imagine. Lan's husband had died of cancer not long after they arrived in Australia. They didn't know he was sick, but the cancer was all through his body by the time they found it. It was all over in a couple of months. He was a manager for a global trading company. The company that brought out the family had been little help since the death.

'So maybe they should go back to China,' I suggested, 'be with their friends and family?'

'Maybe,' Maggie replied. 'Or maybe they just need to stay awhile to grieve. Moving countries is a big deal. They had just settled here. Amy was enjoying school for the first time. You know, Lan's a qualified Chinese language teacher. Mandarin and Cantonese'

'They say it's the languages we should all be learning.'

'She also taught English in China. You'd think the Australian school system would snap her up. But it's all bureaucracy. I think Cheng and Lan are having trouble working out their options. Still coming round for dinner tonight?'

'Sure,' I said, rubbing my eyes. A free meal from Maggie was worth the trip. Hopefully, no one will expect me to stay awake at the table. I confirmed that the media circus had tired John out, who had gone home to collapse.

Closing up the gallery involved corralling remnant visitors out the door. Feeling exceptionally fatigued, I yelled out 'nosing cow' instead of 'closing now'. That took some explaining. But it could have been performance art.

An aroma of cooking chicken in spicy sauces wafted down the hallway as the front door swung open. Bach at a temperate volume joined in from the lounge. Maggie stood at the doorway, emitting a radiance I hadn't seen before. For a moment, I thought she must be pregnant.

'Everything's fine,' Maggie said. 'Howard's back and they've agreed to stay for two more nights.'

I suspect Howard wasn't greeted with radiance by Lan's clan when they heard he had just been wandering the streets. By the time I arrived, Ruben and Cheng were out with the orchids, and Lan was busy making dinner, which explained the smell that was making my mouth water. We walked into the lounge room. Amy, hair now tied in a high ponytail, was on the rug dressing an Anglo-Saxon doll with ridiculous breasts. Barbie. Howard sulked on the couch near some half-packed luggage. Given his father's recent death and current homelessness, the mood was more than justified. Maybe the disappearing act, too.

'Hey guys,' I said.

Howard held up his hand and dropped it.

'Hi,' Amy chimed while negotiating a pink jacket on the doll. It matched the leopard print skirt and yellow boots. An outfit Liz would be proud of. I glanced over to a small painting leaning on the far wall by the suitcase. It was a portrait of a Chinese woman, not well-painted. But I couldn't stop looking at it. The green in the background was at loggerheads with the lighting of the subject. The woman looked flat and grey. Her eyes were close to dead. What an awful paint-

'My god,' I cried, 'it's a Vernon Jones.' Hurrying to get a closer look, I skated across the floorboards

Amy turned and said, 'Yes, it is,' then returned her attention to Barbie's clothing ensemble. Howard didn't move.

'Is this yours, Amy?'

'It belongs to my family. It is of my aunt ancestor who came to Australia a long time ago for a golden new life.'

'For gold *and* a new life,' Huojin Cheng corrected her as he walked in. 'You like?' he asked.

'I have a special interest in Vernon Jones as an artist. Well, I used to,' I corrected myself. 'He was certainly prolific.'

'He wasn't very good,' Amy said loudly from across the room. 'He talked about it.'

'Talked about not being good?' I asked. 'How do you know that?'

'It's in the letters,' she replied.

'Letters?'

'The ones to my aunt ancestor.'

'Romantically involved,' Cheng clarified as he pulled ten letters from a large envelope stuck to the back of the frame and showed them to me. The letters were in Chinese.

'Vernon knew Chinese?'

'Cantonese, yes,' Cheng nodded.

'Vernon said that he couldn't believe people kept buying his portraits,' Amy continued. 'He thought that people just needed to see themselves because they didn't understand where they were. This country.'

'Really?' I replied. 'That's quite a summation.'

'He tried to do a nice one of my aunt ancestor. But I don't think it's very good,' Amy critiqued. I looked again at the painting. It was indeed the most complimentary Vernon Jones painting I had seen, but that didn't say much. From that moment, I knew one thing for sure. There was no returning to a Vernon for my Master's. Cheng looked across to me with pity and said, 'Unfortunately, not a master.'

'Bang Bang chicken is a street vendor's dish from Sichuan,' Lan explained when we settled at the table. 'The street vendor bangs the chicken with a heavy wooden stick. This makes it easy to tear by hand.'

'It's delicious,' Maggie said. 'And the ginger and sesame oil work really well with that nice zing of chilli.'

'A zing of chilli,' Lan smiled. 'I like that.'

It was astonishing how Lan could smile so easily, considering – while grieving for her husband – her family had become homeless, she watched her daughter being physically threatened and had to sit through her son's disappearance all in 24 hours. While we ate, I slowly digested the Vernon Jones revelation, but turned my attention back to matters at hand, asking where the family might want to live next.

'Lan applied for a permanent work visa, but was warned she won't get it,' Cheng explained.

'I'm so sorry. Does that mean you are returning to China?'

'Yes, but we don't look forward to it. They have tagged us for certain activities.'

'These activities wouldn't happen to involve explosives?'

'Explosives?' Cheng gasped. 'No, only peaceful protest, information about Tibet.'

'I just saw a name on the web, explosives engineer Cheng Huojin,' I ventured.

'I don't know him,' Cheng replied with a smile, 'but he was quite well known historically in China.' I was relieved the connection was merely a great leap forward into paranoia. Cheng pulled out a card. 'This is our symbol,' he explained.

'Oh my god,' Maggie exclaimed.

Ruben inspected the card. 'Err…that's a swastika,' he said.

Cheng explained, 'It's a Buddhist symbol, meaning to be fortunate.'

'To us,' Ruben explained, 'it means to be a dangerous fascist.'

Cheng stroked the card, 'The Nazi party adopted the symbol, distorted it, and called it a swastika – a German translation of the original Sanskrit word "srivatsa" meaning endless knot.' Placing the card on the table, he then spun it. 'The symbol is to be seen like this.'

Amy piped up, 'When it spins clockwise, it absorbs energy from the universe. Counter-clockwise, it gives off energy.'

'Very good, Amy,' Cheng nodded.

'I guess the yin-yang symbol is a little less problematic branding-wise,' I said.

'We now have the Wheel of Dharma,' he said, producing another card that looked like a steering wheel of a sailing ship, something that might appear as a nautical motif on one of my mother's polyester scarves. 'Otherwise known by the Tibetans as the wheel of transformation.'

'That's amazing,' Maggie said. 'I don't remember ever seeing this.'

'Well, a picture of Buddha seems to be the thing people relate to,' he shrugged, 'so we go with that.' I suspected Liz would find their branding strategy in serious need of an overhaul.

Ruben turned to Cheng. 'What happens if the authorities find out you are supporting Tibetan independence?'

'Perhaps loss of employment. More likely prison.' Cheng gathered up his cards. The table remained silent.

'Cheng, would you mind reading out some of Vernon's letters?' I asked. A change in subject seemed welcome. Everyone swiftly cleared the table while Cheng retrieved the letters. I watched Cheng as he re-entered the room and settled back at the table. The man moved with such graceful agility.

'Cheng, what's your fitness secret?' I asked. 'Is it tai chi?'

He shook his head while unfolding the bundle of pages. 'I have a lightweight training program.'

Everyone was back at the table, so Cheng began translating each letter aloud. The correspondence was titillating but, in the presence of children, Cheng censored their more 'romantic' passages. Given the letters' authenticity, Vernon indicated clearly on more than one occasion how blessed he was by his success despite his lack of talent. The aunt ancestor called Ming, nicknamed by Vernon as 'Peaches', was possibly his harshest critic. He honoured her in his letters as his most trusted friend and agreed that his clients would be better off carrying a mirror on their person than one of his portraits.

There was mention of Peaches' older sister and how much he enjoyed meeting her.

'My great-great-great-grandmother,' Amy clarified proudly. 'She was in Australia for a year. Took a baby in her belly back to China.'

'Surely not Vernon's child?' Ruben said.

'Yes,' Amy said solemnly.

'Peaches must have been very upset,' I suggested.

Cheng nodded. 'She died within a year of the news.'

'So tragic,' Maggie said.

'Awful. Still, you're alive,' I reasoned, 'Because of Peaches' older sister and Vernon Jones. Could being related to Vernon Jones help with your visa case? You have extraordinary family history here.'

'We tried to explain to immigration, but they don't feel as passionately about Vernon as you do.' I couldn't help but burst out laughing. Passionate about Vernon. If only Perry were here.


Lan put Amy to bed while Maggie, Ruben and I stacked the dishwasher and cleaned up the kitchen. Meanwhile, Cheng prepared for us a special green tea brought from his hometown. With the frantic lead up to the exhibition, then the opening itself, I could feel fatigue descending.

'Must be nice having a daughter as well as a son,' Maggie said to Lan as she poured the tea. I figured she was wondering about China's one-child policy Kevin so respectfully raised outside the gallery. Was that still a thing?

'Amy is not really my daughter,' Lan replied. 'We adopted her. Of course, we love her as our daughter.'

'I can see that,' Maggie replied.

I sipped at the smoky, soothing tea. Maybe this was what I needed after all. 'Howie,' I ventured, 'mind sharing with us your relationship with Kevin Bradley?' Cheng shifted uncomfortably in his seat, but decided not to interrupt.

Howie pursed his lips before saying, 'Kevin said he could get me an exhibition at Noah Webster, which would really help our chances to stay here. We'd look more a part of things, you know?' Howie already sounded a part of things. His slouched-teenager English was impeccable. 'In return, all I had to do was help him import some cleaning stuff from China.'

'Howie's not doing this work anymore,' Cheng said. 'That Kevin is a bad man.'

'From what I saw, I'd agree,' Ruben replied. 'But importing cleaning products isn't a crime, surely? Howie could have done much worse things than keeping Australia hygienic.'

Howie looked down at his cup. 'They can turn the cleaning product from China into a key ingredient for a dangerous illegal drug.'

'Which drug is that?' Ruben asked.

The teenager continued to look down and remained silent. I ended up answering for him. 'It's Zed. As in the letter Z.'

'Z?' Maggie asked.

'Or Zee. Depending on where your national loyalty lies. Big in the club scene,' I explained.

'I didn't know when I started,' Howie said. 'I really thought it was just a cleaning product, but then I realised.'

'You're out of it now, Howie,' Maggie said. 'That's the main thing.' 'Did a guy called Robert have anything to do with this?' I asked. 'A tall, young, good-looking guy?' Howie looked up and nodded.

'Noah Webster, the gallery owner?' I pried further.

'Oh, no,' Howie shook his head. 'Webster knows nothing.'

'He knows nothing?' Cheng said to him. 'You should have told me that. I went to the gallery to talk to Mr Webster about it.'

'Sorry.' Howie hung his head again.

'Howie has a good heart, good intentions,' Cheng said, turning back to the table. 'It just went the wrong way.'

'If we report this to the police -' Maggie started.

'Howie will be linked to it,' Ruben intercepted, 'and they will send the family back for sure.' We agreed to sleep on it.

I asked Howie, 'I hear you're an artist. What's your medium?'

'New media,' he shrugged, 'mostly computer animation.'

'Really?'

'He's very good,' Ruben said. 'Showed me some of his work this morning.'

'Mind if I have a look?' I asked.

After Ruben brought his laptop in from the study, Howie pulled a portable hard drive out of his back pocket, plugged it in and brought up a file 'This is the latest one,' he explained. A detailed animation of a young woman with a tiny coffin in front of her appeared on the screen. The woman was wearing black and crying. The crying became wailing and then subsided to gentle weeping. The sound was chilling in its realism. From time to time, the woman looked at the screen, but then descended into her grief again. In thirty seconds, my reaction moved from intrigue to sympathy. After a minute, I shifted from sadness to discomfort. Another thirty seconds passed, and I felt disinterested. At that point, the woman screamed her pain directly at the camera, making me feel guilty.

'Most people stop feeling compassionate after two minutes,' Howie explained. 'Then she makes you feel bad for not feeling bad,' he chuckled, relaxed for the first time. 'And why should you feel bad in the first place? She's only animated, after all.'

'Good point. Though it makes you realise how a short attention span can also mean a short compassion span.'

'I want to do one of a laughing old man. He'll be able to make you feel really guilty if you don't laugh along,' Howie chuckled again. 'And maybe one of a child wanting your attention to play.'

'This is brilliant, Howie.' I nodded at the woman, who was still weeping.

'I'd like to make it viewer-activated,' Howie explained, becoming animated himself. 'If this was set up in a gallery and someone started walking away from the crying mother, that's when she'd really wail, pulling you back in. Maybe even have all three in a large room, each competing for your attention.'

'Can you stop her now?' Maggie asked, agitated. 'Give her a tissue at least?'

Howie closed the file and silenced the grief. He then stopped and thought for a moment. 'Wouldn't it be great if you could give the woman a tissue? Have a box of tissues and offer it. Some black funnel attached to the monitor. Part of the animation could have her leaning forward and reaching up to take it. But I don't really know how to do that viewer-activated stuff.'

'I know just the person who could help you, Howie,' I said, leaning over and activating the browser. I typed in MaBroAni.com, Marvin's URL.

'You know Marvin Brodie?' Howie said. 'He's huge.'

'You'll be surprised at how small he is when you meet him,' I said, typing in a message for Marvin to contact Howie Houjin, computer animation artist from China, with Howie's mobile and email address.

'Anna,' Maggie said as she walked me to the front door, 'I'm surprised you want to help Marvin. Did something change?'

'You could say that,' I said. 'And I get the feeling he'll have a fresh perspective on the theme.'


My Uber moved through the streets of Sydney like a snake in a cane field, while I sat in the back, exhausted. But weariness didn't stop me from pondering the fate of the Huojin family and the truth about the masterless Vernon Jones.

'We're here,' said the driver. I had nodded off somewhere after North Sydney. Staggering out and up the stairs, I noticed my shoes weren't hurting as much. The apartment was dark. No Liz. I shuffled around her yellow muumuu and her shoes encrusted by hundreds and thousands, brushed my teeth and beelined for my bed.

In the rush to get to the gallery, John had still found time to make the bed. There was a dent on the surface where he sat to put on his shoes before leaving. I undressed, bypassing my pyjamas to slip in naked under the doona. The pillow still smelt faintly of him, a musty aroma. Maybe even blue.

# CHAPTER 23

Shock pushed the coffee directly out through my nose, Fontana de Fair Trade. I was standing in the kitchen contemplating breakfast, when I saw Eva emerging from Liz's bedroom, donned in Liz's superman kimono. The vision had me spluttering over the sink, avoiding staining my work suit by seconds. While wiping my face with a clean Chux, Superman came to my side.

'You okay?'

'Yes, thanks,' I said. It was the first time I'd seen Eva look awkward. Well, even Superman had kryptonite. 'Coffee?' I asked.

'Maybe later. Need to pee,' she said, disappearing into the bathroom.

Liz staggered out of the bedroom, half asleep. She made her way past me, grabbed the coffee packet and breathed in its aroma like oxygen.

'Like to try drinking some?' I asked.

'Ta,' she said, handing over the packet. While putting on a fresh pot, I thanked her for bringing her 'date' to the opening. 'Buying those two sculptures meant a lot to Noah,' I added.

'Well, I felt a smidgeon bad pretending to be a buyer, being an art tease,' Liz answered. 'Bugger of a thing, having a conscience. A bit like herpes, you think it's gone, but you're never really rid of it.'

Then Liz's eyebrows grew large. 'Eva's not a close friend of yours, is she? Otherwise, this might be weird.'

'It's fine,' I shook my head, 'honestly.' Which was a complete porky. Discovering that both my flatmate and Eva are bisexual, or latent lesbians, was clock-drippingly surreal.

'Have you got the number for that guy who did John's video? Ben someone?' Liz asked, 'I might have some work for him.'

'Really? That's great. Ben's fantastic to work with. I'll send his contact details through to you now.' Picking up my phone, I saw the time. 'Shit. Got to get to the gallery soon. Hopefully, it'll be a little calmer today.'

It wasn't. There were more wide-eyed visitors, more enthusiastic sales and more frenzied media looking for the new angle on what was now day-old news. John was fielding questions while Kevin was getting in on the act, complete with burnt orange leather pants. The pants weren't the only difference of the day. Both artists had a decent night's sleep, so they were well primed. Rosalind's second article was double the length, complemented by photos of John's work spread across two pages. John's work had already sold out. But the flow-on effect saw Kevin's selling out by three o'clock. Noah was elsewhere.

Exhaustion crept in as visitors, journalists and Kevin drifted out the door at closing. And once the door was locked, John and I had a moment to stand on the street and look at each other and smile.

'Look at what you've created,' he said, while slipping on his leather jacket.

'I've created?' I snorted. 'You're the creative one, buddy. And all of Australia knows it. Major national glossies in here today, on a Saturday, for god's sake. It's hard to believe it's real, isn't it?'

John stopped my jabbering with a kiss. 'Better,' he said. '*That feels real.*' I could have hung onto his jacket for eternity, as much for affection as for keeping upright. But John's grumbling stomach broke the spell. 'It's official. I'm starving. We missed lunch, I guess. Aren't you hungry?'

Taking a moment to think about it, I realised I could've eaten his leather jacket. 'Sure, let's go get an early dinner. Maybe two. Somewhere around here? There's a nice curry place near home.'

I explained where we were going, all of ten minutes away. After we donned our respective helmets (by now I was an old hand at strapping my gear on), we headed off on the Triumph. I held onto John as we cruised gently down Oxford Street towards Surry Hills. The cafes and bars were, as usual, hiving with activity. Music blended with laughter and the clatter of cutlery.

Turning into Riley Street, I saw blue. It was a benign powder blue. And then some chrome and a window. Time was suspended for a moment, just like in one of John's photographs. I drew a breath, and then I was flying.


'Anna, can you hear me?' A man was looking down at me. Was it god? I didn't expect god to look so young, and so…Lebanese. 'How many fingers am I holding up, Anna?'

'Two,' I said. 'Peace,' I added, and did my best to give him the peace sign back.

'You're alright,' the young Lebanese god smiled.

I looked around, realising we were in an ambulance. Then god got in the way.


It was Emergency. I knew that much. I'd been lying awake alone for a while, wondering how John was. The nurse who had come in earlier didn't know that patient. My left arm, now bandaged, had copped some grazing. It was tender. I could also feel the bruise on my left cheek. A bit sore, but not too bad. The nurse said my helmet saved my life. I was lucky.

'I think I should call someone for you,' he said. 'Your parents? A close friend?'

'No thanks,' I replied. 'I'm okay. Can you find out about John? John Roebelling?'

The dark blue curtains around my bed were firmly drawn behind him. I could hear people walking past, whispering. Then two pairs of shoes stood on the other side of the curtain. One black, one white.

When they entered, they took their seats by my bed.

'Do you have someone coming in, or are they in the waiting room?' Doctor Alice Henry asked.

'No, but I'm fine, thanks. Really. I just want to know about John. John Roebelling. Is he okay?'

'The car was a light blue VW Beetle,' Police Officer May Anderson put forward this odd fact simply, but with an unexpected gentleness. 'It was one of the new ones, only a year old,' she added, looking pained as if the car were a child. It was an unusual amount of detail, but I could tell she was leading up to something. Doctor Henry stepped in. 'The driver of the motorcycle. John. I'm afraid he didn't make it.'

Disbelief hung in the air for a few minutes. The doctor continued, but I only absorbed parts. 'The way he fell….neck….post….died at the scene.'

'God, I feel sick.' I gripped my stomach. Doctor Henry passed me a plastic bowl into which I expelled mostly bile. I hadn't eaten for ages. Neither of us had. We were going to get some dinner. The two sat next to me, quiet sentinels.

'If he wasn't so tired from the exhibition, this probably wouldn't have happened.'

'John did nothing wrong. You did nothing wrong,' Police Officer Anderson said. 'The account of the accident was verified by several witnesses. What happened, it was unavoidable. The brakes of the car failed. The vehicle is under investigation. The young woman, the driver of the car, is devastated,' she added. 'Anna, you mustn't blame yourself. This was caused by a mechanical failure and terrible luck. I'm so sorry.'

'The only thing I remember seeing is blue. Powder blue,' I said.

'Yes,' Officer Anderson replied.

I wondered why I wasn't more upset. 'Shock,' Doctor Henry explained, offering mild sedatives. I took them from her, but didn't take them. Just held them in my hand, waiting.


'The funeral will be early next week,' Eden said. I was back at home after spending the night in hospital for observation. Against doctor's instructions, I decided not to call anyone and made my way home alone. I had an overwhelming need for space. For silence. The police were already contacting John's next of kin. I didn't know who they were. His parents, I suspected. The apartment was empty. Liz was elsewhere.

'John's parents are sorting out the arrangements,' Eden added.

'Okay,' I replied, feeling guilty of having so little knowledge about them. They were Hawks fans, lived in Melbourne. Close in some ways to John, but what ways I had no idea. He'd said he didn't see them much. That distance was a good thing.

'They had to return from their holiday in Amsterdam. His sister's flying up from Melbourne. That's why they weren't at the opening,' he explained. 'John's family are very grateful to you.'

'To me?' I asked. 'What for?'

'For helping their son realise his dream. The opening meant the world to him. I wish I had given him more…more…I dunno. Something more.'

'You said his exhibition was "Zen of the grease-monkey".'

'I said that?' Eden groaned. 'Now I feel even worse.'

'No, it made him laugh when he was feeling really tense. It was perfect.'

'In its imperfection.'

'That's something Ben would say,' I said, feeling the heat of tears rising. 'Does he know?'

'Yes.'

'Shit,' I said, head in my hands. 'Noah doesn't know. I'd better call. He never answers. Maybe that's a good thing,' I rambled. Eden offered to call, but I insisted. It was my job. In a crisis, roles seem to be designated by an invisible force. Eden then suggested I pass on his number to Noah. Then connections with the family can be made. He promised to let me know about the funeral details.

'Call anytime you want to talk, okay?' he said.

'You knew John a lot longer than I did. I should be offering that to you. And I am. I am here for you, Eden. And Ben too.'

'That's kind, Anna. And I know what you're saying. Yeah, Ben and I were close to John. But you guys just seemed to click into this deeper thing. We could all see it. Short but…not sweet. More than that. Dark organic chocolate, maybe.'

I nodded staccato-like, thanked him before hanging up then released a deep groan that came from some place inside that was wild.

'Motorbikes are death traps,' my mother said. She hadn't heard the whole story yet. Just that I'd been a passenger, we had an accident, but I was alright. 'Yes, you are right…' I started, but couldn't complete the sentence. 'How's Dad?'

'He's doing much better. I think he's out the back, tinkering on something in the shed. Want a word?'

'Leave him to it. Send my love,' I said. 'Are you okay?'

'Yes,' she replied. 'But my cheese biscuits won't be if I don't get them out of the oven. Can you wait a minute?'

'I'd better go,' I said. 'I'll call in a few days.' Mum still risked her biscuits to find out when I was coming for a visit. I satisfied her with 'My thesis has become more demanding…end of term?'

Being a Sunday, it was safe to leave a voice message for Sharon at the university for Perry about John. No conversation required. With apologies, I was unable to attend lectures or my thesis meeting on Monday and Tuesday, I said, and didn't know after that. And hung up. It will be what it is, this goldbrick time.

Noah picked up immediately, which I hadn't prepared for. He was flabbergasted at the news but gathered himself enough to ask if I was okay, if I needed anything. He'd speak to Eden, he said, and to the family when they were ready. And then he was gone. But the silence ended there. The news found its way to the world like a grapevine on speed. The media, who had clamoured for John's attention prior to the accident, were recharged with new zest. A new story, a tragic one. John's image appeared in every Sydney newspaper and was scheduled to appear in most national glossy magazines as a tribute to a young star, snatched cruelly before his time.

It turns out disappearing is impossible. On Monday and Tuesday, Maggie and Simon took shifts in hovering over me. The bruise on my face shocked both of them. It had spread and changed colour like a growth. Then they re-focused and got started on the business of being supportive. They brought food and drink, held my hand, talked about John, talked about anything else but John, set up movies for me to watch and watched them with me. Or rather, for me. I didn't really see anything. Liz was there from time to time, too, but was out of her depth. Her presence became the intermittent background music of uncertainty. What Simon was doing about lectures and research, or Maggie about work and her new housemates, I wasn't sure. I had asked, but the answers just didn't stay. On Monday, Sharon texted her condolences and passed on Perry's too (he was having some technical difficulties with his phone).

It was too late on Tuesday when I realised Noah would be in the gallery on his own. He had left a message that morning saying he'd see me at the funeral the next day. Eden had already texted me with the details. Noah added that he would close the gallery that day in John's honour. I would still be paid.


John's parents had agreed to hold the funeral in Sydney. This was for the sake of the large number of close relationships John had formed here. Many were struggling creatives hard-pressed to muster funds for a return Melbourne flight. John's funeral was like many others, except that it was John's. And this was a dream, a bad dream, surely. Made stranger by those conspicuously equipped with microphones and cameras, hanging around a bed of manicured roses next to the old stone church. As subtle as fair bunting in black. Their black t-shirts and black jeans might have been considered a compassionate gesture, except that photographers dressed like this on a daily basis.

Simon insisted on escorting me. He looked elegant in a grey-blue suit I'd not seen before. I was wearing my new black suit, successfully hiding my bandaged arm. My heels didn't hurt anymore, but everything else did. The bruise on my face was fading, but makeup didn't quite hide what was still there. I did what I could. We made our way across the neatly trimmed lawn, ignoring the whir and snap of the cameras, and entered the sparse interior. The white walls and ceiling were ribbed with exposed timber beams. There was no coffin, but a cremation urn had been placed on a small antique table at the altar. Walking slowly on the stone floor, down a side aisle, we wondered where to sit. The wooden pews had been pristinely polished, accessorised by neatly placed hymnbooks on ledges. Simon spotted Ben and Eden sitting one pew back from the front. He had remembered them from the opening. And so steered me towards the space next to them. The two nodded and smiled with sadness as we sat down.

Wide-eyed and clamp-jawed, John's parents, Bruce and Coral, along with his younger sister Mel, sat in the front pew staring out like statues. Bruce, albeit seated, looked tall. His grey hair was immaculately trimmed, his suit perfect for any high-level politician. Coral wore a crisp white shirt and neat dark brown jacket. With short black hair, strong features and dark skin, she could have come from Greek stock, Spanish maybe. It was where those big, empathetic eyes came from. I did a double-take when I saw them.

'Jesus.' That's what came out of my mouth when John's sister turned to look at who was coming into the church. Not a proud moment, but fortunately, I wasn't loud enough for the family to hear. Simon had seen it too and understood my reaction. I was unprepared for the female version of John. Her curly hair was long and blonde. Being female and a fraction younger were other notable differences, but that was it. Peas in a pod, as my mother would say. Mel differentiated herself from her parents by wearing a loose Indian-style shirt, black with gold embroidery. It had flowing sleeves on which she wiped off a tear. John's mother began dabbing at her eyes quietly with a handkerchief, while his father was pale-faced and looked like he needed to vomit.

Gazing back over the pews, I noticed Noah positioned mid-centre. It was not the best of choices. He was surrounded by young artists, most eyeing him as they weighed up the protocol of pitching their work at a funeral. Robert's absence was almost as palpable as John's. Kevin Bradley was nowhere to be seen.

The priest began the service, describing John as intimately as anyone could who was referring to a complete stranger. Ben's eulogy was poetic and precise in touching on aspects of his friend's personality that everyone immediately related to. Bruce read about his son until he broke down, then somehow found the strength to finish. The service seemed much too short for what was required, but the grievers dutifully filed out as they had entered. Lunch was to be held at Irene's place, a family friend who lived only two blocks away. Simon lingered next to me until he saw an old friend across the room. Encouraging him to leave my side, I did my best to convince him I was fine as I saw Noah arriving.

'Thanks for coming,' I said, walking up to him.

'Of course, I would,' he said with gentle gravity. 'How are you, dear?'

'Okay,' I said. 'A little numb, to be honest. I'm sorry I haven't been much use to you lately.'

'Absolutely no problem. It's all under control.'

'Has Robert been able to help out?'

'Ah – no,' he said, his eyes shifting to the bruise on my face. 'You were right about him being mixed up in that business with Kevin. Robert's been in some trouble for a while. Serious trouble involving gambling debts. I felt I had to help him,' he said. 'I was selling my private collection to…assist. But this took the situation too far.' Noah was doing his best to keep himself together, so I didn't push for more details.

'I'm sorry,' was all I could muster.

'We do make quite the sorry pair, don't we? Still, it's nice to see your friend here with you,' Noah said, using his wine glass to gesture towards Simon across the room. 'He was so helpful at John's opening.'

'Simon's a big fan of yours,' I replied. 'Actually, if you ever need extra help, he might be interested. Brilliant at sales, knowledgeable and highly trustworthy.' I left out that he was currently working at Harrington's. Simon could work around that roadblock. The Sydney visual arts sector was a small place. Awkward cross-fertilisation was inevitable.

'Quite the recommendation,' Noah half-nodded. 'I suppose it never hurts to have a Plan B. Ask him to call me,' he said. 'Rest assured, you always come first, Anna.'

'After Jan,' I laughed.

'After Jan,' he nodded.

We looked out over the room while sipping our wine, viewing the emotional kaleidoscope – albeit in suits of grey, brown and black. Some guests allowed flashes of colour. These were mostly the artists, many of whom were now next to Noah attempting an introduction – something artists were, as a rule, terrible at. A relative of John's had also appeared at Noah's shoulder, requesting a 'souvenir' to remember John by, like a painting. Taking Noah's empty glass, I nodded to the exit. He smiled back and fast-tracked to the door. Then I turned to find myself face-to-face with John's family.

'Coral, Bruce, Mel, this is Anna,' Eden gestured. 'John's girlfriend.' I stepped forward, wishing that our cultural tradition didn't expect grieving family members to meet and greet people who feel like crap but, chances are, not as crap as the family.

'Hello,' I said, 'I'm so sorry to meet you under these circumstances.' It was hard not to feel conscious of the bruise on my face. Maybe it would help say more than I could.

'Me too, dear,' Coral replied, 'but I'm so glad we have met.' I hadn't told my parents about John. He hadn't told them about me. But they heard something. John's parents were putting the pieces together. 'Are you okay, from the accident?' She reached out to touch the side of my face. But then stopped herself and pulled back.

'Yes, thank you. I'm okay,' I said, guilt curdling in my stomach. I survived.

'Only the other day,' Coral pressed on, 'a friend in Sydney had emailed me the article about John from *The Herald*. Bruce and I called to congratulate him, but we had to leave a message.'

'He was probably in the middle of doing interviews,' I explained. 'There's been a lot of interest in his work. You have so much to be proud of.'

'I'm so glad you're okay.' Coral reached out to touch my good arm.

Bruce shook my hand and said, 'The exhibition opening – wish we'd been there,' ending with a hurried, 'Thank you.'

Mel gave a hug, while her parents moved off to greet others. 'I know that you only met recently,' she said, 'but you meant a lot to my brother. He doesn't say too much on the phone, but I know him pretty well. Knew him,' she corrected herself, frowning. 'Sometimes it was the things he didn't say that gave him away, you know?'

'Yes, I think I do,' I said, repressing the surge of tears that kept creeping up on me. 'He was going to teach me to swim.' It was a weird thing to say, but Mel was kind enough to nod.

'Would you like a drink?' she said, gesturing towards the open bar. 'I know where Irene stashes her Jameson's. How about an Irish coffee to warm us up?'

Mel soon returned with a couple of glass mugs of hot liquored coffee, topped with cream. I had been surveying Irene's bookshelf. The woman clearly had a penchant for true crime.

I closed my eyes and took a sip of Mel's sweet, warm, white and brown concoction. 'Heaven.'

'Comfort brew,' Mel replied, sipping at hers. 'Anna…Where do you think our Johnny has gone?' she asked. The question was a serious one. She stared at me, expecting an answer. 'Do you believe he's up in some sort of heaven?'

I looked down at my shoes, both of which had started hurting again. 'I'm not really religious.'

'Me neither,' Melissa shook her head, 'but take a shot in the dark. What's your theory?'

I contemplated her answer. Eventually, raising my head, I gave the only answer I could, but with a lump in my throat. 'I don't know.'

'Thanks,' she said, her eyes reddening. 'Thanks for your honesty. I thought I was fine with the idea of mystery,' she said, tears rimming her eyes. 'All of a sudden, I'm finding it hard to make peace with it.'

'Me too,' I said. Then we held onto one another and our hot glasses as if our lives depended on it. 'It doesn't feel over yet,' I said. The thought just slipped out before I even knew I had it. Where did it come from? What did I mean by it?

Mel had some answers. She broke the embrace and frowned. 'I guess he is in his work,' she said. 'And his work will live on, so in that way, it's not over. He's not over.'

I nodded and sipped my drink. But it was even more than that, more than his work as a legacy. John was dead. That wasn't going to change. But the feeling that it wasn't over yet was clear. I couldn't explain it, but I was certain. Something important had started. And it wasn't over yet.

# CHAPTER 24

**M**arvin emerged from Perry's office just as I came out of the lift.

'Hi Anna,' Marvin yelled down the corridor. 'I've been looking out for you. I heard about the accident.' Then, walking closer, I came into full focus. 'Your face…are you okay?'

I touched it self-consciously, covering it. 'Fine,' I said. It's what you say when you're not feeling fine. When you're not feeling anything much. Then I noticed his face. Marvin's complexion had converted from semi-transparent to a warm off-white. And he had put on some weight. More university student, less praying mantis.

'Marvin, you look….good. What happened? Got a girl or something?' I was open to any explanation.

Marvin blushed. Yet more colour. Embarrassment became him. 'No, nothing like that,' he mumbled. 'Met up with Howie. His work is absolutely brilliant. It's turned everything around. I owe you big time,' he said. 'I will do the right thing by Howie, I promise.'

It was time for me to do the right thing by Marvin. 'You need to know something,' I started. 'Howie was involved in some illegal activity involving cleaning products without realising it.'

'Yeah, I know all about the Z thing. Don't worry, it's been cleared up with the police.'

'Thank God for that,' I felt myself slumping against the wall for support. 'Still, it doesn't mean they can stay in Australia, does it?

'I'm going to write a support letter to the Department of Immigration, but I doubt that'll do much. Howie said something about his granddad and a guy called Ruben going into the orchid business together. This Ruben guy's going to sponsor him. Apparently, there's an active orchid trade between Australia and China. It's the kind of thing the government loves.'

'Ruben's turning professional?'

'He said he's been wanting to leave his job for years.'

I shook my head and laughed. Maggie hadn't texted me that bit of news. She knew I wouldn't believe it.


Perry said nothing about my face. The bruise was moving from purple to a yellow-brown, like some sort of organic artwork. He just stared at me while I stared at a section of books behind his head.

'What would John think?' Perry's voice snapped me back to the present.

'What would John think about what?' I asked.

'What would John think about your thesis?'

'Why?'

'He fills your mind, not Dorothy. I'm doing my best to bridge the two. Get you to the other side. Amateur psychology,' he added, taking off his glasses. 'Had John been to the Western Desert?'

'Yes, he had,' I replied, 'when he was a child.'

'What did he say about it?'

'He said he liked it.'

'That's all?'

'Sorry? I don't follow.' And I did not want to follow, not to where this was going.

'Did John suggest you visit the centre, the desert? Uluru and such?'

'Well…yes, but…how did you know?'

'Anyone who's been there says you have to go. Amazing how many Australians haven't been.' Perry mused. 'Maybe a trip to the desert beckons.'

'What? When?'

'How about this Sunday?'

'What? This Sunday?' Any numbness I was feeling at the beginning of the meeting had just been smacked out of me. 'No. It's not possible. It's really hard to leave work right now. The gallery's so busy. All this attention on John's-' I stammered.

'Sunday, Monday, Tuesday, Wednesday, Thursday, Friday,' Perry counted the days on his fingers. 'Noah might give you Wednesday and Friday off. Six days should be enough.'

'It's a terrible time to consider going on a holiday.'

'Research trip,' Perry corrected. 'Our research trip,' he grinned. 'Naturally, I'm coming with you.'

I stared at Perry. There was nothing natural about it at all.

'If you expect us to go to Stumpy Downs,' I said, 'we are going to need a special entry permit through the Central Lands Council. That's what the assistant at the Araluen Centre said.'

'I made some calls after you told me about the fire. Finally tracked down the art coordinator, Helen O'Connor. She's answering her phone now, thank Christ. All we need are dates and we're in.'

'But how?' I asked. 'I heard it was really hard to get a permit.'

'Helen needs some help with a book she wants published. I said I would help,' he said, turning to his computer. 'Okay…leaving Sunday….back Friday….Noah can have you on Saturday, albeit a little dusty.'

'What about your students? It's the middle of semester.'

'They'll manage,' he replied, keeping his eyes on the screen. 'I have fillers.'

'What's the rush?'

'It starts to get very hot there in late October. We won't have another opportunity until maybe April next year. That's too late for your thesis, and god knows how long Helen will be there. The next one in line might not be so generous.'

*Or needy.* 'I need Noah's permission first,' I warned.

Perry picked up the phone and asked me for the gallery number.

'Perhaps I should speak to him privately, later,' I suggested. 'Face-to-face.' I touched my cheek, drawing attention to my wound in the hope of a skerrick of empathy.

'Don't kick a gift horse in the teeth, Lissam,' Perry replied. 'I am an older gent with authority and credibility, about to ask your boss for some time off on your behalf.'

With slumped shoulders, I gave Noah's mobile number. 'He probably won't answer.'

'Noah Webster?' Perry perked down the receiver. 'Yes, it's Thomas Perry here….yes….Australia is still treating me well, thank you. Sorry about your artist…awful….Listen, I'm with Anna Lissam and….yes, she's fine….' Noah said something that made Perry chuckle. 'Really? Well, I'll have to pop in sometime…but on to more pressing matters… We at the university are in the midst of organising an important field trip for selected students, leaving Sunday, and I believe that Anna… where are we going?' Perry looked across to me and shrugged, 'What if I told you we were off to the Northern Territory?' Perry closed both of his eyes tight. 'Really? Just as well we're packing our galoshes and going down to Melbourne, then isn't it?' Perry's forced laugh almost blew the spectacles off his face. 'Melbourne's important…we need to see how damp artists manage to create something of value…yes, I am English. Good point,' Perry smiled at the telephone. 'Anyway, this little jaunt means two days without Anna defending your magnificent castle of creativity…yes, good for her to get away…Saturday as well?' he paused a moment, then smiled. 'Sage idea,' Perry chuckled again while I ran both my hands through my hair nervously. 'Cheers, Webs. Yes. I'll pay you that visit after we get back. Bye now.'

Perry put the receiver back in the cradle with overly demonstrated self-satisfaction.

'You called him "Webs"?' I asked.

'He seemed to like it,' Perry defended. 'Besides, he called me Tom. The conversation begged for monikers.'

'So, we're going to Melbourne now?'

'No, of course not. He just didn't take too kindly to the desert idea. It's like an electric shock goes off in his head when you mention the Northern Territory.'

'Noah has his reasons.'

'So rumour has it,' Perry's eyes twinkled in delight. 'Anyway, thanks to you, Simon's going to be helping Noah in the gallery.' I'd forgotten I'd passed on Noah's mobile to Simon, who was delighted at the prospect of helping Noah Webster. Like Noah, Simon assured me he'd never muscle in on my job. I knew this to be true. But some matches are a natural fit, and this is beyond anyone's control. It was hard not to recognise the obvious.

I turned to focus on the matter at hand. 'Dr Perry, you know that I've hit dead ends at every point with this thesis.'

'This trip is an open door. The open door,' he said.

'Dorothy is in the middle of the desert, deliberately not talking to people like us.'

'Okay, it's an open window, then.'

'An open window?' I shrieked. 'Dr Perry, this is serious. Behaving with respect towards Dorothy Brown and her community is vitally important.'

'I am being serious. If she doesn't want to see us, we'll leave immediately.' Raising his hand to his heart, he added, 'We won't impose, I promise.' A pledge from a liar with what seemed to be a dodgy ticker brought little comfort. While I tried to summon up a counterattack, my opponent noticed my frown.

'Perhaps it's time to stop thinking so much,' Perry offered. 'Accept that you know little, just like the rest of us. Give your brain some space, let it relax at the home of one of the greatest artists of our time.'

There was something I was missing. I was sure of it. I looked hard at Perry and asked, 'Why exactly are you coming?'

'Do you expect me to miss this great adventure? To bypass the chance of meeting the famous Dorothy Brown? My motivations are very simple. There's nothing mysterious about it or me. I am the cheese to Noah's chalk, as it were.'

'If we go, we mustn't take photos while in the settlement,' I said. 'It's disrespectful.'

'I've been informed of this by Helen already.'

'And no pith helmets.'

'Pith helmets?' he asked, perplexed. 'No danger there, girl.' Perry's voice faded before clutching his chest with a grim weariness rather than panic.

I frowned with concern. 'Are you sure you can go, Dr Perry?'

'What do you mean?'

'Well,' I paused. 'Your health…'

'Absolutely no problem there either,' he replied, turning watery eyes to his computer. 'Now, we need tickets, don't we? Let's use the university credit card, and I'll try to get you there as my assistant. It's a bugger you don't work here anymore.' I slid down in my seat and said nothing. 'I will do my best Houdini in this tangle of academic bureaucracy. But if that strategy fails, your costs can be transferred to your student loan. How does that sound?' I sat, wondering if I will have a job once Noah finds out I'm not going to Melbourne, but to the desert. I shrugged my shoulders, figuring I still had some sweets coming. If not, I'll deal with it later. 'Compared to your fees,' Perry said as he searched for flight schedules on the web, 'this small amount will look like a puddle in the ocean. Oops, must have pressed the wrong button…Rockhampton? We don't want to go to Rockhampton…'

'I'll do it,' I said, dragging my chair behind Perry's desk.

'Splendid,' he beamed, shuffling his chair to the left. 'What a team we make, eh?'

I said nothing while I clicked on the mouse. And opened up a new window.

# PART 4
# TASTING

# CHAPTER 25

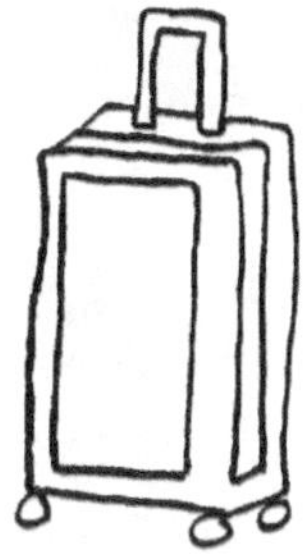

Perry trundled past a screaming baby, a frantic businessman and a daunted woman with a cat cage, all the while looking pleased with himself.

'Lissam, this trip just gets better and better.' Perry was wearing a grey suit with navy striped tie, while wheeling a brown leather suitcase on rollers. Smooth on all fronts. I wondered how long he would stay that way.

'I didn't think the trip had actually started yet,' I replied. We were at Sydney Airport's electronic baggage check-in kiosk. I was working hard at not thinking about John while coming to terms with Liz and Eva, as an unspoken couple, dropping me off at the entrance. Demonstrating such considerate behaviour from either of them was unusual. Maybe they were thinking about John, too. Being a Sunday morning made the gesture historic. Liz still had plenty to say about poisonous snakes, wild dingoes, and drop bears.

'Do you like witchetty grubs?' she asked. 'The Aboriginal people there will force you to eat them. Refusing is considered offensive.' Offensive? The thought sent a chill down my spine. Then I remembered, like so many Australians, Liz had never actually been to the Western Desert. 'They often eat them live. Good protein,' she added. Eva stared out the window and said little. They were a perfect match. Fortunately, neither of them hugged me. A cultural default none of us was prepared for.

Having never flown before, it took me a moment to pull up my digital flight boarding pass on my phone.

'I have a surprise for you,' Perry said while fumbling through his wallet, 'and for Helen. And it's going to deliver Dorothy to us on a platter.'

'A platter?' I asked, sensing an overture of nausea. Naturally, Perry was already a Qantas Club member. By holding the membership card up to the scanner, he was immediately checked in. Well, that was the theory. But the card wouldn't read because he was holding it incorrectly.

'Fuck!' he yelled. The word reverberated off the hard surfaces around him and the frowning nearby passengers. I took over, processing Perry's check-in and tagging his suitcase as if it were my daily routine. I then attended to my own check-in while Perry wheeled himself across the shiny surface to hoick the case onto the conveyor belt. I eventually followed, heaving my backpack with my good arm next to Perry's case. My daypack remained hung over my shoulder. The Freitag had to stay home, which I missed already. Both the bag and my home. *And John.* The thought slipped out fast. I pushed it back and walked.

When booking the tickets, I had been instructed by Perry to pick a flight that lands at Yulara airport. In airport terms, Yulara was also known as Uluru because that was what everyone was flying in to see – previously referred to by non-Aboriginal folk as Ayres Rock. With boarding pass in hand, I met up with Perry, who was waiting for me at the security gate.

'Take my shoes and belt off?' Perry laughed with the female security officer. Except she wasn't laughing. 'I saw a commercial about this on the telly. You'll be asking me to take my trousers off next.' She still wasn't laughing. Perry's chuckling stopped when they found his sterling silver letter opener in his carry-on bag. 'Bastards,' he grumbled. 'My mother gave me that. It's my rabbit's foot.'

The fact that a dead animal's appendage would have an easier time getting through security than a letter opener was not lost on either of us. I smiled at security, hoping that the large red mark on my face from the accident didn't match me with the criminal archetype.

'Aren't we going to Gate 17?' I asked as Perry strode forth in the opposite direction.

'We're early. Might as well go to the club, have a drink or something.'

'But I'm not a member.'

'I can bring a guest,' he said. 'They are very courteous at the club.'

The electric glass doors opened to an enormous wood-panelled counter. While Perry flashed his card at the neatly groomed receptionist, I was staring at what was hanging behind her. A large canvas celebrating thousands of tiny red dots. Different reds that almost verged into orange, or pink, or black. It was the Dorothy Brown I had seen on Noah's computer. But seeing it in reality was something else.

'Not bad, eh?' Perry asked. 'Thought you might like to see the new decor.' I wandered through to the lounge with Perry, soaking up all the other extraordinary Aboriginal paintings from Noah's collection. Rover Thomas, Clifford Possum Tjapaltjarri,

Tim Leurah Tjapaltjarri and Michael Jagamarra Nelson were all instantly recognisable. Noah must have received quite a sum. I assumed there would be an impressive security system setup to keep everything on the walls where they belonged, but it was discreet. Looking around, businessmen and women were typing on laptops, speaking on mobile phones or sitting and talking in low tones with each other. No one was looking at the paintings.

'You don't happen to know where these paintings were sourced from?' I asked Perry lightly. 'It's extraordinary that this hasn't received more media attention.'

'Not a peep,' he shook his head in wonder.

I privately enjoyed sitting in the plush armchair, sipping at my tea (Ben had converted me) while looking at the nearby Rover Thomas painting. Its large sections of colour – brown, black, white – were as strong and as gentle as his country. *John would've loved….* I pushed the thought back.

'What a great country this is,' Perry said, sitting back with his coffee. 'I might just become a member of it too.'

'You're thinking about becoming an Australian citizen?'

'The university is prepared to support the notion,' he said. 'Dual-citizenship would suit me, I think.'

'Best of both worlds?'

'Something like that.' I thought about how Perry could have two countries when others seem to have less than one, like the Houjin family. After a few minutes, Perry snapped me out of the trance by thrusting out his fist and saying, 'To Gate 17,' with crusade-style gusto.

I silently said goodbye to the red Brown and followed Perry through the glass doors. We walked for an eternity, passing gate after gate, back lit billboard after back lit billboard. Then, following the signs, turned left down a curiously narrow corridor away from all the other gates. The labyrinth led us down a second corridor before finding ourselves at the end of the line. The gate to Uluru.

The waiting area for 17 was unglamorous to the point of appearing temporary. Cold lighting laid its dead hand on the rows of badly scratched moulded chairs and worn, mismatched carpet. A section of floor-to-ceiling glass looked out onto the tarmac. Smaller planes arrived and left from this area, which explained the drop in decorative enthusiasm. A television monitor played a children's program, giving some life to the surroundings as passengers waited. We sat nearby, under one of the many exposed air conditioning ducts hanging below the foam ceiling tiles. I considered angling for more information on this 'surprise' Perry had hinted at, but decided it was better not knowing. Ignorance wasn't bliss, but it left me guilt-free. Perry pulled out an international art magazine called *Vision* and buried himself in it. The cover featured a young man in paint-splattered black jeans and a red hooded fleece, staring fiercely into the camera as if his bowels depended on it. The contemporary artist. Not that John would have ever posed like that, I thought. A boarding call for our flight was made over the loudspeaker.

Rather than tell Perry I'd never flown before, I just followed his lead. This was not difficult, as the man had a natural tendency to push himself ahead. Business class boarded first, however. Which meant that Perry had to wait. He had risen from his chair in anticipation, heel tapping in an agitated fashion. I guessed he usually flew business and had downgraded himself to my economy level. When he started twirling his spectacles until they flew out of his hand, I wished he had stayed in his own class. The inertia push of take-off wasn't as strong as the rollercoaster at Luna Park, but for me it was much more exhilarating. Air travel, I decided, was a theme park ride for the more purposeful. Feeling the rush in my body as we lifted through cloud tufts, I smiled across to Perry, but he was already nodding off. Once my ears popped into functioning order, we were cruising in the air. The shrinking city below looked like a model created by an enthusiastic architect with a balsa wood obsession. Then the tight pockets of urban housing gave way to haphazard brown and green patches. Like a quilt by a scrap-saving, poor-sighted grandmother.

I had called my parents before leaving, explaining I was making my way to the Northern Territory on a research trip.

'But isn't your thesis on that man…,' my mother asked. 'What was his name?'

'Vernon Jones,' I replied. 'Ah, this is a separate project. I'm supporting Dr Perry's research.' It was pretty close to the truth.

'I know your father would like a word, but he's just gone down the street.'

'That's a good sign. The hip must be doing well.'

'That pub is a great motivator,' she sighed.

'No problem,' I said. 'I'll talk to him when I get back.'

'Be careful, darling,' my mother warned. 'There's a lot of alcoholism in those Aboriginal community places. It can make people unpredictable.'

I ate my lunch (a roll, juice and mini bar of chocolate, not bad) while watching a movie about the end of the world. I couldn't get into it. Perry, on the other hand, was fixated. Staring out the window, the cloud had become thicker. I couldn't even see the world from where I was. After an hour or so into our 3.5 hour flight, the clouds thinned out, revealing hot orange colours with the odd black wiggly line amongst sporadic splotches of brown and green.

It was as if the land was one giant badly glazed terracotta pot from the 1970s. The lines looked like doodles, but they were patches of plant life following intermittent waterways. I took out a pad and pencil and attempted to draw it, but the page soon looked like an uninspired scattering of dead insects.

Feeling the purr of the engines, I sat. And with the sitting came a sense of peace. But it didn't stay for long. My eyes began searching for something. There was Perry with spectacles resting comfortably on the end of his nose. Dozing, now that the movie was over. He released a snore that competed with both the engines and the grizzling toddler in 12B. The surrounding passengers looked like tourists sold on the Western Desert package: Aboriginal culture, endless red earth and their collaborative mysteries. Just as I had. Except for bullying and manipulation from an over-ambitious Englishman. I settled back in my seat and stared out at the sky and red earth. Perry's snores, the grizzling sounds from 12B, and the hum of the engines all dissolved into nothingness.

Close to the end of the flight, the logo of the tourist package appeared. I had seen it before, on buses, fridge magnets, postcards and even on a money belt made in China with the word 'Melbourne' next to it. But there it was, in plain view. Before I knew it, I was yelling, 'Uluru! Uluru!' I must have sounded demented.

'WHA-?' Perry woke with a start. The surrounding passengers laughed.

'Quick, look. That's Uluru,' I dropped my voice. Nothing seemed as weird or as spectacular as that enormous red rock in the middle of nowhere.

'*Terra nullius*,' Perry mused. 'Land of no one.'

'I don't think the Aboriginal people here would call it that.'

'Well, Lissam, that is probably because they don't speak Latin.'

Peering through the airborne porthole, I noticed that the rock looked like it was asleep, like the heat had got to it a bit. It was the middle of the day, after all. According to the small inflight video screen (post-end of the world) it was 37 degrees down there. I felt the urge to give the rock a water bowl, but apparently, there already was one of an artesian variety, somewhere underneath all that red dirt.

'My god, that's the Olgas!' I yelped when the enormous rock formations came into view. This time, a string of smooth, strong domes. Collectively, their presence was like a dancer lying down on a stage. Waiting.

'They call the range Kata Tjuta now. That's the proper Aboriginal name,' Perry added smugly. I sat back sheepishly in my chair, eyes glued to the landforms. They sat there in the middle of the red expanse, seemingly oblivious to humans. It was easy to imagine them without names from any culture. They were just there.

The overhead speaker announced our imminent landing.

'For all my travel experience,' Perry smiled as we headed downward, 'I still find descent exhilarating. Don't you, Lissam?'

'Umm,' I replied, gripping the armrests. My stomach was rising to meet my throat as the aircraft dropped. This wasn't exhilarating. This was terrifying.

'It probably explains the sense of importance one feels when disembarking. Airports are designed specifically for it,' Perry continued. 'The long, tunnelled walkway to an enormous structure where people are waiting for you. Very much like a musician approaching the stage for a concert, or an athlete entering the oval for a test match.'

'Will people be greeting us?' I asked, as an attempt to get my mind off crashing and burning. Crashing hard. Slowly burning. People greeting.

'No one from Stumpy Downs,' he replied.

I took that as a 'no'. When we came to a standstill, I began to breathe normally, staring in relief at the intact backrest before me. Perry unbuckled and grasped at the storage compartment above us, keen to greet the imaginary fans first. After passing over my daypack, he made his way down the aisle towards the exit. I did my best to keep up. Emerging from the plane, the heat hit my body. The blue sky was baking, and the air was so dry it was like someone had stuck a hairdryer in my mouth. I followed Perry down the stairs and along on the small strip of tarmac that guided us through a surrounding landscape of red dirt and scrub trees. I waved flies away from my face. 'No long, tunnelled walkways here,' I murmured to Perry's back. Sweat stains already appeared under his armpits. Far from being greeted in a stadium-like structure, we approached what looked like a small storage shed. The interior mostly consisted of two baggage carousels and a line of fluorescently illuminated car hire counters. We stood next to the carousel, still and empty, waiting for it to come to life.

'I hate this,' Perry said. 'Waiting for luggage kills disembarking dignity stone dead.' He checked his mobile for messages before continuing his tirade. 'My bag never appears through those little rubber flaps first, or second, or third. Or tenth.' At that point, the belt began to move, and a suitcase appeared. 'I don't believe it. It's mine! The gods finally hear me…hold on,' Perry's shoulders slumped, 'no it's not …blast,' Perry continued stony-faced, eyes fixated on the belt, 'Club Members should receive their bags first, tagged "priority". But they come out…willy-nilly,' He flung his hand out to the rotating bags with exasperation. I nodded absently in return, also consumed with scanning for my backpack. And there it was. I stepped forward to pull it off and dragged it back to where Perry was standing.

'Shouldn't be too long now,' I comforted. 'It was only a small plane.' After the conveyor belt had done its third circuit, Perry stopped gritting his teeth and lurched forward to collect his case, the last bag to appear. Dragging it to sturdy ground, his red face turned up to the ceiling, allowing deep breaths.

'Are you okay?' I had asked this question before. But the answer now had more weight. Being alone with him in the desert brought a gravity to the situation. I could end up travelling with a corpse.

'I'm fine,' he insisted. 'Just give me a moment.' Within a minute, he did seem fine, happily wheeling his suitcase towards the car hire counter.

Uluru was about ten kilometres south of the Yulara airport. But in the desert, the concept of distance changes. According to the map, Stumpy Downs was 800km northeast of Uluru, but Perry was ready to drive into multiple sunsets in a camper van he had hired for us, called 'The Adventurer'. I understood that, coming from the other side of the world, a person would want to make the most of the opportunity. Which was probably why many Australians were notoriously lethargic about taking the trip in the first place, but knew Prague like the back of their hands.

After five minutes of paperwork, Perry was shaking the rental keys with glee. I hurried to catch up. My accident arm began aching as I followed Perry's charge towards the car park. The Adventurer was a jumbo-sized SUV with air conditioning, a roof top pop-up tent, fridge, portable gas stove, solar heated portable shower, outdoor table, chairs, and separate ground tent. Thankfully, at the time of booking, Perry had made it clear that we were to have very separate sleeping quarters.

'This beautiful monster takes diesel,' he continued, 'which is just as well. We can't enter Stumpy Downs with petrol, apparently.'

'Because of the petrol sniffing problem in the community,' I added.

'That's right,' the Englishman confirmed.

Bar the red letters of 'Adventurer' along each side, the vehicle gleamed a pristine white. With the miles of red dirt before us, it wouldn't stay pristine for long. We threw our bags in the back, climbed into the front, and prepared ourselves for rugged desert exploration.

'Shit,' Perry said, looking at the dashboard.

'What?'

'No CD player,' he groaned. 'What kind of backwater is this?'

'The terra nullius kind,' I murmured, wondering who, apart from Perry, owned CDs anymore.

'But I had Vivaldi and everything,' he whined. 'Oh well, we can sing, can't we?' Imagining Perry launching into private boys' school rowing songs, I scrambled a manic search around the dashboard. 'There's a USB port. Do you have music on your phone?' Perry looked at me like I had lost my mind. I was about to offer my phone, but as he put the car in gear and headed out of the car park, Perry said 'Recorded music is inappropriate. This research trip does not require a soundtrack beyond the here and now. Beyond this land.' Glancing sideways, I saw that Perry's complexion was already flushed from the heat. I had heard many of the asphalt roads in the area had no speed limit at all. I made a mental note of the handbrake in case some kind of seizure happened behind the wheel.

'Let's grab some sustenance at the camping ground first. Then we can check out those stones on steroids,' Perry announced. I nodded in agreement while pulling tightly at my seatbelt. And began to pray for both of us.

# CHAPTER 26

The campground was a short distance from the airport. Once we arrived, Perry paid the fee and bought some sandwiches for himself (a second lunch) and cool, flavoured mineral water for both of us. We ate at a table under the shade of a plastic umbrella, looking over a stretch of well-watered grass. Feeling the heat, Perry then decided to change. He emerged from the toilet block wearing a short-sleeved shirt and shorts, betraying virgin-white legs of English heritage. Saying nothing, I slid on my sunglasses and climbed back into the Adventurer. Perry clipped his shades onto his spectacle frames, pulled out of the car park and headed towards the national park.

The Australian desert was not like the endless sand-duned Sahara, or the cactus country of Arizona. This was an expanse of flat orange-red land upon which tufts of blond spinifex and low hardy shrubs squatted. There were also collections of desert oaks – dark, Giacometti-thin trees with fringe-like leaves – and mulga trees with flowers that looked like Buddhist-yellow furry caterpillars. The mulga's skinny trunks and leaves didn't hide much either. It was hard to hide in a place like this. I didn't think of John, but feelings of him surged up from time to time. They were sent back down again. I looked hard at the expanse, doing my best to investigate any interesting detail.

*So where were Kata Tjuta and Uluru?* I wondered, squinting into the landscape. The answer came within minutes when a brown knobbled formation in the distance came into view. As we approached, the knobbles grew larger and larger.

Perry had recommended seeing Kata Tjuta first. 'Sunset at Uluru is reported to be a highlight,' he said, 'of low light,' he added with a smug grin. I had read somewhere that Kata Tjuta meant 'many heads' to the Anangu people, the traditional guardians of the land. Photos on Google make it look like about six large formations, but there were actually thirty-six. Kata Tjuta was like an inverse canyon. Great lumps of pebble sandstone emerged from the red sand as if pushed up by gigantic fingers from under the earth's surface. Parking the Adventurer, we walked along a heavily pebbled track through The Valley of the Winds. A tourist sign explained the domes were over 500 metres tall, topping Uluru's 348 metre height. It was hard to believe that we were looking at the eroded version. Once everything was much taller than this, the sign said. Whenever once was. The whole walk took three hours, which we didn't have time for if we wanted to 'engage with Uluru' (Perry's words) before sunset. Watching Perry stagger and trip down the rocky path, it was doubtful he would have been up to it anyway. But we pushed on and covered what we could manage.

It was spring in Sydney. Here, in the Western Desert, it felt like the middle of summer. Sweat dripped from under my armpits, around my neck, and down my back. Shaking my head to disturb lingering flies, I looked over the wildflowers, tiny and delicate in such an intrepid environment. Despite my research, I didn't know what most of the flowers were called and wasn't in the mood for a lecture from Perry about my own country. But as we wandered about, even Perry fell quiet. The place certainly had a 'gathering' feeling to it. But it also reminded me of melons. Looking up between two curved cliff faces, one side appeared to have been got at with a large melon-baller. The massive round holes had matching balls of conglomerate rock scattered at the base, sitting amongst tiny wildflowers.

Climbing back into the Adventurer, I secretly hoped for a gaudy chocolate box sunset over Uluru. This was putting a bit of pressure on the forces of nature as clouds were rolling in. According to the UK's Daily Mail Online, Uluru looked silver in the rain and that this was quite a rare sight. But the clouds that late afternoon were the wispy, half-baked variety.

Uluru was like so many things. Metaphors tumbled about my head as we circumnavigated it in the Adventurer. It had been photographed enough. Looking striking, certainly, but never quite capturing the natural magic. Up close and personal (without airbrushing), its complexion was surprisingly pimply and pockmarked. This was the real thing. I could imagine John putting away his camera. Not even bothering.

'I don't really want to walk around it, do you?' Perry asked.

After being told by the elders that climbing Uluru was insensitive to their Dreaming, the next best thing for tourists was to say they walked all the way around it. It surprised me Perry didn't want to. I assumed walking around it was what we were doing, just so that Perry could tell people that he had walked all the way around it. Perhaps his health wasn't up to it, a topic he circumvented well.

'No, that's fine.' I shrugged. Perry pulled over to a more solitary spot, away from the buses, camper vans and four-wheel drives, where we could sit on short fence posts and look at what many simply refer to as The Rock. We just sat and stared upwards while others trailed around the rim at the base, like ants surrounding a fruitcake.

Like Kata Tjuta, Uluru was a sacred site. This information gave the experience added kudos. But I felt like a child being told to be quiet in the church. I did my best to behave, but knew I didn't quite understand it. The sacredness. And then I noticed Perry, standing with his white legs wide, arms stretched out in front of him, and clip-on sunglasses looking straight ahead. I realised he was commencing a tai chi formation. He pulled his arms slowly back, then pushed them gently forward once more. Then to one side, back and forth. Then to the next, back and forth. Despite the growing sweat stains under his arms and down the ridge of his back, Perry continued his routine. He was nothing if not thorough. The performance was both comedic and sweet. Finally, resting on a nearby post, Perry said 'Apparently, there are sites much more sacred than Uluru in this area, but we would never be able to pick what they are. Places that are useful for survival in the desert, I imagine. Alternatively, we like the big stuff. Palpable and spectacular.'

'Right now, I have to admit I do,' I replied, gazing out at nature's enormity. When we got back in the car, I noticed a dead bird nearby, half eaten by something over time. The bird looked more like a random collection of feathers and bones. I couldn't decide whether it was ugly or beautiful. I guess it just was.

We drove to the government-designated Uluru sunset spot where, as the signage indicated in multiple languages, we were permitted to take photos. This meant everyone took home the same image. The park was very organised like this. Other tourists had already gathered, armed with folding chairs, digital cameras, lenses and a commando's patience. Perry pulled out his camera. It was one with film. A middle-of-the-range instamatic, possibly from the 1980s. There were grandmothers with more advanced equipment at this lookout. I didn't own a camera, usually opting to use my phone if needed, which was rarely. Remembering John's words, I sat on the Adventurer's bumper bar and soaked up the desert as best as I could.

The clouds had set in and – one by one – people began to doubt. The garish sunset wasn't going to happen. Groaning, the crowd packed their cameras away, got back behind the wheel and began to pull out, including us. Perry's mind was now elsewhere. He had developed a thirst for beer. We were quiet on the way back to the campsite until we both gasped in unison. Kata Tjuta rose above the horizon, lit up in pinks and purples like a full forward's shins after a grand final. It was spectacular. Perry pulled over and hung out of his doorframe, clicking away madly. I just watched as the glory disappeared into the night. It would be back, but I probably won't be.


To buy beer or wine, you need to show your Yalara campground-resort pass. This ensured local Aboriginals were prevented from buying a drink. I overheard in the dinner queue that a couple of beers slip under the radar if the right staff are on duty. I ordered our salads, and upon Perry's command, our raw kangaroo skewers. 'We can say to Dorothy Brown we've eaten kangaroo. It could be a valuable bonding opportunity.' Flashing his pass and a gleeful smile, he added, 'I'll get the beers.'

It was a cook-your-own affair at the resort hotel. Twelve large BBQ grills were set up and sizzling for the hungry onslaught. The onslaught was mostly comprised of well-read German tourists. Beverly, a retired Australian woman standing near the grills with a glass of chardonnay advised me to cook our kangaroo skewers medium-rare for the best eating. Being an expert in instant noodles, I found this task almost as challenging as the notion of eating a damned cute marsupial. Beverly detected my hesitation and guided me through the process.

'What does kangaroo taste like?' I asked.

'These have a spicy marinade, so that's what you will taste,' she replied with a smile. 'Roo is very lean, so not a strong taste on its own. It's like sweet filet mignon,' she added. I thanked her and made my way towards Perry at the communal trestle-styled table. He was talking to a couple of young lads from Bavaria. They seemed to take pride in their inventory of local knowledge; correct pronunciation of Aboriginal areas, flora, fauna, and white settler history. They also knew that the orange-red of the desert sand was the iron from the surrounding mountain areas eroding off the surface and, with exposure to the air, becomes rusted.

'I was right, Lissam,' Perry exclaimed. 'Your country is rusting.'

The Germans replied in a hybrid of English and laughter while they spoke of a famous telegraph line I had never heard of. I took my first bite of kangaroo and found it quite tasty. Beverly was right.

'Kangaroo is very low in saturated fat and high in protein,' one of the Germans said.

'And more environmentally friendly than a lot of other meat,' added another.

Perry nodded, momentarily focused on moving through his meal. Meanwhile, I did my best to convey my erudite knowledge of German beer and sausages. Then the tourists roused Perry into singing Wagnerian operas. It was just as well the tent had been set up before dinner because, several beverages and four Nibelungens later, we were lucky to find our way back to the campsite, let alone coordinate steel posts and nylon. Perry had decided that he would sleep in the tent on the lush mown grass, independent of the Adventurer, while I could scale up the flimsy aluminium ladder to the pop-up rooftop tent, 'away from snakes and such,' Perry added gallantly.

'Tell me something, Lissam,' he said, as he fished around for his toothbrush.

'Yes?'

'Why do you want to go to England?'

'Well, it's a different country, with extraordinary history.'

Perry nodded. 'An adventure?'

'Yes, I suppose so.'

'This might as well be a different country,' he said, giving up on the toothbrush search, 'with extraordinary history. And I think we could deem it an adventure, don't you?'

'Well, an adventure is compulsory according to our vehicle,' I said, thumbing the large red letters. I grabbed my toiletry bag and wandered off in search of water.


Emerging from the toilet block, I shivered as goose bumps rapidly covered my body. The temperature had not just fallen. It had collapsed completely. Jogging towards our site, more accurately, towards my winter fleece and ski socks, I saw something strange. Getting closer, I made out that it was Perry's ample bottom, donned in maroon tracksuit pants, moving into the synthetic igloo. I called out 'night!' before scaling up the Adventurer's ladder. I heard a groan, the sounds of rustling and zipping, then a begrudging 'night' in return. From the rooftop tent, only the lights of the toilet block and a couple of the nearby cabins could be seen. The darkness was inky black, but the twinkling stars between the clouds looked like they had just been installed. New lighting for an old place.

Changing clothes in a tent is never easy. Changing in a tent on top of an SUV was even harder. But I worked my way out of my dusty clothes and into my fleece, navy tracksuit pants and ski socks. Bedding down in my sleeping bag, I revelled in the encroaching warmth while thinking of the Germans and their well-organised lust for knowledge. Meeting Dorothy Brown wasn't something their guidebook covered. As I drifted off, my mind jumbled images of John, Dorothy Brown, and pillows filled with feathers and bones.

Our plan for the next day was to drive directly to Alice Springs. Alice Springs was the Western Desert's largest town. Population: 30,470. Once there, Perry announced, we were to check into a motel. He had a bad night's sleep in the tent, and his back was killing him. 'My shout,' he yelled before edging into the driver's seat. It was going to take the best part of the day to get to Alice. As Alice was on the way to Stumpy Downs, the stop made sense. 'Did you know that Alice Springs is known as *Mparntwe* to its original inhabitants, the Arrernte?' he asked.

'No, I did not,' I replied, juggling the egg and bacon rolls and coffees we had bought as breakfast. Road food. The culture of this place may have been around for over 60,000 years, but Perry was in a hurry. During the drive, I witnessed Perry's remarkably rapid back recovery. It seemed to be through a genuine enthusiasm for the place, mostly because he screeched to a halt every ten kilometres on Lasseter Highway to photograph a dead tree or some red dirt. Fortunately, he didn't feel the urge to perform tai chi. At one point, he tried chasing a willy-willy, the mini cyclones of the Australian desert also called 'Dust Devils'. Watching Perry stop to take yet another photo, it wasn't difficult to imagine being stranded in the desert hours later while he explored the joy of night photography. I spent my time not thinking about John. Looking at rocks. At bushes. At a single crushed beer can. Then thoughts about my father started to spring up out of nowhere.

My father and Puddles. My father and his dodgy hip. My father and his anger. My father helping me with my maths at school. My father and the fights. I walked back to the car, clicked on my seatbelt, and stared out. Perry climbed back in the car not long afterwards.

'You okay, Lissam?'

'Yep,' I said, staring out, focusing on a tree that looked well past the use-by date. Perry started the engine. After hitting the road again, a bird almost flew into the windscreen.

'Jesus!' I cried.

'Pied Butcherbird, I think,' Perry corrected. 'But it shouldn't be out here. Middle of the day, no water.'

I knew how it felt. Nonetheless, Perry saw it as a sign to stop. Again. For what, I wasn't sure. But he was out of the car and walking inland. I followed, focusing on the detail around me rather than the detail inside me. And the dull ache of John. John. John. The flies appeared out of nowhere, like unwanted houseguests. *Who was the houseguest?* I'd heard many flies in Australia were native and served a helpful purpose in the ecosystem. This knowledge didn't stop me from trying to grab them with my fists. It was hopeless. I was too slow and completely outnumbered. My nostrils flared in frustration, and a fly went up one of them. I pressed on the other nostril with my finger and blew air as hard as I could. The fly shot out and buzzed off. I groaned with relief. Meanwhile, Perry was wandering further into the scrubby landscape, unaware of my spectacle and even the flies buzzing about his own head. Giving up the fight, I kept following him, noticing there were as many empty bottles and cans as rocks and clumps of spinifex.

'An Indigenous meeting place?' Perry asked. By the tone, I could tell the question was rhetorical. Old signs of Aboriginal meeting places would have been the remains of a campfire, perhaps some bones from a kangaroo or goanna. Now they had non-biodegradable beverage packaging.

We both stopped when we heard the strange, mournful call of a butcherbird in the near distance. Perry followed the awful sound. God knows why. Still, I followed. We happened upon an area of scrub trees that formed a kind of circle, along with more empty cans and bottles. It felt like this was the focal meeting place. Or maybe I was tripping in the heat. After all, this was more likely to be the handiwork of backpackers 'at large'. The moment felt poignant, nonetheless. The bird disappeared, and Perry wandered further to pee. I stood looking politely elsewhere, wondering if we were trespassing. It was a minor but persistently lingering feeling I'd carried from when we first landed. I swatted at another fly.

We made our way back to the car, segueing inland on the other side of the road to take a photo of a dead tree decorated with old tyres hanging like oversized Christmas baubles. 'A not-so-sacred landmark,' Perry laughed, while puffing slightly from the walk. I stared at the tree. Perhaps it would make more sense in an art gallery.

Once back on the road, it finally happened. Perry started to sing. He chose *The Lion Sleeps Tonight* with a falsetto like fingernails down a galvanised iron fence. I offered to find the original – or any professional recorded version – on my phone and plug it in, but Perry wouldn't have it.

'We don't need technology, Lissam!' he proclaimed. 'We have our lungs and our hearts. We are in raw country. Let us roar!' Which he continued to do, his voice dominating the cabin's interior. Maybe singing would have done me some good, but I wasn't in the mood. Besides, there was no room for backing singers on this stage. Still, Perry's voice helped to silence the ones in my head for a while. When Perry finally ran out of musical puff, he said, 'Pine Gap's not far from here.' I knew about the satellite tracking station, owned partly (and dictated wholly) by the United States Department of Defense. Pine Gap was the Western world's worst-kept secret.

'Just think,' Perry continued. 'The nighttime eyes for America are right here, in the middle of nowhere.' We both looked out to the flat, dusty, scrubby landscape, aware of all we couldn't see. 'You can't fly above Pine Gap,' he said. 'It's prohibited. But what if you could levitate, eh?' he chuckled. 'Like you said, the natives could here.'

'Aboriginal people,' I corrected, then pondered. 'Levitation...I said that?'

'Levitation explains the bird's-eye view in dot painting.'

'That was someone else's theory, not mine.'

Then Perry began to sing again. This time it was *Ain't No Mountain High Enough* as we drove through a landscape as flat as a dinner plate. I imagined Dorothy Brown hearing Perry singing about there not being a river wide enough 'to keep me from you' and running in the opposite direction. When it became unbearable, I suggested starting on the packed sandwiches we had bought at the campsite kiosk. It was close enough to lunchtime. Perry's song petered out, and he pulled over. For a while, all that could be heard was the hum of the air-conditioning and the sound of our energetic munching.

'If Noah gets back into Indigenous art,' Perry piped up, polishing off his egg and lettuce ensemble, 'you can write this off for tax.'

'I doubt that's going to happen,' I replied after swallowing the last of my ham and tomato on Turkish.

'My declared purpose for trips is almost always business,' he said. 'Many begin with the idea to have a holiday, mind you. All I have to do is organise some token networking to write it off, but it never stays that simple. I always get involved somehow, then it really does become a business trip. Someone would want me to rewrite the course outline, or the sponsorship presentation, or the conference guide. They need me to explain it, to present it, to coordinate it, to tour it.'

'Sounds…demanding,' I replied absently.

'Well, how could I refuse them?' Perry asked rhetorically. 'They need me.'

'Do you ever travel with a friend or family?' I asked, hoping for some information about a wife or girlfriend. Or boyfriend, if that were the case. Another life beyond work and Dorothy Brown.

'Sometimes,' he shrugged, but didn't expand. Instead, the weight of the air in the car doubled. Perry peered through the windscreen in the hope of distraction. There was none. It wasn't hard to imagine Perry's holiday companions learning not to need him, spending their time in the sun alone, clocking up enormous expenses on Perry's accounts while he was required elsewhere. He grabbed the bottle of water from the holder and took a swig. 'Pleasure, business.' Perry cocked his head back and forth, weighing them up, then shook off the notion completely. 'As if the two could be separated!'

While Perry pulled back out onto the road and began to hum *Day Dream Believer*, I disposed of our wrappers in the plastic tidy bag. I recalled feeling the same pleasure-work combination. It was when I was at the image library while working on my Vernon Jones thesis. Now I was selling in a commercial art gallery. And writing a thesis on something I knew nothing about. Though that was about to change, according to Perry, my personal Ganesh – creator, sustainer and destroyer (not necessarily in that order), who was currently driving us towards yet more unfamiliar ground.

# CHAPTER 27

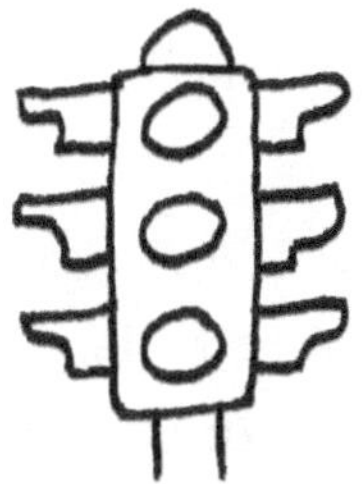

'STOP!' I yelled. Perry halted mid-chorus of *Yellow Submarine* and hit the brakes with force. Our bodies swung forward, then slammed back in our seats. A traffic light had appeared like an alien starship. It was the first we had seen since we landed. A strange placement of mechanical authority and direction. Most importantly, it was red.

'Jesus, son of Christ!' Perry cried. The exercise proved the Adventurer could go from 98 kilometres per hour to zero in a matter of seconds, as advertised. Waiting for the green light, Perry said, 'Did you know that Alice Springs is the only place for over five hundred kilometres to have traffic lights? Tennant Creek is the next town to have them, a considerable hike north of here.'

'No, I didn't know that,' I replied, monitoring my heart rate. Still idling, Perry flipped open a tourist brochure and called the Alice Springs All Seasons Hotel on his mobile. The choice had been inspired by the hotel's expansive bar, as indicated in a full colour photograph. I had already decided what to do if Perry tried the 'Unfortunately, they only had one room left, so we have to share' line. I would sleep in the bar.

'All Seasons,' Perry scoffed while they put him on hold. 'Should be called Both Seasons Hotel, dry or drier.' Flipping the page, he said, 'Damn, we've just missed the Henley-on-Todd Regatta. It's an annual boat race here on the Todd River.'

'Sounds like fun,' I replied.

'The riverbed is dry. They need bottomless boats,' Perry continued.

'A dry boat race?' I asked. 'You're kidding, right?'

He was not. But then a hotel staff member came back on the line, and Perry reinforced his booking request for two separate rooms. From Perry's responses, the booking was confirmed. The traffic light changed, and we drove into the small city, passing suburban houses – some with green lawns – before negotiating the Commercial Centre. Hungry Jacks, KFC, Coles and other familiar enterprises made themselves known amongst unremarkable two-storey brick and concrete buildings. The area was dotted with eucalyptus trees and the odd hardy shrub. While the architectural appearance of the place was not that unlike suburban areas in other parts of Australia, I was unprepared for the number of Aboriginal people wandering around. Even less prepared for the number of Asian residents going about their daily business. My head oscillated as I soaked up the exotic view against what was a rather dull backdrop. After some map navigation on my part, we pulled into the All Seasons Hotel car park. Perry picked up the keys from reception.

'Time for a shower and late siesta,' Perry announced.

I was grateful for the opportunity for some time alone. We agreed to meet at the hotel bar and grill in an hour for drinks and dinner. Discovering the rest of the town was reserved for the following morning. Then we would head for Stumpy Downs.

My room was small but comfortable. I couldn't help but notice the framed photograph of a tropical beach hanging above the double bed. Palm trees lined the white sand that met a predictably clear, almost sanitary, green-blue ocean. It had a mirage-effect after driving all day in the dust and heat. I took a lengthy shower, washing the dust off my body and out of my hair. I spotted the small sign explaining that water was a precious commodity. Too late. After towelling my hair, I luxuriated in the cool air of the open bar fridge, fully stocked with overpriced beer, juice and soft drinks. If I drank anything out of it, who would be paying? As fatigue descended, I called it safe and collapsed on the double ensemble.

I woke with a start. The sun shone through the slit between the yellowing beige curtains. 'Get over here, you gorgeous thing,' it seemed to say. I checked my watch. Perry was probably already downstairs, only by a few minutes. Hauling myself up, I threw on a clean t-shirt and light cotton trousers, combed my half-damp hair, and made it out the door.

Getting to the All Seasons Bar & Grill required venturing a few steps outside first. The heat was still strong late afternoon. The bar's exterior had large panels of smoked glass looking out on the quiet two-lane street. It felt familiar, except for the sign at the door: 'No singlets. No thongs. Suitable footwear required.' As I opened the door, cool air hit my body. The air-conditioning was almost as good as the long shower I shouldn't have taken. Being close to five o'clock on a Monday in this parched-throat town, there was a smattering of what appeared to be a collection of tourists, accountants, and tradesmen. Some were at the wooden and faux-brass bar. Others sat back in bucket seats, upholstered in a faded tropical motif. All patrons were Caucasian. A young, well-groomed barman was chatting with a slightly sunburned, overweight man straddling his barstool like a pogo stick. Walking towards them, I could already hear Perry's lecture. This one was on how 'Man United' was faring in the season so far. They were united enough to be second on the Premier League table, pipped by 'Man City'. The barman, not a follower of soccer, said, 'I don't understand why you'd bother if you can't pick up the ball with your hands.'

'It's a game of skill, Godfrey,' Perry explained. 'With feet.'

'But not to be able to pick up the ball and run is so frustrating,' Godfrey continued.

'Godfrey?' Perry asked.

'Yes, Thomas,' he replied.

'Do they call you God for short?'

'My girlfriend does, at certain times,' he smirked. 'If you know what I mean.'

'Indeed, I do,' Perry chuckled. 'As long as your mother doesn't. That wouldn't be right.'

'She doesn't, but,' Godfrey leaned in, 'wouldn't it be great if the boss called me God?'

'Now you're talking,' Perry's laughter boomed before he noticed he was in greater company. 'Hello there, Lissam. Come and meet God, Alice Springs' reigning snooker champion. God, this is Anna Lissam, my star student.'

'Pool, actually,' Godfrey corrected.

'Excellent,' I replied, unsure whether I should shake his hand or just drop to the floor and bow.

'You can't pick up the ball, any ball, in pool now, can you?' Perry quizzed Godfrey with a grin.

'It's a game of skill, Thomas,' he replied. 'With a stick.'

'Touché,' Perry chuckled. 'Okay, Lissam. What's your poison?'

'A VB would be great, thanks,' I replied, moving onto a stool.

Perry ordered a pint. The golden glow from the large, frosty glass against the backdrop of twilight was almost magical. I opened my purse, but Perry held out his hand, reminding me it was his shout.

'You don't need a pass to buy alcohol here?' I asked Godfrey, who looked back at me quizzically. 'Not like at Yalara,' I explained further.

'Right,' he nodded, then shook his head. 'No, anyone can buy a beer in Alice.'

'But I don't see any Aboriginal people in here,' I said, looking around again.

'Being a plush hotel bar like this...' he started, while I tried not to laugh. 'They feel more comfortable in other places, I guess.'

Perry eased off the stool. 'Shall we recline in those chairs, Lissam?' he said, gesturing towards the tub chairs and coffee tables. I took a healthy sip off the top of my pint and followed Perry towards greater comfort. After a day in the dust of the desert, my beer felt like a sparkling, crystal-clear stream. Given the chance, I would have bathed in it.

'Yes, this is good,' Perry remarked, settling into the pastel-patterned upholstery, and gazing at the glow of his own VB. 'I know we've been sitting in an air-conditioned car all day, but it actually feels like I've earned this.'

'Same,' I nodded, 'and I didn't even do any driving. Maybe it's also knowing that we won't be able to have another for the next few days.'

'No-alcohol zones should be banned,' Perry grumbled, but then attempted to lighten the atmosphere by saying, 'We've got something to celebrate. We'll be meeting Dorothy tomorrow.'

'We don't know that for sure yet, do we?'

'No, but it's likely,' he grinned.

I looked over at Godfrey, who was serving a group of broad-shouldered, stocky young women in shorts and polo shirts. I could tell straight away they were locals. They reminded me of the girls back home at Nagurra. Nodding to Perry's empty glass, I asked if he would like another.

'Why not?' he beamed. For a moment, I felt nausea in my stomach. And wondered why. Then recognized it. *All Seasons was not the Nagurra Hotel*, I reminded myself. *Perry is not my father. Urgh, the thought.*

I ended up buying the next five rounds (five for Perry, another one for me). Dinner never happened. *This is tedious,* I concluded in amongst Perry's art lecture stream-of-consciousness marathon. *I could be spending time with John. No, I can't.* I corrected myself. *God. John.* Three packets of chips helped to absorb the alcohol, but Perry refused to eat them. So I sat, alert for signs of budding discontent.

'I'm watching my cholesterol,' he announced. 'Did you know beer assists in the lowering of cholesterol?'

'I didn't,' I said. 'I know green tea is excellent-'

'Well, it's a theory,' he waved.

Watching my drinking partner down his fifth pint, I took advantage of his inebriation. 'Do you have a heart condition, Dr Perry?' I asked.

'No,' he laughed. 'I just like to take care of myself.' His expression became pained, as if I'd hurt his feelings. And then he looked a little angry. 'Do you know your cholesh-sh-trol level, Lissham?'

Sensing the conversation from here on required porcelain handling, I replied, 'Not by heart.'

'Boom boom!' Perry bellowed, almost falling off his seat with laughter. I began to relax.

'Maybe it's time to hit the hay?' I asked, while catching him by the arm. The man was heavy.

'One more!' he cried, perching himself properly on his chair. Perry then turned to look at me with intention. 'Let's call it a nightcap.'

After pint number six, I faced the challenge of getting Perry back to his room. This would have been a significant problem if Godfrey hadn't been on a break and offered to help. After all, the bartender reasoned, he was partially responsible for the man's condition. With a head under each of Perry's armpits, we lifted the English bulk up the narrow stairs to the apartments.

'We should have had dinner,' I puffed.

'That would've been nice,' Godfrey replied, 'if I hadn't been working.'

'Yes, it would have,' I puffed again, 'but I meant,' I said, stopping to catch my breath, 'it's a problem drinking on an empty stomach.'

'Right,' he nodded, pressing Perry's bulk to the wall. 'Easy to forget to eat. Beer's so filling,' Godfrey said. Perry burped in agreement. 'So you're a student of his?'

'Yep.' I staggered up the next two steps. 'And hostage.'

'Thomas told me earlier about how he taught art history,' Godfrey added as we reached Perry's door. I fished the hotel key out of Perry's pocket and we heaved him onto the double bed, stomach up. 'Well, I might leave the rest up to you then, Anna,' Godfrey said with brisk efficiency.

'Oh no, it's not like that.' I dangled my room key by way of explanation. 'He's going to have to stay fully clothed.' Perry looked happy enough, swaddled in crumpled shorts and shirt. Sandals were removed as a gesture towards sleeping attire before we tiptoed out of the room. Closing the door, I heard Perry chuckle and say, 'Do as the Romans do.'

'As if he doesn't get pissed in Sydney,' I said.

'Right,' Godfrey said, heading down the stairs, 'Rome's getting bigger every day.'

The next morning, Perry was pressed, perky, and keen for an enormous breakfast. There was no shadow of a hangover in sight

'Local fare,' he declared as we walked down Todd Mall. 'It's important to have the authentic experience, don't you think, Lissam?'

'Wherever possible,' I replied, observing how one shop after the other sold tourist-targeted products, from tea towels and t-shirts to opal jewellery and paintings displayed like stacked table placemats. The cafés were just starting to open for the day. We settled at one called 'Bob's' because it appeared the least affected. Wooden tables and chairs were scattered outside amongst an array of potted trees. The menu had been written on a blackboard hanging by the counter. And there were flies. Persistent mascots for the real central Australian experience.

'I don't know what happened last night,' Perry said after ordering himself the Mega-Breakfast and a long black. 'Last thing I remember, I was talking to you about the importance of Tintoretto's canvases at the Scuola Grande di San Rocco in Venice. Ah yes, "The Pillar of Fire" particularly, do you remember?'

'The scene where Moses leads the Jewish people into the desert,' I recited dutifully, remembering the evening lecture clearly.

'Moses looked magnificent,' Perry mused. 'Old Jacopo certainly had great fun with perspective against that dramatic orange-red sky. You really do have to go to Europe, Lissam.'

'Really?' I replied through gritted teeth.

'But this morning,' he continued, 'I miraculously woke up on my bed with my sandals off. It's amazing what you can do while under the influence.'

'Miraculous,' I murmured while counting the change in my purse. I ordered fruit toast and a latté. Despite a dinner of chips, I wasn't that hungry. Perhaps it was the heat. 'Make that a strong short black, please,' I said to the waiter. I figured I was going to need my strength. We were headed for Stumpy Downs.

There had been an attempt the previous evening, during Perry's last pint, to take advantage of his intoxication by asking the question that all his students wanted to know the answer to.

'I understand why you left London, Dr Perry. The National Portrait Gallery saga. But why move to Australia?'

'So many reasons.' He waved an inebriated hand carelessly around him. 'And yet none.' Then chuckled for an inordinately long time. Much to my relief, Perry differed from my father. He was a cheerful drunk, albeit obscure.

'Was it for our Aboriginal culture?' I pressed. 'The oldest culture in the world?' Perry focused hard on the table before him, as if trying to move it with his mind. No words came. 'Did you see Aboriginal art as a publishing opportunity?' I angled.

'I saw many opportunities,' he said, eyes aflame. 'And the possibility of nothing. Which, if you think about it, could be considered an opportunity in a Zen-ish kind of way.' He obviously considered the notion hilarious because, at that point, he almost slipped out of his seat in a fit of giggles.

'Fewer opportunities,' I persisted, helping him back up, 'could be good for your health. Did you come to Australia for health reasons?'

At that, Perry's laughter stopped, eyes red and watery. 'My health,' he began emphatically, 'is only human.'

'You seem to have a heart problem of some kind,' I said. It was worth a second shot. 'Or is it respiratory?'

'I definitely have a problem,' Perry agreed before releasing more waves of laughter. 'My glass is very empty. I don't want to sound negative,' he smiled through the tears, 'but it's not just half empty, you know…it's *completely* empty.'

Deflated, I stood up, glaring at my chuckling companion before returning, once again, to the bar. And that's when I got tired of it. When I realised that I needed to go straight to the source of the matter. Once back in my room, I picked up the phone.

'Goodness, it's almost eleven o'clock, dear. Is everything alright?'

'Yes, everything's alright, Mum. Sorry it's so late. Can I talk to Dad?'

'I think he's asleep. Can it wait until morning?'

'No, I don't think so.'

'Are you calling on your mobile phone? Shall we call you back on a landline?'

'It's okay, I'm in Alice Springs. I don't know the number.'

'I'd better get him then.'

I heard shuffles and grumbles in the background and the thudding sounds of someone making their way to the phone. 'What's up, poppet?'

'The Nagurra Galahs, Dad.'

'The Nagurra Galahs,' he repeated, still waking up. 'You want to know how they're going?'

'They're losing.'

'That's true. Have you been keeping in touch? I guess the scores are online somewhere…'

'No, it was a wild guess,' I said. 'I need to talk to you about when we went to the games together, before I took up netball.'

'It was nice taking you to the games, poppet. Ah, the good ol' days. Shame the team didn't nail a few more wins. Still, we had fun, eh?'

'It wasn't that fun for me, Dad.'

'I know that losing from time to time can be less than fun.'

'From time to time?' I exasperated. 'Winning once would've been nice.'

'Oh, poppet. You must understand that winning isn't everything. That's the problem with your generation. It's all about the result. There's no finding joy in the journey.'

'Was cracking pool cues over the heads of people at Puddles' bar finding joy in the journey, Dad?'

'Aw, come now. We had some rowdy times, me and the lads. But you were safe. Puddles and I made sure of it.'

'Dad, I watched you become physically abusive after every game.'

'Physically abusive? Have you been seeing one of them counsellors? Bandying terms like "physically abusive". Finding reasons to blame your parents for your unhappiness.' He was beginning to sound riled, but then he paused. 'Are you unhappy, poppet?'

'Right now, you could say that,' I replied. 'But back then, while you were throwing your weight around, I was scared stiff.'

'I never hurt you. No one did.'

'I was eight years old!' I yelled. 'I was terrified!'

Dad said nothing. I thought it best to wait, let him absorb the news. After a while, I wondered if he had hung up.

'Dad? You still there?'

'I'm sorry you felt that way, poppet,' he said. 'Why didn't you say something?'

# CHAPTER 28

After breakfast, we bought some pre-packed sandwiches – it was a takeaway town – and wandered further down the mall to experience 'art as souvenir'. Some paintings had been stretched and hung, but most paintings were tacked up on the wall like notes on a pin-board, lying in a pile or hung on racks outside like trousers on sale. This was for practical reasons, no doubt. Suitcase packing convenience. The paintings had close companions: painted boomerangs and didgeridoos, t-shirts, baseball caps and novelty road signs. At least half of what was on display came from Asia.

Still, I was glad for the distraction. I didn't feel like thinking about the call with Dad the night before. The whole point of the conversation was to feel some resolve, to be able to move on from it. Perhaps find a way to hate football on my own terms. But not receiving a proper apology from him left me feeling a new pain. Wishing I'd let sleeping dogs lie, I flipped through a pile of paintings that had less feeling than the postcards on a nearby rack. Or maybe I was missing something.

Further down the mall, we found a space not unlike a Sydney gallery. Hardwood floorboards and large white walls that gave each painting plenty of room to breathe. Within seconds, two things struck me about the exhibition. Firstly, all the paintings, and there were close to forty, were impressive. Contemporary Aboriginal from the region, they were consistently masterful in colour, space and balance. And the second thing that struck me was that each painting had a red dot next to it. Every single painting had been sold. By the labels, I saw prices ranging from eight thousand to twenty thousand. They would sell for more in Sydney. Perhaps that was why they sold so fast. One painting was off the wall, about to be packed in bubble wrap. The exhibition was coming down. We had got there just in time.

A middle-aged man dressed in a chambray shirt and moleskins stood at a large wooden desk in the middle of the room.

'Red Rooster,' he said into the phone. 'Hungry Jack's is too juicy, and KFC is too greasy. The artists work this stuff out with all that back and forth they have to do. On the road, they want Red- ,' he paused to listen. 'The new Jack Kerouacs? They are the original Jack Kerouacs, my friend. And Pirsig has nothing on these guys,' he laughed. 'Zen and the art of feeding artists, yeah.' The man listened as he looked at the ceiling.

'Transcendence?' Perry asked me. We were standing in front of a painting that was a collection of strokes, like white fur on a black background.

'Yes,' I replied, mesmerised by the rippled effect, as if the fur was shifting in a breeze. I cocked my head. 'It's almost Dorothy. Not quite.'

Perry leaned in to look at the label more closely. 'Eunice Brown,' he read. 'You were close, she's a relative.'

Looking further down the wall, each painting was by a female Stumpy Downs artist, each used an intricate dot or dash technique, and each was remarkable in its own right.

'Stumpy Downs has produced some incredible work this last year,' the man at the desk called across the gallery as he put down the phone.

'Sell-out show,' Perry said. 'You must be pleased.'

'It'll be sad to see them split up and go their own way,' the man replied, looking around, hands on hips. 'I've really enjoyed this exhibition.'

'You wouldn't happen to have any new works by Dorothy Brown here?' Perry asked with a grin.

The man laughed. 'No, unfortunately. Dorothy is still rather distant from the game. Haven't seen or heard from her in donkeys. But I spoke to Helen, their art coordinator, about the standard of this new work by the others,' he said, gesturing to his walls. 'Incredible shift in both technique and originality, all of a sudden. Helen can't explain the change. It just happened. And then their art centre burnt down.' The man's shoulders slumped. 'Just as they were really getting going, they came to a halt. We had to buy all these outright just to hold on to them. Otherwise, Helen would be sending them off to Melbourne or Sydney. Still, there's been no problem with re-sale. Just wish I'd kept a couple for myself.'

'We're about to go out to visit Helen,' Perry said, glancing at his watch. 'I'm helping her with a project.'

'Well, if you're going out there, best take some food with you.'

'Certainly.' Perry nodded. 'We shouldn't expect them to feed us.'

'Yes, but also take food for them. You'll have an easier time of it. Sausages, steaks, white bread, tea, milk and sugar.'

'Artist staple, eh?'

'Something like that,' he grinned. 'Give them whatever it takes to keep them painting like this.'

'I have every intention to do that very thing,' Perry smiled back.

The Woolworths shopping experience in Alice Springs was much the same as in Sydney, except that the majority of people wandering the aisles and working the checkout happened to be Aboriginal. I noticed there was a common smell amongst many of these people. I hovered whenever they were near, sniffing as discreetly as I could. It wasn't the usual body odour.

'You getting a cold, girl?' Perry asked as he stacked the trolley with white bread.

'I'm trying to work out the smell,' I whispered.

'It's what we'd probably all smell like if we stopped using deodorant,' Perry whispered, pushing the trolley towards the meat section.

'That's not it. They don't stink.'

'It is body odour, just not our variety,' he explained. 'Apparently, the body naturally adjusts. The same with shampoo. Our hair would go oily, but then adjust.'

'Doesn't seem to happen to homeless people in the city.'

Perry shrugged, 'Perhaps it's because they don't live in a natural environment.'

Then I realised the mystery aroma was similar to freshly turned earth. But by then Perry was already deep in beef. I wandered off to fruit and vegetables.

We eventually pushed the loaded cart towards the checkout, only to find that most people had at least two carts filled to the brim. 'They must live out on properties or communities,' Perry observed with a whisper. But I was watching a man smelling less of the earth and more of alcohol.

'What would you do if someone stole from you?' he was saying to the unfazed checkout assistant. 'You wouldn't like it, would you?' Before the man received an answer, he wandered off through the automatic sliding doors, leaving empty-handed. The expressionless assistant continued to scan the items. Then Perry's mobile rang. It was Helen.

'Yep, sure. We're on our way.' He hung up. 'Helen is telling us to get a wriggle on. We're to meet her at the Stumpy Downs turn off.'

'What's the hurry?'

'Don't know. Perhaps they're hungry for visitors,' he smiled and looked at the healthy pile of sausages.


'Onward and upward,' Perry proclaimed after we had loaded our mini-fridge and storage drawers with foodstuffs. Belting up in the passenger seat, I was glad to get back on the road. But we were heading for Stumpy Downs. Dorothy Brown territory. I was almost certain now was the time to hit reverse. But Perry was grinning. Steering out onto the street, it was clear he had something up his sleeve. A surprise for me and Helen. That was what he had said back at the airport. As we drove through town, dread ran down my sleeve. My palms were already sweating.

Not long after leaving Alice Springs, we came across a group of Aboriginal people at the side of the road, gathered around a Ford Falcon. One of the men waved us down. Perry slowed the Adventurer tentatively.

'We need a spare,' one man said, gesturing towards a flat tyre.

'Sorry, we can't help with that,' Perry replied. 'I'd take you back to Alice, but we're running late.'

'We'll be right, more cars coming into town,' he said with a smile that took up the best part of his face. 'Thanks anyway,'

And then we drove for two hours through the desert scrub on Larapinta Drive, passing three four-wheel drives, another Adventurer, four caravans, two willy-willys, a goanna and six camels.

'Camels!' Perry said, slowing up the car. 'Lissam, why didn't you tell me we were in Mongolia?' I had to admit, they were an odd sight. Still, camels were better designed than us for the terrain.

'I think they were brought out by Afghan traders way back.'

'Where are the Afghans now?'

'Don't know.' Yet again.

'I wonder who owns these fellas.'

'I think they're on their own.' I replied. 'Wild camel. Sounds like a retail chain.'

'Or an energy drink,' Thomas suggested as he returned to the speed limit and the camels disappeared out of view. While staring out the window towards the scrubby desert view, something occurred to me. The unease around meeting Dorothy was not limited to honouring the artist's desire for privacy. I felt the niggling fear of disappointment. What if I didn't feel the connection to Dorothy that I did in paintings like *Meeting Place*? I could be like a rock band fan, finally finding myself at groupie status and discovering my idol is at their best on stage and at a distance.

'There they are,' Perry said, slowing the Adventurer towards the parked minivan on the side of the road. Next to it was a small sign indicating the Stumpy Downs turnoff. A slim, tanned woman with short-cropped blond hair stepped out to greet us. The minibus was crammed with Aboriginal women and children, all staring out. Perry and I climbed out of the Adventurer, red dust covering our shoes as we walked towards her.

'You found us,' she said as she shook our hands. My eyes moved across to the minibus to the faces of Aboriginal women and children through the glass. No one looked like Dorothy. They were smiling, some laughing. At what, I wasn't sure. 'Change in plan, I'm afraid,' Helen said. 'We're heading for a station not far from here, about forty-five minutes away, so they can have a few days for Women's Ceremony. Some are already there. The rest are coming with me now. They said it's okay for you to join us, Dr Perry. Not to be part of ceremony, of course, but to be on the property. Just follow me.' Within seconds, Helen was back behind the wheel and heading for the open road. We pulled out, following the minibus. Children giggled and waved at us through the back window. I laughed and waved back.

'Stop waving and get those sandwiches out, Lissam. I'm starving.' I had to admit, my stomach was in agreement with Perry. The chip dinner and raisin toast breakfast were no longer cutting it. We munched in silence while watching the flat orange landscape dotted with scrub pass by. After a good forty minutes, I looked at the map and said, 'If we go much further, we'll be on the Mereenie Loop. We're supposed to have a separate permit for that.'

'The Mereenie Loop,' Perry replied. 'That leads to the canyon, doesn't it?'

'Yes, King's Canyon.'

'Nice of them to name a chasm after the monarchy, isn't it?' Perry laughed at the symbolism. 'Still, wouldn't mind seeing it.' At that moment, the minibus turned left onto an unsigned dirt road. 'But not today, it seems.' The Adventurer followed the minibus down ten kilometres, dodging a scattering of brumbies and wild camels on the way, until we stopped at an isolated house on the side of the dirt road. Again, Helen emerged from the bus while her passengers stayed put. We climbed out and wandered towards her.

It was early afternoon already. The sun was beating its heat out across a landscape dominated by red cliffs and a scattering of grey-green foliage. More mulgas and desert oaks, also umbrella bushes that don't look much like umbrellas and would protect little from rain or sun. I also spotted a few eucalyptus trees and plenty of short but tough shrubs. They all looked fine without water. 'Don't mind us', the foliage seemed to say, 'we're just sucking on sand.'

Seven cars surrounded the fibro house. However, on closer inspection, five of them were up on blocks. An orange Falcon and a white Toyota ute both looked like they had a chance.

'This is Betty's house,' Helen said. 'Her husband, Lewis, is the guardian of the land we're standing on.'

I looked at the dark windows, trying to identify some movement. Two dogs, possibly a crossbreed of dingo and kelpie, appeared from the doorway, followed by two grey-haired but able-bodied Aboriginal people. A thin man in a chocolate brown Akubra hat and a stout woman in a floral dress. Despite her greater weight, the woman walked faster and reached us first.

'Hi Betts,' Helen said, and looking over the old woman's shoulder, added, 'Hey Lewis.'

Perry held out his right hand. 'Thomas Perry, Prescott University. This is my assistant, Anna Lissam.' In his left hand, the Central Lands Council permit flapped in the breeze like a bureaucratic white flag.

The woman ignored the permit but greeted his handshake with her dark hand. 'Hi, I'm Betty,' she said, though it sounded more like 'Beddy'. The man had finally caught up with his wife and stood slightly behind her, nodding a greeting. 'This is my husband, Lewis.'

'We're grateful to you for allowing us onto this land,' Helen said.

'You're welcome,' Betty replied. She looked over and yelled 'Eh, you mob!' to those in the minivan, giving them a wave. Happy words were yelled out in language, and waving was returned. Betty's face then clouded a little when turning back to Perry. 'We do what we can to keep this place clean, you know.'

Perry looked at the old car wrecks and a plastic bottle lying in the dirt by his feet. I decided to say something before he did. 'No petrol sniffing, alcohol or drugs, right?'

'That's right,' Betty confirmed. 'We take in our people who have had a rough time out there, and we take them camping, teach them some bush medicine, that kind of thing. Back to Country.'

'Lovely,' Perry said, distracted. 'But what about an art centre? Do you have one here?'

'We don't do that.' She squinted back at him. Perry appeared perplexed. But for me, Richard Bell's painting with the words: *Aboriginal Art – It's a white thing* came to mind. This wasn't a place to create things for sale. This place was for something else entirely.

Turning to Helen, Betty said, 'You know where to go, yeah?'

'Just a bit further down the driveway, the houses along the left-hand side.'

'That's right. The school and my family's homes are on the right.' Betty turned to Perry and me. 'Camp at the front of the place on the left if you want. Helen, you take the first house, so you keep an eye on them,' she chuckled before wandering back to the house with silent Lewis.

'Don't be fooled,' Helen said as we walked towards our respective vehicles. 'Lewis has a lot of sway in this region. It's just that his English isn't as fluent as Betty's. They're both elders and the main spokespeople for this area, but Lewis is the one who owns these hundreds of hectares,' Helen nodded.

'Owns or is guardian of?' Perry asked.

'Both. He took a trip to Melbourne and got the title to the whole shebang. But he thinks the paperwork is silly. The community here already knows it's his. Or him,' she added. 'The title is just something needed to communicate with us whites. The government and mining companies, particularly.'

'Why are Betty and Lewis living up here if everyone else is down the road?' he asked. 'Do they need to be gatekeepers of their own property?'

'No, they had to move out of their house because of Sorry Business. Their son died in…an incident two years ago. Very sad.'

'Very.' Perry nodded, but continued his questioning. 'I don't understand why they had to move.'

'It's what they do here when the death of a close relative happens.' Helen shrugged. 'Betty and Lewis can explain all this better than I can. Feel free to talk to them about culture. Perhaps we can line something up tomorrow,' she said, looking back at her passengers. 'Okay, let's get going, so this lot can settle in.' We followed the minibus down the red dirt track, passing a reception tower, wind turbine, an independently standing solar panel, an old muster area with rusted branding gates and chute, and a scattering of more desert oaks and eucalyptus trees.

Through the entrance on the right was a school, as Betty had said. Two small Besser brick houses with concrete-floored verandahs and the odd air conditioning duct protruding from the exterior. Plastic play equipment sat in the red dirt outside. Painted on the buildings were bright colours, shapes, and the numbers one to ten. A mural of an emu and a kangaroo appeared separately around the side of one building. Their own interpretation of the Australian coat of arms. From the roof protruded a satellite dish. On the whole, the view was a mix and match of technology, symbolism and child's play. There was also a sandpit with no sand, but plenty of red dirt around it.

We pulled up at the first house, Helen's allocated domain. Fibro-built with a corrugated iron roof, saddle-bagged by water tanks. Helen was already hauling her backpack towards the small verandah. The women and children spilled out of the bus and made their way to similar-looking houses close by. They had obviously been here before and knew where they belonged. All the front doors were already open, some with screen doors to keep out the flies. As the sun beat down, the houses looked dark inside. Somewhere in this settlement was Dorothy Brown. My nerves tingled at the thought.

Most of the houses also had cars next to them – Ford Falcons, Holden Commodores, dual-cab Toyota utes, Mitsubishi vans. Many were burnt out, smashed, had tyres blown or sat on blocks. Emerging out of the white Adventurer, I noticed an old leather school bag lying in the dirt.

'The digs are pretty basic,' Helen said, re-emerging from the house.

'I can sleep on top of our Adventurer,' I said, 'and we have a tent.'

Perry looked a little startled and turned to Helen, eager for a counteroffer.

'Well, this first house has two bedrooms. I just need one of them. Only single beds and a bit squeaky, nothing special.' A grey kelpie appeared from behind the school.

'This is Rudy,' Helen rubbed the side of the placid animal. Perry stood back while I patted the dog tentatively. I offered again to sleep on top of the Adventurer.

'You sure?' Helen asked.

'I slept very well at the caravan park,' I replied. 'As long as you think…um…it's safe here.'

'Oh yes, we're safe.' Helen smiled. 'If they allowed drugs and alcohol, it might be a different story. As long as you're comfortable up there, that's all.'

'What drugs are problematic?' Perry asked.

'Marijuana, mostly,' she replied.

'Out here in the desert?' he replied, incredulous. 'They must have one hell of a hydroponic system to supply a weed problem.'

'Interesting that it's called weed, isn't it?' Helen pondered. 'There is native cannabis…can't remember what it's called.'

Perry suggested getting settled. Helen turned to chat to a couple of the women, using a language I didn't understand. Meanwhile, Perry took charge of his suitcase. With beating red face and determined grip, he hauled its tiny wheels across the red sandy surface. Rudy and I looked on.

'Well then,' I said to my canine companion, 'we might as well organise the rooftop tent. You any good with ladders?' Rudy gave a little bark. 'Didn't think so,' I replied. Unhooking the heavy plastic cover was akin to opening a giant jam jar, but I eventually managed to free it after straining several fingers. Then there was the challenge of getting the tent rods that were trapped under a large gas bottle in the box on the roof next to the tent. I did my best to pull the tent ladder down. This was supposed to raise the tent, but instead the ladder came apart in two. Fortunately, it was designed to split, and so I worked out how to reconnect it and successfully pull it down as intended. By standing on the edge of the back seat and stretching my body to its limits, I averaged at five attempts to install each of the six tent rods.

Consumed by the demands of the task, it took a while for me to notice the group of children that had emerged to watch. The boys were in shorts, and the girls wore summer dresses that were more like long singlets. Their hair and clothes looked a little dirty. But then I looked down at my white t-shirt, already turning a shade of apricot from the dust in the light wind. A more natural life, particularly one with buried water sources, was likely to be a grubby one. The children flashed their teeth, gleaming despite being a little broken or crooked in parts.

Three large women appeared not long after. The fabric of their t-shirts and skirts stretched across their ample breasts and hips. I presumed they were the mothers of at least some of the children. I smiled and nodded at my audience. The mothers, impassive, stood at a distance. The children, however, ran around the car while chanting, 'hire car, hire car'. Rudy ran with them, yelping in attempted unison. I jumped back onto the ground and pointed to the tent on the roof. 'My home,' I said. Then I pointed to myself and said, 'I am Anna.'

The children introduced themselves in turn. Tony, Daniel, Molly and Jeannie. Their English was as good as my own, so I felt like an idiot with my stilted approach. It was tempting to ask if they had traditional Aboriginal names, but I thought better of it. Too many unknowns. The mothers didn't utter a word. Instead, they sat down where they had been standing and ran their dark fingers through patches of dirt as if it were hair.

Helen emerged again from the house. 'You've met the welcoming committee, I see.'

The children laughed and ran to her chanting, 'Welcoming committee,' as best they could, though the ensemble was a blur of syllables. By then, the women were grinning and murmuring to one another. I detected long-sounding words dominated by the letters g, n, l, a and k. The speech was low and nasal, but the sounds jumped and skipped as if along a constant line.

My education on Aboriginal languages was limited to a tour at the museum during an undergraduate excursion. The group was stopped in front of a case of digging sticks, and our young museum tour guide announced – with a bountiful enthusiasm usually reserved for Junior School groups – that 'When white settlers came, there had been over 250 distinct Australian Aboriginal languages. Now there are approximately 145 in use. All but thirteen are considered endangered.' He gave me a special wink before continuing. 'The disappearance of these languages had been documented as the fastest in the world,' emphasising the word 'fastest' as if it were the fastest car or the fastest internet connection. 'When a language ceases to be spoken, much more is lost than words. Particularly,' the guide said, remembering to lift his index finger as a theatrical highlight, 'when the culture of that language is at least 50,000 years old. Now, any questions?' We all stared back, dumbfounded, before being swiftly moved through to the Oceanic section.

Helen engaged easily with the women, managing their vocabulary with apparent aplomb. I thrust my ineffective hands into the pockets of my shorts and stared down at my white feet that, with every gust of wind, appeared to be turning a darker shade of orange. Rudy looked down at his front paws that had somehow remained grey. The women rounded up their offspring and led them down a path between the houses.

'That was pretty impressive,' I said. 'You speak their language.'

'Their English is better than my Arrernte. But you pick up bits if you hang around long enough. I enjoy learning new languages, and very old ones,' Helen replied. 'Want a cuppa?'

'Sounds good.' I nodded, grateful for anything wet. 'Helen, we've got some food here for the ladies,' I said, opening up the back of the car, then the fridge.

'Goodness! Thank you so much,' Helen beamed. 'Let's pass it out.' I yelled out for Professor Perry, then Helen yelled out something in language, and women appeared, looking curious. 'They can divvy it up amongst themselves,' she said. 'And I'll run some of this up to Betty and Lewis now.' I kept a little back for ourselves, just in case. Thomas joined us to pass out the bags. The women's faces beamed as they thanked us.

'No, thank you,' Perry said. 'This isn't charity. We are grateful to you for your beautiful artworks that have given us so much pleasure. And we thank you for allowing us to stay here with you.' I looked at him, wondering where this polite and humble man had come from.

The group waved at us, the universal language of departure. And we wandered into Helen's allocated house. Inside and out, the place looked as temporary as white civilisation was prepared to go. Perry stood on the worn grey linoleum floor of the lounge room between a torn red couch and a laminated coffee table, deliberating over which would be safer to sit on. He was wearing a white shirt and light brown linen trousers. Folding creases covered him. The scene reminded me of when I first saw Perry in his university office, unsure and unpressed. His kingdom begged for a travel iron.

I put on the kettle in the kitchen. Helen returned and organised cups over to the coffee table while I carried the teaspoons, a bag of sugar, and a carton of milk.

'So you've been trying to get some funding to have the centre re-built?' Perry asked as Helen pulled up an old wooden kitchen chair. I settled next to Perry on the couch.

'Yes, but the timing's a little off. We've just missed the main deadlines for applications.'

'How much were you wanting?'

'I was thinking around forty thousand. We could get away with thirty, I guess. Probably best for it all to be put on hold, anyway. Wait and see what happens with the artists.'

'Getting more paint and canvas is easy,' Perry said. He was holding his mug with both hands and leaning forward, campfire pose. 'We can help with that. I've had a word with the head of Art & Design. That's our art school at the university, where our daubers do their thing.' He ended with a chortle. Helen looked back, blank-faced. 'We've organised funding for art supplies,' Perry pressed on, 'and a student exchange program. Some of our students can come out here to assist in setting up again. Young Anna could be a part of that, help out.' I sat staring at Perry with my mouth open, wondering what else he'd planned for me. Before I could muster a verbal response, he continued the pitch. 'Your artists can paint at our campus, inspire our lot. A new experience is good for everyone to get the creative juices going again, eh? All we need is your thumbs up, and it's lift off.'

Helen shifted in her seat. 'That's really generous of you, Dr Perry, but- '

'Thomas, call me Thomas,' he insisted.

Helen replied. 'The artists aren't painting.'

'Why on earth not?' Perry said, startled. 'We saw their stuff in Alice Springs. It's brilliant. You have Michelangelos in your midst, m'dear. Every painting sold. Don't tell me they see the fire as some warning sign from their ancestors or something.'

Helen shook her head. 'They've just decided it is time to stop for now.'

'Stop?' Perry squeaked, as if unsure what the word meant. Whatever his surprise for Helen was, it seemed to be going south.

'It's a pragmatic decision,' she added, kiboshing the condescension.

Instead, his eyes tightened as he looked at Helen. 'Do you think Dorothy's behind it?'

This was it. The kind of conversation I was dreading, the whole reason for not wanting to get involved. The embarrassment of being associated with Perry, with nowhere to run, nowhere to hide.

'No,' Helen sighed. 'Dorothy had nothing to do with it. The group made their own decision. They really don't want to paint.' Meanwhile, the sun was setting its evening pastels down behind the scrub landscape. 'I'm so sorry you went to all that trouble.'

'How long will this break go for?'

'I have no idea.'

'Are we talking months? Maybe years?' Perry asked.

'Maybe.' She shrugged. 'Who knows?'

'But where will that leave you?' he asked, seeing an opportunity to lever change.

'Me?' she asked with a light laugh. 'Working somewhere else, I suppose.'

'Well, tomorrow's a new day,' Perry chirped. 'The hankering for a finely-bristled brush may come upon them just as suddenly.'

'Maybe, but I wouldn't hold my breath.' Then she changed the subject. 'So, I was thinking about what we could have for dinner this evening. Witchetty grubs, anyone?'

# CHAPTER 29

Sitting in a tight circle around the campfire, I felt my body go cold. The women and children were laughing as a fat, white, live witchetty grub the size of a jumbo glue stick, curled and uncurled right before my eyes. I closed my eyes tight, prised open my mouth, and allowed the gigantic writhing insect to be dropped into my body. I had no choice. It had to be done, just as Liz had predicted. Its culmination of tiny legs wriggled and scratched at my tongue. I wanted to spit it out and scream in horror at the macabre sensation. Instead, I dutifully crunched into its body with my teeth, forcing a raw death that I wished would hurry before throwing up in disgust and shaming myself completely.

This was what I imagined was in store for dinner. But it turned out Helen had a sense of humour. The Aboriginal women were rustling up their own meals elsewhere. Possibly witchetty grubs, but more likely the steaks, sausages and salad we brought from Alice. Helen cooked us steaks, potato and broccoli, also from our food stash. Rudy was at the open door gnawing on a bone like his teeth depended on it, which they possibly did. One thing was clear: a dog could not survive in a place like this on gums alone.

'We're lucky,' Helen said, spooning the potatoes onto each plate. 'Not being all that far from Alice, food is fresher and more plentiful at Stumpy than a lot of other communities. Diet and general health are still issues, mind.'

'Well, this looks like a beautifully balanced meal tonight,' I said, draining the broccoli.

'I was a vegetarian before coming to the Territory,' Helen explained. 'It's too hard out here, being such a meat and carb culture. Fruit and veg can be pretty expensive at the local shop. Organic vegies, forget it. I've saved money on wine, though,' she laughed. 'Okay, grubs up….not witchettys though.'

A green candle halfway through its life sat in the middle of the table, throwing light on the scratched wooden surface.

'The only thing that would complete this delicious meal is a nice bottle of berried Cabernet Sauvignon,' Perry proclaimed.

'We can't- ' Helen started.

'I know, I know.' He held up his enormous palms in defence. 'We certainly are on dry land, aren't we?' Helen smiled politely and continued eating. 'Must be lonely here for you,' Perry said as his jaw gashed through the steak.

'Me?' Helen asked.

'Living amongst these people,' he replied. 'Being in it, but not of it. The women choosing not to paint regardless of how that might affect you.'

'I like them,' Helen emphasised. 'And they seem to like me. I feel privileged being here, watching them make a decision that they have never made as a group before.'

'Yes, I imagine that's very interesting,' he nodded, 'but who do you talk to?'

'Boy, you don't dillydally with the personal questions, do you?' she laughed, eyes wide.

'We're only here for a short time,' Perry grinned.

'So am I – relatively speaking,' she replied. 'Only two years at most.'

'Or much shorter, if they persist in their strike.'

'It's not a strike, they're not asking for higher wages or better working conditions.'

'No, they're asking for a paid holiday,' Perry replied.

'You say that as if you'd never had one, Thomas.'

Perry's eyebrows raised, finally acknowledging that he had crossed a line. 'I'm not saying that they don't deserve it. I'm just conscious that there's only so much time.'

'For what?'

'You know what I mean.'

'No, I really don't,' she tested.

'Before they lose their stories completely, and there's nothing left for them to paint.'

'Is it losing the stories, or losing the paintings that concern you?'

'Both,' he replied quietly with a grin.

Helen rested back in her chair, the energy of debate leaving her body. 'To answer your earlier question, I enjoy talking to the women, to Dorothy in particular. We don't talk often. But when we do, it's good. Had a nice visitor not long ago,' Helen mused, 'just before the fire. She was from Sydney, too. A woman by the name of Jan Hildebrandt.'

'Jan Hildebrandt?' I asked, almost choking on some potato.

'You know her?' Helen and Perry asked in unison.

'I think so,' I replied, wondering how many Jan Hildebrandts from Sydney could there be. 'Was she with a caravan of retirees?'

'No, she was travelling solo in a four-wheel drive. It didn't have Adventurer written on the side,' she said to Perry with a grin. 'Though she did say she had left some friends at a campground in

Alice. Jan mentioned she used to be in the art game, so I suppose it's not unusual for you to have crossed paths.'

'I'm keeping her seat warm at Noah Webster Gallery.'

'You might be in luck. She told me she had just retired.'

'Really?' I asked, imagining Simon more likely to stay with Noah for the long haul than me. What I thought I'd be doing instead, however, was anyone's guess. Most likely, it would be Perry's guess. 'Did Jan say why she was at Stumpy Downs?' I asked.

'Yes, she has a history with the community here. Apparently, she assisted Noah Webster through that whole auction house debacle. Lots of embarrassment over that, which Jan talked about quite openly.'

I recalled telling Jan about my thesis topic, assuming that she had taken up assisting Noah after his Aboriginal period. It never occurred to me to ask her about the Whitlocks. Why would it? Jan never volunteered any special knowledge. Sinking my head in my hands, I heard Perry ask, 'This Hildebrandt woman managed to get a permit to enter Stumpy Downs, then?'

I looked up. Helen nodded. 'It helps to have contacts with the Central Lands Council. She got one quite easily. Anyway, Jan turned out to be very pleasant company for the couple of days she was here.'

I paused before asking, 'Did she hang out with the artists much?'

'Oh, yes. But that was to be expected. They all remembered her fondly.'

'This was just before the fire and the tools down decision?' Perry asked, squirting more barbeque sauce on his steak. 'It does seem an interesting coincidence, doesn't it?'

'Why would Jan have anything to do with these things?' Helen asked. 'According to the assessor's report, the fire was a simple electrical fault. She had left at least a day before the fire started. And the artists, well, what could possibly be her motivation to stop them painting?'

'Probably none,' I replied. 'She seemed very nice when I met her,' I added, doing my best to smooth things over.

Perry shook his head. 'Haven't even met the woman.'

We ate in silence until Perry's hand gripped his chest. His complexion reddened, and bloodshot eyes stared fiercely at his plate before him.

'Thomas?' Helen cried. 'Are you okay?' When he looked at her without a sound, Helen asked me if she should get Betty for assistance.

'No,' Perry finally managed, grimacing. 'Happens from time…to time.'

'What's wrong with him?' Helen asked me.

'No idea,' I replied glumly. 'He will talk about everything else.'

'Do you have a heart condition, Thomas?'

'It's nothing,' he replied, eyes filling with tears. But before long, his body relaxed, and he released a chuckle. 'My god, you should look at your faces.'

'Our faces?' Helen exasperated. 'Are you mad? You should have seen yours a moment ago.'

'I'm fine,' he replied. 'Stop fussing, woman.'

Helen rolled her eyes at me while I tried to not laugh. She then announced that she was going to clear up and make tracks to bed. I sprang from my chair, collected the dishes from the table, and started the washing up before Helen could get there. Perry moved at a slower pace but managed to rise from his chair and gingerly took the tea towel hanging from the oven door as if he hadn't seen one before.

'I can do that, Thomas,' she said, taking the tea towel from him. 'Thanks for the food.'

'If you insist,' he said before swiftly disappearing into the bathroom to brush his teeth. As we washed the dishes, Helen talked about the problem of carpet baggers.

'They trawl around Aboriginal artists out on remote communities, paying cash for paintings they can sell for ten times the price, or more, in the cities.'

'Art centres help artists get paid properly, and ensure their works are sold by ethical dealers and galleries, right?'

"We do our best."

I was about to ask about Dorothy's *Country* quadriptych, but Helen rubbed at her eye and said, 'I'm knackered. Time to crash.' We said goodnight, and I wandered towards the car. Rudy was sitting next to the ladder leading up to the rooftop.

'No, you can't sleep with me,' I said. The dog didn't seem all that disappointed. He just lay his body on the ground and started to doze. I hoped he wasn't feeling too cold. Like the previous night, the air was chilly. After changing, I lay zipped up in the sleeping bag like a cocooned moth waiting for greater things. I was too knackered to worry about Jan, Perry's precarious manners, or my own. But I lay there awhile, feeling exhausted but also wired. I then rummaged through my shorts for my mobile to check the time. Turning it on, it told me I was out of range. I lay down again, ruminating on how Dorothy Brown lay in the darkness in one of the houses nearby, a world away. 'Breathe it in,' John had said. I gave it a go, expecting little. Then dropped off into the unknown.

'Surely you call up friends at home.' Perry asked Helen while munching on Vegemite toast the next morning. Perry's hair was still damp from a recent shower. Helen was still in her pyjamas. 'Perhaps there's someone special waiting for you?' he asked.

'No one special. Sure, I talk to friends on the phone sometimes,' Helen replied, looking weary with her short, blond hair pushed around her head in different directions. I used Helen's bathroom to wash and change back into my shorts and a fresh t-shirt. Black, this time. After waking, I had noticed with disappointment that Rudy was no longer at the foot of my ladder.

'And do you talk to god, Helen?'

'God?' Helen laughed. 'Isn't it a little early in the morning to be talking about god?'

'Well, aren't we on mission land?'

'This place? It used to be a farm run by the Lutherans. It had always belonged to Lewis' family, and that never changed for him.'

'The Lutherans still get involved, don't they? Wasn't sure if you were one of them.'

Helen took a breath. 'No, I'm not. And, yes, they do sometimes get involved these days. In a practical way, mostly.'

'Speaking of getting involved,' Perry dawdled, head to the side. 'May we introduce ourselves to Dorothy today?' I stopped mid-munch for the answer.

'I'll ask her after breakfast,' Helen replied, sipping at her coffee and releasing a yawn. And then we watched her eat her breakfast. We watched every bite and every sip. Helen eating breakfast was interminable. When finally finished, we insisted on doing the dishes so Helen could have a shower and introduce us to Dorothy. After we'd finished the dishes, we sat and waited on the couch. And waited. Rudy appeared at the doorway, looked around sniffing, and then lay down on the step.

'I suppose we should take into account that Helen's due a well-earned break,' I whispered.

'Is she,' Perry replied grimly. It wasn't a question.

'Well, she's probably going through an anti-climax after all the activity of preparing for the exhibition, watching the centre and stock up in flames, brokering grant deals…'

'Only to come back to her artists taking the siesta of the century.' With determined, thick fists clenched and lips rolled inwards, Perry entrapped his patience.

Helen emerged dressed in cargo shorts, sky blue t-shirt and sandals. 'Ready?'

Perry unrolled his lips and fingers in relief. 'I suppose so,' he replied with contrived nonchalance. We made our way to the door. Rudy started to follow, and I halted.

'Maybe Rudy shouldn't come,' I said.

'Why?' Perry asked.

'Dorothy is irritated by dogs.'

'That's true,' Helen said. 'But it's not common knowledge. How did you know?'

I shrugged. 'Must have read it somewhere.'

'Well, Rudy's going to follow us,' Helen continued, 'and the old woman is used to it.'

Where Dorothy was staying was much like the rest. Fibro walls with a small verandah out front, water tank on the side.

'There's a lot of water tanks here for a desert,' Perry noted.

'It does rain,' Helen replied, 'and when it does, you want to catch it.'

'But you've got the Artesian Basin,' he suggested. 'Surely that should be supplying your community generously.'

'It's not limitless,' Helen replied. 'And pumping it up takes energy.'

'So the Indigenous digging stick thing isn't foolproof, then?'

Helen looked at Perry intently. 'The longer I live, the more I realise that nothing – and, it seems, no one – is foolproof.'

We waited outside as instructed, while Helen and Rudy wandered through Dorothy's open doorway. My eyes travelled around the outside of the house, trying to find signs of Dorothy in the materials. The structure wasn't in particularly good condition, but it wasn't particularly bad either. There was an ordinariness to the place, which didn't seem right. Not for Dorothy Brown.

Helen soon emerged saying, 'Not home.'

'Where do you think she might be?' Perry asked.

'Not sure,' Helen replied. 'Let's see if anyone else knows.' We wandered down the walkway between two random rows of houses. Most of the houses looked deserted. Helen walked up to an open doorway. Seeing no one, she turned back to us. 'They might be gathering.'

'Gathering for what?' Perry asked. 'A ceremony?'

'I don't know, maybe just to hang out.'

We walked past about fifteen houses before we stopped, and the bush began. The women were indeed congregating in a shady spot under some gum trees. A few were talking amongst themselves, others listening. The half-naked children were running around scrub trees, playing a game that I couldn't identify. It was possible they were making it up as they went along.

This was the stereotyped view Westerners had of Aboriginal people. Sitting under trees in the red desert, doing very little. For all I knew, if I had come a few weeks earlier, they might have been found painting industriously at the fully functional Stumpy Downs art centre. But here they were, and it made sense. Sitting outside meant they caught the breezes. And under trees, so they didn't bake. I've heard the phrase 'work smarter, not harder' but people in Sydney have a hard time giving up the daily grind. And air-conditioning.

'Anyone know where Dorothy is?' Helen called out to them.

There was silence for a while. The air had no presence. There was no tension. They were just sitting in the silence. I wanted to add, 'While you're thinking about the answer to that one, perhaps you could tell us what Jan Hildebrandt talked to you about.' But I just stood there and looked beyond them, over the scrub to the ranges in the distance, then shifting to the red dirt at my feet. Eventually, there was some murmuring amongst the group, and before long, one woman called out, 'With Betty.'

'That'll be right,' Perry said under his breath. 'The opposite bloody direction.'

'Thanks.' Helen waved before walking back the way we came. Rudy followed.

Rudy stayed in Betty's yard, acquainting himself with the other dogs' rear ends. The rest of us ventured into the darkened home. We found Betty settled on a floral couch in front of the television. On the screen was the Indy car racing tournament. Televised from the Gold Coast, the race showed cars driving around the luxury apartment circuit.

Perry whispered to me, 'I heard that those from Indigenous cultures often embrace the worst of Western civilisation. But I wasn't prepared for this.' The three of us stood next to the couch, watching the screen. The cars continued to go around and around.

After a time, Betty broke the lull with, 'I don't get it.'

'Where's Lewis, Betts?' Helen asked.

'Out back,' she replied.

'In the Outback?' Perry chuckled. 'Aren't we all?'

'Out the back,' she said slowly. 'Trying to resurrect the Falcon.'

A flushing sound could be heard from down the hall, and an old woman eventually appeared at the doorway. Wearing a t-shirt with the Nike symbol and a floral polyester skirt, Dorothy Brown was petite but had an aura of determination. Rudy wandered in. Dorothy growled at him, and he scampered out again.

'Hello there,' Helen said. 'Decided to hang around?'

'I'm Doctor Thomas Perry.' Perry thrust a hand forward, but Dorothy didn't accept it. Instead, she settled herself back on the couch.

'See how Dixon comes in then overtakes from outside?' Dorothy gestured at the screen to Betty. 'That man changes gears like he's whippin' cream. Mad bugger, but good.' Just as a sponsorship plug appeared on screen, Perry's hand gripped his chest, and he began to wheeze. I looked at him, wondering if I should bother to ask if he's okay. The two older Aboriginal women had turned, watching speechless from the couch.

'This happens from time to time,' I explained. But then the colour of Perry's face went from pale rose to beetroot. Wide-eyed, he dropped to his knees.

'Ambulance,' I said to Betty. 'We need an ambulance.'

# CHAPTER 30

Dorothy lay Perry onto his back as Perry gasped for air. 'Angangkere,' Dorothy yelled through the doorway. Helen ran outside, calling for Lewis. 'I'll call for an ambulance,' Betty said, picking up her phone.

'No!' Perry yelled as he caught his breath. 'I'll be…fine.'

'What is with this?' I yelled back. 'For god's sake, get some help. Damned if you're going to die and I'm left here all on my own.'

'I'm…fine,' Perry repeated, panting through clenched teeth like a wild animal. His face was getting paler by the second.

Lewis walked casually past me and crouched down next to Perry. He laid his hands softly on Perry's chest and made a clicking sound in his mouth.

Helen joined us, and Betty explained to me, 'Traditional healer. This is his country. Spirit. Body. Land.' Slowly, Perry's breathing became steadier, but his face was still pale. He stared up at Lewis in a state of shock. I was taken aback, too, when Lewis, with hands still on Perry's chest, began to sing in his traditional language.

'Awelye,' Helen said. 'healing song.' She then paused before adding, 'Lewis, why are you singing Itsy Bitsy Spider in Arrernte?'

Betty and Lewis began to chuckle, and I couldn't help but release a snort. 'This man,' Lewis said, 'he just needs to relax.'

'What? Are you saying it's not serious?' Perry asked. Irritated, he hoisted himself up on his elbows. I noticed his pale complexion returning to a moderate, healthy pink. 'So, what was with the laying on of hands and clicking, the whole performance just then?'

'I am a healer. You just got a check-up.' Lewis shrugged.

'Jesus, I might have had a heart attack,' Perry replied, staring at the lino floor.

'Want us to call you an ambulance?' Lewis asked. Perry took a breath and then shook his head. Lewis got to his feet. 'You come camping with me, and you be good, healthy.'

'Camping?' Perry repeated, aghast. 'I could die out there.'

'You are adventurer. It says on your car, right?' Perry chose not to reply. Lewis held out a hand to Perry. 'We go camping now.'

'Now?' Perry asked, hand hovering near Lewis', not quite committing.

Lewis nodded, grabbing his hand. 'Me and the Falcon need time apart.'


Helen drove us back so Perry could collect some of his things, even though Lewis said, whatever they were, he wouldn't need them. Then Helen and I were to meet up with the rest of the women. Betty and Dorothy were going to join us there. Time to talk women's business, Dorothy had said.

'It was probably a heart attack,' Perry said from the passenger seat, 'triggered by Dorothy Brown's frighteningly expert commentary on one of the most absurd sports invented by Western civilisation – rivalled only by a bottomless boat race held annually in a stone-dry riverbed.'

'Hey, don't trash the Henley-on-Todd. It's great,' Helen said as she drove past the schoolhouse. 'You don't know what you're missing.'

'We haven't had a chance to discuss your manuscript, Helen,' Perry segued.

'Don't worry, there's no rush.'

'The publishing game is a race. Believe me, you have to get in there before the next bastard does.'

'He talks about the importance of speed after having a heart attack.' Helen winked at me through the rear vision mirror.

'Lissam, if for some reason I do come to a complete full stop out there with ol' Lewis,' Perry said, turning his body around to look at me. 'London's overrated. It's as boring as...'

'Bat shit?'

'Exactly,' he nodded. 'The weather's miserable, and the people are parasites. Particularly taxi drivers, property lawyers and certain vice chancellors.'

'Thank you, Professor Perry. I'll remember that,' I replied to the man who had dragged me out to a place that was hard and strange. There was one thing though. I had met Dorothy Brown today.


The women were still gathered behind the houses under the shade of the eucalyptus trees. Helen and I sat away from the group but were still close enough to hear. The discussion was mostly in Arrernte. Helen translated parts, where possible and appropriate. The topics reminded me of debates in parliament, but without the name-calling. Some women raised the issue about drug and alcohol prevention. A few suggested further contemplation on training and education. The idea of re-building the art centre got a mention at various points. Someone made a joke about buying a yacht.

There was the odd moment when Helen wasn't sure what was being said. The most popular word, however, was ceremony. It seemed that ceremony was to be performed before anything solid was decided upon.'

Then they had a question for me. Dorothy asked. 'You're an art history student, right?'

'Yes, I am,' I replied.

'The women aren't painting at the moment,' she said.

'We're now art history,' another woman added, which provoked a fit of laughter among the group.

'You disappointed?' Dorothy asked me.

'More confused,' I said, raising my voice to the group. 'I saw some work at a gallery in Alice Springs, your recent paintings, before the fire happened. They were all so beautiful. I'm curious about whether your group misses creating such special work.' One of the women chuckled and said something in Arrernte.

Helen leaned over and whispered, 'Swansong.'

'They have a word for swansong?'

'Kind of,' Helen answered before another woman said something softly. 'What was that, Eunice?'

The woman replied in very clear English, 'We're having a pretty good time right now, gettin' back to the land, you know? We used to paint outside on the ground. We lay the canvas out to paint. Sometimes you can forget about what's under the canvas.'

'Do you think you'll go back to painting?'

'On canvas?' Eunice asked. 'Dunno. But we're going to paint ourselves. Right, ladies?' There was some twittering amongst the group.

'Quite a few of them are a bit nervous about taking off their tops and painting themselves,' Helen whispered. 'They're psyching themselves up for it.'

'Why would they be nervous?' I asked. 'Isn't it their tradition?'

'A good number are out of the habit,' she replied, 'and some others have never done it.'

I took a breath and asked, 'Do you miss painting on canvas, Dorothy?'

The old woman chewed on a stalk of native lemongrass in contemplation. 'Sometimes, yeah,' she shrugged. 'But I made the decision. It was the right decision for me, for my health and for my family.'

'Did you worry about the health of the other women who were still painting?'

'Nah,' she chuckled, and the rest of her group laughed with her. 'They can take care of themselves with that stuff. They've got to make their own decision about that.' Dorothy shifted her position on the ground. 'We'll have ceremony soon. Sacred ceremony, we can't invite you to it.'

I nodded, feeling strangely relieved. I never quite understood rituals. Ceremony always seemed to be more my mother's thing. From church gathering to Christmas luncheons to that quiet time of prayer before letting her head hit the pillow. Even some of the Aboriginal women looked a little unsure about it. But they were going to step up. They were going to be brave. Me? I couldn't even find the courage to ask about the quadriptych.

'Helen, take this girl out to the campsite,' Dorothy said. 'You remember it?'

'Yes,' Helen replied.

'But don't go past the creek. Sacred place,' she added for my benefit. 'You ladies can be in touch with the land, too, in your own way.' Dorothy grinned. 'Maybe you will find your own ceremony.'

'Maybe,' Helen answered with a smile.

'Make sure this girl gets some time on her own,' she said, nodding in my direction. 'Real time.'

'Okay,' Helen nodded.

Dorothy gestured to me. 'Time for her to be in this place.'

Helen and I got to our feet, and as we began to make our way, Dorothy called out, 'There's a big rain coming, okay?' I looked up at the perfectly blue sky and wondered if they were planning on doing a rain dance to bring it on. While the women prepared to move out to the place their ancestors designated as sacred for women's business, Helen and I walked back to start packing.

I heaved my backpack into the Adventurer. Perry had left the keys with me in case we needed to drive out to find him. It made more sense to use it than the minibus. Rudy seemed to agree. He was already sitting up in the backseat. Helen knew the way, so she took the wheel. We drove up the road towards Betty's but turned right on what was barely a dirt road. Bush scrub flapped at the Adventurer as we passed. Rudy lay down on the back seat, using his body mass to keep anchored as the car bumped along the track.

'I hope I'm not keeping you from working on your manuscript, Helen.'

'No, it's okay. I'm keeping me from my manuscript.' Helen laughed.

'What's it on? Stumpy Downs artists?'

'You've got it. A survey of their paintings in the 21st century, so far. But my primary research went up in the fire. I figured I could scour Australia – the world maybe – for material. But lately, I've felt like taking a leaf out of the artists' book and forgetting the whole thing. What's it all for, anyway?'

It was a good question. I knew exactly how she felt. 'Perry would say it's important. That people all over the world have learnt about Australian Aboriginal culture because of books and exhibitions about their art. New understanding and respect grow from these things.'

'I have to agree,' she nodded. 'I guess that's why I started it.' But I could tell the reason wasn't enough. Then Helen changed tack. 'What's your thesis about?' she asked.

I closed my eyes and let it out. 'Dorothy Brown.' There, I said it.

'Okay,' Helen said, urging me to expand.

'Well, it's about some possible fake Dorothy Browns. It's more Perry's thesis than mine.'

'I'm intrigued.'

Taking a deep breath, I launched into it. 'My thesis was originally on Vernon Jones-'

'Who?'

'A prolific nineteenth-century portrait artist. Anyway, Perry thought I lacked passion about Vernon. In the meantime, he showed me photos of four Dorothy Brown paintings, a quadriptych. They belong to this university in London Perry used to teach. The thing is, I'm the only one who thinks the paintings are fake.'

'Really?' Helen frowned. 'Why do you think they are fakes?'

I hesitated before answering. 'They don't feel right.'

'What do you feel about Dorothy's other work compared to these four?'

'Well, I suppose…space, you know? And a kind of connection. Whereas the series is,' I sat searching for the word for a moment, then came out with, 'broken up.'

'You don't think they're Dorothy on a bad day?' Helen asked. 'Because Dorothy has had some pretty bad days; losing children to authorities and grandchildren to drugs and alcohol, and god knows what else.'

'No, these feel more like someone else on a bad day,' I replied, realising it for the first time myself. 'But to most people who look at them, they are great paintings. They've probably even turned someone's bad day into a good day. So even if I'm right, what does it matter?'

Helen didn't answer. Instead, she asked, 'Thomas knows all about this gut feeling of yours and encouraged you to write your thesis on it?'

'Yes, to work from feeling back to hard evidence,' I explained. 'It's pretty wacko, I know.'

'Not at all,' Helen said, looking out at the scrub. 'I do believe Dr Perry has gone up in my estimation.'

'Really, why?'

'He trusts you.'

'No, he's just using me as an excuse to come out here and create a professional opportunity with you and Dorothy Brown. Or if not Dorothy, then the other women artists.' I stopped myself. 'Who knows? I might be wrong about that, too.'

Helen laughed. 'Blind Freddy can see that Thomas wants to create a professional opportunity out here. The man has ambition coming out the wazoo. He's got so much ambition he doesn't know what to do with it. He's not entirely sure what he's doing here, but he knows it's worth finding out. In that way, he's a bit like you.'

'Perry is like me?'

'He's feeling his way, too. That's all.' Helen shifted in her seat. 'And, yes, on a practical level, with those panic attacks going on, perhaps it was savvy of him to bring a travelling companion.'

'You think they're panic attacks?'

'Maybe. It's what Lewis thinks,' she said. 'My mother used to have them. They looked a bit like what happened back at my place. The episode at Betty's was pretty full-on.' She paused for a few seconds. 'But about your thesis, a more traditional academic would have steered you towards a more conventional study path. Finding a travelling companion isn't that hard, particularly for someone like Thomas. No, I think he trusts you, and he doesn't trust easily.'

'What makes you say that?'

'You're not the only one with a gut feeling, sister.' Helen smiled.

I unpeeled my thighs from the hot plastic seat and lay them down again. We drove up to a large rock with the word 'Here' written on it in ochre, white, and orange. Rudy barked in excitement.

'We're here,' Helen laughed as she turned off the ignition.

'So the thesis is worth doing, you think?' I asked.

'The real question is, do you think it's worth doing?'

'I don't know,' I replied, wincing at the worn-out answer. 'I was supposed to show Dorothy the printouts of the paintings. Doesn't look like that's going to happen.'

'Don't give up just yet,' Helen said before getting out of the car. Rudy jumped to the front seat, leapt out into the red dust, and disappeared through some bushes.

The small dirt road had been worked through the scrub into the shape of a horseshoe. We were surrounded by eucalyptus, mulga trees and some others whose names I'd have to look up. More hard-leaved shrubs and tough-looking grasses that knew nothing of lawnmowers or whipper snippers. This landscape required nothing from humans. Least of all, taming.

The sun was moving in close, so we slapped on sunblock and foraged for hats. I pulled out a green baseball hat from my daypack while Helen donned a cowboy-style straw number. She then walked over to a shrub that had several erect branches emerging from a common base at the red earth. The branches were crowned by smooth, broad, grey-green leaves and flat, dry-looking pods. 'This is a Witchetty Bush,' she announced.

My heart sank. 'Where witchetty grubs live.'

'That's right.' Helen nodded with approval. 'Maku, they're called. You have to dig away the dirt to have a look at the roots. The bulging ones have the grubs.'

'You've eaten one?'

'Yes, they have a pleasant, buttery taste. Like scrambled eggs when cooked. Dorothy says they are good protein,' she added before shifting her attention to the pods. 'Apparently, the seeds from these are very nutritious too. They grind them down into flour.'

'But we're having sausages for dinner, right?'

'Maybe,' Helen answered menacingly. She left for the bushes with a small spade and a roll of toilet paper. Meanwhile, I found the gas bottle and a two-burner cooker. It was time for a cuppa. Helen re-emerged, stabbing the spade in the sand next to a tyre and putting the toilet roll into a plastic bag. Noticing the boiling kettle, she said, 'You've been industrious.' She washed her hands from a fifteen-litre tub of water, then pulled out the cheese and tomato multi-grain sandwiches we had made before setting off. I handed her a plastic mug of tea, and we both settled into camping chairs, eating while staring up at the cloudless sky and waving flies away with our free hands. The birds made a bit of a racket from time to time, but I couldn't hear much else apart from Helen munching and sipping. Even that had stopped a couple of minutes ago. No distant sounds of a women's ceremony.

I looked across at my companion. Albeit wearing dark sunglasses, she appeared to have her eyes closed. I surveyed the line of her cheekbone, the tones of blond in her hair, the ruggedness of her hands. She looked foreign. I didn't know this woman at all. The realisation hit me like a club. For all I knew, I had just been kidnapped. But she looked harmless enough. Then the art coordinator, without artists to coordinate, took a sip of her tea.

'London can be a blast, by the way,' Helen said, breaking the spell. 'I was there way back, mind you, when I was an undergrad. It was just for a year, but fun.'

'Bit different from here.'

'Oh yes, very different.'

'What's it like living in Stumpy Downs? Is it a peaceful community?' Thinking of the fire, I asked, 'Are people safe there?'

'Mostly,' she said. 'On the whole, the community at Stumpy is pretty good. There's a bit of violence, some rape,' she ruminated casually, while horror hit me in the stomach. 'But they really are an amazing bunch. The blokes included.' Looking across at my stunned face, she added, 'It's hard to explain.'

'I guess there's a lot about this place that's hard to explain,' I said.

'Most places are,' she replied before rising to set up her tent. Seeing it as a cue to look busy, I began to assemble my rooftop abode.

'Do you think Rudy's okay?' I asked, looking out across the desert from above.

'Yeah, he'll be back for a feed. Living off the fat of the land only gets that dog so far.'

Helen was right. Rudy returned from his mysterious odyssey during our dinner of beef sausages on multigrain bread and tomato sauce. I also inadvertently ate a few mysterious flying insects that were attracted by the light of the campfire. At least the flies were gone, and the air was cooler. What he had eaten while out in the scrub was anyone's guess, but he looked pretty happy with himself. Lying down at my feet, he worked his way through a sausage of his own.

'I came here not long after arriving at Stumpy,' Helen said. 'Thought I was going to be organising painting materials, stretching the canvases onto frames, sending rolled up ones to exhibitions. But the women brought me here for a couple of days, taking me away from the community I was all geared up to bond with. They wanted me to feel this place first instead.'

'But in my case, the women are busy in ceremony. We've just been in the way. It's exactly what I warned Perry about. I feel… embarrassed.'

'I wouldn't jump to conclusions just yet,' she said, sipping on her tea.

'We fly out on Sunday, Helen,' I replied, agitation setting in. 'It's Thursday tomorrow.'

'It'll be okay. Trust me.'

In digestion mode, I sat back in my chair, stared into the campfire and became mesmerised by the flames. We were like two old men fishing, saying nothing, listening to nature winding down for the evening. Crickets, mostly. Perhaps we were just too tired to speak. There was something in this place that called for additional reserves. But it was hard to know what to prepare for. Indeed, the next day held a new challenge for me, one I failed to anticipate. Another kind of silence was waiting.

# CHAPTER 31

I woke bathed in sweat. It was a big dream, traumatic in some way, but had moved on before my memory could catch it. I was eating its dust. Glad to be awake, I fumbled out of my sleeping bag. As I slipped on my sandals, I could smell breakfast cooking. I shuffled down the ladder from the rooftop. Rudy was at the bottom of the ladder, waiting for me.

'Morning,' Helen said. Already with the kettle on, she was moving scrambled eggs around in a frypan, then flipping the bread toasting on the griller. Sunshine caught her short blond hair while she poured hot water into our cups. The heat of the day had already begun, drying out my strange dream and night sweat. As we settled down in our respective chairs to eat, Rudy crawled under the Adventurer to escape the rays. He scratched some ants off his belly and let out a yawn.

Over breakfast, Helen asked about my work at Noah Webster Gallery. I attempted to give a short story of John's exhibition and the accident, but Helen asked too many questions for the abridged version. We had the time, it seemed. I was starting to feel easy around her, and so I spilled whatever beans were rattling about my head. She squeezed my knee with her hand in sympathy. I also inquired about her relationships. The story went that she had left a theatre director in Melbourne and was now feeling less lonely as a result. He had been too wrapped up in some play about a plague and marriage in suburbia. But she was still holding half a flame for a massage therapist in Darwin. 'To be continued. Maybe,' she said.

Once we finished eating and cleaned up, I asked, 'What do we do now?'

'Do?' Helen replied. 'Whatever you like. I quite like the idea of sitting here for a bit longer. But we could go for a walk soon if you want.'

'Soon sounds good,' I replied. 'Right now I need to go for a different kind of walk.' Armed with the small spade and toilet paper, I headed into the scrub. Squatting over my self-made hole, I remained alert for creatures to come out and threaten me at my most vulnerable. But nothing did, except a colony of ants that scurried around my sandaled feet. With business done, I shovelled dirt to cover the evidence before retreating to the campsite. Nothing makes a person feel more in contact with nature than having to go to the toilet in it.

We sat for a while in silence, and the guilt of non-productivity began to make itself known. I wondered if I should go get my book, at least. Catch up on some reading. The latest Charlotte Wood hadn't been taken out of my bag since I packed it. Neither had my *Guide to Central Australia*. I hadn't felt like reading lately and still didn't. Helen noticed my restlessness and levered me into our walk. 'Before it gets too hot,' she said. The creek Dorothy had mentioned not to cross was dry and blended in with the landscape. So not crossing the creek was harder than it sounded. Fortunately, Helen remembered its path and was able to identify it.

'I don't suppose you know what the significance is of the creek?' I asked.

'I do, but if I told you I'd have to kill you.'

'Really?'

'No, you duffa,' Helen laughed. 'All I know is that rivers and creeks are often traditional boundary lines for different things.'

Walking in the scrub was harder than it sounded, too. Twiggy bushes scratched at my skin as I shimmied around the thicker spots, eyes open for snakes and scorpions. Helen spotted a goanna.

'Where?' I asked, seeing nothing.

'On the corkwood tree.' Helen pointed to a gnarled tree with spindly leaves resembling long spikes. The goanna's reptilian scales were well camouflaged against the dark bark. But when it moved further up the tree, it was hard to see anything else. I had seen the odd goanna in Nagurra. It was a rare event.

'I've heard that when goannas are on the ground, they can mistake you for a tree and run up you.'

'Yes,' she replied. 'And I'm pleased to say that it hasn't happened to me. Just look at those mother claws.' Helen walked closer to the tree. 'You can imagine these guys here over sixty thousand years ago, can't you?'

'There's always been that look about reptiles.' I nodded. 'Like they deserve the pension.'

'We're lucky to still have them around. Though we could have this one for dinner.'

'A protein boost recommended by celebrity chef, Dorothy Brown?'

Helen laughed. 'No, Dorothy doesn't eat goanna. It's her totem.' I made the firm decision then and there that witchetty grubs were my totem. And goanna. And flying insects.

A spectacular flock of small blue-green birds flew overhead. 'Rainbow birds,' Helen said. 'They catch insects on the wing and nest in the sandy ground.'

Helen walked on, leaving the goanna to live another day. I followed, keeping close. At the end of our trek, I looked down at the scratches on my arm. They were red and thin, like a drawing.

'Geez,' Helen said. 'You okay?'

'Yeah, they're just from a tree.'

'Gotta watch those trees.' She nodded sagely. 'They can jump out at any time.'

'They camouflage well against themselves, don't they?' I said.

We returned to the campsite. Rudy was lying by one of the tyres in the sun. I went up to the rooftop tent to get a book, thinking maybe if I started reading the urge would kick in. It was cool up there, so I ended up just lying down for a while.

'Anna?' Helen yelled up at me.

I poked my head out between the flaps and noticed Helen's tent was packed and sitting next to her backpack. Also packed.

'Where are we going next?' I asked.

'I'm going to go out further today. But I think you should stay here.'

'On my own?' I gasped. 'What if I get attacked by something?'

'There's a first aid kit in the back of the car and a CB radio in the front.' I wanted to say that I didn't know how to use the CB radio, but I did know. Being a Nagurra girl, I had played in many trucks as a child, hoping to connect with China or Mars on many occasions. Still, it didn't bring me much comfort. 'What if *you* get attacked by something, Helen?'

'Don't worry about me.'

We turned towards the noise of a car coming down the road. A white Mitsubishi Lancer appeared, covered in red dust, and parked nearby.

'Bloody hell,' Helen said with a smile. Lewis emerged from the vehicle, his Akubra hat still firmly intact on his head. 'You knew it was morning teatime, didn't you?' she said.

Lewis released a smile. 'What you talkin' about, girl? Here to check on you.'

'Yeah, that's the official line.' Helen said, putting the kettle on.

Lewis settled happily in Helen's chair. Rudy sat next to Lewis, his chin resting on the red dirt while his tail lazily dragged back and forth.

'Aren't you supposed to be with the professor?' Helen asked, passing over a packet of ANZAC biscuits.

Lewisshookhisheadwhiletakingabiscuit.'Hetalkstoomuch.' 'He's not alone, is he?' Helen asked.

'Nah, Jimmy showed up. He's with him.'

'Perry's okay then? His health?' I asked, taking a biscuit too.

'Yep, maybe too good,' Lewis chuckled while munching. When finished, he placed a cigarette between his ample lips and lit it. Breathing out the smoke, he then turned to me to ask, 'You like football?'

I had been enjoying the oats and honey of my biscuit until then. 'Not really, sorry,' I replied. Lewis stared back into the distance for a while, allowing three flies to wander about his nose until he raised his cigarette to his lips for another puff. The silence made me uncomfortable. 'Football made my dad a little crazy for a bit,' I offered. Lewis squinted at me. 'When his team lost,' I added, 'he'd drink and get angry.'

'That kind of thing happens here, too. But it's not about losing the game.'

'It isn't?'

'It's about losing something else,' he said, 'in here.' Lewis tapped his fingers where his heart was buried. I thought about my father, about what he might have lost that I'd failed to notice or understand.

After Helen handed our teas over, she dragged her rolled-up tent across to sit on.

'My brother was good at football at school,' Lewis continued. 'Didn't stop six white fellas take him behind the shed, you know?' It was my turn to nod silently. 'Didn't stop him taking them one by one either,' he laughed. 'Aboriginal men are good at football. We have a history of being fast and,' after Lewis searched for the right word, he said, 'agile.' He took another drag of his cigarette. 'To catch prey, you must be. To survive,' he added with emphasis, smoke blowing out of his nose. I sat, trying to ignore the flies, the way Lewis managed to. 'You have to feel your place,' Lewis said, 'and pick your time for action. Careful. Big spaces, small amounts of activity.'

Big spaces, small amounts of activity, I thought, trying to remember where I had heard it before.

'Thanks, Lewis,' I said, still processing his words. 'And thanks for letting me camp on your country.'

Lewis nodded and smiled. 'She's alright, this one,' he said to Helen before finishing his tea. Within minutes, he was back in the car, heading off to check on the noisy bloke.

When Helen threw her gear on her back, I brought up Burke and Wills. 'They died in a place like this.'

'That was a while ago-'

'1860,' I replied, recalling that Vernon Jones was in the country then.

'I'm not going far.'

'Dehydration ravaged their bodies.'

'I'm just going over there,' Helen pointed northward towards a clump of trees in the distance, 'with some water.'

'All their energy left their bodies after expending everything they had on fly swatting,' I said, furiously hand flapping bongo drum style. The flies hadn't responded to my eco-insect repellent, so I'd moved on to the hardcore chemical warfare from Helen's kit. That hadn't worked either. Decades of tourists had seen the desert's flies build up an extraordinary immunity. They continued to hover about my ears, nose and mouth like a nervous medical intern hoping for a future in ENT.

Helen turned to face me. 'I'll be back tomorrow morning so you can cook me breakfast,' pausing before adding, 'Or brunch.'

'They have brunch out here?'

'I do,' she replied. 'Rudy will keep you company.'

I looked across at the dog. He was still sitting where Lewis's feet had been. Helen started walking through the scrub without another word.

'Great,' I said, geeing myself up. 'We have before us an adventure without having to budge an inch.' I looked back across to Rudy. 'Did you know dogs were the first domesticated animal?' I asked. Rudy didn't seem too interested. 'That your ancestors were considered traitors by the animal kingdom for crossing over to humans, helping them fight against them?' The dog wasn't buying any of it.

I turned back to the landscape where Helen's form was becoming smaller and smaller. The woman could move through scrubland like a bargain hunter at the January sales. I sat back and tossed around the idea of taking a proper nap. Deciding to leave it to later when the sun was at its greatest force, I continued to sit and look out over the landscape. 'It's ten o'clock, Rudy, and I'm already ready for a beer.' Rudy looked up and then settled his chin back on the dirt. 'To be honest with you, boy, I feel a bit out of my depth here. Might as well be the ocean. You would think that this would be, in some ways, the perfect place. Warm and dry. But it would take military precision to survive this, Rudy. Learning and preparation. I'm not bad at learning and preparation. Apparently, there's plenty of food out here if you know where to look.' I gazed at the variety of shrubs that surrounded us. I knew the witchetty bush, eucalyptus and the corkwood tree, but that was all. Nearby was a tree that looked like a she-oak, but I wasn't sure.

'I'm not a country girl, Rudy, between you and me. I'm not a city girl either. A townie, that's what they call people like me. I am the great in between. The middle of the three bears, the second of the three blind mice, the house made of wood.' I pondered. 'When we first got "here"'– I chuckled, remembering the sign behind me – 'looking out at this, I have to admit that I thought "there's nothing here". I guess I know a bit now. Well, let's face it, what I know about this land is a grain of sand. At least I know that. I want to travel, Rudy. Move beyond boundaries. There's nothing wrong with that, is there? Hop on a plane, rise above the fences, see what the fuss is all about?'

I decided to get up and wash the breakfast plates and mugs, do something useful while stretching my limbs. Once everything was packed away, I pulled out my *Guide to Central Australia* and spent the rest of the morning discovering my surroundings from the comfort of my chair. I learned that if you felt dizzy in the heat to bind a snake vine around your head. If looking for a sweet fix, a person could suck the gum from an ironwood tree. Much to my delight, the Australian bush had mistletoe. But I soon learned the unromantic fact that it was a parasitic shrub. Native mistletoe wrapped itself around wattle and eucalypt trees in an uninvited manner. And if you ate its berries, you couldn't spit out the pips because, once chewed in the mouth, they stuck to the tongue. When I learned that the bark of the coolibah tree could be used as a snakebite cure, my head jerked up, and I peered in the direction of the dry creek bed to see if there were any coolabahs there. Didn't seem to be, not from where I was sitting. The irony of getting bitten by a snake while trying to find the cure did not escape me. I sat firm.

I was getting hungry. Looking at my watch, I noticed it was lunchtime already. Deferring pummelled seeds, edible tubers and juicy grubs, I prepared a Vegemite sandwich which was inside me within minutes. I looked out over the landscape. The place seemed to ignore me. I had read about artists coming to the desert, attempting some creative connection.

'Where on earth do you start?' I asked Rudy, conscious that an artist would have to segment it somehow, to break it up in order to make it manageable. An artist could focus on the trends of the ridge or the berries from the ruby saltbush if rain had fallen. I drew my lips in while wondering how John would have approached this land without an artificial backdrop and human touchstones. Remembering the egg painting, I realised that he would be just fine with it.

'How could you paint this landscape as a whole?' I asked to Rudy as I gave him a large dog biscuit found in a bag Helen had left behind. 'You'd run off the page, wouldn't you?' I imagined a sketchpad bending back into a tube, an end joining up to a beginning. Of course, the light was the other issue, being so severe. 'Would it be harsh to call this place "harsh", Rudy?' Looking up at me, he seemed in two minds. 'Obviously, this is different from

Sydney, with its bite-sized views. But Nagurra has some broad natural spaces, not that far out of town. Some properties feel so big they could…crush you.'

My eyes filled with tears. Why, I wasn't sure. But it was worse than weeping. I could hear myself howl into my shorts. Where this was coming from, I had no idea. That I must be going mad was all I could rationalise. Along with the tears came the groans. And more groans. I was oblivious to any flies attempting the difficult task of settling on my heaving body. Time became immeasurable, too, as more tears and groans came to the surface. No one came running.

Eventually, the spasms subsided, leaving me in the desert quiet with a strange dampness, utter exhaustion and a strange embarrassment. I wiped my eyes with the back of my hand and sniffed.

'I couldn't imagine drowning out here before,' I laughed to Rudy, who appeared unmoved by what he had witnessed. 'But maybe I was wrong.' I shook my head at myself while getting up to find a tissue from my bag. Recalling I had left a travel packet by my mattress, I climbed the ladder. I crawled onto the mattress, put my head on the pillow and fell asleep instantly, tears still wet on my cheeks.

Cracking my eyes open, not much had changed since I was out to it, except the light was now decidedly low. I must have slept all afternoon. Rudy was asleep at the bottom of the ladder, but woke up as he heard me scaling down. Giving him a friendly rub, I could feel the cool of the evening blanket in. With as much rustic romanticism as one can muster with a local newspaper, sticks and an oven lighter, I managed to revive the campfire. Helen had thoughtfully left a pile of kindling and wood nearby. Drawing my chair closer, the fire offered warmth to me, Rudy, and about sixteen million flying insects whose names didn't appear in the guide.

After a period of unmeasured time, my body asked for food again. I yearned for the familiar, so I boiled up some instant noodles, eating them with a plastic camping fork and spoon. While I slurped, I decided Helen was quite possibly insane, leaving me alone like this. Which was understandable. Being out amongst the desert community without any alcohol for long periods of time was likely to do that to a person. But then Helen looked so normal.

'The craziest people can be like that. Can't they, Rudy?' Rudy looked up at me with the expectation of dinner. He didn't like the noodles I offered him, so he got more biscuits. 'The truly mad can convince you they are the sanest people on the planet. She left me out here alone. Human-alone, Rudy, you understand. Wait 'til Perry hears about this,' I said, looking around as if he was about to appear any minute. 'Who am I kidding? What would he care?' I slumped. It was time to face facts. I had always been on my own.

Washing the dishes by torchlight was more of a braille experience. I then poured the basin of water onto the campfire, as Helen had done the night before. The moon was almost full, so I could see the steam rise from the dimming coals that blinked before they died. The insects eventually retired for the evening. They had a point, I thought, feeling a weary weight in my bones. Doing nothing in this place was exhausting.

Climbing up and crawling into the tent took everything. Getting changed was not on the cards. Rudy remained at the foot of the ladder. It was possible neither of us would survive the night. God knows what was out there. Lying in my sleeping bag, I forced my mind towards more constructive terrain. I wondered if the women's ceremony had finished, or maybe it was just starting up. I had always thought of ceremony as a kind of celebration. But for Dorothy and Betty and the others, it seemed to be more than that. It could also be like going to church, and going to school, and maybe cooking in a kitchen and attending parliament all rolled into one. It was also possibly a studio, theatre and library. Perhaps it was everything. Maybe. I didn't know.

'Rudy?' I called out.

# CHAPTER 32

The morning came. I was still alive. Sticking my head out from the tent, I could see Rudy's body lying next to the ladder. His torso was without the usual rise and fall. I began a scramble down, almost lost my footing, but hung on. When my feet hit the dusty ground, Rudy's head looked up. Then he was fully standing, wagging his tail just as he had done the morning before.

'You scared the crap out of me, boy,' I said.

'Breakfast?' he seemed to reply.

My focus was on a cup of tea, extra strong, but I also cooked up some extra sausages for Rudy and me. Settling into my chair, it was now feeling more familiar, almost a habit. I sipped at my cup and looked out, just as I had done the day before. Rudy was next to me, already working through his second sausage. I wondered if this was becoming a kind of ritual. Both my movements and the surrounding landscape had become predictable, appearing much the same as the morning before. I knew that nature never stays the same, but if you slow down and remove all the busyness as best you can, the real changes will be easier to spot. Then you could move with them. Maybe.

No silhouette of Helen could be seen on any horizon. I looked at my watch. It was 6.24am. Hardly brunch hour, I reasoned with myself. The caffeine from the tea began to work its subtle magic, and my body felt a small surge of energy. Not enough to move out of the chair, however. Rudy slumped next to my feet. I sat, challenging the stillness, or rather the idea of it. It might have been the quick fix of caffeine hitting my system before it was ready, but in a matter of seconds, I was able to imagine the ridge moving. There it was, ploughing through the red earth like a giant barge through the ocean, as it must have done over the millennia. Then I became aware of the smaller things, of birds and ants and leaves and dust, all flying, crawling, waving and shifting. Of particles in the morning air floating, of molecules vibrating…

'Got any more tea there, girl?'

My head snapped up, and there was Dorothy Brown, wearing a blue dress and a Hawks beanie. Gold and brown. John would be dismayed.

'Sure,' I said, gathering my wits and making my way to the camping stove. Dorothy glared at Rudy and settled into Helen's chair.

'Helen's gone bush,' I explained, pointing in the direction Helen had indicated the day before. 'More bush,' I corrected myself, wishing I would stop talking.

'I know,' Dorothy replied.

'I just hope that she's okay out there.'

'She is,' the old woman said, making herself comfortable. 'She'll be back soon.'

I wanted to ask how she knew. Instead, she said, 'Hard time for you, girl. You okay?'

'I think so,' I replied, pulling up a smile.

'You will be,' she said. 'You will be okay.'

I nodded. 'Milk? Sugar?'

'Both,' Dorothy said, adding with a chuckle, 'lots of both.'

I complied with a generous pouring of milk and three teaspoons of sugar. Then added a fourth, stirred, and handed over the mug, wondering if I had added enough. Or too much. 'Are the women thinking of painting again?' I asked, returning to my chair. Was it the right question to ask? Perry would want to know the answer, so maybe it wasn't.

'No,' Dorothy replied, with the slumped posture of someone used to others not understanding. Then time passed. Or stood still. Or went backwards. I was still working it out.

'You know artists, yeah?' Dorothy eventually said, sipping the tea and looking into the milky surface intently. It did nothing to reduce my concerns around the appropriate sugar dose.

'Some artists, yes,' I replied.

'Well, then you know you've got to want to be an artist, to be an artist. If you don't want to…then you better not be an artist. You get me?'

'Yes, I think so,' I replied. 'But artists often say it's a vocation, not something they actually choose. It chooses them.'

Dorothy shook her head. 'You put the brush in your hand, or you don't. You're grown up. You choose. Being an artist when you don't want to be an artist, there's no point to it,' she replied abruptly, raising her large brown eyes from her beverage. Unsure if Dorothy would disappear as quickly as she came, I mustered the courage to do what I came to do. Retrieving the printouts of the four Whitlock paintings from my pack, I handed them over. The old woman squinted at the first two, working her mind through the glare caused by the sun's rays hitting the white pages.

'Can you tell me if these paintings are yours? This quadriptych?'

'Quad, what?' Dorothy looked across at me.

'Quadriptych. Four paintings hung together as one.'

Dorothy shrugged and turned her attention back to the pages. A sign of recognition appeared on her face, then she promptly burst out laughing. I sat stupefied, looking at her gleaming teeth. Dorothy tried to say something through her tears of laughter, but she was unable to contain herself enough to form words. Smiling in polite confusion, I asked, 'What's so funny?'

'These,' she managed to say before collapsing into laughter again. Once her body stopped bobbing with delight, she spoke again. 'Where are they now, these paintings?'

'At an esteemed university in London.' Apparently, that was the punch line. Dorothy broke down in hysterics. Once she collected herself, I asked, 'So these are yours, then?'

'You think these are mine?' Dorothy grinned.

'No, I don't think they are. But they were sold as yours, and that concerned me.'

Dorothy looked back down at the pages and burst out laughing again, causing me to feel even more foolish than before. I took a fast swig of tea and burnt my mouth. Then took another swig. 'Eunice,' Dorothy finally blurted out.

Tea spat from my mouth, narrowly missing my company. 'Eunice? Eunice did these?' It was a mystery how the woman who painted the mesmerising works in the Alice Springs gallery could have also done the Whitlocks. 'Are you sure?'

Dorothy nodded, and her mood soon sobered. 'Poor Eunice, she come from the city, from Sydney. You know?'

'Yes, I live there.'

'Sad place…for Eunice,' Dorothy said before sipping her cup. By the look on her face, something wasn't right. 'Needs more sugar.'

I added two more teaspoons. It seemed to do the trick.

'Eunice?' I prompted.

'Eunice,' Dorothy nodded. 'She wasn't well. Drugs in her body. We got her painting, you know? Pretty wobbly at first, but then she got a real run on.'

'You had your own rehab art therapy program?'

Dorothy wasn't listening. She was smiling at the printouts. 'This isn't Story, so it's okay. She did this as a joke. She was still sick, more empty here. But she thought she'd paint one like me. I laughed and laughed when I saw it, so she did some more. She did four.' Dorothy laughed again, a bit more gently this time. And sipped at her tea. 'These art people. Gallery people,' she continued. 'They were all "Hurry, hurry. We need more, we need more," they kept sayin'. More money, they really mean. I said no, but they didn't listen. They were crazy. "More, more." An' see what happens. They weren't really looking.' At which point she started laughing again.

'You lied, though,' I ventured. 'On certificates of authenticity.'

Dorothy was quiet for a moment. 'New girl sold them. Brenda had just left. Certificates are from gallery, see?' Dorothy points to the Galerie Exotique letterhead. 'Not from here. Miles was in a hurry. Always in a hurry. New girl didn't know what she was doing. She thought she knew. She was in a hurry, too. She didn't stay too long, that one.'

'It was a mistake?'

Dorothy nodded. 'You need paper to know what's real these days? Pretty sad place.'

'Even sadder when the certificates are fake.'

'But funny, too, sometimes.' The old woman chuckled into her mug. Dorothy looked across at my concerned expression. 'Don't worry, girl. It is Story that's important.' Her eyes stared straight into mine. 'No Story here,' Dorothy said, pointing to the pages.

'So these paintings are not important?' I asked. 'These certificates are not important?'

'The women here would not be happy. It says *Country*. Very disrespectful. Eunice didn't call them that. These paintings are not by me. And what's that quad word?'

'Quadriptych?'

'Country chopped up into four pieces?' Dorothy shook her head, all laughter gone. 'Not Country. Not right.' Dorothy passed back the printouts in disgust. 'It's all crazy. Paintings go off, end up in big buildings. Country is here. You are here. I am here.'

'And Jan was here recently?' I asked.

'You know Jan?' she turned to me, smiling. I nodded. 'Yeah, Jan came. Jan's a good woman. She caught those people putting fake paintings through the auction place those years ago.'

'At Harrington's, when Noah Webster was there?'

'Yeah, it was Jan that knew. Tried to tell Noah, but he thought he knew better. Then he learnt his lesson.'

'Did she report the fakes?'

'She had to, to protect Story,' Dorothy said. 'She's a good woman, Jan.'

'Noah must have been furious.'

'She then helped him set up the new gallery. Jan loves Noah like he's her own son, you know? But she's gone off to Pilbara now to see Dale.'

'Dale Spencer from Harrington's?'

'Yeah, they're good mates. He asks her opinion on things sometimes.'

'I should've asked Jan about these,' I said, holding up the certificates. Copies had been in her cupboard. Had she seen them? Did she wonder about them? Dorothy picked up a stick and drew in the dirt.

'Goanna?' I asked.

'Nah, wobbly line.' Dorothy laughed. Her cheeky smile was back. She passed me the stick and gestured for me to draw.

'The power of the doodle,' I said under my breath.

'Eh?' Dorothy asked.

'The doodle. It's a drawing that's done when you're not really thinking about it,' I said, as I drew my own wobbly line. 'I like doodling.'

'Doodle,' Dorothy repeated, rolling it around in her mouth with delight. Then we noticed clouds were rolling in. Fast. Helen came into view, along with the camping gear loaded on her back. Small, perfect circles of dark brown appeared on the ground, random dots around my feet and lines in the dirt. Rain was starting as a light sprinkle. I looked across at Helen, who had obviously felt it too and was hastening her pace.

'You gonna pack up?' Dorothy said. Looking up at the rumbling sky, I felt a splat on my face, and another. It was getting heavier. I got moving. While I was unplugging the gas cylinder, Helen appeared behind me, throwing her pack in the backseat and began packing up the chairs. Dorothy had already headed off down the dusty road that was fast turning to mud.

'You want a lift, Dorothy?' Helen yelled out.

'The car is just down 'ere. Parked it further, so I wouldn't get bogged.'

'You gotta move it, Anna,' Helen said. 'It's about to really come down.'

We threw the last of the gear in the back, collapsed and tied down my rooftop tent, started up the engine and followed Dorothy's old, beaten Toyota back to the camp. If it was hers. Maybe it belonged to someone else.

'This rain could be a long one. We could get flooded in,' Helen warned, looking up at the sky.

'Really?' I asked, staring out at the rain in the desert. The clumps of gum trees and corkwoods, the witchetty bushes and spinifex, supporting the brilliantly camouflaged insects, birds, reptiles and animals that fed off them. And all the vast spaces in between those busy little points. That was when I made my decision. There was nowhere else I would rather learn to swim.

# BOOK CLUB QUESTIONS

1. What part of the book impacted you most? Why? How did it make you feel?

2. Which characters did you like the best? Why?

3. Which characters did you like the least? Why?

4. Did you predict what was going to happen? If so, at what point?

5. What was the power dynamic between Perry and Anna? How did it affect their interaction?

6. Why is the story called 'Pavlova Rising'? What has the pavlova dessert got to do with Australia's national identity?

7. Why is Anna so resistant to getting involved in Aboriginal art? Why might non-Indigenous Australians choose not to engage with First Nations culture?

8. Why is Anna so disappointed when her father didn't apologise for his behaviour in her past? What might this say about the acknowledgment of pain created in the past?

9. Why was Dorothy Brown not worried about her name on the four paintings? What is more important to her? What does her response say about her culture?

10. At the beginning of the story, Anna was more interested in the culture of other countries than her own. Is it because she already knows everything about Australian culture, or is there

more to her ambition to leave? What does she learn by staying?

11. Why was it important for Anna to experience the loss of someone close to her? How did it change what she did next?

12. Is there more interest and support by your community (government, business, general public) in sport than in the arts? If so, why do you think that is?

13. Did the story change your view on Australia and/or First Nations culture?

14. What do you think happened to Anna after the end of the story?

15. Did you feel anything was unresolved about the story? Are there questions you expected to be answered?

16. If you could ask Megan Hills (the author) anything, what would it be?

Feel free to ask Megan via Facebook or Instagram @ MeganHillsBooks or via her website: meganhillsbooks.com

# ENJOYED PAVLOVA RISING?

## PLEASE WRITE A REVIEW

Amazon, Goodreads, wherever you can. It really helps, particularly if it's positive.

## SUBSCRIBE

Subscribe to Megan's somewhat sporadic blog (you won't be bombarded): meganhillsbooks.com/free-story

## FOLLOW AND CHAT

Follow and chat with Megan on Facebook and Instagram @MeganHillsBooks

## READ MEGAN'S SHORT STORY COLLECTION:

Have a taste...

# WHOLE & TORN

*[Sprinkle Cookie]*

The art of Jessica Adams is surprising. Gazing long-distance at her works, one might assume 'photography'. Closer up, one might think 'painting'. Leaning in, breaking the COVID 1.5 metre rule, you blink twice before registering. It's collage.

'Collage on a freakin' towering pedestal of artistic excellence,' one established art critic said to their dog, because no one else was listening.

'Not a whiff of scrapbooking,' a liker quipped on Instagram to 2,365 followers.

It was true that Jess Adams' work comprised an extraordinary number of small bits of coloured paper cut and stuck in a way never seen before. Eyebrows lift involuntarily when seeing Jessica Adams herself. Her refined beauty, her long straight red hair and her wheelchair. Not a big surprise. Just enough to cause a small brow bounce before shifting focus to something else. But on the night of her exhibition opening, there was some special attention firmly on the artist. The kind of male attention unwelcome by women. Particularly by those who can't run.

'Apparently, I'm letting down the disability sector by not creating an exhibition on being a paraplegic,' Jess said to Kelly as they sat in a park near St Kilda beach looking over the water. Right here was Bunurong Country. Behind the women pulsed Melbourne's jumble of high rises, sandstone and tramlines. Melbourne was often cited as "Australia's most European city". Not so much "Wurundjeri Woi

Wurrung Country". A mouthful for English tongues.

'Which brand of arsehole came up with that bullshit?' Kelly replied while focusing her Canon EOS 80D on a nearby tree.

'Someone talking to my mum.' Jess crunched on a Twistie, her fingers dusted in sticky gold. Her hands still looked quite nice, she noted to herself, given they were rough from cutting and sticking tiny bits of paper, and from pushing herself around. She moved around in a manual wheelchair as a preference to electric. There were many reasons for this. Manuals are easy to fold into cars, require less maintenance, and won't run out of charge. They are also easier to navigate in small spaces and crowds. For Jess, there was also the matter of finances, something perpetually at the forefront of her mind, as it is with most artists. But that didn't stop her from salivating over the Pride Jazzy Air 2.0. In eleven seconds, with the touch of a button, she could elevate to the same height as if she were standing. No more awkward moments of people wondering if they should talk from above, bend down or squat. And she could see art as others see it. 'One day,' she murmured to herself on a semi-regular basis. But the versed response to anyone who asks about her choice of chair is, 'This baby keeps me fit,' reinforcing her point by displaying her impressive arm muscles, albeit pale and a bit freckly. She's proud of her elegant but strong upper body, which doesn't look muscular until she flexes. Jess is also grateful that her strength enables collaging small bits of paper over long periods of time, significantly longer than most artists could, given that the back pain wasn't kicking-in. The act of creating may have been her breadwinner, but it was also her medicine. While she worked, all anxiety and self-doubt dissipated. She was in, what some might call, a state of grace.

'Nice of your mum to pass on the toxic message,' Kelly replied, disappearing behind her camera. 'Paraplegic exhibition,' she added in disgust. Jess looked across at her friend's dark hands and curly mop of dark hair, taking the shot. God knows what Kelly was capturing, but it would be something interesting. Kelly called herself a coconut before others did. She grew up urban, but something Wurundjeri had passed down in her DNA or in her spirit or both. Kelly noticed things in nature that Jess or anyone else would miss. She noticed even more things during the COVID lockdowns when nature got to run riot. As Jess and Kelly 'walked' down the street (Kelly swaggered, Jess cruised), they could be chewing the fat on the pandemic, the price of petrol or the fact they were both closing in on forty and still single. But at the end of the street, Kelly could roll-call the insects she saw, the birds she heard, the smell of the plants. When it came to nature, Jess called Kelly's ability 'high-res recall'. The photos Kelly took were for other people, anyone who was willing to look at them. She didn't need them herself, as she already had the images inside her, plus their sound, their smell, their feel. Her photos were interesting. Perhaps not at first glance, but something in them made people double-take.

*To read more, buy the book.*

# ABOUT THE AUTHOR

*Pavlova Rising* is Megan Hills' first novel. She first attempted growing up in Adelaide. Then continued to try doing the same in Melbourne, New York, Sydney, the seaside town of Portsea, and then outside the inland town of Lismore. In some of these places, she worked in the rough and tumble world of private art galleries. She began this novel during her stint in a Sydney art magazine publishing house. And continued it later as the marketing officer at a craft and design association. When she moved to Darwin, Megan worked as a cultural enterprise manager for an Aboriginal organisation and swam occasionally in crocodile-infested waters. And worked more on the novel. Moving to the safer paddling spot of Newcastle, Megan now runs her own creative and cultural consultancy. She works with artists and Aboriginal knowledge holders any chance she gets. Megan has given up on growing up but finally finished *Pavlova Rising*.

# AUTHOR'S THANKS

Big hugs to my friends who generously volunteered to read this book in its various awkward incarnations and gave it to me straight* Jeff Shearer, Liam Price, Kate Gilbert, Julie Squires, Edwina Shaw, Erica Sontheimer, Amanda McCulloch and Lorraine Upton.
*What you didn't like about this book is not their fault. I don't always take good advice.

A respectful boxing glove touch to those two feisty Americans at the Peggy Guggenheim Collection in Venice who heckled me throughout my lecture on Australian Aboriginal art for being a white person talking on this subject. They didn't stop me from presenting, but they got me thinking about non-Aboriginal people speaking on behalf of Aboriginal people. When it's appropriate and when it's arrogance. I still don't have a clear answer on this, but I hope I'm getting closer.

To Laura Duffy. Thank you for helping me create the cover of this book.

Heart acknowledgement to all the Aboriginal and non-Aboriginal artists I've worked with over the years, who bravely create and share expressions of Connection in amongst the strange madness of this 'industry'.

Deep gratitude to Mavis Malbunka of Ipolera who shared her Country and some of her precious knowledge with me, even though I was pretty much a stranger. At my departure, Mavis told me I now had a responsibility to share what I now know. To stand up in the crowd when the opportunity presents itself. She has no idea I've written this book.

Apologies to my family and friends who have suffered hearing about this book for YEARS and YEARS, wondering if it will ever be born. Certainly, it's been the longest pregnancy in captivity. And to Jeff, who helped me through the contractions to Get. It. Out.